FIRST STRIKE

Center Point
Large Print

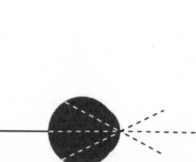

**This Large Print Book carries the
Seal of Approval of N.A.V.H.**

FIRST STRIKE

Ben Coes

CENTER POINT LARGE PRINT
THORNDIKE, MAINE

This Center Point Large Print edition
is published in the year 2017 by arrangement with
St. Martin's Press.

Copyright © 2016 by Ben Coes.

The text of this Large Print edition is unabridged.
In other aspects, this book may vary
from the original edition.
Printed in the United States of America
on permanent paper.
Set in 16-point Times New Roman type.

ISBN: 978-1-68324-262-8

Library of Congress Cataloging-in-Publication Data

Names: Coes, Ben, author.
Title: First strike / Ben Coes.
Description: Center Point Large Print edition. | Thorndike, Maine :
Center Point Large Print, 2017.
Identifiers: LCCN 2016048889 | ISBN 9781683242628
    (hardcover : alk. paper)
Subjects: LCSH: Terrorism—Prevention—Fiction. | Intelligence
officers—Fiction. | Hackers—Fiction. | Large type books. | GSAFD:
Suspense fiction.
Classification: LCC PS3603.O2996 F57 2017 | DDC 813/.6—dc23
LC record available at https://lccn.loc.gov/2016048889

To Susan Coes

My mother, my first reader,
who taught me and many others to love books,
who worked so very hard so that my brother,
sister, and I could aspire, who raised us with love

The question all Americans
must ask themselves lingers painfully:
How does a war like this ever end?

—Jeremy Scahill, *Dirty Wars*

FIRST STRIKE

PROLOGUE

PRESIDENTIAL PALACE
CAIRO, EGYPT
FOUR YEARS AGO

The meeting room in Egypt's presidential palace looked largely the same as it did three centuries before. Ten-foot-tall windows let in soft sunlight through a latticework of finely crafted decorative grating. The walls were covered in ornate green-and-white wallpaper, hand-painted by one of Egypt's most famous artists. A ceiling of coffered gold was imprinted with images from mythology. From its centermost point, a massive marble-and-glass chandelier dangled, refracting the room's natural light in thatches of beams that fluttered as a gentle wind made its white and pink tendrils dance in peaceful rhythm.

The room's timeless beauty was juxtaposed with the chaos outside. Bloodcurdling screams came from Tahrir Square's teeming masses of protesters. Inside the room, angry yelling echoed from President Morsi and his assembled cabinet, crowded around the center of the conference table, houting at each other in bitter recrimination and second guessing.

A year before, the leaders of the Middle East's

most populous country had all toiled in obscurity as the senior wing of the Muslim Brotherhood. Now they were cabinet members serving in the presidential administration of Mohammed Morsi. The Brotherhood had succeeded in climbing to power. Egypt—one of the largest, wealthiest, and most powerful countries in the Middle East—had elected Morsi president. He was the Arab Spring's most tangible result, and with his election the Brotherhood had gone from the fringes of jihad to political relevance.

But that was all about to end. The Arab Spring had come and gone. Leading an actual country quickly exposed Morsi for what he was: a bumbling, ineffectual, megalomaniac a hundred times more despotic than Hosni Mubarak, the dictator he replaced. Since his election in June, Morsi had made one terrible decision after another, shutting down the judiciary, then disbanding parliament, and ultimately decreeing his actions to be above the law because he *was the law.*

Populist fever still teemed in Cairo's streets, but now it was coming for Morsi. His time—their time—was slipping away, and they all knew it. They all felt it. Cairo . . . the presidency . . . Egypt . . . everything they'd worked for, sacrificed for, lied, cheated, and killed for . . . soon it would be gone.

Power would be gone.

Morsi sat at the end of the table. He looked tired. He had on thick-lens glasses with metal rims. He ran his fingers over his neatly trimmed beard. He slouched forward, listening to the debate.

It was Garotin, the Muslim Brotherhood's young military strategist, who held the floor.

"The Egyptian military is aligning themselves against you, Mr. President," he said. "The old factions have buried their differences."

The sweat on Garotin's forehead, the anger in his voice; all of it revealed a sense of desperation and futility.

"We control the military," said Morsi.

"We do?" asked Garotin, annoyance and disgust in his voice. "You do understand the military has the guns and the soldiers, Mr. President?"

The shouting from Tahrir Square coming through the windows grew louder and more savage.

"Almawt i Marsi! Almawt i Marsi!"

Death to Morsi!

"You're the minister of defense," said Morsi. "It's your job to rein them in."

"General Catabalis will not accept my calls. Meetings are canceled without explanation. The generals are not listening."

"The commander general of the armed forces reports to you, not the other way around," said Burj, Morsi's foreign minister.

"Yes, that's right," added Morsi. "Tell the generals to clear out Tahrir Square and bring stability back to the city. Surely they don't want a repeat of the Arab Spring?"

Garotin shook his head in shock.

"Are you all blind?" he said, his voice rising. "It's obvious, Mr. President. The military is taking back the country and making it look like they're saving it, all because of your . . . your . . ."

Garotin could not finish the sentence. The entire room was waiting for him. He stared at Morsi but was unable to utter the word.

Another man spoke up, finishing Garotin's sentence: "Incompetence."

All eyes in the room shot to a man in the corner. He stood near the windows. A black eye patch covered his right eye. He muttered the word barely above a whisper, yet it cut across the pandemonium like a knife through butter.

Tristan Nazir, at thirty, looked no older than a college student. He was thin and wore a blue button-down shirt. He had close-cropped black hair. He was good-looking, not handsome so much as professional-looking, clean-cut, perfectly put together, as if he'd just stepped out of a meeting of the university debate club. The eye patch, however, lent an altogether darker air to his demeanor: empathy for whatever injury had befallen him, fear for the violence it implied.

Nazir stared at Morsi. "I believe that is what you mean to say, Minister Garotin, is it not?"

The silence didn't last long.

"How dare you!"

El-Farka, Morsi's chief of staff, lurched from his seat and charged toward the corner of the room, pushing past the others, trying to get to Nazir.

"Call the presidential guard!" yelled Burj.

Morsi, for the first time, raised his voice.

"Stop your silliness, Hosni!" he said, speaking to his hothead chief of staff and pointing at the chair. "Sit down at once, or *you* will be the one arrested."

Silence replaced the chaos and shouting.

Morsi waved his hand, calling Nazir over. Nazir stepped around the table, past El-Farka, and walked to Morsi's side. He bowed slightly out of respect, then straightened up and met Morsi's gaze.

"Tristan?" said Morsi, barely remembering his name. "The finance expert, yes? Oxford?"

"Yes, Mr. President."

"Incompetent?" said Morsi, quoting him. "Is this what you think of me, Tristan?"

Nazir stared into Morsi's eyes. He glanced at Garotin, then El-Farka, then went back to Morsi.

"Yes," he answered. He betrayed neither anger, fear, disgust, nor for that matter, emotion. He answered Morsi matter-of-factly. "While I was merely trying to help Minister Garotin complete his sentence, yes, I would call you incompetent, Mr. President. It does not mean that I don't like you, sir."

A chorus of yells took over the room, yet Morsi didn't seem to notice. He locked eyes with Nazir. When the shouting in the room didn't end, he raised his hand.

"Will you all shut up," he said.

"But surely you cannot allow this impudence?"

"I would rather hear a man's honest opinion than a bunch of flattery and lies."

He nodded to Nazir. "Tell me, son, what would you do if you were in my position?"

"Excuse me, sir?"

"Tristan, if you were president of Egypt, what would you do?"

"Yes, what would you do, traitor?" someone shouted.

Nazir looked calmly in the direction of the remark.

"And you, Minister Burj, who has architected President Morsi's self-destruction, what are you then, if not a traitor?"

"I . . . I am a patriot," he stammered. *"A patriot!"*

"A patriot to what?" asked Nazir coldly. "To Egypt? To the Muslim Brotherhood? The former is about to imprison you, and the latter will soon cease to exist."

Another pause as collective shock swept the room.

"To the caliphate!" said Burj, standing up, pounding the table in sync with his words, stammering. "To a country ruled by Islam!"

"A noble idea to be sure, but what good is an idea if it is only that?" asked Nazir. "Ruling is about power—the acquisition of power, the maintenance of power, and the custody of power. It is about having the strength to demand that your own people sacrifice their lives in a larger struggle. It's about the willingness to kill."

"The bloodshed must end!"

"The United States was born in the blood of murdered Indians and British and the sacrifice of their own people," said Nazir calmly. "It was done because they had one supreme objective: a country."

Nazir's words were stated in a quiet voice. When he finished, a long silence took over the room.

"This is blasphemy," yelled El-Farka from across the conference table. "We are not the United States. Praise Allah!"

"Right now, we have one of the largest militaries in the world," said Nazir. "We have more than four billion barrels of oil reserves in the central territories. These are the structural necessities of power and permanent statehood, yet we're content to watch them slip through our fingers, like sand."

Morsi held up his hand to shut up El-Farka. He looked at Nazir.

"Your tongue is sharp, Tristan. Be careful. It will get you in trouble. I asked you a question: What would you do?"

"I apologize, sir," said Nazir. "What would I

do? If I were president, I would go to Catabalis's home and take his family. I would then have the leverage to ask Catabalis to impose martial law. Immediately. Today. Right now. After that, I would fire all military officers above the rank of colonel and have them imprisoned."

He paused and looked around the room.

"I would behead them all."

Shocked groans came from several people in the room.

"In five years, few would remember my actions. Those who did would fear me. But we would have a country. A nation. *A caliphate.* That is all that matters."

"A popular revolution brought me to power," said Morsi. "I cannot abandon those who elected me. I certainly would not *behead* people in order to preserve my own power."

Nazir glanced above the conference table in the direction of the window, where he had been standing.

"Marwan," said Nazir. "Come here."

Al-Jaheishi, who was dressed similarly to Nazir, looked up. His face turned red. His eyes darted about nervously.

"Don't be nervous. Come here."

Al-Jaheishi walked tentatively from the corner of the room to Nazir. He glanced nervously at Morsi, then to the conference table, then stared at the floor.

18

"Put your hand on the table," said Nazir quietly. The young man slowly moved his hand to the table.

Nazir glanced at Garotin. "Minister, might I borrow your knife?"

Garotin reached beneath the table and pulled a knife from the sheath at his ankle. He placed it on the table and slid it to Nazir, who picked it up.

Nazir looked into the boy's eyes.

"Would you sacrifice yourself, Marwan, if it was part of something bigger than you?"

"Yes, Tristan. You know this."

Nazir looked at Morsi.

"When George Washington was fighting the British, he did not have enough money to buy shoes or socks for his men, even in the dead of winter. The greatest military victory of the Revolutionary War occurred when Washington led his troops, many in bare feet, across the Delaware River in temperatures that no man at this gathering has ever experienced. Bitter cold, the kind that kills men. Most of Washington's troops either died or lost their legs to frostbite and gangrene. But Washington knew what needed to be done."

Nazir raised the blade over his head and slashed down. The sharp tip of the knife cut into the top of al-Jaheishi's hand. It sliced through skin, muscle, and sinew. There was a horrendous, dull noise in the moment the blade entered. Then a low thump as the steel entered the wood table. Al-Jaheishi winced but said nothing as blood spilled out.

Pandemonium erupted throughout the room, though al-Jaheishi himself remained calm.

Nazir looked around as blood gushed onto the table. He looked at Morsi, then extended his arms out in front of himself, prepared for arrest. The doors to the room burst open. Two presidential guards charged inside. Their eyes went to the table. Dark crimson was now spreading.

Carnage.

Several people pointed at Nazir. The guards turned. He was waiting, calmly, his hands extended.

"Arrest him," said Morsi. "He's insane."

BLT STEAK
WASHINGTON, D.C.
SIX MONTHS LATER

In a city with more than its fair share of fancy steakhouses, BLT was a cut above the rest. It was Washington's most popular, where professional athletes, businessmen, senators, diplomats, and lobbyists filled the tables. Even the president of the United States was known to dine here at least once a month.

On this particular Friday evening, BLT was crowded and busy. The mood was boisterous, with laughter echoing against the Makassar ebony of the ceiling and walls, a few shouts from table to table as diners recognized each other, chefs and waitstaff communicating in barked give-and-take, always a sense of underlying fun, as if meeting the high demands of BLT's reputation was some form of athletic contest.

At the back of the restaurant, a set of mahogany doors led to the large private dining room. Behind the closed doors, a massive wood table was designed to accommodate several dozen people.

This night, the table was empty—except for two men in dark suits.

The din from the restaurant penetrated the walls, creating a low, comforting hum inside the elegant room.

They sat at one end of the table. The table was bare except for a bottle of red wine, two glasses, and a steel briefcase, unopened. It was between the two men, though it was a little closer to the man on the right, Stedman. A thin tungsten cable ran from a padlock on the briefcase to the man's wrist. The case hadn't left his wrist since departing London seven hours before.

Stedman's dirty-blond hair was parted in the middle and swept back. His face was weathered and handsome. His chair was pulled slightly back from the table and he was leaning casually back, his legs crossed in front of him. Stedman studied the large room, a quizzical look on his face.

He turned to the other man. "What is the

American obsession with steakhouses?" he asked, his British accent sharp and crisp, Eton- educated, confident, and, above all, aristocratic.

The other man, Cannon, grinned but said nothing.

"It just baffles me," Stedman continued. "I would hardly place the destruction, preparation, and consumption of cow in such glory."

"That's because the English could never figure out how to catch the cows," said Cannon, a slight Texas twang in his voice. "They outrun you guys."

Stedman laughed. Then his smile disappeared.

"Where is he?"

Cannon took a sip of wine.

"His country is currently fighting two, some would argue three, wars," said Cannon calmly. "I could be wrong, but I'm guessing the deputy secretary of defense might be a little busy."

At that moment, the door slid open and a short, slightly roundish middle-aged man with brown hair stepped inside and slid the door shut: Mark Raditz, the deputy U.S. secretary of defense.

"James, Bill," said Raditz apologetically, stepping toward them with his arm outstretched, "I apologize. I was at the White House."

"I think that's a pretty decent excuse," said Cannon, shaking his hand. "Anything you can tell us?"

"Nothing you don't already know," said Raditz,

an anxious look on his face. "Afghanistan is a fucking mess. Iraq's even worse."

Raditz took a seat at the end of the table just as a waitress stepped into the room.

"Good evening, Mr. Raditz," she said. "May I get you something to drink?"

"Sure, Jenny. A bourbon would be great."

Raditz noticed the briefcase on the table. His eyes moved to the steel cable attached to Stedman's wrist.

"What's up?"

Stedman reached into his pocket, removed a set of keys, and opened the briefcase. He removed a stack of paper. He dropped it with a thud on the table in front of Raditz.

DRAFT TOP SECRET//NOFORN DRAFT

U.S. SENATE SELECT COMMITTEE ON INTELLIGENCE
The Metrics of Jihad:
Committee Study on the
Current State of Radical Islam

Forward by Senate Select Committee
on Intelligence
Chairman Saul Kennedy

Rates of Enlistment
Financial Strength
Force Ranking of the Different Groups

DRAFT TOP SECRET//NOFORN DRAFT

Raditz stared at the cover sheet.

"Saul Kennedy called me last fall," said Cannon, referring to the senior senator from California, who was chairman of the senate intelligence committee. "In October, SSCI hired RAND to conduct a bottoms-up assessment of the current state of jihad."

"What do you mean by 'bottoms-up'?"

"Numbers," said Cannon. "Nothing but numbers."

"We analyzed all militant Islamic groups in the Middle East, Africa, and Europe," said Stedman. "We used a specific set of metrics and then we benchmarked the various groups. Rates of enlistment, finances, technical skills, and a bunch of other quantitative measurements. We went deep into the field. We had an unlimited budget. Needless to say, we spent a great deal of money. Intelligence is not cheap. SSCI wanted a comprehensive picture of radical Islam's health, as well as the relative strengths and weaknesses of the various jihadist groups compared against one another."

The door slid open. The waitress returned. She handed Raditz a glass.

"Let me guess. It's a shit show."

"Radical Islam is gaining momentum," said Stedman, "even in places where the West has focused its resources. In virtually every category and across every metric, in every geography, the battle against jihad is being lost, and lost badly."

"It's worse than that," said Cannon. "Where the U.S. invested money in the form of troops, or even in such things as schools, well building, and food programs, growth was especially acute."

Raditz skimmed over the five-page executive summary. When he was finished, he rubbed his eyes for a few moments, then looked up. He drank the bourbon in one large swig, reached for the bottle of wine, and filled his bourbon glass. He pushed his chair back.

Raditz had spent his entire career fighting terrorism. What did he have to show for it? America's vaunted war on terror was like dust in the wind, only the wind in this case was a hurricane. The two wars, the drone strikes, the kill teams, the covert operations, Gitmo, enhanced interrogation, NSA eavesdropping, and tracking had all, if anything, spurred the jihadists on and made them stronger, tougher, more capable—and more committed. Like the pruning of a tree, each American attempt at cutting off jihad's limbs had only made it stronger.

"You could've just e-mailed this to me."

Cannon reached into his coat pocket and removed a small black object that looked like a radio. It was a signals-jamming device, designed to prevent electronic eavesdropping. He turned it on.

"We have an idea we want to run by you."

SADDATTHA REGIONALE FACILITÉ PENALE
YOQUM, EGYPT
ONE YEAR LATER

Raditz was led by the prison director to a windowless suite in the basement of the sprawling prison near the border of the Sinai. The director said little. His instructions from Cairo were very clear: Give the man what he wants.

The prisoner Raditz was there to see had been at Saddattha for a little more than half a year. He was one of a dozen individuals RAND had identified as potential "up-and-coming" radicals to be tracked for possible backing in an off-balance-sheet "arms-for-influence" program.

During his brief time in Egypt's most notorious prison, the man had become the de facto leader of the prison's sizable secretive jihadist community. No one foresaw how quickly he would rise and how much power such a young, quiet, calm, almost professorial man could aggregate.

That his ascension within the bitterly competitive ranks of the prison's radical militant community came almost exclusively from his writings, and that those writings were for the most part reasonable, respectful to the West, and devoid of the usual bile and hatred only increased his mystique—and Raditz's interest.

Raditz stepped through a steel door into the anteroom of an interrogation chamber. Through the two-way mirror, he saw Nazir. Dressed in khaki prison garb, with his hands shackled in front of him, he was staring down at the wooden table. When he glanced in the direction of the mirror, Raditz noticed the eye patch.

Raditz made a gesture to the director with his right hand, turning an invisible key, indicating he wanted the key to the prisoner's cuffs.

"He's a dangerous man," said the director, squinting. "He's the—"

"I know who he is."

Raditz entered the small blue-walled interrogation room. Nazir looked up at him. His skin was olive. He was clean-shaven, and his hair, like that of most of the prisoners, was cut short. He looked clean-cut. He smiled.

"Hello," said Nazir.

Raditz sat down across from him. "Hi, Tristan."

Raditz leaned forward and unlocked Nazir's

cuffs. He removed his cell phone, a customized device with a variety of applications built by DARPA, the Defense Advanced Research Projects Agency. He turned on an app that made it impossible to record the conversation that was about to occur.

"My name is Mark Raditz. I work for the U.S. government."

Nazir nodded politely.

"Is this the visit just before you send me to Guantánamo Bay?"

"That's up to you."

Nazir grinned.

"Have you read something that I've written?"

Raditz nodded. "All of it. Even the stuff at Oxford. Are you a jihadist?"

"No, I'm not a jihadist, at least not in the definition *you* have," Nazir said. "I do believe in the idea of a Muslim state. However, I would base the government itself, the system, that is, on your country. Representative government. A judiciary. An executive branch. A constitution."

"But first you need the country."

"That's right."

"Why did you drop out of Oxford?" asked Raditz.

Nazir's mood shifted noticeably. His eyes seemed to darken and his light mood became sad.

"I would rather not talk about it. It has nothing to do with any of this."

"Your brother drowned."

Nazir's eye shot to Raditz. But if Raditz expected to see anger, the expression he saw instead was cold, black, and emotionless, like stone.

"I'm sorry."

"Stop trying to figure me out."

Raditz leaned back. "If you were given your freedom, what would you do?" he asked.

Nazir smiled. "I'd like to eat a good meal. That's the first thing."

Raditz waited.

"If you're asking if I would join Al Qaeda or some such thing, the answer is no."

"Why should I believe you?"

"I'm not saying you should believe me. I'm just answering your question."

"Why wouldn't you?"

Nazir paused, deep in thought.

"Because I have a vision for how a country could exist. A Muslim country. *They* don't. All they care about is headlines, vengeance, fueling their hatred. Until we establish a set of goals worthy of aspiration, Islam will never have stability. A country will never have permanence unless its goals are aspirational in nature."

"But you've written that terror has a place."

"Yes, I believe it does. Exterminating the Native Americans, for example. That was critical to the creation of your country, Mr. Raditz."

Raditz locked eyes with Nazir, a slight crease on his lips acknowledging the point.

"Are you a pragmatist?"

"What do you mean?"

"Would you work with the United States if it meant you could build a country?"

"I still don't know what you mean."

Over the next half hour, Raditz laid out how it would work.

As one of three individuals at the Pentagon with the power to divert so-called black pool money that was appropriated to the Department of Defense but not subject to line-item congressional oversight, Raditz had begun to fund offshore accounts. At the same time, he had been looking for the right individual or group to back. If he found one, Raditz would then send funds through the offshore accounts to certain foreign arms manufacturers, who would manage the logistics of moving the shipments overseas. The chosen group had to meet certain criteria: It had to be trustworthy and able to keep the relationship secret. It could not threaten American allies, such as Israel, or commit acts of terror or aggression against America. It had to be well-run and capable of using the weapons to "win" the battle to be the strongest militant group in the Middle East. Raditz didn't want to give a group money simply because the members talked the talk. Ultimately, the United States wanted out of the Middle

East—and the program would be the beginning.

"Does anyone else in the United States government know of this, Mr. Raditz?"

"No."

For several minutes, Nazir sat in silence, deep in thought. Finally, he looked at Raditz.

"I am just a political theorist," he said. "A writer. A student. What would I really like to do? Study the history of governments, how they came about, and then teach. I don't know how to build a country."

"I'm giving you the chance. You might not know how, but you're already demonstrating the skills. It's happening inside the prison."

"Don't be silly. The prison director doesn't know what he's talking about."

"Tell me, Tristan, if you were to call for a hunger strike, what would happen?"

He shrugged, a little bashful. "People would stop eating."

"What if you were to call for riots?"

Nazir looked at Raditz. "There would be blood."

"You see?"

"Where would I even start?"

"Syria."

"Don't you get along with Assad?"

"Assad, just like his father, is a vile human being."

Nazir's body language was clear—the idea intrigued him.

"You stay out of Iraq," said Raditz, making the presumptive close. "You leave Israel alone. Most important, you leave America the hell alone."

"Thank you for asking me, Mr. Raditz," said Nazir. "I think that I would like to try. If I might ask, how much of this 'black money' has been put aside?"

"Two billion dollars."

1

AEROPUERTO INTERNACIONAL DE CARTAGENA
CARTAGENA, COLOMBIA
THIS AFTERNOON

Dewey Andreas slept for the first hour after takeoff. When he awoke, he found the liquor cabinet on board the unmarked black-and-white Gulfstream G200. The jet was the property of a Florida-based corporation called Flexor-Danton LLC, which was, in turn, controlled by the Central Intelligence Agency. He pulled out a bottle of bourbon, unscrewed the cap, looked to make sure the pilots weren't watching, then took several large gulps. He put the bottle back and opened two cans of beer.

Dewey was dressed in a short-sleeve polo shirt, black with yellow piping. It was a new shirt, Fred

Perry's largest size, but Dewey's shoulders and chest stretched out the material and made it look too small. The sleeves clung tightly to his massive biceps. A Tudor watch with a striped canvas strap was the only thing adorning his tanned arms. He had on jeans and Nike running shoes.

Dewey's brown hair was long and pushed straight back, parted roughly in the middle, and slightly messed up, as if it hadn't been brushed in weeks. An unruly thick brown beard and mustache covered his face. His distinctive light blue eyes, which stuck out from his gruff appearance, projected a coldness and distance. Dewey had a hard, rough quality in the way he dressed, in how he carried himself, but most of all in his eyes.

Dewey stared at one of his cans of beer for a few moments, then lifted it to his lips and chugged it. He crushed the can and tossed it in a trash can next to the cabinet. He took the other beer and sat down. On the seat across from him was a manila folder.

It was his second trip to South America in the same week. The first trip—to Chile—had been a bust. The intelligence had been bad. Or perhaps it had been good and the target had gotten wind of the trip. This was one of the challenges when the target was a former agent.

Dewey opened the folder. He picked up the cover sheet, which was yellow with age:

DATE: May 18, 1988
PROJECT: 09H-6
REFERENCE: Roberts, Sage
              COS. Moscow
SANCTION: Adjudant Judge Leon Whitcomb
              Ref. White House finding 334.67A
DECISION: Disavowal and Termination
              EXTREME PREJUDICE

Dewey didn't bother reading the old case order. He knew its contents already. This wasn't an emergency priority. In fact, it had been sealed away more than a decade ago, classified a "cold file" and stuck in the bowels of a building along the Potomac River owned by a group of people who had more urgent fish to fry.

Technically, Dewey was using some well-deserved vacation time, his reward for stopping the Russian terrorist Pyotr Vargarin, aka Cloud, who'd nearly succeeded in detonating a thirty-kiloton nuclear bomb in New York City just a stone's throw from the Statue of Liberty. The vacation time—along with the use of the jet, no questions asked—had been granted to him by Hector Calibrisi, the director of the Central Intelligence Agency.

Dewey had killed Vargarin himself. But the seeds of the monster the Russian had become were planted by America, specifically a murderous rogue CIA agent named Sage Roberts. Dewey told himself that he felt nothing for Pyotr Vargarin, but it wasn't true. He felt sorry for him—sorry for the boy who at age five had watched his parents get shot in front of his eyes, murdered in cold blood by Roberts. As much as Dewey hated what Pyotr became, he hated even more the thought that Roberts still walked the earth.

Dewey flipped through the thick sheaf of papers until he came to a photograph. It was a headshot of Roberts. It was an old photo, his last agency file photo, taken in 1987. He had thick brown hair, parted on the right and combed neatly to the side. His face was long, with dark shadows beneath his eyes and a scar beneath his left eye. He would be much older now.

Dewey flipped it over. Taped to the back of the photo was a small brass key. Scribbled in handwriting just below was an address.

Dewey took a sip of beer and stood up. He walked to the cockpit and stuck his head inside.

"How long until we get there?"

Both pilots turned. "Twenty minutes," said the pilot on the left.

Dewey found the lockers inside the first-class lounge at Cartagena Airport. He inserted the key in locker 17. Inside was a small duffel bag.

He rented a car and changed his shirt as he drove. He parked on the street, in front of a high-rise building that sat at the ocean's edge. Reaching into the duffel, he removed the gun: a Colt M1911A1, a matte-gray SAI silencer already screwed into the muzzle. He tucked it into a concealed holster inside his leather jacket.

The elevator took him to the penthouse. When he knocked on the door, a pretty middle-aged woman answered.

"*Hola*," she said, smiling.

"*Estoy buscando a su marido*," said Dewey.

"*Hoy en día se juega al polo*," she said.

"*Ah, sí, se me olvidó.*"

The Cartagena Polo Club was a half-hour drive from downtown. Dewey parked his rental in the lot out front.

The club was crowded with people. Banners covered the side of the main entrance, emblazoned with corporate logos: Rolex, BMW, Bacardi, Tanqueray, and others.

The largest banner read EL CAMPEONATO DE CARTAGENA.

The match was already in progress. Teams of riders moved in frenetic clusters down the field, the ground thundering as the majestic sweep of horses trampled the green grass. Dewey scanned the field, marking him within twenty seconds. He was the oldest one on the field, the edges of his gray hair dangling down beneath his helmet, a tad flamboyant. Too flamboyant. He rode with the natural confidence of one who grew up on horses.

Dewey walked along the sidelines until he came to a young woman who had binoculars in her hands.

"*Puedo le prestado?*" he asked politely.

Dewey trained the binoculars on the game. He found Roberts, the number 21 in gold on the front of his striped shirt.

He took a program from a table near the club-house and went inside. He went down a hallway to the men's locker room. It was empty. The room was dark, wood-paneled, with thick carpet and old photos on the walls of men on horseback playing polo. Each locker had a brass nameplate attached to the front.

He scanned the program and found the team rosters.

#21—Roberto Segundo

Clever.

Dewey moved along the line of lockers until he found Roberts's. Looking around to make sure no one had entered the room, he removed a small, powerful flashlight and shone it along the edges of the locker door. Near the bottom of the door, the light showed a nearly invisible piece of thread.

Old school.

Dewey lifted the thread and kept it in his hand. He took a pick gun from his pocket and put it against the keyhole of the padlock, then pressed the button. A few seconds later, the lock popped open. Dewey opened the locker. On the top shelf was a sleek, smallish silver-colored pistol, Walther PPK. Dewey popped the mag, emptied the bullets into his pocket, then slammed the empty mag back inside the gun and put it back.

He searched the rest of the locker, finding nothing.

Dewey closed Roberts's locker and locked it. He knelt and placed the thread back over the seam of the door, hiding evidence of his intrusion.

Back outside, he found the outdoor bar and got a beer, then watched the match from the back of the crowd. When it was over, a trophy was presented to the winning team.

Roberts stood in the line of players as the crowd applauded from the sidelines. Dewey watched him as he mingled with other players and fans. Eventually, as the crowd thinned out, he walked toward the clubhouse.

Dewey came into the clubhouse from a porch near the swimming pool on the other side of the building from the polo fields. He entered the men's locker room. He scanned the group of players, hand on his pistol, but Roberts wasn't there.

Off the locker room, Dewey stepped into a bathroom. There were two men using the urinals. One of them, a young Colombian in tennis apparel, was flushing. After he left, Dewey shut the door and locked it.

He reached to his torso, then turned, clutching

the suppressed Colt .45. He raised the gun and trained it on Roberts, its six-inch silencer jutting menacingly from the end just inches from him.

"*Bonito partido de hoy, Sage*," said Dewey.

Nice match today, Sage.

Without turning, Roberts answered in English. "I saw you on the field," he said as he continued to urinate.

"Sure you did," said Dewey.

Roberts turned so fast it was almost undetectable, swiveling with the Walther PPK out and aimed at Dewey before Dewey had time to fire . . .

"You stood out like a sore thumb," said Roberts with a malevolent look on his face.

There was a moment of silence. Both men stood still—aiming their pistols at each other just feet apart—each man in the crosshairs of the other's gun.

Dewey looked into Roberts's eyes. He noticed the scar beneath the left eye. For a brief moment, Dewey seemed to lose his focus. It was just a fraction of a second, but Roberts sensed it. He pumped the trigger before Dewey had time to react.

The dull click of the gun's empty chamber echoed off the terra-cotta walls. Roberts's face lost its triumphant arrogance at the same instant a shit-eating grin hit Dewey's lips.

"So did you," said Dewey.

Dewey pumped the trigger. The slug spat into

Roberts's chest, kicking him back against the urinal. He tried to grab for the wall but fell to the floor. Blood covered his white-and-red striped polo shirt. His hands reached to his chest as he struggled to breathe. Blood gushed from his nose.

"That one was from the United States of America," said Dewey, taking a step closer. He put the end of the suppressor to Roberts's head, inches away. Dewey waited for several moments. Finally, Roberts looked up.

"This one's from Pyotr."

2

U.S. CONSULATE
VIA PRINCIPE AMEDEO
MILAN

Rick Mallory was dressed in a double-breasted Paul Smith suit, navy blue with thin red pinstripes, a light yellow shirt, and no tie. He was the only man in the consulate's large, ornate drawing room not wearing a tuxedo. Mallory's blond hair was cut short, longer than it was in the Marines but still barely half an inch in length. He wore rectangular-framed eyeglasses that he'd bought at the Prada boutique down the street.

Mallory stood at the back of the room, in a corner, beneath a large oil painting by Ernesto

Serra of a woman asleep on a chaise, her blouse open, exposing her naked body. While it was perhaps a tad racy to be on display at a U.S. consulate, the painting was his favorite in the building, and not just because of the model's beauty. She reminded Mallory of his late wife, Allison. Mallory clutched his third vodka of the evening and forced himself to look away from the painting. He scanned the room. The reception was in full swing. It was the consul general's annual party in observance of Festa di Tutti i Santi, All Saints' Day, a national holiday in Italy.

The crowd consisted of Milan high society. In attendance were businessmen and -women, their spouses and partners, many from the fashion world, government officials, a few celebrities, several members of the Milano football team, and members of the press.

Mallory's eyes suddenly shot to his left. A woman was staring at him. She turned away and started speaking to a man near the bar. As she raised her wineglass to take a sip, her eyes darted back to him and they made eye contact.

She had short brown hair and wore a white dress that clung to her body. Her lips were bright red. She was young, perhaps in her midtwenties, and very pretty. Mallory's heart raced slightly as she moved across the room. Along with the wineglass, she held a small jewel-encrusted clutch. As she came closer, she extended her hand.

"*Buona sera*," she said. She had a soft Italian accent.

He reached his hand out. "*Ciao, signorina*," he said, shaking her hand.

"My name is Sophia Paschiano," she said.

"Nice to meet you. I'm Rick Mallory."

"Hello, Mr. Mallory." She smiled.

"What brings you to the party? Wait, let me guess."

Mallory let her hand go, then swept his eyes politely, but also admiringly, down the length of her gown.

"You're a model, am I correct?"

She laughed. "You're very kind. Thank you, but no. I'm a reporter for *Il Giornali*."

"A reporter?" asked Mallory. "I'm the public affairs officer here at the consulate."

Her smile vanished, and her eyes took on a more sinister air.

"No, you're not," she said. "You're Agency. Is there someplace we can talk? I must speak to you immediately."

Mallory shut the door to his third-floor office and gestured to a tan leather sofa beneath the window that looked out to the public gardens a few streets away. Sophia sat down. Mallory sat behind his desk, still clutching his drink. He said nothing for some time. Finally, she spoke.

"When I was a student at Oxford, I dated a

boy. His name was Marwan al-Jaheishi. He was involved in activities."

"Activities?"

"Islamic. They were always peaceful."

"I'm listening."

"He remained in London for a few years, then moved to Cairo."

Mallory tapped the side of his glass as he waited.

"He called me yesterday," said Sophia. "He asked if I could facilitate a meeting between him and you."

"Me . . . or the consulate?"

"You, Mr. Mallory. He said it was very urgent."

"How does he know me?"

"Cairo. He was with the Muslim Brotherhood."

A cold chill emerged at the back of Mallory's neck, which caused him to shudder ever so slightly.

"He wants to give you something."

"Let me guess. A box with a ticking noise coming from the inside?"

Sophia shook her head, then laughed softly.

"You think I'm lying," she concluded.

"Everyone lies."

"I don't."

Mallory grinned, shook his head, then looked out the window.

For all he knew, *she* was a terrorist, though probably not. A battery of background checks usually ensured that anyone allowed entrance into a U.S. consulate had no ties, but who the hell knew anymore? Quietly, unnoticed, he put his hand on the butt of the gun beneath his left armpit.

More likely, she was telling the truth, and the ex-boyfriend was using her so that he could get close enough to kill him.

"I'm afraid I can't help you," said Mallory.

Sophia paused, then stood up.

"I understand. I don't blame you. But he was a nice boy, for what it's worth."

She removed a small card from her clutch. She placed it on the desk. "His phone number, should you change your mind."

She walked to the door. She twisted the doorknob, but before she opened the door she turned and looked at Mallory.

"He's inside ISIS. He wants asylum."

The cold chill that had been at the base of Mallory's neck shot down his spine as he reached for the card.

"When you say inside . . ."

"He reports directly to Tristan Nazir."

3

Nazir stood still as his cell phone vibrated in his pocket. He didn't answer it.

A lone lamp on the desk cast dim, rusty light. Nazir held a white teacup, which was chipped on one side. Other than to take the occasional sip of tea, he hadn't moved for half an hour. His one good eye was focused straight ahead at the wall. His eye was like a black stone, emotionless and cold. He seemed dazed, mesmerized, and, above all, sad. Only Nazir knew that in fact, at that moment, he felt nothing but jubilation.

On the wall was a large map of Syria and Iraq. Spread across the two countries were hundreds of colored thumbtacks.

Nazir could remember the first one he inserted. It was two years before, a red tack that he had stuck into a small Syrian town called Arihah. It was the first military offensive by the polyglot group of jihadists Nazir had brought together under one vision, a group he named ISIS. Arihah was the first victory over the Syrian government.

45

Now, the map was a colorful rainbow of thumb-tacks, spread across northern Syria and central Iraq, like cancer.

Nazir took a sip from the cup. His tea had long ago turned cold, but he didn't care.

Finally, he stepped away. He walked quickly to his desk and picked up a pen. Leaning forward, he started writing in a leather-bound journal:

> Marx wrote that the final achievement of power goes from gradual to sudden, as victories create momentum that instills disillusionment and self-doubt in the enemy; the loser thus weakens and collapses. However, experience reveals that Marx was wrong. The ultimate achievement of power goes from gradual to protracted. Enemies in their last gasps pool like molten metal and harden into whatever cavity or tight space is still to be fought over. Do not make the mistake of easing off as victory is in sight! In these final moments, fear, intimidation, bribery, and, above all, VIOLENCE AND BRUTALITY must be doubled and even tripled. It thus works as such: the closer you are to achieving power, the harder it will be to achieve it.
>
> —T. Nazir, 4 Sept.

Nazir closed the journal and glanced at his watch. It was three forty in the morning. He reached into his pocket, pulled out his cell, and looked at the number. Then he dialed.

"You called. What do you want?" he asked.

"They arrive on the morning flight. He's a journalist."

"What about security?"

"It's been compromised. We're inside."

4

DAMASCUS INTERNATIONAL AIRPORT
DAMASCUS, SYRIA

Ben Sheets, a fifty-six-year-old freelance photographer, looked calmly out the window as the Air Arabia jet descended toward the black tarmac at Damascus International Airport. He reached for his carry-on, which was on the floor between his legs.

"I love Damascus," came a soft whisper behind him. Sheets turned. His wife had been asleep for most of the flight from Dubai, but something had awakened her. She smiled.

"Me too," he said.

"This must be our sixth time."

"Tenth, honey."

"Ten?" she said sleepily, stretching her arms. "There's no way."

"It's ten. Seven times on assignment, two vacations, one honeymoon."

"Maybe you were with another woman?" she said kiddingly.

Sheets laughed. "Never."

"When will the story be running?" she asked.

"December."

He reached out and gently grabbed his wife's hand.

"Where do you want to eat tonight?" she asked.

"I know you like the Grove," he said.

"Is that part of Damascus still safe?"

Sheets nodded knowingly.

"Yes, honey," he said. "All of Damascus is safe. We just probably shouldn't go around waving any American flags. Besides, the magazine hired a security team. We're meeting them near baggage claim."

Sheets pulled the canvas bag from the floor and removed an unusual-looking black Nikon camera. He pressed it against the window and aimed it toward the city skyline in the distance. Damascus was a tannish melee of low-flung red, white, and brown buildings, like an island in a sea of empty sand. Behind it stood a shelf of mountain: the Golan Heights. Israel. Every place else was empty as far as the eye could see, with thin strips of roads that appeared white from so high. Syria appeared peaceful, at least from the air. Sheets pressed the button on the camera and snapped several dozen photos.

"The *Times* said ISIS is within a few hundred miles," she whispered.

"Would I ever put you at risk?"

She stared into his eyes, searching, doubtful. She leaned toward him and placed her head on his shoulder.

"No."

As they waited for their suitcases to come around on the carousel, Sheets scanned the baggage claim area. He saw two men, both in dark suits, staring at them from across the crowded atrium. One of the men nodded imperceptibly and started walking toward Sheets and his wife. The other man went left, toward the airport exit.

"There's yours," said his wife.

The suitcases were next to each other. Sheets pulled them from the carousel, then glanced back in the direction of the two men. The man was approaching.

"Mr. Sheets?" he asked. He had a thick Syrian accent.

"Who are you?" asked Sheets.

"I am from the security company," he said. "My name is Farulah."

The Syrian smiled and extended his hand.

Sheets did nothing.

"*National Geographic* magazine, yes?" the

security man added. "Nicole Brountas arranged for my services."

"Nice to meet you," said Sheets, shaking his hand. "This is my wife, Margaret."

Farulah bowed slightly to her and extended his hand.

"My colleague has gone around to retrieve the car. Do you have your suitcases?"

Sheets and his wife trailed Farulah toward the airport exit, then followed him across a concrete walkway crowded with people waiting for taxis and buses.

Sheets glanced around. He'd been to nearly every country in the world and most dozens of times. He'd long ago stopped ever feeling nervous. But that didn't mean he didn't pay attention.

As they passed a tourist bus taking on passengers, a silver Range Rover pulled up in the next lane.

"There he is," said Farulah.

They approached the Range Rover as its driver climbed out and moved to the rear of the vehicle, opening the hatch.

Suddenly, Sheets's eyes were drawn to a taxicab parked behind the SUV. The passenger door opened. A bearded man climbed out and started shouting at Farulah's colleague, waving his arms.

As their driver started to say something to the angry passenger, a dull, nearly silent series of thumps echoed from behind Sheets. He pivoted and saw a suppressor sticking out the window of a third vehicle. The Range Rover driver was struck in the head by a bullet. A moment later, bullets ripped into the taxi driver's chest. Sheets lurched left, looking for Farulah, only to see his body spasm as a suppressed slug hit the back of his head.

"Margaret!" he screamed, turning to his right.

Sheets caught only a glimpse of her being forcibly pushed into the car before something hard slammed the back of his neck. His last sight before unconsciousness was a black T-shirt and black mask, and eyes the color of darkness.

5

ISIS CAMP NO. 16
UNREGISTERED TERRITORY Z8–39
EAST OF QU'OUH, SYRIA

Nazir took a quick shower, dressed, and left his apartment. It was 5:30 a.m. He walked quickly for three blocks, glancing constantly about, and entered a parking garage. He climbed the stairs to the second floor and walked along a row of parked cars until he came to a white Toyota Land Cruiser. The vehicle was dark, its engine off. Nazir made eye contact with the man in the driver's seat. He climbed in the front passenger seat. Two gunmen sat in back.

The Toyota drove into the small central business district of Latakia and sped along the deserted streets, still empty at this early hour. At some point, a Toyota Tundra pickup truck moved into position in front. Behind them appeared a black Lexus SUV. The convoy moved quietly, keeping distance between the vehicles. The sky to the east had begun to turn a dull purple as sunrise approached.

The three vehicles moved east. Small clusters of tiny prefab homes around clover-shaped cul-de-sacs gave way to low fields of shrub grass, then brown unpopulated plains that soon became high desert. Minutes became hours. The dark sky disappeared into orange and yellow.

After many hours of driving, the pickup truck in the lead moved off the main road, followed by the two SUVs. Soon the three vehicles were crossing a beautiful hillock of burnt orange dirt at more than 50 mph, off road, clouds of dust flaming behind the cars. They came to a high, shrub-pocked hill that suddenly dropped away. A vast valley of flat desert sat below. In the middle of the valley, several miles away, there was activity. Like a village of ants, a small cluster of buildings could be seen. There were trucks, cranes, and at least a dozen trailers. It looked like the beginning of a settlement or a construction site.

As they moved closer, men started walking toward them in a line that spanned several hundred feet. The men were dressed in black, their heads covered. There were at least a hundred of them. Soldiers.

The three vehicles continued to rip across the orange and brown dirt.

As the vehicles charged at the line of gunmen, they went from walking to running, weapons out. As the vehicles drew closer, the figures grew clearer. Every single soldier was sprinting directly at the vehicles. Each clutched an assault rifle, which he trained out in front of him as he ran.

Nazir looked up as the distance between the vehicles and the soldiers disappeared. The pickup truck abruptly sped up so that it was in the lead. The other SUV fell in behind the Land Cruiser. They came closer and closer to the line of gunmen. Every muzzle along the line was arrayed in a steady fracture, like dark eyes. A quarter mile became a tenth of a mile became a hundred yards became a hundred feet. The gunmen stopped running. In unison, they raised their rifles and trained them at the three vehicles, preparing to fire. And then, with a suddenness that made even Nazir jerk in his seat, the two SUVs shot out— one to the left, one to the right, and the three vehicles crossed the line of soldiers at the same time, cutting between black-clad gunmen who, as the vehicles crossed between them, raised their muzzles in unison, aiming them at the sky, then shot off rounds into the air as they all screamed: "Nazir! Nazir! Nazir! Nazir!"

The vehicles ripped past the men toward the collection of trailers, vehicles, and soldiers.

There were eighteen trailers in all. Most of them were steel shipping containers, arrayed in a line. There were also a few mobile homes with windows.

Smoke came from a burn pit several hundred feet away.

Hundreds of men milled about. The temperature, by 8 a.m., was in the eighties.

The vehicles emptied, save for Nazir, who remained inside.

The soldiers greeted the arriving ISIS men with handshakes and hugs. After more than a minute, Nazir opened the door and climbed out.

He was dressed in a light blue short-sleeve shirt and light gray trousers. Nazir's hair was parted on the right and combed neatly back. He was the only individual not wearing the uniform that had come to be, throughout the world, the feared uniform of ISIS: black pants, black shirt, black bandanna wrapped around the head.

As Nazir emerged, everyone turned and let out a raucous, sustained cheer. Several soldiers fired their guns into the sky.

Nazir didn't react.

He moved into the throng of men, greeting them

with handshakes, which he gave as he looked each in the eye and said nothing. He moved down the line of men. At some point, he noticed something to his right, in the distance. In the middle of the trailers was a large steel cage. It was empty.

"Where are they?" asked Nazir after he finished greeting his soldiers.

"In the trailer, sir," said one of the men.

"Is the cameraman in place?"

"Yes, sir."

"Good," said Nazir. "Proceed."

The soldier nodded to one of the guards near the first trailer. The guard acknowledged the silent order and walked down the line of trailers, opening the door to the third one. After almost a minute, a gunman stepped back out. He was followed by two more gunmen. Then came the American couple.

The woman had long blond hair. She was slightly overweight. She was dressed in jeans and a white T-shirt. Black tape was wrapped around her mouth. Her hands and feet were tied with rope. She moved slowly, inch by inch, as one of the gunmen pressed the muzzle of his gun to her back.

Her husband came next, followed by two more gunmen. He was tall, bald, with a beard and mustache. He was shirtless. His wrists and ankles were bound. But, unlike his wife, the man's mouth wasn't taped. It was no longer necessary. Blood trickled over his lower lip. A wash of crimson stained his beard and chest from where they'd cut out his tongue.

This was Sheets.

He refused to walk. He fell over, lying on the ground. The two gunmen grabbed him by the rope around his ankles and dragged him across the dirt toward the steel cage.

Nazir stepped through the line of soldiers and walked slowly toward the cage. He had a cold expression on his face, with a trace of anger. Nazir's men moved aside to let him through. As they dragged the American toward the cage, Nazir watched.

Every soldier turned and looked at him as he walked forward, toward the man who was now lying on the ground.

They'd captured him in Damascus. A photographer from *National Geographic*. What kind of idiot takes his wife with him to Syria?

They pushed them both inside the cage. The man lay on the ground. A low, muffled groan came from him. The woman stood. Somehow, she had a look of calm. She stared at Nazir as he came closer.

Outside the cage, a soldier stood behind a video camera, framing the picture. With his eye pressed to the viewfinder, he signaled with his left hand.

Another soldier entered the cage with a red

plastic gas can and emptied it around the feet of the American woman, then doused the photographer.

The smell of gasoline caught Nazir's nostrils as he came within a dozen feet of the cage, just behind the photographer.

The cameraman leaned back. He turned to Nazir and nodded politely. Nazir nodded back. When he did, the cameraman placed his eye again to the camera, then, a moment later, held up his left thumb. This signaled another gunman, who was standing to the left of the cage, smoking a cigarette. He took a last drag, then, with his middle finger, flicked the butt. It somersaulted through the air, crossing between two grates on the cage, and came to a soft landing a foot from the woman. All eyes were on the smoldering butt as it came to rest on the gasoline-soaked steel platform. All eyes, that is, but Nazir's and the woman's. She stared at Nazir, the man she knew was her executioner. And he stared back, without emotion, without apology, without guilt. He did not look happy; his look was simply that of a warrior, whose actions had been, on some level, predetermined. He was acting out the script that had long ago been written. It was a story of political ascendancy. Actions necessary when one's objectives are clear. A story of jihad.

A loud chorus of cheers began behind Nazir, but he said nothing.

Then came the spark. Flames shot up around the American couple. Red-orange flames climbed into the sky as terrible, inhuman screams fogged the din.

6

DANIEL ROAD
CHEVY CHASE, MARYLAND

At 11:45 p.m., Chevy Chase Village was quiet, its shops and restaurants long since shut for the evening. It was one of the capital's most exclusive enclaves, a gorgeous place of wealth and prosperity, its inhabitants powerful and rich, its small village a collection of excellent restaurants and high-end retailers, Starbucks and Tiffany's within a few blocks of each other.

The village's pretty colonial homes sat dark and still. Streetlights every few blocks cast what little light there was, and on some roads, such as those abutting Rock Creek Park, the weak light intermingled with the overhanging tree branches, creating a spectral atmosphere, like the scene in a horror movie just before the kill.

Daniel Road ran alongside Rock Creek Park. Its homes were larger than on other streets in the village, its lots bigger. Its owners more private. Each was set back from the street by a long driveway. Most were bordered by picket fences. Large old trees with heaving branches cantilevered above the road.

On a particularly dark stretch of Daniel Road, a white van was parked beneath the overhanging branches of a large maple tree. The van looked abandoned. The front seat was empty. A layer of pollen and bug guts was thick on the windshield.

Five individuals were crowded into the back of the van. The air was fetid with sweat. A man named Sirhan was nearest to the front. He was in charge. He sat on the floor with his back against the door. On his lap was a sawed-off 12-gauge shotgun. Next to him were two more men of similar appearance. Ali and Tariq. Both were Middle Eastern, Arabs, in their early twenties. Ali was dressed in jeans and a white T-shirt. Tariq had on a light blue button-down shirt with patches on the chest and arms, his uniform for his job as a security guard, though at the moment he was off duty.

"Is it time?" asked Tariq, seated behind the driver's seat. He was slouched down in case anyone walked by.

There was enough light from a distant lamppost to cast soft glow through the back window. The light allowed Sirhan to stare at the two other people in the van. One was a middle-aged woman with short dirty-blond hair, dressed in a red bathrobe and an untied tennis sneaker on one foot.

She lay on her side on the steel floor, near the back, contorted awkwardly. Her arms and legs were bound by rope. A leather belt was cinched around her head and across her open mouth, pulled tight so that she couldn't close her mouth or speak. From a gash above her left eye, blood trickled down her forehead and beneath her ear. Her hair, face, and clothing were drenched in sweat. She was breathing rapidly.

Next to her lay a teenage girl with long hair. She was dressed in jeans and a sweatshirt. She too was bound and gagged. Blood oozed from her nostrils. She was soaked in perspiration.

"No," said Sirhan. "Not yet."

Inside the home on Daniel Road, Mark Raditz was seated on a large, deep, light-tan leather couch. To his left, on a cushion, was a thick stack of briefing papers, which he'd yet to read. To his right was a similar stack of papers, those he'd already been through.

The low din coming from voices on the TV was the only sound in the room. An Orioles game was on. Raditz, the deputy secretary of the Department of Defense, loved baseball, though he wasn't paying attention.

On Raditz's knees was a laptop computer. He watched the video for the fourth time. It showed a man and a woman being burned alive.

ISIS was growing stronger. Raditz and every

other high-ranking Pentagon official were spending all their time trying to stop its spread across Syria and Iraq. That day, Raditz had been to the White House to meet twice with the president.

"What are we doing to stop them?" the president had asked, again and again. "Why haven't we found Nazir? What sort of animal would behead innocent people?"

Raditz had answered each question in the same frustrated tone.

"We're doing everything we can, Mr. President. Nazir is a ghost; he moves anonymously, from town to town, like a drifter, a common citizen; like the wind. What kind of animal, sir? I don't know."

But Raditz did know. He was the one who'd created the monster.

With every town and village ISIS took, with every church destroyed and innocent person killed, that knowledge—of his own complicity—ripped away at Raditz's mind, overwhelming him. Raditz knew the guilt would soon destroy him—unless he was somehow caught—in which case it would be his own government that did it. They'd call it treason, even though it had been precisely the opposite that drove him to do what he'd done.

If only he could find Nazir before they found out the truth . . .

It's not your fault. You didn't know. How could you know? Your motives were pure!

But Raditz's inner voice—the only ally he had left—was fading.

In his left hand, he held a glass of red wine. In his right, Raditz clutched a Smith & Wesson .45. For months now, it had been his nightly ritual. A bottle of wine, sometimes more, and his gun, which he held like a talisman, moving it inevitably to his mouth, to his nostril, to the side of his head, always with his finger on the trigger. Sometimes, in the darkest moments, he felt his finger pressing against the trigger. But he couldn't do it.

A soft chime came from one of four cell phones on the table in front of the sofa. He leaned forward and picked up the phone. He stared at the screen.

:: UNKNOWN ID ::

He pressed the green button and put the phone to his ear "Raditz," he said.

He leaned back and took a sip of wine, waiting to see who it was, assuming it would be his boss, Harry Black, the secretary of defense, or Josh Brubaker, the White House national security advisor. He waited for someone to say something. All he heard was silence.

"Mark Raditz," he repeated, a hint of impatience in his voice. "Who is it? If someone's there, I can't hear you."

"You can hear me, Mark," said Nazir.

Raditz paused for a very long time, as he debated whether or not to hang up.

"What the *hell* do you want?" he said. "You have some nerve calling me."

"I think we both know I have plenty of nerve," said Nazir.

Raditz's nostrils flared.

"Fuck you! What do you want?"

"We need ammunition. Guns and ammo. Shoulder-fired missiles. Nothing fancy. But I need a lot of it."

Raditz let out a cackle.

"I wouldn't send you a fucking cap gun," he said. "You lied to me. You lied to the United States of America. Right now, I have at least a dozen UAVs scouring Syria and Iraq for your scrawny little one-eyed cadaver. When I find you, I'm going to fuck you in the ass with a Hellfire missile."

"Sounds like fun," said Nazir. "The problem is, I have evidence that I think would prove rather embarrassing for you and for your country. Until you do kill me, that evidence could easily find its way into the hands of a reporter."

"You have as much to lose in that equation as we do."

"You yourself said America wants out of the Middle East. ISIS *is* your way out. I never lied to you. I just refuse to do things the way you want me to."

"Cutting people's heads off? Destroying

antiquities? You're no better than Hitler. In fact, you're worse. At least he *kept* the art after he stole it from the Jews."

Raditz's voice was rising as his face flushed crimson. He pointed at his laptop, despite the fact that Nazir couldn't see it.

"And now . . . now . . . *burning people alive? You're a sick fuck.*"

Nazir said nothing for several seconds. Finally, he cleared his throat. "You need to let go."

"You invaded Iraq," said Raditz. "Weapons that we paid for have been used to kill American soldiers. We had a deal: we give you arms, you leave us alone, you leave Israel alone, you leave Jordan and Saudi Arabia alone. You leave us *the hell alone.* You broke that deal, not to mention the atrocities your men are committing. You really think that's how you build a movement?"

"Not a movement, a country," said Nazir. "It might not be the way *you* would do it, Mark, but it is the way I am doing it."

"Beheading reporters? Burning them alive?"

"Every time we air the tape, recruitment goes through the roof."

"Which just shows how fucked-up you Muslims are."

"What can I say? Yes, I lied to you. But that was then. This is now. I need guns and ammunition. Missiles. One more shipment. If you do this, you have my word—"

"Stop," said Raditz. "Your word is shit. You want to embarrass me? Embarrass the United States? Go ahead. Why haven't you done it yet?"

"Because I knew I would need one last thing. This is what I need."

"I'll tell you what," said Raditz. "I'll do it."

"That's more like it."

"Tell me where you are and I'll send an Exocet right now," said Raditz, laughing. "Immediate delivery."

Nazir joined him in laughing.

"So is that your answer?" asked Nazir.

"Yes, that's my answer, fuckhead. Go fuck yourself. I have to go. It's my bedtime."

"Very well," said Nazir, clearing his throat. "I'll leave you alone."

"Don't call me again."

"I won't," said Nazir. "I'll respect your wishes. Oh, one more thing. Can you deliver a message to my friends?"

Raditz's mouth opened as a shot of cold fear hit his chest. He was momentarily speechless. Slowly, he put the wineglass down.

"What have you done?" whispered Raditz.

"Go to the window."

"Are you threatening me? You don't get it, do you, Tristan? *I'm already dead. Dead!* This will come out and I am a dead man, even though all I was trying to do was stop you lunatics from taking over the world. There won't be a trial or even a discussion. Go ahead and kill me. Send 'em in."

"I need you alive," said Nazir. "They're not there to kill you."

"What have you done?" Raditz asked anxiously.

"Go look," said Nazir. "When the answer is yes, I will release them. I would decide relatively soon, though. Your ex-wife is fine but your daughter doesn't seem too happy."

Silence took over the call.

Raditz felt tears abruptly dampen his eyes.

"You miserable fuck . . . they didn't do anything." Raditz's voice trailed off amid pathetic sobs.

Nazir waited for several moments.

"Mark?"

Raditz was silent, except for his low crying, a sound he himself had never even heard—animal desperation, like a wolf caught in the steel maw of a hunter's trap.

"Is the answer yes?"

"What about my family?"

"Open your garage. I'll have them back the van in."

"It'll take a few days," said Raditz, barely above a whisper.

"Fine, I understand. I know it's complicated. I'm going to take you at your word that it will happen. You see, Mark, I'm trusting you. But if you fail me, next time they'll be delivered in bits and pieces."

7

U.S. CONSULATE
VIA PRINCIPE AMEDEO
MILAN

Mallory couldn't sleep. He looked at his watch: 2:18 a.m. He turned on the light and walked to the chair where he'd thrown his pants. Searching the pockets, he found the card, reached for his cell, and dialed. After three rings, someone picked up.

"Hello?"

"Al-Jaheishi?" asked Mallory.

"Yes, who is this?"

"The reporter gave me your number."

"Why has it taken you so long to call? Do you understand my life is at risk?"

"What do you want?" asked Mallory, ignoring the question.

"I have information."

"What do you have . . . and what do you want for it?"

"I need to meet you."

"Okay, this call is done," said Mallory.

"Wait!" he pleaded. "I need to meet you to give you information. I have evidence. You have to know this: The United States Government is

behind ISIS. Your government. You provided the money and the weapons."

"That's absurd."

"It's true."

"How do you know?"

"I know. That's all you need to know. Do you not care?"

Mallory paused. Within the quiet, and the dim light of his bedroom, he experienced the same feeling he had earlier: confusion bordering on futility, crossed with fear.

"My government is not involved with ISIS, Al Qaeda, or any other group of terrorists. We hate you all."

"You are," said al-Jaheishi. "I'm sending you a photo."

A few moments later, Mallory's phone chimed. He opened the photo. There were two men, standing before a large shipping container, its end open. Stacks of RPGs were visible. The two men were shaking hands. One was unmistakable: the most wanted man on earth, Tristan Nazir, leader of ISIS. The other man was in a suit and tie. His face had a black mark across it, redacted.

"This proves nothing."

"He is one of the highest-ranking officials in your government, Mr. Mallory."

"Send me the information."

"No. As soon as I give it to you, I'm a dead man.

I want asylum. I will put it all onto a SIM card. Meet me in Damascus."

"How soon?"

"Tomorrow."

8

BIRCH HILL
MCLEAN, VIRGINIA

A black Jaguar F-Type R convertible roared along a secluded country road, then came to a stop at a pair of brick pillars separated by iron gates. Beyond, brick walls covered in ivy ran in both directions, surrounding the property and shielding whatever was behind it. Security cameras were visible atop each gate and every dozen feet along the wall.

A small, weathered sign on one of the pillars said BIRCH HILL in ornately scrolled brass lettering.

Across the street, a black Chevy Suburban was parked, its windows tinted dark. It was one of four such SUVs dotting the roads around the property. Inside each vehicle sat CIA paramilitary.

The driver of the Jaguar reached out and hit a six-digit code into the intercom keypad next to the driveway. The gate clicked, then swung slowly open. The driver sped forward.

The driveway curved gracefully between two

symmetrical rows of old birch trees whose branches hung over the drive, creating a shadowy canopy. Past the trees spread lawn to the property's border, demarcated by the brick wall in the far distance. At the end of the driveway, in a clearing at the top of a small rise, stood a rambling whitewashed brick mansion. A circular parking area was in front. In the middle was a small flower garden.

A young woman in jeans and a T-shirt was leaning over a spray of bright red peonies and cutting them.

The Jaguar coughed a few times as its driver forgot to downshift, nearly conking out. When he finally downshifted, the car shot forward, engine revving furiously, tires kicking up stones.

The woman watched with a bemused smile as the car sputtered up the driveway.

She had long brown hair and was barefoot. She took a few steps toward the approaching car, her hands holding a large bunch of flowers, as the Jaguar came to a stop just in front of her.

She stepped to the side of the car and leaned down toward him.

He had on sunglasses and a run-down camouflage baseball hat. His skin was a deep, rich brown.

"Hi, Dewey," she said.

"Hi, Daisy."

"Nice driving."

Dewey fumbled for the handle and stepped out

of the car. He removed his sunglasses and looked at Daisy Calibrisi with a slightly embarrassed expression.

"It's not mine."

Daisy stepped toward him and reached out her arms.

"I'm glad you're here," she said, hugging him. "Thanks for coming. At the rate Dad's going, he won't be done until Christmas."

"Where is he?"

"In back."

Dewey leaned down to give her a polite kiss on the cheek. At the last moment, she moved her face slightly to the right so that their lips met. Dewey kissed her quickly and took a step back.

Daisy grinned. There ensued a few moments of awkward silence.

"You're tan," Daisy said. "You been sunbathing?"

"I don't sunbathe, Daisy."

"Well how'd you get so tan?"

"I don't know. I played golf the other day."

"Golf? You?"

"Yeah, *me*. Why so surprised?"

"It just seems like an old man's game."

"I *am* an old man."

Daisy smiled.

She glanced down at Dewey's flip-flops, then let her eyes move up his legs, which were tan, a little hairy, and, above all, thick with muscle. Her eyes stopped when they hit a pair of old plaid Bermuda shorts with paint stains on them and a rip near one of the hems.

"Are you any good?" she asked.

"Let's put it this way: I got three hole in ones once."

"My God. Really?"

"Yeah. One round."

"You're serious?"

"Yes, Daisy. I know how to play."

She gave Dewey a suspicious look, not sure if she should believe him. She nodded slowly.

"Well, if it *is* true," she said, "that's pretty amazing."

"Thanks."

"Where was it? One of the courses around here?"

"No. It was in Maine."

"Maine?" she asked disparagingly. "They have golf in Maine?"

"Yes, they have golf in Maine, dickhead."

"So where was this so-called golf course where you supposedly got this hole in one?"

"Plural," said Dewey. "Three of them."

"Okay, what's the name of the course?"

"Bangor Acres. It's an eighteen-hole golf course. I grew up going there."

"Bangor Acres? That sounds like a cemetery."

"It's the best miniature golf course in northern Maine. It's off Main Street, out near the railroad. Take a right. It's a little run-down, but it only costs five bucks to play."

Daisy started laughing uncontrollably.

"*Miniature* golf?"

"I've always been able to get it through the windmill."

Daisy was still laughing.

"Sometimes I think about what could've been if I'd focused on golf. You know, the wealth, limos, that sort of thing."

"You're a jackass," she said.

Dewey kicked his foot against the pebbles. Then he glanced at her. Daisy's dark hair was in a ponytail. Her nose was sharp, long, and pretty. Her eyes were deep brown, with long lashes. She looked warm, elegant, and mysterious. A young Sophia Loren.

Dewey found himself staring at her for perhaps a moment too long, and he forced himself to look away, glancing past her, at the plot of dirt she'd been digging.

"What are you planting?" he asked, nodding toward the dirt. "You guys getting in on that medical marijuana thing?"

Daisy didn't answer. Instead, she waited for his eyes to return to hers. When at last they finally did, she gave him a Cheshire Cat grin.

"What?" he asked innocently.

She smiled and shook her head.

"Nothing."

Dewey didn't say anything for several moments.

"I hear you graduated," Dewey finally coughed out.

"Yeah."

"Congratulations."

"Thanks."

"Law school. That's a biggie."

"Let me guess," Daisy said. "*Thank God the world has another lawyer,* right?"

"I wasn't going to say that," he protested.

"You weren't?"

Dewey shook his head.

"No. I think lawyers are misunderstood."

"Really? You're serious? I totally agree."

"Yeah, ninety-nine percent of lawyers make the other one percent look bad."

"Jerk," she said. "Total jerk. Why do I fall for your jokes every time?"

"All kidding aside, I'm proud of you, actually," said Dewey.

"Thanks," she whispered.

He followed her around the side of the house to the backyard. A tall orange ladder was propped against the house, Calibrisi at the top, slapping black paint on a shutter on the second floor. Calibrisi's face had a smattering of black paint spots and smudges.

"Hi, Hector," said Dewey.

"Dewey!" yelled Calibrisi. He jerked his head around to see Dewey. "You just get heeeeeere—"

Calibrisi's voice inflected into a high-pitched, panicked howl as he suddenly felt the ladder shift to the left. He reached out to grab hold of

74

something to prevent his falling. His hand grabbed the shutter, which was covered in wet paint and slippery. The ladder shifted some more and now Calibrisi reached out with both hands, scrambling desperately for something hard to stem the fall. The wet hand left a black handprint as he continued to slide, creating a hideous track of paint across the white wall.

"Heeeeeeelllllppppp!" he groaned as the ladder picked up speed.

Dewey charged toward the ladder and grabbed it, but he couldn't stop it. Calibrisi's weight, the sharp angle, the length of the ladder—it all had too much momentum.

"Dewey! Stop it!" Daisy screamed.

Dewey's eyes went left. If Calibrisi fell, he would land on a blue stone terrace. From two floors up, there might be a broken bone or two. Dewey thrust his left leg between two rungs and slammed his shoulder into the side of the ladder, letting out a loud grunt as the steel crunched against him and stopped. It teetered at a precarious forty-five-degree angle.

With his left shoulder and left thigh against the ladder, Dewey held it, preventing it from moving any more.

He glanced up. Calibrisi had one hand on the copper gutter and the other on the ladder, holding on desperately. His brow was furrowed, his face beet red.

For a few moments, there was only silence and the sound of Calibrisi's heavy panting.

Suddenly, the back door of the house opened. Vivian Calibrisi stepped outside. She saw Dewey, intertwined like a pretzel with the ladder, and her eyes scanned up the brick wall, where they followed the black smears of paint to where they concluded, at the corner of the house, and her husband, now at the top of the ladder, dangling from a combination of ladder and gutter. She slowly shook her head.

"Serves you right, stubborn old mule."

Dewey glanced in her direction. "Hi, Vivian," he said matter-of-factly.

"Hi, Dewey."

She walked over to Daisy. Together, they stood looking at Calibrisi clinging on to the gutter for dear life, with Dewey pressed against the ladder like a linebacker against a tackling dummy, holding it still.

"Are you going to just stand there?" asked Calibrisi, a hint of annoyance in his voice.

"Who are you talking to?" asked Dewey.

"All of you!"

Dewey glanced at Daisy, then, ever so slightly, let up on the ladder. It slid a few inches.

"Stop!" yelled Calibrisi. "What the hell are you—"

"I told him to hire a painting company," said Vivian.

"Last time I did that, they spilled paint all over the flowers! Now get me down!"

"There's more than one painting company," said Vivian, shaking her head. She stepped back toward the door.

"I agree," said Dewey.

"Fuck you," whispered Calibrisi.

"Can you stay for dinner?" Vivian asked, smiling at Dewey.

Dewey nodded. "Sure."

Vivian looked up at Calibrisi. "By the way, you have a phone call."

Calibrisi's face went from beet red to a slightly darker shade.

"Vivian!" he yelled. *"Take a message!"*

Dewey let the ladder slide another few inches.

"That's not a very nice way to speak to your wife," said Dewey.

Dewey let go again, the ladder sliding another inch or two. He turned and caught Daisy's eyes. She was laughing.

Calibrisi shut his eyes. He was quiet for several moments. Finally, he opened them and looked down.

"My apologies," he said to Dewey, calmer now.

"Apology accepted," said Dewey. "Now how about your wife?"

Dewey nodded toward the door, where Vivian was still standing, about to go back inside.

"Vivian," said Calibrisi, "love of my life, my

sincere apologies. And if it wouldn't impose too much hardship on thee, would you be so kind as to take a message?"

"Will you hire a painting company?"

"Yes, dear," he said.

Dewey looked up at Calibrisi.

"Okay," said Dewey. "Chill out. On three. Pull yourself along the gutter."

Dewey took three deep breaths.

"One, two, *three!*" He launched and hit the ladder with his left shoulder. The ladder flung right a few inches. Dewey repeated it. With each strike, the ladder moved a few inches until, finally, it was straight.

Calibrisi climbed down. He stood in front of Dewey.

"Thanks."

Dewey nodded. He reached for his shoulder.

"You okay?"

"Fine."

"So how was your trip?" asked Calibrisi.

"Good."

Just then, Vivian opened the door.

"He won't let me take a message," she said. "He says it's important."

Calibrisi looked at Dewey.

"Who is it?"

"Rick Mallory."

9

OLD QUARTER
ALEPPO, SYRIA

The Old Quarter was really not a neighbor-hood. That is, if a neighborhood was considered homes, families, schools, and shops, a place where people lived, where children grew up, where fathers and mothers left for work in the morning and returned at night, where gardens were planted out in front of homes and tended to with pride. No, this was not a neighborhood. Not anymore.

It was wreckage now, every building pocked with holes, and many little more than concrete rubble, the occasional steel rebar beam jutting into the air. The dull staccato of automatic weapon fire was the sound track. Even now, after midnight, every few minutes the silence was interrupted by a fusillade, as fighters on both sides battled for title to the neighborhood that had once been. The families were long gone. All that was left was the Syrian Army, a few dozen American UAVs flying overhead, and ISIS.

Garotin sat in the backseat of an extended-cab pickup truck, staring at the screen of his iPad. On it was a blueprint grid of the square mile directly in front of him. His soldiers were represented by small red dots; the enemy forces were green. Garotin had a cold, hard expression. He didn't smile much, but if he did, he would certainly be smiling now. By dawn they would take the Old Quarter. Which meant they would control the southern and eastern flanks of Aleppo. After that, the Syrian Army would have no choice but to withdraw.

The forces of ISIS were coming ineluctably closer and closer to Damascus.

"Drone!" came a voice over the walkie-talkie. "Thirty–one–two. Above the train station."

The man next to Garotin, Bakr, his deputy, glanced at him.

"Should we move the men?"

"No," said Garotin.

"There are at least twenty men near the station," said Bakr.

"If we move the men, the United States will understand that we can see the drones at night," said Garotin. "It is worth much more than twenty men to have them not know. Do as I say."

The truck was dark, save for the glow of the iPad. Garotin lit a cigarette and sat back and watched. For several minutes, the scene was eerily dark, punctuated by the sound of gunfire every now and then. Suddenly, the telltale high-pitched scream of a missile could be heard, followed by an explosion, just a few blocks away. This was followed by another missile, then another explosion. There were four in all.

Screams came from the walkie-talkie. After several moments, someone came on the line.

"We're hit."

Bakr could see flames dance above the rubble a few blocks away. He raised the walkie-talkie to his mouth. "Move toward the train station."

"I have casualties. I don't know how many men are alive."

Garotin reached over and took the walkie-talkie from him.

"Move to the station," he barked. *"Now!"*

Garotin tossed the walkie-talkie back to Bakr.

"Tell ammunitions to meet them with RPGs," ordered Garotin.

"We have a week's worth of RPGs," said Bakr. "Maybe less. We're running out."

"What do you mean, we're running out?"

"I told you this, Commander. I told you this yesterday. We're almost out."

Garotin nodded, remembering. He took a last drag on his cigarette, then flicked it out the window.

"Yes, you did," he said. "We'll have to do this with what we have."

"Bullets are in short supply as well," said Bakr.

Garotin paused, deep in thought. His face showed disappointment.

"How much do we have?"

"Two weeks at most," said Bakr. "I don't see how we can move across the river without more ammunition."

Garotin nodded, understanding. He gestured to the door, indicating for Bakr to leave him alone.

"Just get them to the train station," said Garotin. "By dawn I want a line of attack to the east of the hospital. Let me worry about the ammunition."

10

PORT OF TAMPICO
MEXICO

The guns were sanitized. There were no manufacturer engravings or other identifiers on any of them. And they were all precisely the same model: M4 carbine, blackish-gray, gas-operated, magazine-fed, telescoping stock, Picatinny rail, vertical forward grip, 14.5-inch barrel, semiautomatic and three-round burst firing capability, .223-caliber or 5.56×45mm NATO cartridge.

It was a favorite of most counterterrorist and Special Forces units because of its combination of compact size and vicious firepower; it was the model of choice for close-quarters combat and urban warfare.

There were no individual cases to hold each

weapon, thus maximizing volume inside the forty-foot-long steel shipping container. Like sardines in the proverbial can, they were arrayed in rows and stacked to the roof of the box. The container held about eight hundred guns in all and was the thirty-second container loaded to the teeth. Twenty-five thousand guns in all.

The weapons were manufactured in Mexico by a company called MH Armas, whose engineers had replicated the original design by Colt Manufacturing. They were knockoffs, but no less lethal than the standard offering.

A black-and-yellow mobile gantry crane lowered the container to the ship, stacking it on top of an already bulging checkerboard of forty-foot steel containers.

In addition to the containers filled with M4s, fifty-eight containers were filled with bullets. Ammo cans the size of mailboxes were loaded with 5.56×45mm slugs, then packed together in wirebound wooden crates and stacked on pallets. Pallets of the crates were stacked to the roof of the containers. In all, there were more than 330 million slugs about to leave for the trip to the Middle East.

But guns weren't the only fare on the weighed-down, freshly painted, 662-foot-long container ship. The containers closest to the front of the boat held contents much more valuable and much more lethal: stacks of HEATs, high-explosive antitank missiles. There were seventy containers filled with antitank missiles and ten containers with shoulder-fired, recoilless rocket launchers. They could take out tanks and other battlefield armament but were also extremely effective in urban environments. One well-targeted HEAT missile could take down half a building and easily kill a dozen men. Many cities throughout the Middle East were pockmarked with the legacy of the ubiquitous weapon.

Dawn approached as the final container was battened with steel cord to the ship. It would be a scalding-hot day; already the temperature was above ninety degrees. The sky was changing rapidly from gray to deep red as the sun approached at the eastern horizon. In many ways, a perfect day.

A tall bearded man named Miguel stood next to the base of the gantry crane. He took a last drag on a cigarette as he watched the final container settle into place. Next to him was a short, stocky man in khakis, a white polo shirt, and black cowboy boots: Mark Raditz. His skin, after less than a day in Mexico, was blaze red with burn. He was overweight.

"Were you able to deliver the other things I asked you for?" asked Raditz.

"Yes. The passport is with the money. It's Mexican, I don't know what name they used, but it's been cleared up through the proper authorities."

"Can you trust the people who did it?"

"You can't trust anyone," said Miguel. "I don't know the government official who arranged everything. But I wouldn't worry. If these officials didn't have their little bribes and corruption, they would all starve to death."

"How much did it cost?"

"One hundred thousand dollars."

"That's less than your fee."

"Much less," said Miguel, "but if you don't like it, perhaps I can send a refund to your office, Mr. Deputy Defense Secretary?"

Raditz sneered.

"How much money is left over?"

"The total amount of funds that you wired was eight hundred and eight million dollars. That was ten million more than the job, the weapons, et cetera. Subtract the fee for the passport as well as my fee for arranging the passport, and there is nine million six hundred and fifty thousand dollars left over. As you asked, I washed nine million into a new bank account. The details are with the passport. I converted the rest into euros, Visa gift cards, and pesos."

Raditz nodded, staring at the ground.

There was an awkward moment of silence.

"I'm curious, Mark," said Miguel. "You've never taken anything before. Suddenly you decide to take a lot of money. You arrange for a new identity. It's fairly obvious what's happening. My question is, why?"

"That's none of your fucking business," Raditz said. "You know the rules. Drop the boxes and keep your mouth shut."

"They might come looking for you."

"They *will* come looking for me."

"Do you expect me to not say anything?"

"That's up to you," said Raditz. "But America does things to people who deliver guns and missiles to terrorists."

"I'm like the FedEx man, that's all."

Raditz shot Miguel a look.

"They'd kill Santa Claus if they found out he was delivering guns to ISIS. You should be able to retire after this one, with what I've paid you."

"With what *you've* paid me?" asked Miguel, grinning. "You mean with what the United States of America paid me."

"Whatever. But I wouldn't come back, not if you value your life. I'm saying that to protect you. You can listen or not. It doesn't matter to me."

Miguel flicked another cigarette stub into the water and leapt onto the ship. He nodded to a crewman standing along the starboard gunnel, indicating he wanted him to untie the ship so that they could put to sea.

"Fine," said Miguel. "By the way, you don't look so good, Mark. You look like you're one cheeseburger away from a massive heart attack."

Raditz smiled. "Fuck you. How many days will it take you to get to Syria?"

"That's none of your business," answered Miguel, grinning.

Raditz's smile disappeared. If he found amusement in Miguel's flippant answer, he didn't show it.

"We'll have the Gulf Stream behind us. Eight days to Gibraltar and another three to al-Bayda," he said, referring to the port on the Syrian coast.

The ship made an almost imperceptible tremor, indicating it was moving.

"Safe travels," said Raditz.

11

DAMASCUS, SYRIA

As Marwan al-Jaheishi waited for the video to download on his laptop, he removed a manila folder from his briefcase. He opened the folder. The top page was a contact sheet filled with small photos, all showing the same two men: Nazir and an American VIP. Grainy black-and-white photos showed the two men as they sat on a sofa in the lobby of a hotel, from a discreet distance. Al-Jaheishi remembered taking the photos, at Nazir's instruction. The following pages were the transcript of the men's conversation.

The agents who had accompanied the American had patted down Nazir, then scanned him with a magnetometer, but al-Jaheishi, again at Nazir's direction, had planted six listening devices around the hotel lobby the evening before, and one, taped to the underside of the sofa they sat on, caught the entire conversation. The transcript of the meeting was twenty-six pages long. The remaining pages in the folder, perhaps a hundred in all, listed the contents of a large shipment of weapons that had arrived a few months later. Each sheet of paper was an individual container, with its contents listed. This, too, al-Jaheishi had been in charge of, again at Nazir's direction. The American gave them little warning, other than to tell them they would need a crane and the ability to move at least a hundred forty-foot containers. The American had assumed Nazir and his men would be too busy, stressed, or lazy to contemplate the book-keeping of the arms shipment, but he was wrong. Al-Jaheishi had cataloged everything.

Al-Jaheishi lifted his phone, turned on the camera, then leaned down and framed the first page and snapped a photo. Methodically, as quickly as he could, he moved through the entire sheaf of papers, photographing every one. He saved the photos onto the SIM card, then popped the card from the phone and put it in his pocket.

The video completed downloading to his laptop. He watched the entire thing; it was a little more than twelve minutes long. When it was done, he shut his eyes, trying to control an overwhelming sense of nausea. It was the first time they'd burned anyone alive. He felt revulsion. At that moment, he wanted to kill himself.

He looked at his hand, first the top, then the palm. Scars ran on both sides. They were pinkish and faded, each about two inches long and half an inch wide. It was the place Nazir had stabbed him so many years ago in Cairo. He felt even worse as he considered the level of degradation and humiliation he'd been willing to tolerate.

Then he heard the words inside his own head: *You want to live, Marwan.*

He opened his eyes. He was so close.

As he did with all of the videos, al-Jaheishi cleaned up the beginning, adding ISIS's telltale opening: a ten-second clip showing the ISIS logo in bold white across a black screen, with the soft melody of an Arabian folk song playing in the background.

He edited the rest of the tape to remove any moments that appeared to be badly filmed or in some way unprofessional. He cut the remaining video into precise sequences—couple moving from trailer, gasoline, immolation—creating sharp intercuts between them. He then applied a sophisticated film-editing hue to the entire film, similar to what TV news editors did. When he was done, the video was seven minutes long and looked as if it had been made by someone at CNN.

He watched it one last time. As the flames engulfed the American man and woman, al-Jaheishi felt a sense of shame and self-loathing.

"I'm sorry," he said aloud.

But his words were not intended for the Americans, whose muted screams now filled the room. No, al-Jaheishi's words were intended for the one in whose name it was happening, the one whom he'd been brought up to believe was not cruel, the one for whom he would now risk everything in order to stop it.

Al-Jaheishi picked up his phone. He breathed deeply, counting to ten, trying to calm his nerves. He hit Speed Dial. The phone rang several times, then clicked.

"Yes," came the voice.

"Tristan," he said.

"Marwan," answered Nazir. "Have you down-loaded it yet?"

"Yes. I downloaded it and edited it. Everything is done."

"Very good. Does it meet your approval?"

"It's like the others, Tristan," he said, immediately regretting the hint of disapproval he knew his answer had implied.

"You don't like it?" said Nazir.

"No, I didn't mean that at all."

"It's too violent? You think perhaps we go too far? Tell me."

Al-Jaheishi paused.

"No, I like it. They are infidels. We must continue to—"

"Stop feeding me your lines of bullshit," snapped Nazir. "It's not a video anyone will like, but it is necessary. *Necessary,* Marwan."

"You will be pleased. Would you like to see it before I upload it?"

Nazir was quiet for a few moments.

"No," he said. "Get it out immediately."

An hour later, al-Jaheishi was dressed in a gray pin-striped suit, a white button-down, and a yellow tie. He entered the office building and showed his ID card to the security guard, then took the elevator to the eighteenth floor. He walked to the end of the hallway, past several office suites of companies with names like Parish Capital Ltd. and Simoan Trans-Atlantic Holdings, until he arrived at a frosted glass door with the name ASSYRIAN RELIEF ASSETS LTD.

The entrance area was large and quiet. A long, elegant glass receptionist's desk sat directly to the left, an empty leather chair behind it. This was where Assra, the receptionist, usually sat, but today she was not there. Two modern black-leather-and-chrome couches were to the right, facing each other around a low oval glass coffee table with newspapers and magazines piled neatly on top.

The back of the entrance foyer was a long floor-to-ceiling window. The sprawling city of Damascus was visible beyond.

Al-Jaheishi walked down the hall, past half a dozen offices. He said hello to his coworkers as he quickly passed the open doors. At the end of the hallway, he opened his door, stepped inside, and flipped on the lights.

A man was seated in his chair. He had his shoes up on top of al-Jaheishi's desk, legs crossed at the ankles.

"Good morning, Marwan. You're late."

"I was at prayers, Tristan."

Al-Jaheishi felt perspiration surface at his hand, upon his forehead, even on his upper lip. He tried not to look at Nazir as he removed his coat and hung it on the back of his door. He said nothing as he walked to his desk and placed his leather briefcase on the corner.

"They're calling us butchers," said Nazir. "Isn't that what they should've called us after the beheadings, Marwan?"

Al-Jaheishi laughed.

"Now, perhaps they should call us arsonists," continued Nazir.

Al-Jaheishi laughed again.

"It turns your stomach, doesn't it, Marwan?" asked Nazir.

"No," said al-Jaheishi. "It's necessary."

"Is it?" asked Nazir. "And what will we do when

we have a country of our own? If it is necessary now, will it not still be necessary then?"

"There are stages to the development of the state," said al-Jaheishi, lying. "When it is no longer necessary, you won't do it, and you will look benevolent in comparison, Tristan."

Al-Jaheishi stared at Nazir. Nazir's eyes were like black lasers. *Does he know?*

"But it's brutality, Marwan. We could just kill them. Instead, we behead them. We burn them alive. Surely, between us, you can see the terrible things we're doing?"

He's testing you, Marwan.

"What will never be forgotten is the brutality," answered al-Jaheishi, "but it is like steel in the sword of our rule and our power. We can perhaps someday stop, but the brutality will instill fear forever."

Nazir nodded, then, ever so slowly, smiled. "Very good," he said.

Nazir removed his feet from the desk, swung them around, and stood.

Al-Jaheishi looked right, past Nazir, to a filing cabinet. A screwdriver jutted from the top drawer, wedged in, as if someone had been trying to pry it open.

Al-Jaheishi's eyes moved from the screwdriver back to Nazir.

"The combination is your birthday, Tristan," said al-Jaheishi. "All you had to do was ask."

"Where are they?" asked Nazir.

"Where are what?"

"The records."

"What records?"

"You know damn well what records. Everything to do with the arms shipments from the Americans."

Al-Jaheishi looked into Nazir's angry eyes. He felt his own eyes drawn like metal to a magnet, wanting to look at his briefcase. But he held Nazir's stare.

"They're in there," said al-Jaheishi.

Al-Jaheishi's mind, in less than two seconds, ratcheted through the dilemma he now faced.

He stepped in front of Nazir. He went to the second drawer from the top and started to turn the lock, even though he knew the records—all 158 pages of them—were inside his briefcase. But if he admitted to taking them from the office, Nazir would want to know why. And when al-Jaheishi attempted to make something up, Nazir would see through it. He would be tortured for the truth, and dead within the hour.

The problem was, if the records weren't in the filing cabinet, a similar fate would likely befall him. But perhaps he could create an excuse. As he dialed the combination, there was a calm look on his face, yet inside he was so scared he felt faint. He unlocked the drawer and, just as he started to pull it out, heard the monotone beeping of Nazir's cell.

Al-Jaheishi reached into the drawer as he listened.

"Yes," said Nazir, just a foot behind him. "What?"

Al-Jaheishi grabbed a sheaf of files that had nothing to do with the arms shipments, pulling them out and turning . . .

Nazir was already at the door. He had the phone to his ear. He turned, covering the phone with one hand.

"Bring them to my office," Nazir said as al-Jaheishi motioned toward him with the stack of files.

Al-Jaheishi nodded and watched as Nazir walked quickly down the hall. He waited an extra moment, then another, and then one more. He opened the locks on his briefcase and popped it open, frantically switching the files inside with those in his hand. He shut the briefcase and bounded for the doorway.

12

RAMAT DAVID AIRBASE
ISRAELI AIR FORCE
JEZREEL VALLEY, ISRAEL

Dewey was the only passenger aboard the CIA Gulfstream 150, part of the Agency's fleet of aircraft scattered around the world, a quasi airline referred to internally as Air America.

The cabin was dimly lit as the jet cut across the last miles of the nine-hour trip. Both sides of the cabin were filled with luxurious cream-colored leather captain's chairs. Near the front, two large, deep built-in sofas stretched beneath the windows. Some of the Agency's planes were stripped down and lacked creature comforts, but a few, like this one, were posh, used primarily when the Agency was escorting members of Congress into a hot zone.

It was the kind of supremely comfortable plane where a passenger could easily fall asleep for the entire flight. But Dewey hadn't slept at all. Now, nine hours in and less than one to go before landing in northern Israel, he realized he'd made a mistake by not trying to grab a nod or two.

He read, for the third time, the brief Political Activities Division report on ISIS and its leader, Tristan Nazir.

TOP SECRET TOP SECRET TOP SECRET
FLASH PROFILE: *TERROR ALERT*
CONTEXT: TERRORIST ENTITY 445 ISIS
TAG(S): Nazir, Tristan; Garotin; Muslim
Brotherhood; ISIS; Beheadings
LAST UPDATE: JULY 8
BG RR4:
ISIS was founded in 2013 following the collapse of the Muslim Brotherhood in Egypt. The main architecture of the group is Iraqi Baathist, but its leadership—a cult of personality—is Muslim Brotherhood.

The group has, in a very short amount of time, aggregated disparate elements of the radical Islamic diaspora across Iraq and Syria into a cohesive, tightly run, disciplined operating entity. All military activities fall under the rubric of Ahmad Garotin, a 31-year-old Egyptian who previously served as military strategist for the Brotherhood in Egypt. It is assumed Garotin and Nazir connected during this tumultuous period in Cairo.

The history of ISIS is really about its founder, Tristan Nazir.

By age 26, Nazir was already a member of the Muslim Brotherhood's Executive Office, as well as a member of the Brotherhood's Shura Council, its governing body. Nazir was immensely valuable to the Brotherhood due primarily to his financial training and expertise. Although he did not graduate, Nazir attended the London School of Economics 2009-10 and Oxford 2007-08. Nazir was in charge of the Brotherhood's finances and fund-raising prior to Morsi's election. He managed the appropriation of all Brotherhood money and thus negotiated larger contracts with vendors, including arms manufacturers.

Quiet, taciturn, calm, and confident, even arrogant, Nazir was the brains behind much of the ascendancy of the Muslim Brotherhood in Egypt. Beneath his polished demeanor Nazir was a radical with extreme anti-American and anti-West beliefs. He preached a strategy of "accretion and permanence." If the Brotherhood wanted to be more than just a mouthpiece for Islam and actually govern,

Nazir argued, it required structural sources of recurring income. Al Qaeda, Nazir argued, would ultimately be a temporary entity due to the fact that it failed to create an ongoing source of revenue. Taxation was how countries did it. The Muslim Brotherhood couldn't tax anyone and thus needed "bridge" financing. Oil production—acquired via military action—was the only way. Early on, Nazir was vocal in his calls for the military wing of the Brotherhood to use its strength to take petroleum-related assets that could then be resold. "Political power is meaning-less if not accompanied by territory and natural resources. These hard assets will enable the Brotherhood to build permanence," he said.

To the extent the Arab Spring was artificially manufactured and stoked, especially in its early days, Nazir was one of the main architects of that effort, knowing it could create opportunities for the Brotherhood. Following the Arab Spring and the ascension of Morsi to the Egyptian presidency, most members of the

Shura Council argued that Morsi—and the Brotherhood generally—needed to show that he/it could tolerate opposition and that he/it would govern with moderation and thus show the world that sharia could work. Nazir was the only member of the Shura Council who argued for brutality, calling for the execution of all Egyptian military officers and political leaders and the imposition of martial law until such time as the Brotherhood was firmly ensconced in power. Nazir was ultimately fired from Morsi's inner circle. He achieved freedom through dubious circumstances SAD/COMSTET have been unable to determine. He resurfaced two years later after ISIS was well on its way to consolidating power in Syrian and Iraqi militant [non-AQ] circles. It is believed he engineered a partnership with Yasim Hussein, one of the Iraqi Baathists . . .

The jet arced left and Dewey put the folder down. He glanced out the porthole. It was nighttime. Clouds obscured any lights that might have been visible on the ground.

Dewey had been to the Middle East on several

occasions. Some memories were better than others, though calling one better than another was like saying getting stabbed was better than getting shot. Now, reading about ISIS gave Dewey that same sick feeling he had whenever he was back. It was the feeling of lacking control, of being at the edge of chaos, of being among people who wanted you dead.

It was the same feeling he had when he climbed into the back of a truck in Afghanistan two years before. The memory made his heart race and his stomach clench.

Dewey had spent a tumultuous three days executing the overthrow of Omar El-Khayab, a radical Islamist who'd been elected Pakistan's president and was threatening nuclear war with India. After successfully executing the coup, Dewey had been double-crossed, taken hostage, and sent to the terrorist Aswan Fortuna, nearly dying on a blood-soaked tarmac in Beirut.

Israel had saved his life. Now he was back.

The Gulfstream landed at 2 a.m. Israel time, touching down on one of the runways at Ramat David Airbase. Of the Israeli Air Force's nine bases, Ramat David was one of the busiest, largest, and most vulnerable, sitting just a handful of miles from both Lebanon and Syria.

The plane came to a stop near a white brick building at the end of the runway. Dewey walked to the front of the plane and stepped into the cockpit. He leaned forward, between the two pilots, trying to get a look out the front window.

In the distance, a door at the front of the building opened and a small group of men stepped out. They moved directly toward the plane. The first two were Israeli soldiers, each clutching a submachine gun trained away and at the tarmac. They were followed by an older man, slightly overweight, also in uniform. A fourth man stepped out right behind him. He wore tan camouflage tactical gear. He was young and walked with a slight limp. He had brown hair and a beard and mustache. What skin on his face was visible was painted black.

"What are your orders?" Dewey asked the pilots.

"We're to wait for you, sir," said the pilot on the left.

"Can you check COMMSPEC for any messages from Hector?"

"Sure." The pilot swiveled to his left to a small screen. He typed into a keyboard, waited, then looked at Dewey.

"There's a SPEC SHEET alteration, sir," he said. "You want me to send it to your phone?"

"Print it," said Dewey.

A moment later, a printer on a shelf came to life. It stopped after printing one page. Dewey grabbed the end of the piece of paper and ripped it off the printer. His eyes quickly scanned the sheet.

SPEC SHEET:
MISSION ARCHITECTURE V.14s

1. ANDREAS to infiltrate Syria via IAF/S13 joint task force, drop off Tishreen Park approx. 2 miles from Damascus central and RV one.
2. ANDREAS moves to east central Damascus ON FOOT to neighborhood Karsbi. Meet-up will take place at café DIRECTLY ACROSS FROM STATUE (photo #1).
3. [Seychelles UAV tactical Group 14: LIVE]
4. MALLORY (photo #2) arrives between 0830 A.M. and 0900 A.M.
5. *ALTERATION* AL-JAHEISHI (photo #3) arrives and will exfiltrate with MALLORY.
6. PARAMETER 4: MALLORY acquires SIM card from AL-JAHEISHI prior to exfiltration.
7. ANDREAS, MALLORY, AL-JAHEISHI move on foot to Passahq Park. Exfiltration to Ramat David IAF Israel.

At the top of the sheet was a black-and-white photo of a café. The photo showed a collection of half-empty tables, with Arabic writing on the café's signage. The statue was visible across a sidewalk.

The second photo showed Mallory. He was a white man in his thirties, good-looking, with short-cropped blond hair. The third and last photo was al-Jaheishi. He looked young, in his early twenties. He had black hair combed neatly to the side, olive skin, and a kind smile on his face.

Dewey folded the paper and stuffed it in the pocket of his jeans. He made eye contact with both pilots.

"They'll put you up somewhere," said Dewey. "I'll be back sometime tomorrow afternoon."

"Good luck," said the female pilot.

Dewey turned just as the hydraulic for the Gulfstream's door made a series of low chimes, then pushed the door open and down, as a set of air stairs unfolded. He pulled out his phone and hit Speed Dial, calling Calibrisi once more.

"I'm about to go in," said Dewey.

"You get the add-on to the SPEC?"

"Yeah, that's why I called. Tell your drone guys to back off. I don't want to tip our hand."

"Got it."

"I gotta run."

He descended the steps just as a group of Israelis from the barracks building arrived beneath the jet. Two armed soldiers separated and formed a two-point cordon around Dewey and the two Israelis.

"Dewey," came the booming, gravelly baritone voice of the older man, Menachem Dayan, Israel's top military commander.

"General Dayan," said Dewey as he stepped onto the tarmac. He grabbed Dayan's hand and shook it vigorously.

Dewey's eyes moved to Dayan's left.

"Hi, Dewey," said the younger man in tactical camo, Kohl Meir.

Dewey grinned, stepped to Meir, and grabbed his hand.

"Hi, Kohl. I wasn't expecting you to be here."

"You think I'm going to let you go inside Syria without me? You'll be dead in fifteen minutes."

"Probably."

"We need to get you rigged up and moving," said Dayan. "We have a tight window to get over the valley."

Dewey followed them to the barracks. He was led to a brightly lit room lined on both sides with lockers. In the middle of the room stood an elevated chair, like a barber's chair. A tall woman in a white uniform was already in the room. Dayan nodded to her and she moved to Dewey's side, quickly measuring him, then searched a long rack of clothing at the back of the room. She returned with an outfit, which Dewey changed into: a dark gray robe with red piping and a red sash.

Dewey stepped to a mirror and examined himself, a slightly quizzical appearance on his face.

"Religious garb," said Dayan. "You will be dressed like an aging cleric."

"Does this mean I can perform weddings?" asked Dewey.

Dayan and Meir ignored Dewey's joke.

"The SLA usually leave the clerics alone," said Meir. "If you were smaller, perhaps we could dress you up like a woman, but I don't think there are any six-foot-four, two-hundred-and-fifty-pound Syrian women running around."

"Two twenty-five," said Dewey.

Meir arched his eyebrows as he scanned Dewey from head to toe.

"Sure, Dewey." He nodded, a big shit-eating grin on his face. Meir looked at Dayan.

"He must be, how do you say, 'big boned,'" added Dayan, grinning.

Dewey laughed, shaking his head.

The woman snapped a finger and motioned for Dewey to take a seat in the elevated chair.

She studied his skin for several seconds. "You're tan," she said. "That's helpful."

She dusted Dewey's face with a light layer of makeup, which had hints of black, making his skin appear more weathered and old. Then she colored his hair with dry dye, making Dewey's hair mostly gray with some remnant black. Unlike wet dye, it would wash out. She did the same with his mustache and beard.

"This is designed to hold for a short period of time," she said. "If you need to, it will all wash out and clean off with water and soap. It will not last more than a day."

As she worked on Dewey, Dayan and Meir stood in front of him. Dayan lit a cigarette. Meir stood, arms crossed.

"What if someone says something to me?" asked Dewey.

Dayan shook his head, grinning.

"Don't open your fucking mouth," he said. "Trust me. You're like baseball, hot dogs, apple pie, and Chevrolet all rolled up into a gorilla. Even the clerics will try to kill you."

Dayan and Meir briefed him on the upcoming helicopter trip.

"Syria has always been a level-one, on-the-dirt environment," Dayan said. "It's not safe. When I was in Sayeret Metkal, I preferred going to Beirut over Damascus. The Syrians are a bizarre, violent, untrustworthy people. Now it's far more dangerous. You have a very paranoid Syrian Army, you have Russians, and you have local police and militia who are loyal to the Assads running around killing anyone they suspect could be affiliated with ISIS. I don't like it. Whatever you're going to Damascus for, it better be damn well worth your life."

"Damascus is very chaotic right now," added Meir. "Refugees are everywhere. NGOs, aid groups. Mercenaries protecting them. It's a humanitarian crisis. So it will be busy, hectic, and overflowing with people. Everyone from the smaller cities is coming there to get away from the war zones. Within the overall chaos, it should be relatively straightforward. You'll blend in fine. I tend to worry less about the Syrian regulars. What you need to watch out for is ISIS. They're inside Damascus, according to our sources."

"Can you tell us anything about the operation?" asked Dayan.

"It's an exfiltration. Two VIPs, an American and an A-Rab."

"Who is he?"

Dewey glanced at Dayan and Meir. "A top-level informant inside ISIS."

Meir was quiet as he registered Dewey's words.

"His name?" asked Dayan.

"His name's irrelevant."

"If he played the run-up to the meeting incorrectly and ISIS suspects something, you'll be compromised too," said Dayan. "Is there some sort of check-in before you hang your neck out?"

Dewey shook his head.

"Dewey," said Dayan with a concerned look on his face, "I don't need to tell you what happens if they capture you."

"They'll kill you," said Meir. "Or worse."

"What's worse than getting killed, Kohl?"

"I would say being burned alive or having your head chopped off would be worse."

Dayan glanced at his watch.

"Let's go."

They walked past the CIA jet to a helicopter—dull black, side door ajar, rotors slashing the air in violent rhythm. Dewey recognized the model: Eurocopter AS565 Panther, a medium-duty very fast combat chopper that constituted the heart of the Israeli Special Forces chopper capability set.

Dewey turned to Dayan at the side door. "Bless you, son," he said, bowing, getting into the spirit of his costume.

Dayan laughed.

"Jackass," he said, shaking Dewey's hand. "See you guys tomorrow. Be careful."

The chopper rose beneath a black, wind-whipped sky. Dewey looked out the window at the massive spread of Ramat David Airbase, alight with activity: jets taking off, jets landing, refuel trucks moving, lines of soldiers running in formation around the edges of the buildings, barracks lit up. A hundred feet above the tarmac, the Panther suddenly tilted hard right, then ripped sideways as the pilot cut north toward the Golan Heights and, beyond, the Syrian border.

13

ALEPPO, SYRIA

Aleppo, at three o'clock in the afternoon, was dry, dusty, and hot. That was normal in the desert city located in the windswept plains at the center of the country. What wasn't normal were the swirling chimneys of smoke floating in all directions, dissipating at rooflines into dystopian clouds of smog. Fires burned in more than a dozen places. Automatic weapon fire rattled the air and provided a steady drumbeat to the afternoon. The mechanical *rat-a-tat-tat* of gunfire was interrupted by the occasional deep bassoon of a rocket-propelled grenade exploding or the high-pitched falsetto of a shoulder-fired missile as it tore into the limelight for a half second before slamming into a tank, a vehicle, a building, or simply a cluster of air, shaking the ground. Screams were rare, but when they rose above the chaos they were bloodcurdling.

There were no sirens. Ambulances were a prime target of the insurgents, and the few ambulance drivers remaining in Aleppo had long ago learned to drive as quickly and as quietly as they could. Most had already absconded with their ambu-lances, packing them with family and belongings, fleeing to the Syrian Army strongholds in the south.

Like most cities in Syria and the Middle East, Aleppo was surrounded by empty desert. Where the crowded city started was not a gradual beginning. Dense blocks of buildings appeared like a wall, then ran for miles. Aleppo's urban core was shaped like a large oval. It spanned approximately four miles across and two up and down. Buildings of sandstone mortar, concrete, and steel. Normally, this was where most of the population was. Normally, the streets were busy with pedestrians competing with bicycles and motorcycles, all of them competing with the beat-up cars, trucks, and buses.

But Aleppo's usual hustle and bustle was absent. Those who had the foresight and the means to flee were already long gone. Those who remained cowered in their apartments. Whole blocks had been leveled. Buildings were rubble. Streets were pockmarked with craters. Fires sprouted from random spots, dotting the horizon like an Indian camp in the Wild West.

It was the fifth day of battle. It was the bloodiest five-day siege in Syrian history. More than thirty thousand were already dead.

On one side, to the east, was the Syrian Army. On the other, the radical Islamic insurgents known as ISIS.

The outside world knew little of the battle for

Aleppo. There were no journalists anywhere near the city, save for a cameraman and a reporter from French channel TF1. But they were both dead—captured within hours of their arrival by the Muslim insurgents and beheaded. The black-clad fighters from ISIS had made the beheading of reporters their calling card.

Garotin sat in the back of a white Toyota Land Cruiser. At thirty-one he was too young to command an army, and yet it was Garotin who commanded this army. He wore dark blue canvas pants, black boots, and a red polo shirt, on top of which was a black flak jacket. His black hair was tousled and roughly parted in the middle. He had a sharp nose, bushy eyebrows, and was clean-shaven. Garotin was handsome, though he had a mean look, a look of hatred, even when relaxing.

Nazir, ISIS's leader, had placed Garotin in charge of all ISIS military activities, and Garotin had led his soldiers on a devastating onslaught of Syria and Iraq. What he lacked in training and experience, he more than made up for with sheer balls. Like Nazir, Garotin shared a deep belief in the preemptive power of violence and savagery. ISIS took no prisoners, instead ending its victorious battles with long firing lines in which surrendering troops were slaughtered. This knowledge was a powerful weapon.

ISIS counted more than two hundred thousand troops. It was an undisciplined, undertrained, motley collection of teenagers and twenty-somethings from across the Arab world, fighting for jihad and for a group that had become, in only two years, the most feared fighting force in the world. This was not because of their skill, not even because Garotin was shrewd. It was numbers. ISIS was enlisting fighters at an astonishing clip. Indeed, Garotin's biggest logistical challenge had nothing to do with military strategy. It was the simple fact that he didn't have enough guns and ammunition for the thousands of young Arabs who wanted to be a part of the history that was being written—the history of a terrorist group more vicious than Al Qaeda on the verge of claiming a whole country.

The Toyota was positioned four blocks behind the left flank of his soldiers.

The screen of Garotin's laptop computer showed, in precise detail, an aerial map of the central square city mile that had become the flashpoint for the battle. The map was fed by a program linked to the SIM cards of cell phones carried by his troops. The screen was a panoply of red dots in a half-moon.

By Garotin's estimates, Assad's men numbered fewer than a thousand. ISIS, which continued to bus and truck fresh fighters in from the west, had at least ten times that number. The taking of Aleppo was inevitable now.

Next to Garotin sat one of his lieutenants, Bakr.

Two more of his lieutenants were in the front. All three men clutched walkie-talkies. The windows were up, but the sound of the battle just a few blocks away permeated the SUV. The crackle of the walkie-talkies was almost constant, as Garotin was fed, through his lieutenants, real-time information on the battle from various strategic viewpoints.

"Where is team eleven?" asked Garotin, not looking up from his screen. "They should be coming up to the south of their right guard. They're just fucking sitting there."

Bakr keyed his handheld.

"Eleven, over," barked Bakr. "Eleven, Marsi, where are you?"

A pregnant silence took over the SUV, then was interrupted by the squawk of Bakr's walkie-talkie.

"We're at the hospital," came a voice, desperate and hurried. "But they're—"

A loud explosion came over the walkie-talkie.

". . . they're hitting us with grenades. We've lost a lot of men. The only way to take them will be to destroy the hospital—"

"No!" shouted Garotin, grabbing the walkie-talkie. "Do not touch the hospital. Keep fighting. We'll get you support. Where exactly is their battalion?"

"The street that leads from the front of the building," he said as another explosion ripped the air. A mile away, they could hear it a few seconds later in the Toyota.

Garotin studied the map.

"Give it to me," he ordered, looking at the man in the driver's seat, who handed him his walkie-talkie.

"Forty-four dawn," said Garotin. "Mohammed, where are you?"

"We're along Tradda Boulevard," said Mohammed. "We've cleared them out. Very little is happening right now."

"Do you have any missiles left?"

"Yes. We have a few."

"I'm going to give you precise coordinates. It is imperative that you not miss."

"Yes, Commander."

Garotin punched a few keys on his laptop.

"The coordinates will be on your phone. Enter them precisely as I've written them. The enemy has built a last stronghold. They're just in front of the hospital. Do not hit the hospital."

Garotin handed the walkie-talkie back to the driver.

"Let's go," Garotin said, flashing a smile.

From a corner room on the fourth floor of the hospital, Colonel Asif stood. He was alone, having left his small command center down the hall to call Assad and explain to him that the Syrian Army was within hours of losing Aleppo.

Asif stood at the window. In his hands he clutched binoculars and studied the swarms of ISIS troops amassed in a 270-degree perimeter, a perimeter he knew would soon be a full circle. Occasionally, he saw men from ISIS running between buildings as they came closer and closer, but for the most part he studied muzzle flash, pairing it instinctively with what he heard to create a gut-level sense of what was now inevitable.

The battle was over the moment Bashir El-Assad had ordered the depleted Syrian Air Force to stand down. ISIS had shot down three Syrian jets and Assad believed he could not afford to lose any more.

"Aleppo is a battle, and this is a war," Assad had explained to Asif two days ago. "We need jets more than we need Aleppo."

What was left of Asif's command was arranged in a quarter-moon along the perimeter of the hospital. Asif had positioned his battalion with the hospital behind them, thinking the hospital would act as a shield. To an extent, it had. The five-story white brick facility had sustained only minor damage. But ISIS had too many men. They were swarming, waves of young fighters throughout the day and night, unafraid to die.

Asif knew the story was being repeated in other places across the country. The men of ISIS were fueled by a loyalty and a belief that no state army could compete with. They believed they were fighting for Allah. For Asif's men, the fury was not nearly as deeply rooted; to a man, every soldier in Syria knew he was fighting so that Bashir El-Assad could maintain his luxurious lifestyle and dictatorship over the Syrian people.

Asif lifted his cell phone and dialed.

"Get me President Assad," he said.

A moment later, the nasally voice of Bashir El-Assad came on the line.

"Colonel Asif," said Assad. "What is the news? Have we beaten back these bastards?"

"No, Mr. President. No, we have not. I'm afraid we are within hours of losing Aleppo."

A long pause.

"It's unacceptable," seethed Assad. "For God's sake, I'm surrounded by incompetents and fools."

Asif said nothing for a few moments. Then he heard something to his left. He charged to the window. Just above a long block of apartment buildings, he saw the telltale black comet trails. He scanned quickly to the missiles themselves, difficult to see, their light color blending with the gray sky. There were three missiles in all, soaring directly toward the hospital.

"Goodbye, sir," said Asif. "It has been my honor to serve you."

Asif dropped the phone just as the first missile ripped the last hundred yards through the sky and then arced and shot downward, stabbing into the largest cluster of troops he still had. Asif winced as the ground shook and the screams rose above the din. A moment later, another missile hit just in front of the first, and he was kicked sideways and down by the powerful tremor that cratered a hundred yards in front of the hospital and shook the ground. He waited for the third missile, which came less than two seconds later, and again he was bounced violently.

Asif stood up. The scene in front of the hospital was terrible: three craters the size of swimming pools, fires charring everything within fifty feet, the screams of those soldiers who were still alive.

To the right, a line of soldiers moved toward the hospital. They all wore the same thing: black shirts, black pants, black bandannas around their heads. There were too many to count. They gunned down soldiers who attempted to surrender.

Asif pulled his revolver from his belt, stuck it in his mouth, and fired.

The Land Cruiser pulled into the parking lot behind the hospital. Garotin climbed out. He lit a cigarette, took a puff, and tossed it to the ground.

He entered the building behind two armed ISIS soldiers. The hallway was brightly lit. Both sides were lined with doctors and nurses. They stood in terror and silence, appraising Garotin as he walked slowly between them, meeting their eyes with noncommittal stares.

Garotin reached the end of the hall, then turned back to the gathered doctors and nurses.

"Good afternoon," he said. "This is now a military hospital. You are all now in the service of ISIS."

Garotin removed a handgun from beneath his left armpit. He took two steps. An elderly patient was seated in a wheelchair. Garotin aimed the gun at the man's chest, then fired. The slug ripped through the old man and sprayed blood on the wall.

Several nurses let out muffled screams.

Garotin's eyes swept down the hallway, as if daring someone to say something. When no one did, he turned to Bakr.

"Have the troops clean out the rooms," he said. "Then bring the injured inside. *Our* injured."

14

NICOSIA, CYPRUS

Mallory was seated in the back row of the plane for the three-and-a-half-hour flight from Milan to Nicosia. He bought his ticket at the airport just minutes before they shut the door to the plane, paying in cash. His head was shaved and he was wearing contacts. He was flying under double-cover, using a doctored passport from Ireland, which had been acquired by an MI6 agent with whom Mallory had traded a similarly back-channeled passport from Canada, effectively destroying any chance of detection. He wore a denim jacket, jeans, and work boots. He looked like a soccer hooligan or perhaps an unemployed Irish bricklayer.

Bill Polk, the director of the CIA's National Clandestine Service, had suggested that he enter directly into Damascus under the guise of aid worker, but Mallory had decided against it. In Cairo, he'd witnessed firsthand the murderous chaos of the so-called Arab Spring. It didn't matter why you were there or what you were trying to do. The pope himself would've been ripped limb from limb had he ventured down the wrong alley during those violent weeks. By all accounts, Syria was worse.

The plane landed at a few minutes before noon. Mallory bought a disposable cell at a newsstand and dialed a number for the Cyprus switch, a relay that would direct him to Langley.

He glanced around the small airport, crowded with tourists, as he waited. Three clicks, then a monotone beep. He dialed a series of digits, twelve in all. A few seconds later, he heard ringing.

"Control," came a male voice. "Region eight."

"Switch MX dash five."

"Identify."

"Seven nine eight two one one, Mallory."

"Hold, sir."

A few seconds later, another voice came on the line.

"NCS Mission CON," said a woman. "Mallory?"

"Yes."

"Third-grade teacher?"

"Miss Starr."

"Birthplace of wife?"

Mallory swallowed.

"Cedar Rapids."

"Hold for one message, sir."

A few moments later, a recording started playing. It was a deep male voice, clear and slightly robotic:

"Exfiltration Café Mosul M-O-S-U-L. You will be met by Andreas comma Dewey. He has in-theater command control. Advisory one: expect Andreas as of twenty-thirty hours. In-theater code black if go, green abort. Exfiltration will be through Israel unless improvised by Andreas. Informant has been provisioned for Tier Two extraction; evidence is Tier One. Repeat, evidence is Tier One mission priority."

Mallory listened again, then hung up. He knew where Café Mosul was; he'd been there before. The café was in the middle of a crowded square, with several roads, lanes, and alleyways leading into it. It offered flexibility in terms of approach and extraction as well as the anonymity that came with crowds.

Mallory rented a car and drove to Larnaca, a small city on the southern coast of the island. He arrived as the sun was setting. He checked into a tourist motel near the beach, then went out. At the local post office, he sent the Irish passport to his apartment in Milan. At a pawnshop, Mallory purchased a used Skyph 9mm. Down the street, he went into a boutique, where he purchased black pants, a black T-shirt, and a headscarf.

Back at the motel, Mallory applied self-tanning lotion to his face, neck, arms, and hands, along with black mascara and shoe polish for his eyebrows. He compared his reflection to his photo in the second passport he'd brought along— a hastily made Syrian passport. It would not withstand any sort of INTERPOL or other database back-pull, but Mallory knew the Syrian border was in a state of chaos right now. The airports were the only places with any sort of technological capability. Had he flown directly to Damascus, he likely would've been caught. But Tartus and its dilapidated ferry terminal offered a more open gateway. They would, at most, do a simple eyeball of his passport. Mallory also knew that a passport from any other Middle Eastern country would put him at risk. ISIS was drawing its recruits primarily from Iran, Egypt, Saudi Arabia, and Algeria.

He changed into the new clothing and left the motel at 9 p.m., throwing his old clothing in a

Dumpster behind the motel. He was on the 10:07 p.m. ferry out of Larnaca to Tartus.

The ferry was surprisingly modern—a triple-pontoon craft built for speed with a large passenger hold built atop the pontoons. The ferry was packed with people. Mallory sat inside reading a book called *Angel's Envy* in Arabic. Almost everyone aboard the vessel was Syrian, and they were overwhelmingly male and young. A few days in Cyprus was a cheap respite from the war raging inside Syria.

Normally, a meet-up like this would have involved some sort of tertiary support, such as a Delta or two, in the background. But other than Calibrisi and Polk, nobody knew of Mallory's plans. If al-Jaheishi's information was accurate, it meant a covert arms program had taken place directly under Langley's nose, without ever being detected. It also meant it was an extremely high-level operation, possibly involving the Pentagon or State Department. The information al-Jaheishi possessed would, if true, get people in very hot water. They couldn't run the risk of tipping off whoever was inside the U.S. government about al-Jaheishi.

Mallory had grave doubts as to whether al-Jaheishi would show up, and if he did, if the evidence was even real. But as long as there existed the possibility that someone inside the U.S. government was funding ISIS, he had to go to Damascus and work the contact alone.

But the lack of backup was not what worried Mallory most. What worried him was the fact that al-Jaheishi had known him from Damascus and then had somehow had the guile to locate him in Milan.

As he sat alone, beneath the dim lights of the ferry's interior, surrounded by sleeping people, he realized it was likely a setup. A suicide mission. It was at those moments when Mallory thought not of his country but rather of Allison. The hole he'd felt for more than a year now was not going away. If he died, maybe there was a heaven. If there was, she would be waiting for him. It would be just her style to be right there, waiting, with her carefree Iowa smile on her face. Mallory shut his eyes and folded the book shut on his lap, feeling the cold wet of tears on his cheeks.

Mallory was awakened by a hard push on his shoulder. He opened his eyes, startled, then looked up to see a soldier staring at him. He had the olive-and-red beret of the Syrian Army.

"*Waraqa*," the soldier barked, extending his hand.

Papers.

"*La bd li raqduu*," said Mallory, in flawless Arabic.

I must have fallen asleep.

He pulled the passport from his pocket.

"May I stand up?" asked Mallory politely.

The soldier ignored him.

"What brings you to Tartus?"

"I live in Damascus," said Mallory.

"Where in Damascus?"

"Rija."

"What number?"

"One hundred seventy-seven."

The soldier pored over the passport for nearly half a minute.

"What do you do in Damascus?"

"I worked at my brother's store, but he was killed by the terrorists. I look for work, always."

"The terrorists?"

Mallory nodded. "ISIS," he said.

The soldier handed the passport back to Mallory. He stared a few extra seconds at him.

"You should be in the army if you care about your country. They killed your brother? You're a coward."

Mallory nodded, bowing his head. "I know," he whispered, staring at the floor.

The soldier shook his head in disgust, then turned and walked to another Syrian, still asleep.

Mallory exited the ferry. The sky was still dark. He looked at his watch: 4:45 a.m.

In the parking lot bordering the terminal, he approached a cluster of men loitering against their cars.

"Damascus?" he asked. "I will pay for a ride to Damascus."

An old man with short gray hair nodded, then walked to his car, a dented yellow sedan.

"Forty dollars."

As he climbed into the backseat of a small, beat-up Citroën, Mallory glanced at the ferry, now moored in the distance, then the ocean beyond.

"Twenty," said Mallory.

"Twenty-five."

15

DAMASCUS, SYRIA

Al-Jaheishi entered Nazir's office. In his hand, he held a manila folder. Nazir still clutched his cell phone to his ear. He stared without emotion at al-Jaheishi.

Here it is. Al-Jaheishi mouthed the words.

Nazir nodded to the door, indicating that he wanted him to shut it. After he'd done that, al-Jaheishi stepped to Nazir and handed him the folder.

"It must be written just as I have said," said Nazir into the phone. "If you can't write it, I will find someone else."

Nazir covered the mouthpiece and glanced at al-Jaheishi.

"Sit down. This will only be a minute."

Nazir removed his hand.

"It must be as simple as the United States Constitution. The Bill of Rights. Do you understand? The same structure, Mohammed, but with entirely different content. This will be the foundational document of a caliphate. It must be every bit as charismatic and timeless. It must show strength and . . ."

Nazir glanced suspiciously at al-Jaheishi.

". . . compassion."

Nazir hung up and dropped the phone on the desk. He opened the folder.

"Is this the only record of our transaction with the Americans?"

"Yes," said al-Jaheishi. "Have I done something wrong?"

"Have you photographed this?" asked Nazir, ignoring the question as he flipped through the pages, then flashed a cold look at al-Jaheishi.

A warm burst of heat spiked at the base of al-Jaheishi's skull, then bloomed in his head.

Fear.

"No, Tristan. Of course not."

Nazir seemed to study him for a few extra moments, then let a slight grin come to his lips.

"Let me see your phone."

His hand shaking, al-Jaheishi reached to his pocket. He handed his phone to Nazir. Nazir turned it on.

"What is the code, Marwan?"

"Nine nine eight one."

Nazir typed in the code, then thumbed through al-Jaheishi's phone. He opened his photo collection and quickly scanned through it. It took more than a minute. When he was finished, he tossed the phone to al-Jaheishi.

Nazir took the folder. He grabbed a section and reached to the right of his desk, stuffing the section into the shredder. The grinding noise was loud. As al-Jaheishi watched, Nazir stuffed the entire contents into the machine.

"I thought this was our leverage, Tristan—"

"Don't think," said Nazir. "I'll do the thinking, Marwan."

"Yes. I'm sorry."

Nazir nodded to the door, telling al-Jaheishi to leave.

After al-Jaheishi was gone, Nazir sifted through the thin strips of paper in the trash can beneath the shredder.

His mind raced. He thought the hard part had already taken place. People, weapons, money—all those hurdles were past him. Now he was in the part of the process that came after the hard part. It was the interplay of people, countries, and other factors beyond his control, factors like al-Jaheishi's loyalty fighting against his weakness, Raditz's courage and patriotism at war with his desire for self-preservation.

What is your battle, Tristan? he asked himself.

"It is the battle between my desire for infamy," he whispered aloud, staring into the shreds of paper, though seeing nothing, "and my hatred."

Nazir's mind flashed to the mountain, Everest. He'd been a member of the Oxford Mountaineering Club. The spring and summer of his junior year, he'd climbed Everest, or most of it. To get within a hundred feet of the summit required a year's preparation, two months in Nepal, a week in Base Camp, and countless days at various points along the way, acclimating. The final hundred feet—that was what no time could achieve for any man. For once you began, your body could not acclimate; it began to wither in the oxygenless heights. No, to climb the last hundred feet was about luck, fate, and confidence. The bitterness of his failure to climb the last hundred feet ate at Nazir every day, every hour. He tasted it now. He realized that ISIS was similar—the creation of a country—and he now stood at the same high precipice as so many years ago; the oxygen was thin, few had ever stood where he now stood, he could die due to factors beyond his control.

Yes, the first part was hard. But now you are at the place beyond the hard. The summit is in sight.

He thought of Raditz. It was an interesting fact—another fascinating fact in this whole thing—that something valuable can, in an instant, become worthless. That someone who offered protection could become your greatest enemy.

The evidence of his deal with Raditz had offered Nazir protection and, he thought, tremendous leverage. But no longer. Raditz was a destroyed man. He didn't care anymore.

Now, Nazir understood, the evidence could threaten everything he had created. Like a backpack filled with food and oxygen on Everest, the deal with Raditz had taken him to within a hundred feet of glory, but he could nevertheless die atop the summit. The evidence of the deal with Mark Raditz threatened everything.

In his head, Nazir replayed Raditz's words: "Go ahead, expose me. I'm already dead. But the moment the world finds out who paid for ISIS's guns, what then, Tristan?"

Nazir had scoffed at Raditz's words, but they stung, and now he realized truer words had not been uttered. If Raditz had done a deal with the enemy, Nazir had done one with the devil himself. If the world knew, it would alter the purity of ISIS's beginnings. The 150,000 men who'd enlisted without even the offer of pay? They would abandon it all—then come for him. The philosophical purity that was the underpinning of ISIS—equal parts religious fervor, loyalty, and, above all, hatred for America—would splinter into disarray and infighting. To compromise was not the way of ISIS. To compromise, and even work, with America . . . well, Nazir knew, that would be the end.

A knock came at the door, startling Nazir. "What is it?"

"It's Que'san."

"Come in."

Que'san, who was in charge of Nazir's personal security team, entered. He shut the door behind him.

"Have you changed the rules on the removal of files from the office, Tristan?" asked Que'san.

"No."

"Even for Marwan?"

"For nobody. Files are *never* to be removed."

"Then I believe we have a problem."

"Marwan?"

"It's from the video camera inside his office," said Que'san. "I think you should see it."

Al-Jaheishi walked back to his office. He felt as if the floor was made of quicksand. Every step seemed to take hours. Every pair of eyes down the hall seemed to watch him walk as if they knew.

No one knows. Calm down. He doesn't know.

He sat down and took several large gulps from a water bottle, then removed his jacket.

He looked at the clock on his desk: 7:41.

Why is time moving so slowly?

He flipped up his laptop and went to his e-mail. But before the application had even loaded, he saw Que'san at the end of the long hallway, knocking on Nazir's door. It meant nothing. It happened twenty times a day, and yet, just as he turned the latch, Que'san flashed a sideways glance down the hall.

Al-Jaheishi waited for the door to Nazir's office to shut, then stood up.

He walked back down the hallway. If the steps a few minutes ago had been hard, these were like torture.

Does he know? He doesn't know, Marwan. He would have already killed you!

Nazir watched the video clip for the second time. It showed al-Jaheishi as he frantically took papers from the filing cabinet and switched them with those in the briefcase.

"When was this taken?"

"Less than an hour ago."

Virtually every intelligence agency in the world was searching for ISIS and specifically Nazir. Nazir knew that everything depended on secrecy and that even one false move, such as accidentally leaving a piece of paper in a coffee shop, could expose him. Everyone inside the offices knew that the removal of files was considered an act of treason, punishable by death. It was difficult to believe anybody could be stupid enough to violate the rules. Al-Jaheishi wasn't stupid.

He already suspected al-Jaheishi had taken files

in the past, but al-Jaheishi had always denied it. The video's confirmation was shocking, like a kick in the teeth.

Yet a part of him still gave his oldest friend the benefit of the doubt.

"There could be an explanation," said Nazir. "Go ask him to come here."

Each step al-Jaheishi took seemed to echo along the green marble of the corridor. He came to the door just before Nazir's. He glanced into the office. Azrael looked back, nodding. As he neared the door of Nazir's office, he heard the dull click of the latch. The knob was turning.

Before the door could open, al-Jaheishi passed the door, then charged for the lobby. He cut across the reception area, then entered the hallway at a full sprint. He ran to the elevators and hit the button.

He looked back. The hallway was silent. He put his hand into his pocket and touched the small thin SIM card.

"Come on," he whispered to the elevator.

Faint chimes, indicating one of the cars was coming, chirped from the shaft.

Suddenly, he heard voices. He looked down the hallway just as the loud *ding* of the elevator's arrival punctuated the corridor.

Que'san burst through the suite door. He held a gun.

Oh, my God, what have you done?

As the elevator doors slowly parted, al-Jaheishi lurched inside.

"Marwan!" Que'san yelled. *"Stop!"*

Al-Jaheishi searched for the buttons, his hands quaking with fear. As he fumbled, his eyes again went down the hallway. Que'san's handgun was trained at the open doors. The metallic *thwack* of suppressed gunfire was accompanied by the thud as a slug ripped into the back wall of the car.

Al-Jaheishi tucked into the front corner, shielding himself from Que'san's bullets. He found the Close Door button just as another slug ripped the wood at the back of the elevator.

Que'san's footsteps grew louder as he came closer.

Al-Jaheishi hit the button repeatedly as several more bullets boomed into the elevator, their damage moving in a line along the wall, moving closer and closer to him. Then the lights of the hallway seemed to flicker as Que'san's large frame crossed beneath the closest hall light. Al-Jaheishi could hear his breath, filled with anger.

The elevator doors seemed to be stuck . . . and then they moved inward.

The gunfire grew rapid now. Slugs hit just inches above al-Jaheishi. The doors groaned shut. Then came a loud series of *clangs* as slugs struck the outer door and the elevator began its descent to the lobby, eighteen floors below.

16

RAMAT DAVID AIRBASE
ISRAELI AIR FORCE
JEZREEL VALLEY, ISRAEL

In a small building at Ramat David Airbase, a windowless room held four workstations and a wall of plasmas. Two plasmas showed a topographical map, in real time, of the Syrian border east of the Golan Heights. Imposed upon the plasmas was a set of red and green grid lines, with various lights flickering. What the maps displayed was Syrian Defense Forces, including missile batteries, lined up like chess pieces along the border, waiting for signs of Israeli incursion by plane or helicopter.

The plasmas also showed Israeli asset groups in the same area.

"They just crossed Green Line."

The Green Line was the original border between Israel and Syria.

The speaker was a young, pretty blond-haired IAF officer named Adina Safer. She was the mission officer and had tactical command authority for what would soon be penetration of the Syrian border by the Panther carrying Dewey and Kohl, which at that moment, was a red dot flickering brightly at the center of the plasma as it moved at a blistering 300 mph clip above the forbidding mountain crags of the Golan Heights.

"Electromagnetic deception," Safer continued. "Jonathan, are you ready?"

To Safer's left, another uniformed Israeli, Jonathan Tarshaw, studied a small computer screen in front of him as his fingers maneuvered furiously across his keyboard.

"I'm locked in," Tarshaw said. "On your go, Dina."

Safer cued her mike. "Panther Ten, you are two minutes from Purple Line, over."

Purple Line was the actual border between Israel and Syria, created after Israel took the Golan Heights from Syria in the Six-Day War. After crossing the Purple Line, the Panther would be fair game for a kill shot from a Syrian missile battery.

The speakers in the mission control room crackled with static from the helicopter, then one of the pilots came on: "Roger that, control, over."

"Check your systems, Matthew."

"Systems clear."

"Wait for the free and clear," said Safer, nodding to Tarshaw.

"Initiating signals," said Tarshaw.

"On your count, Lieutenant."

Tarshaw stiffened slightly, then leaned in. "Hard count," he said loudly. "Beginning now."

Tarshaw held up his left hand, five fingers, as, with his right, he typed. "Five," he said, then dropped a finger as he counted down. "Four . . . three . . . two . . . one. And we are live. That's a go."

He hit the keyboard.

On the screen, the red flicker of the Panther abruptly disappeared.

"You're dark, Panther Ten," said Safer. "Free and clear, over."

"Affirmative," came the voice of one of the two pilots in the cockpit. "Panther Ten has the con, over and out."

Safer crossed her arms, then took a step toward the plasma screen.

The pilot's voice popped again inside the control room.

"Path cut to two-seventy dot four nine in ten . . . nine . . . eight . . ."

The Israeli chopper banked right and climbed sharply as it crossed an empty stretch of hills that, ten thousand feet below, constituted the border between Israel and Syria.

The speaker inside the cabin came on with the voice of one of the pilots.

"Syrian airspace, boys. Start packing up."

Dewey registered the words as he stared out the window at the ground now three miles below the speeding helicopter. It was all dark except for occasional clusters of lights from villages.

With him was Kohl Meir along with two more commandos from Shayetet 13, Leibman and Barsky.

"Why don't they shoot us down?" asked Dewey.

"Technology," said Meir.

"Stealth?"

"No," said Meir. "It's called electromagnetic deception. We know where the Syrian radar is and we send false signals. At least, we think we know where it is. Hopefully Assad hasn't moved the tracking stations."

"What do you mean, 'hopefully'?" asked Dewey, a little surprise in his voice.

"Hopefully," said Meir matter-of-factly. "You know, like hopefully that girl likes me, hopefully it's nice weather at the beach, hopefully that guy shooting at me is a bad shot. Hopefully, the Syrians haven't moved their radar transmission systems."

"That's reassuring."

"You asked."

"And if they *have* moved them?"

"If they moved them, it will be a dramatically shorter flight."

Dewey shook his head.

"Anyway," continued Meir, grinning, "the guys are pretty smart back in Tel Aviv so I'm not too worried. We direct data streams into the emitters, including false targets. We figured out how to make their radar see things it isn't really seeing. We're invisible."

"Why haven't the Syrians figured it out?" asked Dewey. "Seems like the kind of thing that you can get away with once."

"We'll know if they figure it out."

"How?"

"There will be about a dozen missiles flying up from the ground," said Meir, smiling nonchalantly. "Keep your eyes peeled, will you, Dewey?"

"That's funny."

"It wasn't meant to be."

Dewey nodded toward the cockpit. "Can these guys evade a Syrian missile?"

"Oh, yes, of course." Meir nodded. "They're very good. One missile, perhaps even two. But . . ."

"*But?* What the fuck does that mean?"

"If the Syrians shoot more than one or two missiles . . . well, I think at that point I'll probably put on a parachute."

Meir was now laughing.

Dewey shook his head.

"I'm glad you find this amusing."

"I'm just fucking with you," said Meir, still laughing.

The other commandos, seated on the floor of the cabin, were also laughing now.

Dewey breathed a sigh of relief.

"So we know for a fact they haven't moved the radar?" asked Dewey.

"No," said Meir. "I mean the pilots can't evade two missiles. Even one would be next to impossible. It's a fucking helicopter. A fighter jet, yes, but this thing is slow. It's like a flying elephant. Hitting it with a missile would be like hitting the side of a barn with a watermelon."

Meir, joined by Leibman and Barsky, was now red-faced with laughter.

"Fuck you," said Dewey, smiling and shaking his head as laughter from Meir and the others filled the cabin. "I forgot how fucked-up Israeli humor is."

"You'd have a fucked-up sense of humor too if everyone was trying to kill you."

Dewey pressed his nose to the glass and looked out the window. Other than a small patchwork of yellow in one spot on the ground, everything was black.

"What am I looking at?" asked Dewey.

"Golan Heights," said Meir, who was also looking down from a window on the opposite side of the cabin. "My father fought there. So did Matthew's." Meir pointed his thumb toward Leibman, on the floor behind him. "It was a terrible war, but we won. Afterward, Israel offered to give most of it back to Syria in exchange for peace. But of course they said no. The Syrians would rather kill Israelis than enjoy a picnic with their family on the beautiful hills."

They were interrupted by the crack of the cabin intercom.

"Lights out," came the pilot. "We'll be above Izraa in ten minutes. Keep the noise down too."

17

DAMASCUS, SYRIA

Al-Jaheishi entered the lobby. It wasn't crowded, but there were at least a half dozen people, including a pair of security guards, as well as businesspeople just arriving for the day.

It had been Nazir's idea to locate one of the ISIS offices in Damascus, in the heart of Assad-controlled territory. He had believed that if they wore the right clothing and used accounts that were untraceable, they would simply blend in. He'd been right, of course, but it always gave al-Jaheishi a chill to enter the lobby, afraid of what he might find.

It will soon be over. You will be in America. Uncle will remember you.

Al-Jaheishi walked through the lobby and out to the street, then went right and fell into the crowd of pedestrians. He walked for several blocks. When he saw a taxi stop at the corner in front of him, he ran to the door. Just before he climbed inside, he glanced back at the office building. The sidewalk in front was crowded. A line of people arriving for work was queued up outside the revolving glass doors. Then Que'san emerged from the revolving doors and charged through the middle of the line, nearly knocking over several people.

Al-Jaheishi quickly ducked into the cab and shut the door. His eyes shot to the back window.

"Where to, sir?" asked the driver.

Behind Que'san stepped his deputy, Azrael.

Al-Jaheishi shuddered.

It was Que'san who came up with the idea of the beheadings. It was Azrael who performed the first one.

The two men stood on the granite steps in front of the building, looming unnaturally and darkly, scanning the sidewalks and streets for al-Jaheishi. Both had on suits. Both had their right hands tucked inside their jackets, clutching guns. Que'san was looking left, but it was Azrael's eyes who seemed to home in on the taxi. His arm moved into the air, pointing in al-Jaheishi's direction; pointing, it felt like, directly at him.

"East quarter," said al-Jaheishi. "Café Mosul."

Mallory was dropped off at the central train station. The area in front of the station was packed with people, though there were also pockets of empty space. Soldiers. They stood in the olive-and-red uniforms of the Syrian Army. Mallory quickly counted eight before he'd made it halfway to the front doors. Each soldier clutched a submachine gun. They covered the entrance at ten-foot intervals, eyes scanning the crowds.

Mallory walked with his head bent slightly, eyes to the ground. He entered the crowded station and cut across the main waiting area, heading for an exit at the far side. He moved slowly, so as not to raise suspicion, crossing another line of gunmen, then fell in line with a pack of pedestrians just off one of the commuter trains. He crossed the street, then cut back toward the main entrance, where he'd been let out. The Citroën was still in front. Bending over, pretending to tie a shoelace, Mallory looked across the busy boulevard, between cars and buses, until he had a clear view. The driver was still sitting in the front seat, his head turned toward the entrance, as if watching for him. Mallory stood and moved up a side street, away from the train station, walking quickly. He took his next left, then a right, then another left, zigzagging into a pretty neighborhood of sandstone homes, with neat courtyards in front and brightly colored shutters.

"Good day to you," said an old man from his porch, where he sat with a cat on his lap.

"Good morning, my friend," said Mallory, waving.

Mallory had been to Damascus on several occasions during his CIA career. In some ways, its crowds, traffic, smog, and noise reminded him of Cairo. But if Cairo's buildings spoke of history and wonder, of architectural achievements hard to imagine having taken place so long ago, Damascus had a simple beauty that was beguiling. Cairo had inhabitants; the city was there for them, too large and sprawling to ever feel a sense of ownership, only awe and fear. Damascus was clean in the way a local city is, a city that was more like a large town, and the pride that came with that was obvious in its cleanliness, in the way its people nodded politely, the way shopkeepers kept their windows spotless and, just off the commercial areas, the way red and yellow flowers dangled from flower boxes perched on small porches. Legend had it that on a journey from Mecca, the Prophet Mohammed saw Damascus but refused to enter the city because he wanted to enter paradise only once, when he died.

Mallory looked at his watch. It was five minutes after eight. He used the distant white peak of Mount Qassioun to orient himself. He spotted the Presidential Palace in the distance. When he reached the outer circle surrounding the fountains at the center of Umayyad Square, he noted a loose line of soldiers pacing around the fountain. Cars sped by, horns blasting almost constantly.

Mallory walked until he came to Al Madhi Ibn Barakeh, a busy street running west. After a few minutes, he could see the telltale blue glass of the

Blue Tower Hotel. A half dozen blocks later, he saw a fountain down a small side street; then, beyond, a line of shops. In the middle of the line of shops, he saw a bunch of tables filled with people, eating and drinking.

He glanced at his watch: 8:36.

He looked again. He didn't see Andreas, but that meant nothing. Mallory assumed that Andreas was camouflaged, but there were so many people.

The chopper coursed in a high line several hundred miles south of Damascus, weaving between small towns—Izraa, Shaqra, Elbobar, then north, near Hazm, until it was a direct line north to Al Ghuzlaniyah, a large suburb near Damascus. They flew at twenty thousand feet. Despite the fact that the cabin was pressurized, Dewey felt the cold air seeping in.

All lights on the Israeli chopper were extinguished.

Dewey watched out the window for much of the time. It was still dark, but the clusters of lights grew larger, brighter. It meant they were passing over increasingly populated areas. It gave him a deeply uneasy feeling.

"I assume our radar is silent," said Dewey, glancing at Meir in the dim gray.

"Yes," said Meir.

"How are they piloting?"

"Eyes."

Dewey nodded.

"This is nobody's idea of a cakewalk," added Meir. "I'll be glad when we're on the ground."

A few minutes later, the chopper shuddered and tilted toward the ground, swooping left.

A dim blue light went on in the cabin. One of the pilots came out of the cabin.

"We were picked up," he said, kneeling and looking at Meir, then Dewey. "A regional airport. They've asked twice for identification."

"What's the protocol?" asked Dewey.

Meir looked at Dewey, then the pilot. He had an odd look on his face, whatever humor and calm that had been there disappeared in an instant.

A high-pitched beeping noise echoed through the chopper.

"Lock on!" screamed the pilot in the cockpit. The other pilot lurched backward, toward the cockpit, scrambling into his seat. "Hold on!"

The chopper bent left, but instead of correcting, kept moving in what seemed like an impossible arc, down and down. Dewey, Meir, and the other commandos were thrown to the back wall. Dewey grabbed a canvas handle.

"The parachute," barked Meir, blood coming from his nose, which had somehow been struck during the chopper swerve. "Get it on!"

The chopper leveled, then broke up, then sharp right as the roar of a jet engine scorched overhead.

Dewey grabbed the chute. He looked at Leibman. "I need guns."

At Ramat David Airbase, Safer watched the pair of Syrian jets leave Ramadahh Airbase. She had no way of communicating with Panther Ten.

She hit her ear, triggering commo.

"Black Torch Four, Black Torch Five," she said calmly, her nostrils flaring ever so slightly as her face belied her, flushing red. "Get going. This is a live operation. We have a midair recon situation south of Big D. Repeat: this is a live operation. Priority One Recon."

The mission room, housed just off the main runway at Ramat David, shook as the force of the departing F-18 rocked the air, accompanied, a moment later, by the sonic roar of the engines. A few seconds later, the second jet did it again.

"MC, this is Black Torch Two, over," came the voice of the pilot of the lead jet. "What do we got?"

"We have a stranded helicopter twelve klicks south of Damascus," said Safer. "This is Panther Ten. Three members of S Thirteen are on board. Local Syrian radar must've spotted them."

"Roger that," said the pilot. "Will we be dark?"

Safer turned to Tarshaw. He nodded and put his thumbs up.

"They're already at Green Line," he said. "Jesus."

Tarshaw typed furiously and didn't bother counting down. He nodded to Safer, who moved her eyes to the plasma. Two green dots, moving toward Syria, suddenly disappeared.

"You're dark, Black Torch One and Black Torch Two," she said. "Over."

Leibman pulled open the door to the weapons cache in back of the chopper. The cabinet looked like the behind-the-counter display at a firearms dealer. Carbines spread across the top, stacked vertically, all Colt M4 with grenade launchers, optics, etc. The row below was a mix of submachine guns—Uzis and HKs. The next row, at waist level, was crowded with handguns, lined up, butts out. Below were rows of ammunition. Dewey's eyes caught a black glint from above the carbines. A pair of Hecate sniper rifles sat horizontally.

"You need to get below a thousand feet," Meir yelled.

Dewey's eyes shot to the cockpit. Meir was telling the pilots to go down low enough for Dewey to jump and not die. Short chute. He remembered Rangers. Even at a thousand feet, it was almost suicide.

Don't think about it. You liked Rangers.

Dewey grabbed a weapons vest from the floor, pulling it over his T-shirt. He strapped an M4 tightly across his torso, muzzle aimed at the ground. With Leibman's help, he strapped an HK MP7A1 submachine gun to his back. He stuffed each armpit holster with a handgun.

"They're all loaded," said Leibman, helping Dewey stuff mags into the vest. "They're good to go."

Dewey nodded as Barsky wrapped the black robe around his shoulders.

"Looks good," said Barsky, attempting a smile.

Dewey grinned.

"No pictures," said Dewey. "If my mom saw this, she'd be a little upset."

"'Cause you're about to die?" asked Meir, approaching from the front, laughing.

"No, because I'm dressed up like Ayatollah Khomeini."

The chopper banked suddenly as the growing decibel of an incoming missile sounded from somewhere outside.

"Hold on!" yelled one of the pilots.

The chopper shook as one of the pilots triggered the undermounted guns. The *rat-a-tat-tat* of the machine guns' powerful fusillade rocked the cabin.

An explosion to the right, bright red and orange; all eyes shot in its direction. In the distance, one of the Syrian jets was like a fiery apparition in the early morning sky.

Meir stepped past Dewey and reached into the bottom right section of the weapons cabinet. He searched for a few moments, then came back with his hands full.

"Here," he said, handing two grenades to Dewey. "You might need them."

Interruption from the intercom: *"T-minus five,"* yelled the pilot. *"We need to get the fuck out of here."*

"I'm fine."

". . . four . . ."

"All I know is I usually don't need a grenade, but when I want one, it is very nice when it's there, Dewey."

". . . three . . ."

Dewey put the grenades in the pocket of the vest.

Meir showed him what looked like a large ChapStick tied to a nylon string.

". . . two . . ."

"What the fuck is that?" asked Dewey. "Lipstick? I guess I've never been tortured in the Middle East."

". . . one . . ."

Meir laughed.

"There was an insult in there somewhere," he said, grinning, then pushing the object to Dewey. "You will have to explain it to me someday."

"Deal," said Dewey.

"This is an Iridium tracker," said Meir. "Strap it around your neck. I'll be back to get you."

"Commander, we are past drop line and we have

inbound enemy guns," said the pilot. *"We need to get out of here."*

"You're not coming back to get me, Kohl," said Dewey as he pulled the parachute over his shoulders and stepped toward the cabin door. "I'll find my way out."

Meir grabbed the right strap of Dewey's parachute as Dewey neared the door, pushing Dewey back against the wall.

"Wear it," said Meir. "I'm coming back. Whether it's to collect your dead body or give you a ride, well, that's up to you."

"Fine."

He tied it quickly around his neck.

Dewey glanced at Leibman and Barsky, standing at the back wall, clutching handles. "Thanks, guys."

He turned to Meir and put his hand up. They grabbed hands, clutching them for a few moments.

Meir slammed a button above the side door of the chopper. The door slid back. A gale of warm wind scored the cabin.

Dewey took a running step toward the open door, then one more, his foot striking the outermost steel at the edge of the chopper, jumping out into the air, then dropping into the void, disappearing, as the Panther ripped up into the sky and away from Syria.

18

CAFÉ MOSUL
DAMASCUS, SYRIA

Mallory arrived at the café.

"A table, sir?" asked a woman.

"Yes, please," said Mallory in flawless Arabic. "Over there."

His seat was at the outer perimeter of the tables. He ordered a cup of coffee. Mallory's eyes scanned the restaurant, the street in front, the sidewalks leading to the café. It was warm out, at least eighty, despite the early hour. He saw nothing, save for traffic and pedestrians, people on bikes and motorcycles.

He was taking the first sip of his coffee when the sound of gunfire cracked nearby.

Mallory breathed deeply, trying to calm down, but it was no use. The adrenaline was now flowing. It had been so long. At least a year. He realized, now, that time away from it was bad. Mallory had atrophied. Or more to the point, Mallory felt he'd atrophied, and that inner doubt was much more harmful than any operating rust.

He thought of Allison. A memory flashed. It was a charred limousine, the limousine meant for him, which he'd chivalrously given to her to take to a tennis match at the Cairo Cricket & Field Club.

"I'll walk, sweetheart," he said. His last words to her.

He was interrupted from his thoughts.

"Sayidi, alshshay," said the waiter, who placed a small tea cup in front of Mallory.

"Shukraan," said Mallory.

Mallory took a sip just as noise came from his right, near the edge of the square. His eyes went immediately to a tall man, running desperately toward the café. Mallory recognized him from the INTERPOL photo.

Al-Jaheishi.

And then everything went to hell.

Dewey tumbled through the bitter-cold dawn air, the freezing wind ripping his face. He somersaulted for the first dozen seconds, then gradually planed out and righted himself into a dive. He kept his eyes shut except for brief moments to gauge his altitude. The earth moved at a startling speed up toward him, and the morning light revealed brown, green, and orange country, mixed with roads and buildings. He knew he was practically invisible now, but as soon as he opened the chute he could be seen by anyone looking up. The key was to open it at the last possible moment. The higher the opening, the more people who would be able to spot him. But being spotted was less risky than opening the chute too late.

The early hour was his saving grace. The haze of sunbreak was still in the air, and the streets below looked empty for the most part.

He reached for the parachute handles and waited. His eyes focused on a parking lot, the cars like Matchbox cars. He tightened his grip on the release line. The cars grew larger, but still he waited, as tears from the wind coursed down his cheeks. He could see trees, bushes, a woman. He would hit the ground any second. One more moment . . . then one more . . .

Dewey ripped the cord. The chute popped behind him, the loud snap like a gun going off, and he was yanked violently back, halting his speed, and just in time. Adjusting his eyes, he was less than twenty feet above the ground and dropping quickly. He slammed into the dirt pack of the parking lot, hitting feetfirst, bending at his knees to help absorb the impact, then diving into a tuck and roll.

As he stopped rolling, Dewey removed his fixed-blade combat knife from the sheath at his ankle, slicing through the cording of the chute, then removing it all, folding up the materials in a tight ball. He moved toward a line of cars and stuffed everything beneath a car.

He scanned the parking lot, his hand moving instinctively inside the folds in the hijab to the shoulder holster beneath his left armpit and gripping the butt of the handgun. He saw no one.

Dewey was breathing hard now. The cold air he felt a mile up in the sky above Damascus was but a memory. The air at ground level was hot, and he was soon drenched beneath the black garment.

The parking lot was located behind a clean-looking warehouse in a quiet section. Dewey walked to the back corner of the building, trying to get a glimpse down the driveway to the main road. In front was another parking lot. Two men in work gear climbed from a pickup truck and walked toward the front of the warehouse.

Dewey couldn't read the writing on the building, but the company had to be some sort of utility. The parking lot was half-filled with vans and pickups, every vehicle with the same white paint and orange-and-brown logo.

Dewey walked quickly to the back row, searching for the oldest pickup he could find. A late-model Nissan sat at the end of a row. He smashed the driver's side window with the butt of his gun, unlocked the door, climbed inside, and scanned for anyone who might've seen him or heard the glass break. No one had.

Dewey inserted the blade of his knife beneath the steering column, popping the plastic cover off, then found the harness connector and, inside it, a bundle of wires. He touched the starter wire to the other wires. The car's engine rumbled to life. Dewey cranked the steering wheel hard in both directions, breaking the steering lock, and drove slowly to the corner of the building and along the driveway. When he got to the far corner, he stopped. He counted seven people walking toward the front entrance. They were oblivious of Dewey's presence, except for one man who looked in Dewey's direction, stared for an extra second or two, then kept moving toward the door.

On the main road, Dewey fell into a line of cars. He pulled the cell phone Meir had given him from his pocket, already open to the mapping application and the café preprogrammed. He was less than five and a half miles away. He looked at his watch: 8:28.

The traffic in Damascus was a helter-skelter of pedestrians, people on bikes, taxicabs, trucks, and cars, the blare of horns incessant. Vehicles traveled on the right side of the road, but whenever the opposite lane was open, cars swerved into oncoming traffic, trying to pass slower cars. The occasional traffic light was ignored.

Sprinkled at seemingly every corner were Syrian soldiers, all clutching machine guns or carbines. The city was clean, the buildings neat and well-kept. But the mood reminded Dewey of Islamabad in the days before the overthrow of the Pakistani president Omar El-Khayab. It wasn't just the presence of the soldiers, their weapons sweeping constantly across traffic and sidewalks, storefronts and cafés; it was something less visible, something ethereal—tension, fear, the knowledge that Syria was in the middle of a war it was losing. Damascus may have been the safest city in Syria for the moment, but the fear of its men and women, as they walked quickly, eyes darting about, was unmistakable.

Get in, get out. Keep it simple.

Dewey took advantage of the chaos to drive almost recklessly across the city toward Umayyad Square.

Off the fountain of the square, he went down a busy boulevard. When he was just a block away from the café, Dewey turned onto a narrow side street and parked.

On foot now, Dewey walked to the corner. He took a left, walked a block, then took another left, so that he was walking directly toward the café where he was to meet Mallory and the Syrian, al-Jaheishi.

Al-Jaheishi looked at his watch: 8:25. He was supposed to be at the café in five minutes, but he was still a mile away. He'd set the meeting place far away from the offices in order to ensure that he wouldn't accidentally bump into anyone, but now he regretted it. He looked around, his head swinging nervously left and right, searching for Que'san and Azrael. He'd lost them.

He took a few breaths and began to run. In seconds, he felt the pain come on, the familiar pain.

A memory flashed: *Wimbledon Commons. A rainstorm.*

The memory was of the annual Oxford vs. Cambridge Varsity Match, sophomore year, the first year he won it for Oxford. Al-Jaheishi had run for Oxford's cross-country club. By junior year, he was Oxford's top-ranked runner.

His arms, nervous and clenched, somehow melted into a calm rhythm, swinging languidly at his sides. His legs took the sidewalk in deep, long strides. He had on a shirt and tie, pants, and wingtips, and yet he was back at Four Lawn, running across the verdant polo fields, running like a teenager, running like the wind. For a few precious moments, he heard nothing except the crickets back in England, the sound of his breathing, the lovely beat of his heart, tested and willing. For a moment, al-Jaheishi was free.

Then, at the next street, Que'san's deep voice brought him back.

"Stop! Marwan!"

Al-Jaheishi rounded the corner at full sprint as, behind him, he heard shouts, a woman's scream, then Que'san.

"Stop that man!"

Al-Jaheishi focused ahead. Café Mosul was two blocks away. Then he saw Mallory. Their eyes met, and Mallory stood up and turned.

Then, in the same moment that he heard the unmuted sound of gunfire, al-Jaheishi was kicked in the leg. He looked down. In that half second he saw blood and the missing chunk of his own calf, then the pain hit and he tumbled to the ground.

For a moment, Mallory let himself believe the gunshots had nothing to do with him. But he knew.

Something's wrong.

Mallory moved in the direction of the noise. There he was. The first shot had missed.

Bystanders did not understand what was happening. There were a few panicked looks, but no screams. Not yet, anyway. That would come.

Mallory registered a gunman, a block north, targeting al-Jaheishi. It was a trained infantry stance, run then stop; hold, breathe, target, fire.

Again, unmuted gunfire cracked the air. This time it was followed by more screams from pedestrians. Panicked men and women started charging toward the square.

Mallory tried to see through the chaos, searching for al-Jaheishi.

On the ground, near a storefront. There he was.

Is he dead?

Mallory stopped in his tracks. On both sides of him, men and women rushed by, their eyes wide with fear, frantically trying to escape the gunfire.

Mallory watched, transfixed, as the first gunman was joined by a second. The two killers closed in on al-Jaheishi.

Get up!

As if he could hear Mallory's thoughts, al-Jaheishi climbed to his feet.

The second shooter—a tall man with a bushy mustache and wearing a business suit—took the lead. He dropped the rifle and, in stride, pulled a pistol from beneath his left shoulder.

Al-Jaheishi crabbed along the ground toward a storefront, a market, clutching his leg, dragging it along with him.

Mallory took a few languid steps toward the store, watching as the gunman followed in pursuit, gun in hand. The thug charged into the store and disappeared. A few seconds later, there was more gunfire, muffled slightly. It blended into the din and chaos. People poured out from the store.

Screams enveloped the square. For the first time, sirens sounded in the distance.

Mallory stopped. He glanced up the street, marking the other gunman, who stood calmly by a car with his rifle raised and aimed at the storefront, lest al-Jaheishi should reemerge. But he wouldn't.

"*Hu mmayit,*" said Mallory aloud.

He's dead.

Mallory moved backward, eyes strobing between storefront and gunman. The meet-up had gone bad. Shit happens.

He remembered the words, from training.

The biggest mistake operators make is believing

in a mission after it's dead. An operator dies because he keeps operating after a mission goes bad. There's nothing wrong in saying a mission is dead. Live to fight another day.

His priority now was getting out of the immediate neighborhood without drawing attention. Then Damascus proper. Then Syria. That would be the hard one, unless he could find Andreas. Mallory scanned the hectic scene, looking for him. Was he here? Had he even made it over the Golan?

Mallory's cell phone vibrated in his pocket. He pulled it out.

The screen showed a series of letters and numbers, confusing to anyone but Mallory, who looked for the pattern:

A856Y47P2292MKF
A85
A
CENCOM; the code was from Langley, most likely an automatic status exchange, such as a GPS trigger in relation to Andreas.
8
The code set; cipher through based on that set.
5
Start message in five characters, then go ahead five in sequence.

He scanned the code five places:

P22

P
A GPS flag; Andreas position status.

2
Border of Syria penetration; Andreas was in-country.

2
Landing zone achieved; Andreas is on the ground.

He looked five characters along; this last code would be the rules of engagement. He saw the letter *F.* A combination of anxiety and adrenaline shot through him.

No rules; priority of the package is national security priority level Emergency. Do whatever you need to do.

Any in-theater command control and other operational protocols were irrelevant now, including al-Jaheishi's status. Mallory would have to attempt to get the package whether al-Jaheishi was dead or still alive.

Mallory joined a phalanx of onlookers, moving backward. He crouched near a dented Peugeot, watching and planning his next move. He would need to engage the ISIS gunmen . . . unless al-Jaheishi somehow emerged from the wreckage.

• • •

Al-Jaheishi pushed himself up from the ground, using his good leg to stand on. He grabbed his destroyed right leg at the knee and pulled it, limping toward the door to the market. He tried not to look down but couldn't stop himself. Blood seeped from his leg, already sopping the lower part of his slacks. He reached for the door. At the last moment his eyes shot left and he saw Mallory. He remembered Mallory from Cairo. It had been just one meeting, at the Cairo Hilton. President Morsi and his top advisors were there to sit down with the American delegation. Hatred was in the air, yet Mallory, like him a silent witness to discussions by others from his government, had smiled at him and introduced himself.

Another gunshot ripped the air. Al-Jaheishi was hit in the shoulder. In the same moment, a glass window shattered in front of him. The slug had passed through his shoulder and smashed the glass. Screams came from every direction. Al-Jaheishi let out a low yelp and ducked inside the market.

He reached reflexively to his shoulder, feeling grotesque wetness, his flesh now opened and gushing blood. He hobbled inside, trying not to look down, trying not to look at his destroyed calf. He stumbled to the back of the store, pulling his leg by the pants material above his knee.

Inside the store, a few shoppers still huddled in

fear. They had believed—falsely—that remaining there offered refuge. Al-Jaheishi swept past an old woman and then a young father with his daughter. They stared in silence, horrified at the sight of his destroyed shoulder and leg.

The old lady reached for him.

"*Abni*," she whispered, tears in her eyes, as he pushed by her.

My son.

At the back of the store was a wall of freezers. He ducked behind the endcap of the row of groceries, clutching the aluminum shelf, trying to hide, trying not to make any noise, though all he wanted to do was scream as terrible, unrelenting pain washed over his entire body.

The door slammed open, then there was a loud commotion at the front.

"*Ayn hu?*" the man screamed.

Where is he?

He recognized the deep voice. Que'san.

Al-Jaheishi glanced about, spying a mirror in the corner, below the ceiling, there for the shop-keeper to catch shoplifters. From his crouched position, he could see Que'san moving to the counter, weapon out, trained at a short man behind the counter who had his arms up. He heard mumbling. Then, a moment later, gunfire. It was like a bomb, followed by screams. The shopkeeper dropped to the ground.

Al-Jaheishi glanced down the aisle. For the first

time, he registered a trail of crimson weaving down the floor, left there by his badly bleeding leg.

Screams and shouting came from the front of the store. Anyone still remaining dropped their bags and ran.

Al-Jaheishi remained back at the freezers. He watched the top of Que'san's head as he moved toward the rear of the store. With pain shooting through him, al-Jaheishi got down on his knees, hiding on one side of the aisle as Que'san moved slowly and methodically along the opposite side, weapon out, searching for him.

Al-Jaheishi skulked along the aisle toward the front of the store, then rounded the corner and doubled back down the next aisle, behind Que'san. A trail of blood formed shimmering lines of crimson on the white linoleum behind him as he crawled. Que'san was now in front of him, his back to al-Jaheishi. His big frame loomed as he scanned for him. The hunter, looking for his wounded prey.

Al-Jaheishi had never killed anyone. Not even close.

Sirens, for the first time, pitched in the distance.

He lifted himself up, in silence, and ran down the aisle and jumped onto Que'san's back, wrapping his right arm around Que'san's neck, then pulling back with all of his strength, trying to break his neck or choke him.

But Que'san was powerful. Al-Jaheishi struggled to stay on Que'san's back as the larger man fought to get free. A vicious elbow from Que'san slammed into al-Jaheishi's ribs, then another, knocking the wind out of him. Still, al-Jaheishi held on, in pain, unable to breathe, yet holding on, trying with all of his strength to choke Que'san.

Que'san grunted, trying to say something, his voice low and hoarse. Al-Jaheishi was hurting him. Then he heard it: the pistol in Que'san's hands dropped to the ground.

Al-Jaheishi was still piggyback on Que'san, desperately holding on as Que'san, struggling for air, reached his hands above his head, trying to punch at al-Jaheishi. One of Que'san's hands found al-Jaheishi's hair, grabbing it, yanking it hard. Que'san's other hand clawed at al-Jaheishi's neck, fighting to pull al-Jaheishi from on top of his shoulders.

Al-Jaheishi struggled to hold on as Que'san pulled him forward, trying to extricate himself. Al-Jaheishi felt the power in Que'san's arms. He fought to wrench Que'san's neck backward, but he wasn't strong enough. Que'san raised him slowly up. He felt his legs coming off Que'san's back. Que'san had him; he hurled al-Jaheishi off his shoulders, through the air. Al-Jaheishi tried to get his hands up, but it was futile. He slammed headfirst into the freezer, then dropped to the hard floor, groaning in pain.

Al-Jaheishi looked up, dazed. Everything was blurry, black and white, as if in slow motion. Pain struck him a few seconds later at the crown of his skull. He tried to focus.

Get up!

The cloudiness enveloped his view, until he saw movement. Que'san was charging at him, both arms out. His face was contorted in hatred and anger.

Then al-Jaheishi saw the gun. It was lying there, so close, just a few feet from his foot, black and glinting beneath the fluorescent lights.

Move now!

Que'san flew at him, yelling, fists raised. Al-Jaheishi lurched left, reaching for the gun, barely avoiding Que'san's right hand. Al-Jaheishi grabbed the gun, turned, and fired. Unmuted gunfire cracked the air, followed by a pained grunt. Crawling, al-Jaheishi tried to get a few feet away. He looked. The bullet had struck Que'san in the stomach. Blood covered his shirt, and his hand moved to the wound. Then Que'san found al-Jaheishi with his murderous eyes. Heaving, he fell forward, his arms swinging for al-Jaheishi. Al-Jaheishi tried to scurry away across the linoleum as Que'san fell, but Que'san landed on his legs, his eyes angrier than even the moment before, the anger of a man who was not supposed to be killed by one so weak as al-Jaheishi.

Hand trembling, al-Jaheishi triggered the gun

again. The bullet ripped into Que'san's chin, blowing off the front of his head, splattering blood across a row of cereal boxes and loaves of bread.

Al-Jaheishi stared for a moment in shock and disbelief. Then he struggled out from beneath Que'san's arms. He hobbled to the front of the store as sirens grew louder. He reached into his pocket, finding the SIM card, clutching it in his blood-drenched hand. He charged through the front door, weaving like a drunk man.

As two more muffled gunshots echoed from the store, Mallory stood up and moved. He registered the second gunman, who continued to focus on the store, waiting to see who would emerge and, if it was al-Jaheishi, to put a few more slugs into him.

The door swung open. It was al-Jaheishi. Their eyes locked.

Mallory charged toward him, pushing. His eyes shot back to the second gunman across the street just as he fired. Blood arced from the center of al-Jaheishi's chest as the slug nailed him. He tumbled to the sidewalk.

Mallory ran to al-Jaheishi, pushing aside fleeing pedestrians.

"*Ana tabib,*" he shouted. "*Alhusul ealaa wata alttariq!*"

Get out of the way! I am a doctor.

Mallory reached al-Jaheishi's corpse. He grabbed at his hands just as he heard a voice.

"*Ila yamassuh!*"

Don't touch him.

Mallory placed his left hand against al-Jaheishi's neck, pretending to feel for a pulse even though he knew he was dead. Meanwhile, he groped with his right hand, searching for the SIM card, patting al-Jaheishi's front pockets as he looked for the tiny object.

In his peripheral vision, he saw the gunmen as they ran toward him. He couldn't find the card. His mind raced. They were getting closer.

"*Tataharrak!*" shouted one of the men, just as Mallory noticed al-Jaheishi's outstretched arm. His fist was clenched.

Move!

"'*Annah jurih*," Mallory said, not looking up, groping desperately for the hand, prying the fingers open. Inside al-Jaheishi's hand was SIM card. "*Ana tabib.*"

He's injured. I am a doctor.

He grabbed the card just as a sharp kick struck him in the back. Mallory spilled over sideways, then looked up.

The gunman studied Mallory with a slightly panicked look, not knowing what to do, whether he should just shoot Mallory right then and there.

Two more men came to the dead body of al-Jaheishi. He hadn't seen them. Whereas the gunman wore a button-down and dark business slacks, these two had on jeans and black T-shirts, and held Uzis.

ISIS.

Multiple sirens came from several directions. Mallory saw a red flash from the first police car as it arrived on the chaotic scene.

Slowly, Mallory stood up, raising his hands, playing the scared citizen, looking at the three gunmen just as policemen shouted from up the street and the gunmen reflexively tucked their firearms against their bodies.

Mallory stepped away from the dead man. He turned and walked slowly back toward the café. A small crowd remained, watching from afar. He pushed his way through.

Mission accomplished. Now get the fuck out of here.

When he was past the café, he looked back. It was a hollow feeling, hollow in a way that was indescribable except by the man who is staring at death. The man in the suit was less than five feet behind him, flanked by the two thugs.

"Aietaqadat 'annak nazarat mudhak."

I thought you looked funny.

Mallory ran. One gunman fired. The bullet hit Mallory in the back—a low shot, beneath his heart. He knew what he was doing.

Mallory crumpled to the ground, landing on his back.

"Where is it?" the man asked, this time in broken English.

Mallory stared up at him as the pain consumed him.

"Where is it?" the gunman yelled, leaning down, jamming the muzzle of the gun into Mallory's forehead.

Mallory said nothing. He stared up at the terrorist. He clutched the SIM card in his hand as blood pooled in his throat and caused him to cough and choke. He felt the thick liquid gurgling in his throat, blocking his breathing. The pain was deep, throbbing, and it spread across his body, but all he could think about was the fact that he couldn't get a breath in, he was drowning in his own blood, and he couldn't move.

Mallory closed his eyes just as crimson began to trickle from his mouth, nose, and ears.

Gunfire. He heard it. It had come from a distance. The police?

Mallory opened his eyes. He felt detached, a silent witness, like he was watching a movie. His eyes found the killers. All three of the gunmen—the man in the button-down and the two black-clad thugs—turned toward where the new shots had come from. Mallory saw confusion on their faces. The two men in black shirts pivoted and raised their Uzis. The man who'd shot him—the one in business attire—leaned down and extended the handgun, preparing to fire at him.

The killer was irate. He was saying something to Mallory, but Mallory didn't hear it. He didn't move. He felt the pain dissipate. He still had yet to take a breath, but that didn't matter anymore and he stopped trying. A calm feeling came over him.

19

CAFÉ MOSUL
DAMASCUS, SYRIA

Dewey was half a block away from the square when he heard the gunshots. Low booms, a high-caliber rifle fired outdoors.

Without thinking, he jumped from the sidewalk to the road.

He heard two more gunshots and then screams.

Dewey hit the square at a hard sprint. A central rectangle with a statue in the middle was surrounded by streets on all four sides. The streets were lined with shops and restaurants. The sidewalks were jammed with people. The square itself was also crowded.

He entered the square at six o'clock and immediately found the café directly opposite at twelve o'clock, across two streets, on the other side of the square, several hundred yards away.

The square was in a pandemonium. People were

running in seemingly every direction, crazed by the sound of the gunshots. He smelled the aroma of gunfire. Then he heard sirens in the distance, still a few blocks out.

Dewey's eyes were drawn to a row of shops at a far corner of the square. The movement was frenetic, even panicked. This was where the shooting had occurred. It was now total chaos. People poured from shops, sprinting toward the square—and the café.

More gunshots. They were like firecrackers, muffled; a pistol fired inside one of the stores. High-pitched screams and shouting. The peal of tires ripping into tar as cars tried to flee the scene.

The street was awash in people running from Dewey's right—where the gunshots had occurred—to his left—on sidewalks, in the street, across the square.

Sirens roared in short, loud, high-pitched bursts.

Dewey charged down the middle of the street in the direction of the gunfire, into a thicket of fleeing Syrians. He didn't see the taxi that was also trying to escape the chaos. It was speeding directly at him. By the time he registered the impending collision, Dewey couldn't get out of the way. The taxi swerved, but then it lurched back at him; the driver's head was turned completely around, looking back at the stores where the gunfire had started. Dewey leapt as it was about to strike; he landed hard on the front hood, caving it slightly, then rolled off. He landed on his feet and continued to race toward the far corner of the square.

The noise was fevered. Car horns mixed with sirens, the patter of feet scrambling frantically, screams and shouting.

Dewey's eyes shot right and focused: a lone individual was moving slowly along the sidewalk, struggling away from the block of shops. He was young, his hair short. Then he saw it: the man's shoulder was drenched in blood. The man dragged his leg as he struggled to move. A break in the crowd enabled Dewey to see his leg; it too was covered in blood from the knee down.

Al-Jaheishi.

Behind him, a tall man trailed at a distance. He clutched a handgun and had it trained at the injured man a few dozen feet in front of him.

Dewey stepped forward, his eyes moving left as his hand reached into the folds of the hijab. His fingers went to the strap around his right shoulder.

Sirens grew louder and multiple; without looking, Dewey registered the flashing red to a block away.

He was now across the street from al-Jaheishi and the tracker. Suddenly two more gunmen came into view. Both were dressed in black. They jogged. Each man held a short weapon that Dewey recognized immediately: Uzi.

As he moved calmly toward the scene, Dewey

unclasped the strap attached to the rail of the M4. His eyes picked up the path of al-Jaheishi's eyes as he ran—or limped—for his life. Dewey followed the sight line. He saw Mallory.

Another loud crack interrupted the chaotic scene as the gunman fired. Al-Jaheishi fell to the ground. Dewey watched as Mallory moved to him.

Without looking, beneath his hijab Dewey slid the fire selector on his weapon to manual. In front of him, he saw Mallory reach al-Jaheishi, kneeling over him as if seeing if he was all right. The gesture looked Good Samaritan, but Dewey knew the CIA man was searching for the package.

He walked onto the square, aiming for the café. His finger was on the trigger, ready to kill if necessary but hoping he wouldn't have to.

Al-Jaheishi was dead, but Mallory was over him, soon joined by a pair of others, also trying to help. The gunmen—all three—came up behind them, but they didn't fire. Mallory looked up and said something to the tall man. Mallory reached for al-Jaheishi's shirt and started unbuttoning it, pretending to give medical aid, a performance intended solely for the three gunmen, who now loomed, weapons out and trained on Mallory.

Suddenly, the tall one kicked Mallory in the back. He tumbled over. After a moment, Mallory stood up cautiously as the two men in black descended on al-Jaheishi and ransacked his pockets.

Mallory moved backward, hands out, indicating to the gunman that he would leave. He walked away from the corpse.

Mallory's performance seemed to work. The killers paused over al-Jaheishi.

He heard shouting in Arabic from up the street. Several Damascus policemen had arrived on the scene.

Mallory was nearly to the crowd in front of the café. A few more yards and he would be clear. They would be able to get away relatively unscathed, shielded by the chaos. Dewey would return to Israel without firing a bullet.

And then the tall gunman turned to Mallory, now at least twenty or thirty feet away. He said something; the two black-clad thugs stood. All three started sprinting in Mallory's direction.

When Mallory turned, it confirmed the killer's suspicion. Dewey knew it was all over.

His left hand gripped the stock of the carbine as his right hand undid the other clasp holding the strap to the M4, letting the strap drop to the ground. Dewey swept the rifle in front of him as he ran across the square toward Mallory.

The three killers charged toward Mallory.

"No!" Dewey yelled, just as the gunman fired. The slug hit Mallory in the back, knocking him to the ground.

The sidewalk cleared out as those lurkers who'd remained in the café dispersed.

Dewey sprinted toward Mallory just as the tall gunman leaned down, no doubt looking for the SIM card. Dewey reached the road in front of the café. He was less than twenty yards away. He put his finger to the ceramic trigger and, in midsprint, fired. The suppressed carbine made a dull *spit*. A slug struck the tall gunman a half inch above his ear, blowing out a chunk of his brain.

The other killers swiveled; both men marked Dewey immediately. They swept their weapons through the air, but Dewey was a half second ahead of them. He flipped the fire selector to full-auto and fired, pulling the trigger hard. The dull *thwack thwack thwack* of suppressed slugs could barely be heard. The spray of bullets tore a zigzag line across the men. One of them screamed as his chest was pulverized. The second man was hit at the same moment, the slugs tearing into his neck and face, dropping him, killing him instantly.

Dewey ran toward Mallory, scanning to his right, back up the street. The café, the sidewalks, everything had emptied out as terrified Syrians fled the carnage. He kicked one of the terrorist's weapons, an Uzi submachine gun, toward a concrete bench and reached down to grab Mallory's shirt collar, dragging him to the bench, which offered a degree of protection from the gunmen, who were moving in on all sides. He dropped to the ground next to him.

He counted three police cruisers, stopped in the

middle of the road back near the shops. Officers climbed in and the police cruiser lurched forward, lights flashing, siren blaring, and raced toward him. Another cruiser followed.

Dewey picked up the Uzi. He now had two guns. He would soon need to change out mags on the M4. The mag on the Uzi was almost full.

He looked down at Mallory, whose eyes were shut. Something caused Dewey to turn and scan the street near the stores, behind the third police cruiser, which hadn't moved.

What is it?

He'd seen something. He surveyed the terrain behind the police cars. All around him, the pandemonium transitioned into the quiet of fear and death, a war zone, still fluid.

Then he saw him. He was alone, standing behind a parked car almost a block back from the corner. He was dressed in business attire but held a rifle tight to his right side, out of view. He was watching Dewey with a monocular. That was what Dewey had seen—the glint of the monocular. *Sniper.*

The first police car came to a screeching halt a few dozen yards from the café. Two policemen in dark blue uniforms climbed out, guns in hand, less than fifty feet from Dewey. A second cruiser stopped immediately to the left of the first, walling Dewey in to the east.

The sniper in the far distance moved out from

behind the sedan and slunk along the storefronts, down the sidewalk. He stopped at the corner of the building. He raised the rifle. Dewey watched as he acquired him in the crosshairs.

Dewey dropped to his stomach next to Mallory and placed the M4 in front of him, on the ground, taking aim at the gunman. A low thunderclap boomed from the gunman's rifle. The slug clanged behind Dewey, missing and hitting a car. Dewey yanked the trigger back hard. A burst of suppressed slugs struck the building just above the killer's head. He ducked into an alcove. Dewey moved the fire selector to semiauto and pulled the trigger. A cloud of slugs hit the front of the store, shattering glass everywhere around the alcove. The gunman was out of the target zone but the three-burst had bought Dewey some time.

To Dewey's right, police were climbing out of their vehicles and taking up position behind their doors, weapons raised.

The gunman broke from the alcove and started running back up the block, away from Dewey, crisscrossing wildly, ducking behind cars and other objects, making it difficult for Dewey to take aim. He had already spent too much ammo; the last thing he wanted to do was waste a mag throwing lead haphazardly in the air, attempting to hit an elusive target.

The gunman was looking for stability; he would attempt a snipe.

One of the police officers yelled to Dewey in Arabic, telling him to stop.

Dewey turned to Mallory. His eyes remained closed. Blood trickled from his nostrils and mouth. He felt Mallory's hand. It was soaked in blood. In the palm, still clutched tight, he found a small object, no bigger than a fingernail. SIM card. *The package.* He picked it out of Mallory's hand, stuck it in his pants pocket, and turned back to the field of fire.

The police were now arrayed in a line, all four officers crouching behind the open doors of their cars. He counted four muzzles, all aimed at him.

In the distance, the lone gunman ducked into another alcove. A second later, he kicked out the glass of a storefront. The long muzzle of the rifle emerged. He raised it and targeted Dewey.

Just then, a black police van entered the square on the opposite side of Dewey and Mallory, behind them. The van sped along the edge of the square and screeched to a stop a hundred feet away. Three SWAT-clad officers with carbines jumped from the back and took up position.

The sniper is the immediate threat.

Dewey swiveled. He ducked against the rifle, his right eye to the sight. Then he fired, just as unmuted gunfire exploded from the gunman in the shadows. The man's aim was off by less than a foot, and Dewey heard the clank of a slug hitting the concrete a few inches to his left. Dewey let up for a moment, then retriggered, remaining still as he did so, blasting a circular arc around where he knew the sniper was positioned. The sniper rifle's muzzle retracted. The slugs quieted the gunman, who now tried to avoid the fusillade. Dewey watched through the sight as slugs tore through glass and mortar all around the gunman. Then he heard a low scream as one of the bullets struck.

The police officer barked again at Dewey, first in French, then English.

"Put the weapon down!"

Dewey glanced behind him. The three tactical agents repositioned closer.

Dewey looked at Mallory. He reached his free hand out. He slapped Mallory lightly on the cheek.

"Rick," he said. "Hold on. Help is on the way."

Dewey hit him again, harder this time, and Mallory opened his eyes.

"Hey, buddy," said Dewey.

Mallory's eyes were like jelly, unfocused and discombobulated. Then he found Dewey.

"Do you have it?" whispered Mallory.

"Yes."

"It's over, isn't it."

"No, we're fine," lied Dewey. "We're just waiting for RECON. Hang in there."

"It's okay," said Mallory, looking at Dewey. "I just want to know the truth."

Dewey was startled by a premonition; his head

turned. The three policemen were closer now. That he expected. But behind them, on one of the side streets feeding into the square, a white van appeared. It arrived quietly, unbeknownst to the policemen. More gunmen poured from the vehicle. They were dressed in black. He counted two, three, four . . .

He turned back to Mallory.

"This part of the trip is over," said Dewey, looking into Mallory's eyes. "But it was only the beginning. It's not over."

Gunfire interrupted his words. Slugs struck concrete a few feet from Mallory's head as yelling in Arabic—yelling Dewey assumed was meant to get him to surrender—filled the streetscape.

Dewey gripped Mallory's hand, tight enough almost to break a bone. Then he let go.

Dewey dropped the M4 and picked up the Uzi. He sprayed a line of slugs across the patrol cars, hitting two of the officers, causing the other two to duck for cover. The noise was high and electric, like a swarm of angry bees. The first shots from the tactical agents struck the concrete above his head. Dewey rolled beneath the bench and pivoted his torso, then lifted the Uzi and aimed it at the SWAT-clad gunmen. He yanked the trigger—still set to auto-hail—and swept the muzzle in a smooth line across the edge of the square. He hit two of the gunmen. Frantically, he turned and fired at the police cruisers on the other side of him. He struck one of the officers in the head, another in the neck. Dewey turned yet again, firing at the third SWAT-clad agent, hitting him in the cheek, dropping him in a contorted tumble to the street.

The violent *rat-a-tat-tat* of automatic gunfire was like a war zone.

Dewey turned to face the last policeman, triggering the carbine, getting only an empty click. The officer fired. A bullet hit his leg—right thigh—and he swore as he desperately reached for the Uzi and turned it on the policeman, who was shielded by the door of the cruiser. Dewey ripped slugs beneath the door, striking the man's feet; he dropped, screaming, and Dewey finished him off with another quick burst of gunfire.

In pain, he popped the mag from the M4 and slammed in a new one. He swiveled and aimed at the black-clothed killers behind him. He moved the fire selector to three-burst and swept the badly kicking carbine as smoothly as he could. The first burst hit one of them; the others took cover and started firing.

Dewey skirted backward, behind the concrete bench, just as gunfire from the terrorists cracked the air. He reached frantically for the MP7A1—still strapped to his back—pulling it over his head, gripping it, aiming at the killers. Then he pressed the trigger. The sound was familiar, unlike any other firearm, at least in Dewey's mind. From the torpor of pain now roiling him, he found a hint of satisfaction in the menacing sound of the gun. The submachine gun burst lead in a frenetic, metallic, high-pitched drumbeat. He hit another of the men, who screamed as he fell. The others ducked back.

You have to move. Now!

Dewey stood up. A pained groan came from deep in his throat. His leg gave out and he nearly fell over. But it was his only acknowledgment of the pain that now shot through his leg, then up through his body, like fire.

He retargeted the black-clad gunmen now converging to the west. He slammed his finger against the trigger, gritted his teeth, and took a step on his right leg, testing the strength. The slug had hit muscle. The femur was intact. He let himself glance down at the wound. It was a graze, a thin dollop of thigh was missing a few inches above the knee, but that was it.

Dewey ran from the scene, limping noticeably. He moved to an alley beside the café. He ran until the alley intersected with a road, and then turned down the road, slowing a bit. He jogged a few blocks along a narrow, winding empty residential street as the sound of sirens echoed from several blocks away. He tucked the submachine gun inside the hijab as he moved as quickly as he could away from the horrific scene. After two blocks, he slowed to a walk and slouched, pretending to be an old man. He kept his right hand on the MP7, finger on the steel ring guarding the trigger, just above the trigger itself.

The sound of sirens grew faint and muted. After walking several more blocks in a zigzag pattern, trying to get as far away as possible, he heard the squeal of brakes somewhere behind him. He glanced back furtively, finger moving from the trigger guard to the trigger. He saw nothing; they were out of his sight line. He kept moving. Then his eyes caught another car ripping down a street ahead. The car screeched to a sudden stop at the end of the street. Trying to act natural, Dewey watched as the driver studied him.

In the same moment, Dewey became aware of an approaching vehicle behind him. He didn't need to turn; the two cars were working in conjunction, and they had marked Dewey, and he knew it.

The car in front of him—a yellow sedan—abruptly moved, jerking left as the driver turned the car and drove toward him.

His eyes swept the street. The roadway was barely wide enough for one vehicle, which meant there were no parked cars to potentially hide behind. Sidewalks on both sides of the roadway were tiny, perhaps two feet wide. To Dewey, it felt like a tunnel, with the light at both ends dimming, a gauntlet that, in that moment, Dewey understood would likely be the place he died.

Now that escape was unlikely, Dewey swore at

himself for the few moments of freedom he'd had just after fleeing the square. He should've uploaded the contents of the SIM card while he had the time. He thought he could get clear and just carry it out. Mallory's life, the entire mission—all of it would be pointless if the data on the SIM card was lost.

The yellow car began speeding down the narrow street.

Urban combat. Tight quarters. Daytime. You're outnumbered and exposed. What's your move, Andreas?

The words from training echoed inside his head. He was in Damascus, trapped on a narrow, curving residential side street, walled in on both sides by sandstone, cut off on both ends by men who wanted him dead.

His mind flashed to a long ago memory. Training. Fort Bragg. Close quarters combat—those exhausting, terrifying, occasionally exhilarating weeks learning urban guerrilla fighting tactics.

Find egress. A doorway, steps to a basement, anything that offers a physical or visual shield.

Dewey scanned the street as the yellow sedan came closer. He registered the vehicle behind him. It was a dark van, and it was closing in as well. The van's front window was tinted black; he couldn't see how many men were inside. Looking to the sedan, encroaching from in front of him,

Dewey counted a driver, passenger, and two more men in back.

There were no windows, doorways, passageways, alleys, or other exits. The only thing he saw was a slight bend in the wall of homes twenty feet away, across the street, which created a small indentation. But it was not egress; his only hope was to shoot his way through one of the flanks.

He was trapped.

Being trapped is a state of mind. Even if you're incarcerated, a gun against your head, even if a rope is tied to your neck, you're never trapped. Unless you allow yourself to think you are. If you believe you're trapped, you're done.

Dewey ripped off the hijab, letting it fall to the sidewalk, and charged up the street, away from the van, toward the oncoming sedan, raising the MP7 as he ran, then firing at the oncoming vehicle. The spray of automatic weapon fire was like a thousand buzzing bees, electric and frantic, echoing along the sandstone walls. Slugs struck the front grille of the car, then the windshield, ripping a checkerboard of holes in the glass. The driver's head was pulverized by the wash of bullets, but the passenger ducked, as did the men in back. Driverless, the speeding car veered sharply and slammed into the lip of the sidewalk, tires jumping the curb, just before barreling into the wall beneath a shutter-covered back window of a home.

Dewey sprinted the remaining yards to the small indent as the three occupants of the car jumped out, rifles in hand, and took refuge behind the wrecked automobile. Bullets from a carbine boomed behind him, and he dived, hitting the sidewalk with a shoulder, rolling and turning so that his back was against the wall. He was now in the small indent, just as a fusillade of slugs pounded the wall above his head.

In one motion, Dewey whipped the muzzle of the submachine gun toward the gunfire, triggering the MP7 as his left hand reached for a mag from the vest. Instead of a new magazine, he found a lump. A grenade. He grabbed it, putting it to his mouth as he fired. The van was now parked in the middle of the street, thirty feet away, two gunmen on either side, another in the front seat, shooting through the windshield. He was the first gunman. Dewey let up on the trigger, ratcheted the muzzle right, then fired; a loud, pained grunt came from the van as bullets took out the first gunman.

With his left hand, Dewey threw the grenade toward the van. Before the explosive even landed, his head pivoted, his eyes catching a glint of reflection near the wrecked car. Sunglasses. Black steel. Then a loud boom. The grenade exploded just a few feet from the side of the van. The explosion rocked the van sharply, flipping it onto its side and leveling the two men closest to the blast. The ground shuddered and the concussion made the street shake. A gunman who'd marked Dewey fired the moment after the grenade exploded. His slug—an easy shot for any half-decent marksman—ripped the sandstone inches from Dewey's shoulder, barely missing, raining grit and pebbles onto his head. Before he could fire again, Dewey triggered the MP7 and took the man's head off with a well-aimed burst of slugs, before the mag clicked empty.

Dewey searched for a new magazine, but bullets were flying from both directions. He made his profile as small as he could against the wall and searched frantically for the mag but found, in the chaos, only the butt of one of the handguns. Dropping the submachine gun, he ripped the pistol from beneath his armpit; he leaned out to get a quick view, then ducked in just as slugs hit the wall. He fired blindly toward the van, then swept it in the other direction, sending a three-slug cover line toward the car.

Dewey wasn't trapped, but he was fucked.

Directly across from him, he saw a set of wooden shutters. He shot a hole in the bottom section, and a few more holes, widening it, then again sent cover fire in both directions, again blindly, trying to buy himself time until, at some point, the mag was spent.

He dropped the pistol from his right hand. With his left, he ripped the second handgun from beneath his right armpit as, with his right hand, he retrieved the other grenade, pulling it to his mouth, teething out the pin, and throwing it at the hole in the shutter, praying the house was empty. The grenade hit the hole and passed through—bull's-eye—and Dewey covered his head just as the explosion blasted out the lower part of the wall, sending bricks, rocks, rubble, dust, and dirt, along with a fierce kick of air, in his direction. He moved, first firing cover shots at the van, then the car, then sprinting across the dust-shrouded street. Turning as he sprinted, he saw one of the gunmen running down the street; with his left hand, Dewey swung the pistol toward him and fired, striking him in the neck, just as he leapt into the destroyed house.

Dewey was in an empty bedroom, much of it destroyed, though on the bed, stuffed animals were piled in the corner. A child's room, thankfully empty.

He heard yelling from the street as the remaining gunmen swarmed from both directions.

Dewey ran into the living room and then down a small entrance hallway, charging toward the front door, which led to the next street over. He pulled the door open. In front, three Damascus Metro Police cars were lined up, lights flashing; behind them stood a small army of SWAT-clad gunmen. Seeing the door open, and Dewey, two of the officers raised their rifles and started firing, just as Dewey ducked and slammed the door shut.

He sprinted back through the house and up a staircase. At the top, a man and a woman were on the floor, arms around each other, silent, staring at him in fear.

Dewey charged past them, pushing open doors until he found the bathroom. He shut the door, locked it, and sat on the floor. The bathroom was tiny. He put his feet against the door and his back against the toilet, creating a barrier.

He heard voices downstairs, then the ominous sound of steel-toed boots pounding the stairs.

Dewey dropped the gun.

He worked quickly. He took the cell phone from his pocket as the footsteps grew louder. He popped the SIM card from the side of the cell phone, then lay the phone on the floor. He reached into his pocket and found the SIM card from al-Jaheishi. It was covered in a layer of dried blood.

Someone shouted from down the hall. The voice was deep and furious: "*Ayn hu*?"

A woman mumbled something between hysterical sobs.

The terrorists again barked at her. She said something, a sobbing plea, then screamed. The crack of gunfire stopped her screaming. The first shot was followed by another, and still one more, as the terrorists murdered the family.

Dewey put the bloody SIM card to his mouth, wet it, then wiped it on his shirt. Blood still covered part of the circuit near the edge. He wet it again as boots thundered down the hallway, growing louder. There were at least two men. They moved down the hall to the bathroom, just outside the door. One of the killers pounded his fist against the door, yelling frantically in Arabic.

Dewey's eyes caught his blood-soaked thigh. The pain was acute, but he hadn't thought about it for several minutes. All he could think about was getting the contents of the SIM card to Langley.

Automatic weapon fire came from somewhere downstairs. Through the open window, Dewey heard the clanking of bullets ripping into the police cars as the terrorists sought to remove complications from the scene. There was a loud scream as someone was hit, then return gunfire from the police.

Dewey wiped the card on his shirt, as hard as he could, trying to scrape away the dried blood. He jammed the card into the side of the cell phone.

The handle of the bathroom door jiggled, followed by a sharp kick, which punched the door above the latch, splintering the wood. Another kick followed, just as Dewey found the green message icon, attached the SIM card's data files, then typed in a twelve-digit number. He hit Send just as a powerful third kick shattered the center of the door. He threw the cell phone into a straw clothes hamper near the window. The muzzle of an assault rifle appeared in the broken frame of the door, easily finding Dewey on the floor. The gunman trained the weapon at Dewey's skull.

Above the rifle, Dewey registered a set of eyes—dark, cold, surrounded by long black hair, a sharp nose, dark skin covered in a sheen of sweat, a mustache and beard.

One terrorist pulled away the broken door and stepped into the bathroom. The other man followed. He removed a knife from a sheath and jammed it toward Dewey as the first gunman kept the muzzle of his AK-47 aimed squarely at Dewey's head. He put the knife beneath the GPS tracker given to Dewey by Kohl Meir. He tore the knife up, severing the tracker cord. He dropped the device to the floor and stomped on it with his boot.

More gunfire continued between the terrorists and the police, a steady *rat-a-tat-tat* cloaking the only sound Dewey cared about at that moment—the faint, high-pitched monotone from the cell phone at the bottom of the clothes hamper, indicating his message was going through.

20

CIA HEADQUARTERS
NATIONAL CLANDESTINE SERVICE (NCS)
PRE-TACTICAL OPERATIONAL CONTROL (PRE TAC)
LANGLEY, VIRGINIA

At three in the morning, Bill O'Flaherty stared into an ocular scanner at the same time as he placed his hand beneath a red fingerprint reader, both of which were outside a large unmarked steel door. After a couple of seconds, the locks clicked and the door opened. O'Flaherty, cup of coffee in his free hand, stepped inside.

Pre-Tactical Operational Control was a cavernous, windowless, dimly lit room, its eighteen-foot ceilings accommodating three walls of large plasma screens. Two lines of workstations faced the screens, each offering a different view of CIA activities throughout the world.

The room was eerily quiet, all audio having been routed through headphones and earbuds.

PRE TAC's mission was to monitor the activities of NCS operators and agents in various parts of the world and keep key members of the NCS and CIA hierarchy apprised of developments. This included activities of the Political Activities Division, usually agents working in hostile territory to advance America's foreign policy goals in nonlethal ways, such as currency manipulation and political destabilization. Its main focus, however, was Special Operations Group, the paramilitary arm of the CIA.

PRE TAC was the air traffic control system for covert operations conducted by the CIA. It was not where operators were managed out of—that was one floor below, in the Tactical Command Center—TACCOM—but it was always PRE TAC's analysts who knew when developments were reaching crisis point. Whereas TACCOM could sit unused for days or even weeks, PRE TAC was always teeming with activity, always in near silence. PRE TAC provided live support, real-time third-eye analysis, and, when necessary, coordination of on-the-ground exigencies with the Pentagon and ally intelligence services, such as MI6 and Mossad.

Most important, the highly trained analysts inside PRE TAC were responsible for maintaining chain-of-command protocols, meaning that they had to know when to elevate matters if something was going sideways.

O'Flaherty stepped into the room and the door shut behind him.

"Morning, everyone," he said, a big smile on his face.

O'Flaherty was the senior Middle East analyst inside PRE TAC.

Mary Moseley, a black woman with headphones on, turned from one of the workstations and smiled. "Hi, Bill," she said. "How was your weekend?"

Such was the arbitrary nature of the schedules of the PRE TAC analysts that words like "weekend" and "vacation" and even "morning" had long ago lost all meaning. It was the middle of the night on a weekday, but for O'Flaherty it was Monday morning.

"It was awesome," he said, putting his coffee cup down and taking a seat next to her. He popped open his briefcase and removed a white wax paper bag with *Krispy Kreme* scrolled in red along the front. "Brought you a donut, gorgeous."

"Jelly?"

"Yup."

"Lemon?"

"Raspberry."

"Aw," said Moseley. "You're the best, kid."

"No, you are," said O'Flaherty, his eyes moving to one of the plasmas on the front wall, his expression becoming businesslike.

The plasma showed a frame from a video, Arabic writing below. In the frame, a man was seated, a woman was standing, they were in a large steel cage. Flames could be seen on the ground at the man's feet.

Moseley saw his look—though a pro, he couldn't hide his horror.

"Yesterday," she said.

"Who are they?"

"Americans. He's a freelance photographer on assignment for *National Geographic*, Ben Sheets. That's his wife. Do you want to see all of it?"

"No," whispered O'Flaherty. He tried to smile. "I'll look at it after you leave. You've probably seen it a hundred times by now."

"Actually, a hundred and one." She stood up. "Don't ever stop being that way," she said, patting O'Flaherty on the shoulder as she pushed her chair in.

He was again staring up at the screen.

"What way?" he asked, taking a bite from a glazed donut.

"A gentleman."

He turned, mouth full. "Get out of here," he said.

A plasma at the far side of the room suddenly cut from an Al Jazeera reporter, volume muted, discussing the execution of the American couple, to bright red, which flashed. Three loud alarm bells rang out.

A computer-generated female voice—calm, officious, and slightly futuristic—came over the intercom:

Special Activities Division, Section Q, 03:07: We have a CRISIS DISPATCH:

Immediate Priority: Switch Protocol: Alpha—Bravo—Epsilon. N.O.C. 2—4—9—5. Repeat: Switch Protocol: Alpha—Bravo—Epsilon. N.O.C. 2—4—9—5 . . .

The pause lasted less than three seconds before the alarm bells rang again and the computer-generated voice came over the intercom:

Special Activities Division, Section Q, 03:07: We have CRISIS DISPATCH: Immediate Priority: Switch Protocol: Alpha—Bravo—Epsilon. N.O.C. 2—4—9—5. Repeat: Switch Protocol: Alpha—Bravo—Epsilon. N.O.C. 2—4—9—5.

O'Flaherty looked at Moseley, who hadn't left and stood now by the door.

"Uh-oh," she said.

"I got it."

O'Flaherty reached forward, pulled on a head-set, and hit his keyboard, stopping the woman's voice, then started typing.

"Roger, Control," said O'Flaherty, speaking into his mike. "Give me an origin point on that transmission, please."

The computer-generated female voice wasted no time answering:

Origin point: Damascus, Syria.

"Thank you, Control," said O'Flaherty, continuing to type.

The red screen cut to a photograph of a document. The top page showed a black-and-white photograph. Two men were seated in a hotel lobby somewhere.

"Control, do you have any diagnostics on the device?" asked O'Flaherty.

Device is tracing to a live Non Qualification: Andreas, Dewey.

O'Flaherty immediately recognized the younger man, with neatly combed dark hair, dressed in a business suit, Middle Eastern. He stiffened in his chair, unnerved by the sight of the most wanted man in the world. It was ISIS's leader, Tristan Nazir. Slowly, O'Flaherty's eyes moved to the man seated next to him. He didn't recognize him at first, not because he didn't know who the man was, but because it was so stunning, out-of-context, and shocking.

"I need a non-SIM UCC read, Control," said O'Flaherty.

His request was greeted by several moments of silence, then came the voice:

Device is Yemeni, batch 11889AF4556.

"Batch trace, Control, come on," he said, impatience in his voice.

Registration 49AS5 dash 3. Al-Jaheishi, Marwan.

O'Flaherty put the next few pages on the screen directly in front of him, quickly reading through the transcript of the conversation between the men in the photo.

"Control, I want a remote erasure procedure on that SIM card and I want transmission reprovision. Get this off any servers that it passed through."

Erasure procedure commencing. Estimate completion in six . . . five . . . four . . .

Moseley stood behind him, staring at the screen. She lifted her hand and pointed.

"Billy," she said, a horrified look on her face, "is that—?"

"Mark Raditz," interrupted O'Flaherty as he typed. The remaining pages of the document spread like cards across the other plasmas.

"You need to get this to Polk," she said, referring to Bill Polk, the deputy CIA director who ran NCS.

But O'Flaherty wasn't listening. Instead, he tapped the wireless headset three times.

"Control, I need DCIA, this is PRE TAC O'Flaherty, over."

"Protocol?"

"Alpha. Bravo. Epsilon."

"Hold, please."

A few moments later, O'Flaherty heard ringing in his headset, then a deep voice.

"Yeah."

"Director Calibrisi," said O'Flaherty, an emotionless look on his face, "it's Bill O'Flaherty. I'm sorry to wake you, sir, but we just received a crisis dispatch."

"Where's it from?"

"Damascus. It's a non-official cover protocol."

Calibrisi was silent.

"Do you want the ID on the NOC, sir?"

"I know who it is," said Calibrisi. "Call Anson Britt and tell him to start looking at recon scenarios. Then call Bill and tell him to meet me in PRE TAC in fifteen minutes."

"Yes, sir."

"If there's anyone else in PRE TAC with you, tell them they're not to leave until I get there. This is a sanitized 'black' event. No one comes in or out of that room until I say so."

21

UNITED AIRLINES FLIGHT 234
IN THE AIR

The man in seat 5B was young and obviously wealthy. He looked sophisticated, even elegant. He wore a tan suit and a red-and-white gingham shirt. A small navy blue handkerchief stuck up from the chest pocket of the blazer, which he kept on for the entire flight from Dallas to Mexico City. He had on stylish white-framed eyeglasses and John Lobb wingtips that looked freshly shined. His hair was blond, his skin light olive. He looked like a European returning from vacation. His French passport was tucked into the inside chest pocket. The hair dye had worked wonders.

The steward approached.

"Mr. Lagrange, would you like another champagne?"

Allawi looked up. The name Lagrange was fake; a cover name on a forged passport provided by a contact of Nazir's.

"Yes, that would be perfect."

His eye shot briefly to a man in the row in front of him, across the aisle.

Raditz.

He was still asleep.

"*Mal yanam qabl 'an yatimm dhibhah*," he said under his breath.

The lamb sleeps before it is slaughtered.

"How long until Mexico City?" he asked when the steward returned with his champagne.

"Approximately one hour."

As if Raditz had heard Allawi's thoughts, he suddenly stirred. His arms went over his head in a waking stretch. Then he stood up. Raditz looked around, though Allawi had already turned toward the window, pretending to stare out at the sky while his left hand reached into his pants pocket, removing a paper-thin object the size of a stick of gum.

A few moments later, the soft chime of the restroom door being locked.

Allawi glanced around, making sure nobody was looking. He peeled a strip of yellow plastic covering from the object. What was left was transparent unless held under the light, its circuitry embedded in a thin layer of polycarbonate. It was a tiny transmitter, capable of emitting a localized signal that someone with the proper equipment could track, as long as it was within about a square mile.

Allawi stood and moved to the overhead compartment above Raditz's seat. His own leather bag was stowed inside. He unzipped it with his right hand as, with his left, he felt for the zipper on the canvas duffel he'd seen Raditz holding in the first-class lounge. He unzipped it, just as the faint whoosh of the toilet flushing could be heard. As Allawi was about to stick the piece of plastic into Raditz's bag, as far down and out of the way as he could, his hand found something even better: Raditz's wallet.

The lock on the restroom door clicked.

Allawi lifted the wallet. He inserted the small plastic wafer inside one of the unused pockets.

The door to the restroom opened.

Frantically, he put the wallet back in the bag and zipped it up just as he heard Raditz's foot-steps coming down the aisle.

Allawi lifted out his bag and removed a book from it. Raditz stepped to his side, waiting for him to get out of the way.

"*Pardon, monsieur,*" Allawi said in a French accent.

"Take your time," said Raditz.

Allawi shut the overhead compartment. After putting the book on his seat, he went to the restroom. Inside, with the door closed, he stared into the mirror. His heart was beating fast.

He pictured Nazir.

"*He must not know he's being followed. After the ship has left with the weapons, follow him for a few days, then kill him.*"

"*I understand, Tristan.*"

22

Calibrisi was picked up at his house in McLean ten minutes after hanging up with O'Flaherty, his hair still wet from a quick shower. With few cars on the road, and the speedometer pushing 80 mph, the drive to CIA headquarters took less than five minutes.

He entered PRE TAC a little before four in the morning. O'Flaherty was seated at a workstation in front of his computer. Polk was standing next to him, looking over his shoulder at the computer screen.

Calibrisi scanned the cavernous room, counting a dozen other people in addition to O'Flaherty and Polk.

"I logged the room," said Polk. "We're sanitized."

"Where's Anson?"

Polk gestured toward the far corner. Britt was seated next to Mary Moseley beneath a plasma that showed grainy video of Damascus.

Anson Britt, a forty-two-year-old former member of the Marine's Force Recon, was in charge of reconnaissance operations for the National Clandestine Service. Britt's NCS unit was responsible for retrieving Langley assets who were trapped or lost behind enemy lines. Britt noticed Calibrisi and walked quickly across the room.

"Well?" asked Calibrisi.

"There's not a lot to go on. There's no UAV feed."

"Call RAF and see if they have anything."

"Already did. I also reached out to my source inside Damascus Metro. He's calling me back in a few minutes."

"Get hold of Kohl Meir. See if he and Dewey arranged meet-up."

Britt nodded.

Calibrisi stepped to Polk. He was looking over O'Flaherty's shoulder at a computer screen filled with numbers.

"How bad is it?"

"How bad? On a scale of one to ten, it's a hundred and fifty-eight. It's a shit show." Polk pointed to O'Flaherty's screen. "Those are spread-sheets detailing weapons shipments to ISIS over the past three years. RPGs, guns, ammo—massive amounts of all three. More than a billion dollars by my rough math. They used a down-market Mexican arms manufacturer, then moved the weapons by boat to the Syrian coast."

"Did you establish the link to the United States?" asked Calibrisi.

Polk looked up. His face was expressionless. He glanced back at O'Flaherty.

"Show 'em."

O'Flaherty tapped his keyboard a few times. One of the plasmas on the wall lit up with a large color photo of two men, both dressed in button-downs and khakis, standing on a pier before a medium-size rust-covered container ship that towered above them. Tristan Nazir stood to the left. Next to him was Mark Raditz.

O'Flaherty tapped again and another photo appeared. It was taken from the deck of the ship and showed a close-up of a stack of containers. Several were open. They were loaded with steel boxes that Calibrisi immediately recognized: RPGs.

"My God," whispered Calibrisi, disbelief and fury in his voice. "That son of a bitch."

O'Flaherty tapped his keyboard again. The line of plasmas filled with various pictures of Raditz and Nazir.

Calibrisi stepped slowly in front of the plasmas, staring in astonishment. Finally he turned to Polk.

"When was the last shipment?"

"According to the files, a year ago."

"Start looking for him."

Polk nodded.

"I have two forensics teams already on it. His office and his home are clear. He hasn't been at either in at least a week. His cell is shut down. I should also mention that we put a tracker on his family. He has an ex-wife and a teenage daughter. They're gone too."

"We need to find him," said Calibrisi. "How about the manufacturer?"

"It's a contract shop called MH Armas," said Polk.

Calibrisi was quiet for a few seconds.

"Don't get too close," he said. "I don't want to tip him off."

"It might be too late for that. He has to know. Nazir must've tipped him off about the files."

"You said he's been gone a week. It doesn't add up. Al-Jaheishi had yet to even make contact."

"I see your point," said Polk. "There's something else. Either it's a coincidence and he's been planning his escape, or there's something else."

"Like what?"

Polk shrugged. "Could be anything. Maybe he's in danger. Maybe the stress just got to him."

Calibrisi walked to the door. He looked once again at a photo of Raditz and Nazir, this one showing the pair seated on a couch in a hotel lobby.

He picked up his cell and hit Speed Dial. As he waited for his call to go through, he turned. "Anson, upstairs. You too, Bill. Get your ISIS C.O. and Mexico teams up there too."

Calibrisi put the phone to his ear as he pushed his way through the door.

"This is Hector Calibrisi," he said. "I need Jim Bruckheimer. Tell him it's urgent."

23

NATIONAL SECURITY AGENCY (NSA) SIGNALS INTELLIGENCE DIRECTORATE (SID) FORT MEADE, MARYLAND

On the third floor of an office building a short drive from Washington, D.C., Jim Bruckheimer reached for his ringing cell phone.

The building was one of four ominous-looking black-glass structures off a private exit from the Baltimore–Washington Parkway. The buildings were referred to as the Big Four and were the headquarters of the National Security Agency, America's code breakers, cybersleuths, eavesdroppers, and watchers from afar. Bruckheimer was the forty-seven-year-old head of the NSA's Signals Intelligence Directorate, whose job it was to process all foreign signals intelligence. SID's powerful computers, cameras, and satellites were America's primary electronic signature collector and aggregator. Its tentacles spanned the globe: e-mail, credit card transactions, cell phone activity, and, in general, any activity in which human beings came in contact with computers. This so-called SIGINT—electronic signals intelligence—was then processed by the NSA's massive computers and winnowed down to meaningful intelligence for use by the president of the United States, the Pentagon, CIA, and other intelligence and national security officials.

Bruckheimer didn't recognize the number on caller ID.

"Bruckheimer."

"Jim, it's Hector."

"Hey, Chief. What's up?"

"I need to find someone," said Calibrisi.

"That narrows it down," said Bruckheimer. "Can you at least tell me if it's male or female?"

"It's Mark Raditz."

"Mark Raditz as in the deputy defense secretary?"

"Yeah, that one. I'll brief you later, but right now I need your best people on this. We need to find this son of a bitch. Get any credit cards, aliases, passports, and run them against PRISM. Look at his ex-wife and daughter too. I'm sending you some photos. I need you to run them through any facial recognition applications you have out there. Look domestically as well as abroad."

There was a brief pause.

"Hector, I know you said you'll brief me later, and I trust you, of course, but if I start slamming PRISM against Raditz inside the U.S.—"

"Raditz gave ISIS more than a billion dollars' worth of guns and missiles, Jim. It was a secret program he ran out of a Pentagon dark pool. We need to find him."

"Any guess as to where he might be? It would save us time."

"Middle East," said Calibrisi. "Mexico. Maybe Central America or South America. Raditz has visited pretty much every country in the world. That said, he's not an operator. He doesn't know what he's doing."

"Hector, not that I care, but will there be a trial?"

"No way. This would do a lot of damage if it ever got out. That doesn't mean we're going to kill him, though. Frankly, he might be useful. Thanks for your help. Someone in our counsel's office will get you the FISA warrant."

"I'll call you when we have something."

24

LANGLEY, VIRGINIA

Anson Britt, Margaret Lyne, Stacy Conneely, and Fernando Rocha were seated on a pair of red leather Chesterfield couches in Hector Calibrisi's glass-walled corner office.

Britt sat next to Lyne, the CIA's assistant director for intergovernmental affairs. Lyne was Langley's chief lobbyist and primary interface with Congress and other governmental agencies. Her main role was working with the Pentagon.

Conneely, a linguistics prodigy, was the agency's top ISIS analyst.

Rocha was a Special Activities Division deputy director. His main area of focus was finance, including money laundering and currency manipulation.

All four had received the flash brief on the Raditz files.

Calibrisi and Polk entered the office. Calibrisi looked visibly upset. He took off his coat and tossed it onto the floor near the window. He pulled his tie off and did the same. His face was bright red. Sweat dripped off his forehead.

Polk appeared to be slightly calmer.

Calibrisi stood behind his desk for several quiet moments.

"Before we get into this clusterfuck of a situation, I want to know what's going on with Dewey and Rick. Anson?"

Britt paused. He looked at Polk and then Calibrisi, a serious expression on his face

"Rick is dead," he said. "Dewey's status is unknown, though in all likelihood he's dead too."

"Who's your source?" asked Polk.

"Damascus Metro Police," said Britt. "I also spoke with IDF. Dewey had a tracker on him. It moved in sync with the activity in the square. They had him a few blocks away. Then it went dark. Either they captured him and ripped it off or—"

"And Metro?"

"Mallory is confirmed dead. He was shot in the back, bled out on the street. My source at Metro also says Dewey is presumed dead. There was a pretty intense gunfight involving him and some guys from ISIS. Metro was there too. Apparently, Dewey was cornered by a contingent of ISIS gunmen. The location corroborates with the Israeli tracking device. Based on the time lines, ISIS cornered him immediately after the transmission of the files. My source has no further intel."

"They didn't see the body?"

"No, sir. The ISIS contingent engaged Metro. They killed several policemen. At some point, Metro dropped a shitload of artillery on the location from a chopper. It's rubble. If he's there, they're not going to dig him out for days."

"What if he's not there?" asked Calibrisi. "What if ISIS got him out?"

"It's a possibility," said Britt.

"Can Metro help us find out?"

Britt shook his head.

"No fucking way. Metro lost nine men. According to my source, Dewey killed at least five of them. They're not about to cooperate. In fact, they're pretty pissed off."

"How do they know it was us?" asked Polk. "Mallory was untraceable. Dewey is non-official cover."

In other words, Polk was questioning why Britt even divulged Langley's involvement.

"If we want the bodies back, I had to tell them," said Britt.

"All I'm saying—" Polk began.

"Take it off-line," snapped Calibrisi, cutting him off. "Who the hell cares if they know? Get Mallory's body out of Syria so he can be given a proper burial."

"Already done, Chief. He's being flown to Baghdad. He'll be on a flight to Andrews by dinner."

"What about Dewey? How do we find out if he's alive?"

"We moved some high-altitude UAVs into the theater," said Britt. "Looking at movements out of Damascus for the past hour, there are a couple of noteworthy convoys. We're talking vans and pickups. If they haven't killed him, they took him somewhere. We have the end points for those convoys locked and under S8 surveillance. One's Aleppo, the other is a camp out in the middle of the desert nowhere."

Calibrisi looked at Conneely.

"Stacy?"

"My guess would be Aleppo," she said. "Since ISIS took the city, they turned the hospital into a central staging area. It's the closest nexus point for them. Garotin is there. If Dewey's alive, that's probably where they took him."

"That corresponds with one of the convoys," said Britt. "The hospital was the terminal point."

Calibrisi shot Polk a look.

Polk was usually a quiet, unemotional man, yet today his face looked pained. He shrugged helplessly. He moved to a map on the wall that showed the Middle East.

"We have assets in the theater," said Polk, gesturing to the map. "We have operators in Baghdad and southern Turkey. That's before we even talk to JSOC, who could ready up a strike team very quickly. The issue is mission vulnerability. It doesn't matter who we send in or what size the team is. If he's in an ISIS stronghold—Aleppo or anywhere else, for that matter—all we'd be doing is sending those men to their deaths. Our only hope is some sort of ransom, though I highly doubt Nazir would forgo the opportunity to do something very dramatic and very public with an American agent."

"They're going to behead him," said Conneely. "Then they'll put it on YouTube, Al Jazeera, et cetera."

Calibrisi glanced to the window, which looked out on a picturesque stand of birch trees.

"Anson, I want you to elevate it to JSOC. Call Joe Terry. DEVGRU, CAG, 24th STS—tell him it's emergency priority. Have him come back with a recon scenario or two. In addition, reach out to GID," said Calibrisi, referring to Jordan's General

Intelligence Directorate. "I'll call Menachem Dayan."

"And what do I tell them?"

"We need an entity that has channels of communication with ISIS. We're going to negotiate with them. If they're willing to ransom Dewey, the president can decide whether to actually do it, but at least it'll buy us time. Focus on *proof of life.*"

"I can reach out to Lee Gluck at *60 Minutes*," said Conneely.

"And say what?" asked Polk.

"My guess is Lee has better contacts into ISIS than we do. I'll ask him to facilitate a message into Nazir's inner circle."

"Do it," said Calibrisi.

Britt stood up and gave Calibrisi a nod as he rushed to the door. Conneely followed him.

"What are the parameters?" she asked.

"What do you mean?" asked Calibrisi.

"What if we establish a direct line of communication?"

"No parameters. Take it if you can get it."

Britt and Conneely left.

Polk was standing next to a bookshelf near the door. He gave Calibrisi a long stare but said nothing. He didn't need to. After so many years working together, Calibrisi understood that Polk thought Dewey was probably dead already.

"Let's talk about Raditz," said Calibrisi.

He moved around to the front of the desk and took a seat in one of the chairs. He was quiet for several moments as he looked at the faces of the people in the room.

"I'm not sure where to begin," said Calibrisi, looking at Lyne. "This is such a fucking mess. Have you spoken with anyone yet?"

"Yes," said Lyne. "Harry Black and Josh Brubaker."

Black was the U.S. secretary of defense, Raditz's boss. Brubaker was the National Security Advisor.

"What did they say?"

"Josh wanted the files. He's going to brief the president. He also wanted to know what we're doing to rescue Dewey. He said you would already know this, but to tell you to do *whatever* you have to do to get him out of there alive. He wants you over at the Oval as soon as you're done here."

Calibrisi nodded.

"What about Harry?" he asked.

Lyne crossed her legs. "His exact words were, 'When I find Raditz, I'm going to cut off his balls and stuff them down his fucking throat.'"

"How the hell did this happen?" said Calibrisi, addressing Rocha. "Where did he get the money?"

"It came out of a Pentagon dark pool," said Rocha. "This is so-called program money, out-side the Pentagon budget, allocated by Congress specifically for activities they agree to give DOD that will not be scrutinized. It's never a big number, but Raditz aggregated it over a four-year period. We're still poring through it, but it appears Raditz succeeded in sheltering around two billion dollars. I should probably mention that each dark pool allocation requires both the secretary and deputy secretary to approve. Harry Black signed off on all of it."

"Did he know where it was going?"

"Not necessarily," said Rocha. "We were able to access the charters. There were four in all. Under the program description, they all said the same thing: 'An Initiative to Fight Terrorism.' "

"For what it's worth, Harry mentioned this," said Lyne. "He guessed this is where Raditz got the funds. He's opening up their files for us to look at."

" 'Fighting terrorism,' " said Calibrisi, shaking his head in disgust. "Ironic."

Lindsay, Calibrisi's assistant, opened the door.

"It's Jim Bruckheimer. He says it's urgent."

Calibrisi pointed at his desk phone, indicating to send the call there. A moment later, the phone started beeping. Calibrisi hit the speaker button.

"Hi, Jim."

"Hector, sorry to interrupt," said Bruckheimer, "but I have some information."

"Good."

"Well, you were partially right, I'm not sure he

knows what the hell he's doing. His passport hit the grid five days ago. United Airlines DFW to Mexico City, seat 4A."

Calibrisi looked at Polk, then muted the phone.

"We're going to need someone down there," said Calibrisi.

Polk nodded, pulling out his cell phone.

Calibrisi unmuted the phone. "Is he still in Mexico?"

"I don't know definitively," said Bruckheimer, "but if I had to guess, I'd say yes. He bought a round-trip ticket but wasn't on the return flight. And other than the passport ringing the bell, there's been no electronic signature event. We have his credit cards, his ex-wife's credit cards, cell phones, bank accounts, and everything we know of, and there hasn't been any activity whatsoever. He's probably using cash or traveler's checks, though we can't find any big cash withdrawals going back six months and no purchases of traveler's checks either."

"He's been working with a company called MH Armas," said Calibrisi. "It's a weapons manufacturer in Tampico, on the coast. He probably visited there several times over the past couple of years. I need your guys digging deep into signals intelligence coming out of Tampico. Run Raditz's photo against any media you've intercepted from the U.S. border down to Central America."

"Got it," said Bruckheimer. "PRISM's going to

be our best hope of finding him. It's designed to correlate seemingly random electronic activity by module."

"What does that mean?"

"It means we can pinpoint an individual based on past activity even if the current activity uses a different electronic signature. For example, if we can find a record from last year, such as a credit card purchase or a cell call that was definitively executed by Raditz, PRISM will correlate the activity to present-day signals intelligence. If he called a number with his old cell phone a year ago and then called that same number with a new, unknown phone, we'll be able to lock onto him, track him, define a new set of electronic signatures, and find him."

"I can't imagine he'd be so stupid—"

"You'd be surprised."

"He knows how PRISM works."

"You didn't," said Bruckheimer.

Calibrisi grinned. "Asshole."

"If he stayed at a hotel, if he bought a meal, if he so much as bought a pack of gum a year ago and he uses a traveler's check from outside of Mexico, or visits the same hotel or store, we'll flag it. Doesn't mean it's him, but it might be. You'd be surprised how quickly it narrows it down. People are creatures of habit."

Calibrisi reached for the phone. "Anything else?"

"Yes," said Bruckheimer. "The urgent part. Just

for the hell of it, I had one of my analysts look at the passenger manifests on that United Airlines flight from Dallas. One of the other passengers aboard the flight tripped an algorithm. Approximately ten minutes after the flight landed in Mexico City, someone other than Raditz made a phone call to a PBX switch located in Berlin that previously correlated to Raditz. In other words, PRISM flagged the call because it already had Raditz's cell records."

"How do you know it wasn't him?"

"Because we listened in. We caught the last few seconds. The PBX is some sort of cloaking device, a conduit frag—hides both users and then encrypts their conversation. But before the encryption took hold, we heard him. He was Arab."

"Did you run it through voice recognition?"

"Yes. It didn't match anything in our files. But it wasn't Raditz."

"Okay, I'm following."

"The point is," Bruckheimer continued, "Raditz himself has either called or been called through the exact same switch at least a dozen times, including a week ago. Anyway, we marked the correlation and then ran the caller's cell activity against the passenger manifest in order to try to narrow down who it was. An hour ago, the owner of the cell used his passport to check into a hotel in Mexico City. Because we're tracking the cell by SAT, we know it's the same individual."

Calibrisi glanced at Polk, who pointed at his cell and gave him a thumbs-up, indicating he had someone on the line.

"Anyway, so here's the interesting part."

"It's already interesting, Jim."

"I know. I mean *really* interesting. It's a French passport that belongs to someone named Pierre Lagrange. He's a thirty-year-old male from Marseilles. That all checked out, but when we processed his photo, that is, when we ran it against our facial recognition platform, it popped. We have a match on four photos, all showing this guy with Nazir. He's in the background. He's an Iraqi named Haider Allawi."

"What the hell does it mean?" asked Calibrisi, speaking to no one in particular.

"It means Nazir is cleaning up his mess," said Polk.

"Why hasn't he killed him yet?" asked Calibrisi.

"Maybe he has," said Polk. "Or maybe it's a RECON—"

"You guys are jumping to conclusions," interrupted Bruckheimer. "It doesn't mean Raditz is there too. It's circumstantial. I just want to be clear."

"Do you have this guy's location in real time?" asked Polk.

"Yeah," said Bruckheimer. "He's at the St. Regis Hotel in Mexico City."

"Call us if you find anything on Raditz," said Calibrisi, "and thanks, Jim. It's damn fine work."

Calibrisi ended the call and looked at Polk.

"They must need Raditz alive," he said.

Polk picked up a small remote and hit a button, lowering a plasma screen from the ceiling. A moment later, the face of a young, handsome Hispanic man appeared. He was outdoors. He had longish black hair, a beard and mustache, and was shirtless, his chest, shoulders, and arms ripped. He wore sunglasses and was leaning back in a white lounge chair, the blue water of a swimming pool behind him, along with several bikini-clad women. He communicated through an earbud as his cell streamed his image back to Langley.

"Hello?"

If he was at all self-conscious about lounging by a pool, half-dressed, surrounded by beautiful women, he didn't show it.

"Franco, it's Bill."

Franco was Franco Gutierrez, a member of CIA paramilitary under the direction of Special Operations Group. Gutierrez was based in Rio de Janeiro, though his area of activity stretched from the U.S. border with Mexico down through Central and South America.

"Hey, boss," Franco said, grinning. He had a soft Spanish accent.

"Where are you?" asked Polk.

"Medellín."

"You need to pack up and get to the airport," said Polk.

Gutierrez's smile vanished. He stood up and started walking through the throng of young women and men socializing by the rooftop pool, pulling on a short-sleeve linen shirt as he moved.

"Do I need to arrange transportation?"

"No, we'll take care of it. Get to the private terminal. You'll get your orders when you're in the air."

"Can you at least tell me where I'm going?"

"Mexico City."

25

MEXICO CITY

Allawi was in traffic when he received the text message from Nazir:

:: UNLEASH THE DOGS ::

He slammed his hand into the steering wheel. He knew this might happen.

It had been two days now. Allawi had been tracking Raditz, first to Mexico City, then to Tampico to meet with the ship captain, then back to Mexico City. Raditz, as far as Allawi could tell, didn't have a clue.

On the outskirts of the city, he'd been pulled over by the police for speeding. That was when he lost him. Because the tracking technology required proximity of about a thousand feet.

For eighteen hours now, Allawi had driven what seemed like every street in the city, searching for Raditz.

His iPad was on at all times, propped up on the passenger seat. The tracking app was on. Allawi should've been able to see Raditz's location if he was within a thousand feet. Now, the screen was empty.

:: UNLEASH THE DOGS ::

He hadn't informed Nazir that he'd lost him. Now he would have to. Raditz could be gone from Mexico City. He could've discovered the thin wafer of plastic inside his wallet. He could be anywhere by now. China. Africa. Anywhere.

Yet Allawi remained in Mexico City, searching. False hope, perhaps, but at least there was a chance.

Allawi was exhausted. He knew how disappointed Nazir would be, but he had no choice. He had to tell him.

He took a right off of Rio Hudson and looked for a place to park. He didn't want to be driving when he spoke with Nazir.

He saw the hotel ahead. He took a left and went

past the entrance to the employee parking lot, then stopped. He reached for his phone, frustration, anger, above all, fatigue on his face. As he started to dial, his eyes shot to the passenger seat. There, on the screen, a red digital light was flashing.

He'd found Raditz.

26

IN THE AIR

Two hours after lifting off from Medellín in the Air America GV, Franco's cell phone buzzed as an encrypted message arrived from Langley. The message was blank except for a link to the encrypted document, which he double-tapped:

ACCESS CONTROL: 741
DOCUMENT REENCRYPTION 00:59:48

A prompt appeared that asked him to press his thumb against the screen. A moment later, a different prompt asked him to stare into the camera on his phone as a remote application scanned his irises. The document opened:

TOP SECRET
NCS
NAT SEC PRIORITY: DDCIA * NOC4899-W

SPEC SHEET: MISSION ARCHITECTURE
RECONNAISSANCE OF VIP
PRIORITY LEVEL TAU

1. GUTIERREZ arrives IATA (Mexico City Benito Juárez International Airport) via COMPANY transport *BRAE BURN TWO* (GV121 ex. Medellín, COL). Flight time 4:12. CREW: OC34OWEN + CR22MEADE.
2. *BRAE BURN TWO* remains at IATA and prepares for exfiltration.
3. GUTIERREZ moves to DROP POINT [St. Regis Hotel (as of 17:35:00) subject to change]. Room under alias MARTINEZ, JESUS (Passport control).
4. GUTIERREZ receives precise location information for recon of TARGET when available.
5. TARGET is MARK RADITZ, U.S. Citizen [VIP], see photograph and notes below.
6. RADITZ is *in flight* and faces long-term incarceration for violations of multiple national security laws. He should be considered a CATEGORY 1 FLIGHT RISK.
7. RADITZ is combatant level 6 and has specific aptitude with various weapons though no known combat experience and no hand-to-hand skills or experience. He should be considered *moderately* dangerous.

8. This is a PRIORITY TAU action [DCIA 55]: RADITZ has high-value intelligence and should be exfiltrated with extreme intent <u>but alive.</u>

9. <u>SPECIAL NOTE 1:</u> We believe RADITZ is in the immediate vicinity of HAIDER ALLAWI, an Iraqi and known ISIS official. See photos below.

10. ALLAWI is traveling under French alias PIERRE LAGRANGE. It is not known *why* ALLAWI and RADITZ are traveling together. The two men could be meeting or RADITZ could be under watch and at risk.

11. *Rules of engagement:* RADITZ has deep knowledge of U.S. SFO operating protocols. <u>Use any means necessary</u> {NOC J-099 RE "1998 transborder exemption"} to secure RADITZ and remove from DROP TARGET and exfiltrate to IATA *BRAE BURN TWO* for flight to U.S.

12. ALLAWI is <u>not</u> target. Tactical consequence should in no way contravene main mission architecture. However, if opportunity presents itself, ALLAWI can and should be *<u>terminated with extreme prejudice.</u>*

13. RADITZ should be secured once on board for flight to U.S.

14. Exfiltration to Joint Base Andrews, Maryland, USA via *BRAE BURN TWO.*

Franco reread the mission spec a few more times, then scanned the photos attached to the file. He didn't recognize Raditz, but he knew damn well who he was.

"You fucked up," Franco muttered aloud as he studied the photos.

Next he looked at the photos of Allawi. Like all of them, Allawi was young, with a look of cold determination on his face.

Franco's mind swirled with questions. Why would Raditz be running? If Allawi was nearby and wanted to kill Raditz, why hadn't he already? Of course, maybe he had. And if Allawi was there to meet Raditz, why?

Franco had long ago gotten used to the way information was segregated and filtered out when it came to operations. The fact that the orders contained no further information about Raditz and what he'd done, Franco knew, was to protect the United States. Whatever Raditz had done was bad, so bad they didn't want it ever to see the light of day. SOP.

Standard operating procedure. Yet something about the assignment troubled him.

"Twenty minutes out, Franco," said one of the pilots over the Gulfstream's intercom.

Franco reread the brief one last time. As he

moved once again to the photos, the screen shot abruptly red and the document reencrypted and disappeared.

He went to the back of the cabin. A steel cabinet, four feet high, six feet wide, was bolted to the right wall. Inside were several rows of weapons, all arranged neatly. The top two shelves were various carbines, submachine guns, and sniper rifles. The next two rows contained handguns of many shapes and varieties. Another row was lined with knives, suppressors, lights, holsters, disposable international cell phones, and a few other accessories. The bottom four rows were stacked with ammo.

Franco picked out a Kimber Super Match II .45 ACP with an undermounted halogen light. He slammed in a fourteen-round extended magazine. He didn't expect Raditz to require the use of the gun, but that's not who it was for. He also grabbed an SRD45 suppressor—eight inches long, titanium—and a custom-made drop-leg holster that could accommodate the pistol with the suppressor locked into the muzzle. He found a SOG S37K SEAL Team fixed-blade combat knife and sheathed it around his left calf. He scanned quickly and then, just in case, took a backup gun: a small, highly concealable Ruger LC9, which he sheathed to his right calf.

He grabbed two disposable cell phones.

Franco shut the doors. He opened a cabinet

across from the weapons store. It was the jet's field trauma kit, filled with various tools, bandages, and medicines. He reached for a small bottle filled with a milklike liquid: propofol, a short-acting, intravenously administered amnestic agent. He also took a syringe.

A few minutes later, the Gulfstream taxied to a stop near a nondescript building.

Franco unlocked the cabin door and hit the hydraulic button. The door began moving out and a set of air stairs lowered to the tarmac.

Franco leaned into the cockpit. "Hopefully, it'll be quick," said Franco.

"Any time estimate?"

Franco shook his head.

"A few hours. It could take longer. It's a priority exfiltration. Get this thing refueled."

27

SOUTH BENTALOU STREET
BALTIMORE, MARYLAND

South Bentalou ran through one of the poorest neighborhoods in Baltimore. It was a street more accustomed to police cruisers than BMWs, but that's what Daisy Calibrisi was driving, her mother's shiny red BMW X5 SUV. Both sides of the block were lined with small two-story homes

231

made of brick or concrete. Most were dilapidated, with peeling paint and broken windows, and a few had long ago been abandoned, their doors and windows covered in boards or plastic. In some places, garbage lay strewn on the sidewalk, empty beer cans and wine bottles, chairs missing legs and with torn fabric, a hubcap here, even a mattress leaning against a neglected tree. People milled about on the sidewalks. In a few places, front steps were occupied by people sitting and watching the street as if it were a television set.

Daisy parked the SUV in front of a brick home about halfway down the block. In front, two black children passed a worn football. Daisy turned off the car and climbed out.

One of the boys turned to look at her. An enthusiastic smile flashed across his lips. "Daisy!" he yelled.

"Hey, slugger," she said, as the boy ran to her and threw his arms around her waist.

"She said you were coming," he said.

"Of course I'm coming, Anthony," said Daisy, holding him an extra moment. She glanced at the other boy, who was small and wore glasses. He stood still, holding the football, a dour expression on his face.

"Hi," she said.

"Hi," the boy responded shyly.

"You must be Rex?"

A slight grin hit his lips. "Yeah."

Daisy stepped toward him and extended her hand.

"I'm Daisy," she said, kneeling down so that she was at eye level with him, then taking his hand and shaking it firmly.

"I know. Gramma told me about you."

"Well, she told me about you, Rex, and it sounds like you're one of the smartest students in your whole grade."

He smiled, saying nothing.

"He ain't smarter than me," said Anthony from behind Daisy.

Rex continued to look at Daisy, then rolled his eyes knowingly.

"Anthony, you're the smartest in *your* grade," she said, standing up and signaling to Rex for the football. He underhanded it to her.

"But what's even more important than being the smartest?" she asked, holding the football.

Anthony rolled his eyes. He'd heard this sermon before.

"Hard work," he said.

"That's important," she agreed, "but there's something even more important."

"Staying in school," said Rex.

"Oh, yeah, that's *very* important," said Daisy as she took a step back and held the football, preparing to throw it. "But it's not the most important thing."

"Don't do drugs," said Anthony.

Daisy shook her head.

"That's *incredibly* important. But it's not what I'm thinking of."

Daisy took a few more steps back, then nodded to Anthony, indicating she wanted him to go out for a pass.

"I give up," Anthony said.

"Man, I'm really surprised," she said as Anthony continued back until he was down the block a ways. "The most important thing—"

Daisy leaned back, brought her arm behind her head, and prepared to throw.

". . . is being the best female quarterback in the United States of America and most likely the world."

Daisy's arm whipped smoothly forward. A clean spiral lofted through the warm morning air. The ball arced high, then dropped in a perfect slope into Anthony's arms.

"You're telling me Joe Flacco can throw like that?" she asked.

Rex laughed, while Anthony shook his head.

After a few minutes of catch, Daisy climbed the steps to the front door. Tacked to the door was a light blue pennant emblazoned with the words COLUMBIA UNIVERSITY.

She knocked. After a moment, a thin gray-haired woman with glasses opened the door. Her face melted into a smile.

"Hi, Miss Betty," said Daisy.

"Well, God bless you, dear," said the woman, who threw open the door and wrapped her arms around Daisy. "She is so excited to see you."

"Where is she?"

"In her room. Now stand back, let me look at you."

The woman scanned Daisy from head to toe, shaking her head.

"You get more beautiful every day, child, I swear."

"You're pretty cute yourself, Miss Betty."

The woman erupted into a loud, enthusiastic laugh.

Daisy walked through the apartment, through the kitchen, then down a hallway. She arrived at the last door, which was open. Several cardboard boxes were stacked near the door, along with a few duffel bags.

Seated on the bed was a girl. She wore glasses, a white T-shirt, and khakis. She was thin. If there was anything unusual about her, it was her hair, which arose in an unruly, beautiful Afro. She said nothing as she took in Daisy.

"Hey, Little Sister," said Daisy.

"Hey, Big Sister," said the girl, whose name was Andromeda, though everyone called her Andy.

"So, you ready to become a big-time, hotshot, fancy-pants Ivy Leaguer?" asked Daisy, entering the room and sitting on the bed.

Andy looked at her but said nothing. She had a morose expression on her face.

Daisy put her hand softly on her shoulder.

"You forgot to pack your fancy pants, didn't you?" she asked, shaking her playfully.

Andy said nothing. She stared at the floor.

Daisy knew her well. After eleven years, of course she knew her, like the way an older sister knows a younger sister, or a mother a daughter. Andy wasn't crying, but Daisy could see the light salty white of dried tears on her cheeks.

"I'm scared," whispered Andy.

"Every freshman at every college is nervous before they get there," said Daisy, wrapping her arm around Andy's neck and pulling her closer. "I almost threw up."

"I've never been away from Baltimore."

"So coming to my house doesn't count? What am I, chopped liver?"

Andy smiled. "I mean living away."

"You're a brilliant, beautiful, one-in-a-million girl," said Daisy. "You are going to blossom at Columbia. I think I'm more excited than you are."

"I'm not good enough to be in the Ivy League."

Daisy stood up. She stepped to one of the boxes and put her hands beneath it. She turned around and caught Andy's eyes.

"Andy, you're *in* the Ivy League. Present tense. Whether you like it or not, your name— Andromeda Anne Robinson—is on a great big list at one of the greatest universities in the world, and no one can ever change that. You *are* an Ivy Leaguer. It's already happened. It's done. Now, we can certainly debate as to whether or not Columbia is as good as UVA, but that's missing the point."

Daisy flashed Andy a devilish grin, then hoisted the box.

"UVA?" said Andy, standing up and lifting another box. She smiled, then laughed. "Is that even a college? Everyone knows Columbia is better."

"Maybe at fencing," offered Daisy, moving toward the door with the box.

"Fencing?"

"You know, with swords."

"It's called épée."

"Épée, schmépée," said Daisy, stepping into the hall.

"Columbia has produced like a kajillion Nobel Prize winners," said Andy.

"Good point. Nerds. Columbia definitely is better at producing nerds."

"They're called geniuses," said Andy.

"Didn't some Columbia student steal uranium from the science building last year?" asked Daisy, her laughter filling the hallway.

"Oh, man," said Andy, giggling. She followed Daisy through the door and down the hallway. "This is going to be a long ride."

28

ST. REGIS HOTEL
MEXICO CITY

Raditz was reclined on the king-size bed. He stared up at the coffered ceiling. A drinking glass filled with minibar champagne rested on his bare chest, his left hand around it, holding it steady. His right hand was beneath his head. He was deep in thought.

He would spend two, possibly three days in Mexico City, then move on. He would buy a car with cash, and drive. First Central America, then South America, where he would ultimately disappear.

The money would last him the rest of his life. In fact, he would likely die long before he spent all of it. A dark thought—which he tried to push away—came to him.

You won't spend any of it. They're coming . . .

"No," he said, tipping the glass to his lips, taking another gulp, spilling a little on his chin, which proceeded to dribble down his neck.

He would get to Brazil. Land of the Lost. A retired agent told him that. He would disappear. In Rio or a smaller city. He would buy a house. Or perhaps a farm somewhere in the country on the way to Chile, maybe even in Chile. Or Argentina. He would disappear.

He thought of his daughter, the day he'd said goodbye. Raditz had taken everything he had from his Fidelity account and handed her the check: $353,402.90.

"Take care of your mom."

What they did to her. What they did to her!

What you did to her.

"Oh, God," he whispered, as guilt washed over him. The sight of her on the concrete of the garage that night.

What have you done?

Raditz imagined a thick envelope being handed to his daughter one day. She is thirty, thirty-five. A child or two is near her as she opens the door. Her husband is a kind man. He doesn't know any of it. Or he does, and he understands that mistakes are made by good people. That his wife's father is a good person. She opens the envelope and there is more money than she has ever seen. A million dollars. Two million.

Raditz was weeping now as he thought of the life he had once had, the life he worked so hard for, the life he destroyed. He sobbed for several minutes. He walked into the bathroom and turned on the cold water, splashing his face several times, trying to wash away the tears, the feelings of guilt.

In the morning, he would leave. He didn't want to. He was a good man. He made an intellectual mistake. An honest mistake on behalf of his country. But he knew how the system worked. Any chance he had of forgiveness and clemency had long ago been destroyed by not telling anyone about what he'd done. Framing out Harry Black. Hiding it all. Now he would be called a traitor.

Go downstairs and have a drink. Tomorrow, you can disappear.

The worst was over. He could learn to live with the guilt. It would pass. Raditz would put it all behind him.

Allawi put down the phone. A sadistic smirk spread across his lips.

Unleash the dogs? Don't worry, Tristan, I will unleash the dogs.

It didn't take long for Allawi to home in on the St. Regis. He used the iPad to guide him, continuing down the side street, cutting left: At the next corner, he saw the building ST. REGIS HOTEL MEXICO CITY.

Allawi passed the front entrance and parked in the employee lot behind the building, in a space close to the entrance, between two cars, under the bright lights of the garage. He knew the best way to hide was to blend in, and the best way to blend in was to act like you belonged. The cars in far corners were, ironically, the ones that stood out the most. Nobody paid attention to the closest ones.

Allawi reached for his duffel from the backseat. He pulled out a KBP GSh-18 9×19mm pistol, then threaded a custom-made suppressor into the muzzle. He strapped on a shoulder holster and tucked in the gun. He pulled on a leather jacket. He opened up the app on his iPhone so that he didn't have to lug around the iPad.

The tracking technology was accurate to within six inches. He wouldn't need to get a room. He would find him, wait for the right opportunity, and kill him. He would do it carefully, but it wouldn't take long. According to Nazir, Raditz was fat, an office worker, a politician. He would kill Raditz quickly but with discretion. This was why Nazir had sent him.

Allawi didn't view himself as a terrorist. He was an *assassin*. An *intelligence agent*. When ISIS was a country, he would help build its intelligence service. He wanted to go home. He was willing to sacrifice himself—but now was not the time. It wasn't necessary.

The hunger for the kill made him walk quickly to the elevators. As he climbed into one of the elevator cars, the red tracker light moved closer to the center of the phone screen. He hit the top floor and the elevator started to climb. At seven, the red light reached the midpoint of the screen and Allawi shot his hand out. The elevator stopped and the doors opened.

He went left as, with his fingers, he increased

the magnification of the screen. He moved down the hallway, watching as he came closer and closer to the room. Then the light hit the very center of the screen. His eyes moved slowly to the door: SUITE 712.

Allawi put the cell in his coat pocket and reached his right hand inside his coat, grabbing the butt of the gun. He removed it from the holster but kept it inside the coat, flicking the safety off. He knocked on the door, then placed his left thumb over the eyehole as his right index finger found the trigger.

Franco walked behind the private terminal and found a dark sedan parked near the back of the lot. He drove into Mexico City and pulled up to the front entrance of the St. Regis just as the early evening sky was edging toward a hypnotic brownish-red.

He climbed from the sedan, dressed in a blue T-shirt, jeans, and Puma tennis sneakers. He pulled on a blue nylon jacket. Three weapons were concealed on his person: the knife, the Ruger, and the Kimber .45.

Franco approached every project slightly differently depending on the mood he was in. This one was no exception. He knew agents were supposed to develop successful patterns and adhere to the ones that worked, but Franco believed the unpredictability of his approach to mission work gave him an advantage. It made him more alert, spontaneous, and creative. It gave him a nervous edge. It also prevented him from developing lazy habits.

Walking to the entrance of the St. Regis, he turned on one of the disposable cells and dialed a four-digit number. When he heard a high-pitched beeping noise, he typed in a ten-digit code, then hung up. Half a dozen seconds later, a text made the phone vibrate.

V C X g W S S a I P b C W

NSA pinpointed Raditz; he was in room 712.

"What a fucking idiot," he whispered as he entered the hotel.

Franco was seldom surprised by the stupidity and arrogance of people.

If Raditz was running, he obviously understood the risk. He should've been several days into a decades'-long parallax in remote country, getting accustomed to constant movement, in gritty, underpopulated places where the arrival of an intelligence officer would stand out. The St. Regis Mexico City was the kind of hotel a man on the run would stay in if he believed he would never be caught, or else believed getting caught was inevitable. It was a devil-may-care attitude—the kind of attitude that Franco was very familiar with, because it was his own.

Of course, he could afford that kind of arrogance. He didn't do things that might make the U.S. government want him dead. As to those various scumbags, foreign officials, and angry husbands who did want him dead, unlike Raditz, Franco had the skills to back up the checks his devil-may-care attitude was writing.

As the elevator climbed, Franco reached to his belt and felt for the gun's safety, turning it off. He put his hand in the pocket of his windbreaker, making sure the loaded syringe was ready. He placed his thumb on the end of the plunger—inside the pocket—and gripped the plastic cartridge. He stepped off the elevator on the seventh floor and went left.

He passed an older couple, stepping aside, nodding hello, then rounded the corner, practically knocking over a man coming in the opposite direction. Franco's eyes shot to the man, scanning the face, cheekbones, eyes. He was young, clean-cut, and he smiled bashfully to apologize for walking too close to the wrong side of the hallway. Franco wasn't fooled by the man's innocent smile.

Franco let go of the syringe and moved his right hand to his belt in the same instant he lurched with his left elbow, meeting the steel of Allawi's weapon as Allawi swung it across the air, and knocking it sideways as the killer fired. The gun made a high-pitched spit as the bullet ripped just inches from Franco's ear, then another. In a sinuous parry, Franco ducked left as his right hand drew the Kimber and fired point-blank at Allawi before he could recover from Franco's small but effective elbow. Slugs ripped into Allawi's chest and neck, spraying blood on the wall behind him as he was pummeled backward. He let out an angry groan. As he fell, Allawi held up his pistol at Franco, but Franco saw it coming and caught Allawi's arm with his left hand just as Allawi completed his fall to the green-and-tan carpet.

Allawi was riddled with lead, though still alive. Franco was crouched over him, left hand clutching Allawi's wrist, right hand moving the Kimber to Allawi's lips and then slamming it into his mouth as he stared at the Syrian's dark bloodshot eyes. He pushed the suppressor as hard as he could into the terrorist's throat, waited a moment, then fired twice.

The chime of the elevator startled him and he looked over his shoulder. He stood quickly, leaving the gun on the ground, and walked, pulling out his cell from his left pocket and pretending to talk as his right hand went back to the syringe.

"My dear, I will be right there. Of course I love you! Yes, yes . . ."

He rounded the corner slowly, oblivious of everything around him, like someone on his honeymoon. Raditz was coming toward him, staring suspiciously.

"I am getting on the elevator. Please, sir"—he held the cell out to Raditz, smiling—"will you tell my beautiful wife I am getting on the elevator and I will be there in a minute?"

Raditz seemed to lose his reserve; a smile creased his lips as he held up his hand, saying no thank you but laughing at the moment. Franco slashed the syringe into Raditz's neck as he passed, watching as Raditz's mouth went agape, then catching him as he fell to the ground.

Franco ran to Allawi and took his gun. He returned to Raditz and picked him up, tossing him over his shoulder.

"Fuck, you're a load," he muttered.

He took the elevator to the second floor, twice telling people who tried to get on it was a medical emergency. At the second floor, he walked to the stairs, lugging Raditz the entire time. He took the stairs to the basement, cut through the basement to the service loading dock, and dropped Raditz behind a bush. He went and got his car and came back and lifted Raditz into the trunk.

Forty-five minutes later, Franco carried Raditz up the stairs of the GV, whose engines were already firing and ready to rip. He tossed Raditz onto a sofa, hit the hydraulic button that closed the stairs, then leaned into the cockpit.

"Wheels up."

29

MONCRIEF COUNTY ROAD
CHANTILLY, VIRGINIA

The farmhouse sat in a clearing at the end of a mile-long, winding gravel driveway off a seldom-traveled winding country road in a part of Virginia where old-line horse country wealth started its slide into Appalachia.

It was a pretty if modest brick house, built in 1950, with black shutters, a slate roof, and neatly trimmed hedges surrounding it, and a lawn that spread out for a few hundred yards, transitioning into fields that rolled off to the horizon. The house sat on eight hundred acres of land. There were no other houses for miles.

At the end of the driveway, a steel gate was locked tight. A few hundred feet inside the gate, out of view of anyone who happened to drive by, was a black Chevy Suburban, inside of which sat two men, both employees of the Central Intelligence Agency.

A mile on, at the end of the driveway, sat two more vehicles: a shiny black van and a dark sedan.

Standing in the middle of the driveway were two additional men. Both had on khakis, short-sleeve polo shirts, sunglasses, and flak jackets.

Both clutched submachine guns tipped with suppressors, which they kept trained at the dirt.

The sound of insects, of the occasional bird-song, of wind rustling the leaves, was interrupted by a low grumble from up the driveway. The two men stiffened slightly. A few moments later, another black sedan came into view, its tires kicking up dust as it charged into the parking area and stopped in front of them.

Calibrisi climbed from the back of the sedan, nodded at the two operators from CIA para-military, then walked to the house. He went through the front door, took a left, walked down a corridor, then opened a door and took a staircase down into the basement.

Three bright klieg lights cast electric blue across a cramped, low-ceilinged room. The lights were positioned on a stanchion in the center of the room and were aimed at a man seated in a steel chair. The heat from the lights was intense, and after three hours, the man's hair, face, and clothing were drenched in sweat.

He was strapped to the chair. Metal bands were clamped around his wrists, ankles, and waist. Electrodes were affixed to his forehead, chest, and feet, their wires dangling out to the side. The wires ran along the ground and disappeared beneath a door.

An IV was spiked into his left arm, its tube connected to a bag containing a liquid.

As Calibrisi entered, the man stared up at him with a sorrowful, defeated expression. Calibrisi held the man's eyes with an icy stare.

The man tried to speak but couldn't. All he could do was grunt. A red ball gag was stuffed in his mouth, held in place by a nylon strap wrapped around his head.

Calibrisi followed the colorful wires from behind the man, which led to a large mirror at the back of the room. He opened the door next to the mirror, went inside, then shut the door behind him.

The room was small. It had been built by a private contractor with top secret security clearance based on specifications provided by the CIA. The back and side walls were stacked with a variety of monitors and computer equipment, like the control room on a nuclear submarine. The front of the room was a large two-way mirror. The room was soundproofed and air-conditioned.

Two individuals were seated in front of the mirror.

"Did we run the pharmaceuticals?"

"Yes," said the woman. "We initiated the suite two hours ago. We gave him a second round just now."

Calibrisi looked at the man seated next to her.

"And the polygraph is ready?"

The man nodded. "Yes, sir. I ran him through

three sessions of control questions as well as a GKT," he said, referring to an agency interrogation protocol known as a *guilty knowledge test*.

"What are shock levels?"

"Five milliamperes for the first violation. Second is ten. Third is fifteen."

"Make the first sixteen," said Calibrisi.

"What about the second?"

"There won't be a second."

Calibrisi returned to the interrogation room. He went behind the man and unlatched the nylon at the back of his head, releasing the gag. He stepped around the table and stood behind the lights.

The man panted. He flexed his jaw as he stared up at Calibrisi. Calibrisi remained silent for more than a minute. Calmly, he stared at the man in the chair.

"What took you so long?" asked Raditz.

"Traffic," said Calibrisi. "Sorry, am I inconveniencing you, Mark? I can reschedule if you want."

Raditz shook his head, stretching out his mouth.

"That's not what I meant."

"What did you mean?"

"I thought you would find out sooner. That someone would."

Calibrisi stood still, arms crossed.

"My apologies," said Calibrisi. "We were busy trying to stop ISIS from killing more innocent Americans."

Calibrisi shook his head in pure anger, then stepped forward, raising his right hand to his left shoulder and swinging right to left, viciously slapping Raditz across the cheek.

"How the hell could you do this?" asked Calibrisi. "What were you thinking? I never, never would've tagged you as a traitor, not in a million years."

Raditz looked crestfallen, embarrassed, and humiliated.

"I'm not a traitor, Hector," said Raditz.

"You supplied ISIS with more than a billion dollars' worth of guns, missiles, and ammo. Garotin has now taken half of Iraq and Syria with those guns."

Raditz nodded. "I know. If you're here to make me feel worse, there's nothing you could say or do to make me feel any worse than I already do."

Calibrisi glanced at the control room. The agent manning the polygraph nodded: so far, he was telling the truth.

"Who else is involved?"

Raditz shook his head. "Nobody."

The agent on the polygraph held up two fingers. Raditz was lying.

"You did this yourself?" he asked, holding up a finger to the control room. *Don't hit him yet.* "And by the way, I set the amps to sixteen."

Raditz knew what it meant.

"I did it alone. I mean, people were involved,

but they didn't understand what they were involved in."

"What the hell does that mean?"

"The authorizations on the dark pool money, for example. I was the only one who knew where that piece of it was going. The manufacturers didn't have a clue."

"Harry Black needs to sign off on all black pool funds."

"And he did sign the protocols, but he had no idea."

"How could he not have any idea?"

"Because I lied. I told him it was for weapons, but that they were to be used to fight terrorists. Because that's what I was doing . . . It's what I was trying to do."

"I still don't understand why."

"You were there," said Raditz. "It was the RAND report."

Calibrisi considered what Raditz said.

"I remember."

"That was a watershed moment for me," said Raditz. "I've spent half my life fighting radical Islam, and yet what did I have to show for it? Nothing."

"If you can't beat 'em, join 'em."

Raditz shut his eyes, shaking his head.

"No!" he yelled angrily. "Is that what you think?"

"That's certainly what it looks like."

Raditz took a deep breath.

"I know it does," he said, calming. "But the idea was just the opposite. Vet up-and-coming players, find one we could work with, aggressively fund someone who had the potential to scale. In other words, back winners in the region not as radicalized as Al Qaeda. A group that might be sympathetic to U.S. interests, at least in private. Arms for influence. Nazir fit the bill."

Calibrisi listened with a blank expression.

"When was the last time you communicated with Nazir?" asked Calibrisi.

Raditz's mouth opened. He looked at Calibrisi, then he turned and looked at the two-way mirror.

"Over a year ago."

Raditz screamed in the same instant his entire body contorted as if he was having a seizure. It lasted two seconds.

Raditz looked up, panting, his face beet red and wet with perspiration.

Calibrisi waited, giving him a few seconds to recover.

"Sunday," he panted.

Raditz started to cry.

"They took Zoe," said Raditz, referring to his daughter. "They came and took Zoe and Susan."

Calibrisi took a step forward, a stunned look on his face.

"Who's they?"

"They have a cell here," said Raditz.

Calibrisi pulled his cell phone from his pocket, hitting a button.

"How many men?"

Raditz glanced back at the mirror.

"I don't know. I swear, Hector. A van full. They came to my house. Threatened me."

"Did they take them?"

Raditz nodded.

Calibrisi heard the phone pick up.

"Get me George Kratovil at the FBI," said Calibrisi into the phone, then put his hand over the speaker.

He looked at Raditz, who was now sobbing pathetically.

"They took your daughter and your ex-wife and you didn't let anyone know?" he asked. "You would let them die just to keep this whole thing secret? You're contemptible—"

Raditz was still panting. Every few seconds his body made an involuntary twitch.

He looked up at Calibrisi. "No, they let them go."

"Hector—" The FBI director came on the line. Calibrisi removed his hand from the phone.

"Hold a sec, George," said Calibrisi as he stared at Raditz, studying him, as if his mind was trying to put the pieces together. There was something here; he couldn't put his finger on it.

It was Raditz who broke the silence.

"Just kill me," he whispered, pleading, tears of

shame on his face. "We both know where this is going. I didn't mean for it to end up this way, but it did, and I accept responsibility."

But Calibrisi wasn't listening to Raditz. His mind continued to process. Finally, the quizzical look disappeared.

"Why did Nazir release them?"

Raditz shook his head back and forth, his eyes shutting.

"Why, Mark?" asked Calibrisi calmly.

"No," cried Raditz. "No, I can't—"

Calibrisi nodded at the mirror.

"No!" screamed Raditz. "I'll tell you."

Calibrisi brushed the air with his hand, telling the control room to hold off.

"Why did Nazir release them?" snapped Calibrisi.

"Because I did what they asked."

Calibrisi paused. He put the phone back to his ear.

"George, I need to call you back," he said.

He took a step toward Raditz. "Money?"

Raditz shook his head.

"My God," said Calibrisi, anger rising. "You didn't—"

Raditz had an awful expression on his face. He fought against involuntary sobs that caused him to convulse.

"Yes," said Raditz.

"Guns?"

"Yes, guns. Ammo. And . . . missiles."

"You fucking idiot. How much?"

Raditz returned Calibrisi's stare. He remained silent. After several moments, he finally relented.

"Almost nine hundred million dollars' worth."

Calibrisi's eyes went wide. He was speechless.

"Nine hundred million!" he stammered.

"Forty thousand rifles, thirty million rounds."

"Do you have the ship contact info?"

"There's a cooler in my basement, a YETI. The SAT number is taped to the bottom."

Calibrisi walked quickly to the door, grabbing the handle.

"You need to understand something," said Raditz. "The cell is still active."

Calibrisi jerked his head around. He glared at Raditz with contempt.

"Where're your daughter and wife?" asked Calibrisi.

"I don't know."

"Where are they?"

"Hector, be reasonable. I don't want them involved," Raditz begged.

"Too late. You should've thought about that a long time ago."

"I don't know. I told them to disappear."

Calibrisi took an angry step toward Raditz. "Where are they?"

"No, leave them alone."

"We need to get them in front of a sketch artist,"

said Calibrisi. *"Immediately.* We need to know how big the cell is and what they look like."

"You have to promise me—"

Calibrisi nodded to the window. Raditz screamed as his body was kicked by another intense blast of electricity. After three seconds, Calibrisi waved his hand across his neck, telling them to stop.

Raditz was shaking uncontrollably as sobs hiccupped from his throat.

"I'm not going to promise you a goddam thing," said Calibrisi, "but I would never hurt two innocent people. Because of you, we now have an active cell of terrorists on U.S. soil. We need to find that cell and we need your family's help." Calibrisi was seething. He leaned close to Raditz and spoke barely above a whisper. "I'm going to give you one more chance to tell me where they are or I swear to God I'll put enough electricity through you to make you look like a fucking Christmas tree."

Calibrisi walked quickly across the driveway, redialing George Kratovil at the FBI. An agent pulled open the back door of the black Cadillac DTS and Calibrisi climbed in, the phone to his ear.

"Move it," he said.

Kratovil came on the line a few seconds later.

"Hector," said Kratovil. "What do you have for me?"

"Do you still have people at Raditz's house?"

"Yes."

"Tell them to go into the basement. There's some sort of cooler down there, a YETI. They need to find it. Taped to the bottom of the cooler is a number. As soon as you get it, text it to me."

"Got it. We'll take care of it."

Calibrisi hung up on Kratovil and dialed CIA CENCOM.

"Identify."

"This is Hector Calibrisi," he said.

"Hold, Director Calibrisi."

Several beeping noises could be heard on the line, followed by another operator.

"This is CENCOM. Go, sir."

"I need you to patch me through to Torey Krug at EUCOM along with Tammy Krutchkoff in DST."

EUCOM was the U.S. European Command. DST was the CIA's Directorate of Science and Technology.

"Bridge it, sir?"

"Yes. Hurry."

As Calibrisi waited, he thought about how best to bring in Raditz's ex-wife and daughter. Raditz had finally admitted they were in Montreal. Calibrisi could've told Kratovil to dispatch a team, but he thought better of it. He trusted Kratovil, but it was impossible to predict what would happen if information was delegated beneath him at the FBI. Calibrisi had worked for five years at the FBI and he knew how good some of the agents were and how bad some of the agents were.

The reconnaissance of Susan and Zoe Raditz had to be handled delicately. At this point, they were the only link to a cell of terrorists on U.S. soil. If it was not done correctly, they could run or not cooperate, and the last thing Calibrisi wanted to do was strap either of them to a machine like the one Raditz was currently attached to. But he would.

Even more important, the fact that a cell was on U.S. soil was explosive information, the kind of thing an ambitious FBI agent might feel compelled to leak to a reporter or member of Congress.

Calibrisi also worried about his Montreal chief of station, Charlie Couture. There was no question Couture could get the job done. He was one of the most trustworthy agents Calibrisi had. But he could be a little rough around the edges.

The phone beeped several times, then the voice of the CENCOM operator came on the line.

"This is CENCOM four two four, encryption protocol Panama Epsilon. Director Calibrisi, you're live."

"General Krug," said Calibrisi, "you have me and Tammy Krutchkoff from the CIA."

"Hi, Hector. What's going on?

259

Just then, Calibrisi's cell phone vibrated with a text from Kratovil at the FBI. The number flashed across the screen.

"We have a ship somewhere in the Mediterranean or on its way to the Mediterranean that needs to be stopped. It's a container ship out of Mexico and it's loaded with weapons on their way to Syria, and not the good guys either."

"What does loaded mean?"

"Almost a billion dollars' worth of guns, missiles, ammo."

Krug whistled. "That's a big shipment. Do you know where it is?"

"That's why Tammy is on the line," said Calibrisi. "Tammy, can we pinpoint a SAT phone by its number?"

"Depends," said Krutchkoff. "The answer is usually yes; all SAT phones have some sort of GPS. But the scrambling technology is changing every day. Whose phone is it?"

"The ship captain."

"Is he friendly?"

"Why?"

"Because we could call. If he answers, it enables us to go around certain encryption layers."

"Assume he's not friendly."

"Then it'll be harder. He won't answer. He knows he should only return calls. Second, if he's been operating in a conflict theater like the MED, he's going to be sophisticated enough to have invested in some cutting-edge encryption. He could be tough to find. Do you have the number?"

"I'm texting it to you right now," said Calibrisi, typing and shooting Krutchkoff the text.

"We'll get working on it."

"What do you want me to do?" asked Krug. "You want me to sink it?"

"No, not yet. Just lock it down."

30

MEDITERRANEAN SEA

The container ship was moving at a brisk twenty-eight-knot clip across the Mediterranean. Since departing Mexico, Miguel had pushed the ship to its maximum speed and not let up. Other than a brief but violent rainstorm somewhere in the Atlantic, it had been smooth sailing.

That didn't mean Miguel had enjoyed it. To the contrary. Raditz's last words had left an indelible sense of anxiety.

"I wouldn't come back, not if you value your life."

Miguel had moved all kinds of illegal cargo in his long, lucrative career. In fact, for more than two decades he hadn't moved anything that wasn't against the law. Moving legal cargo simply didn't pay very well. But he couldn't recall feeling such a sense of dread as he did the day he shoved out of Tampico. His first large shipment of cocaine, from Cartagena to Sicily, had been stressful, but not like this.

Miguel's ship was a converted oil tanker built in 1957. It was 662 feet long and piled high with containers, a so-called feeder ship. It was one of three vessels he owned. All the boats shared a few similarities. They were rusted and old. The names had long ago faded. And they had been bought after bankruptcies of their former owners. The truth is, there were more ships than people able to captain them. There were literally thousands of abandoned ships throughout the world, some in dry dock waiting for a better day, others rotting husks on rocks and remote shores, near towns few had ever been to in places like Poland, Ukraine, in virtually every country in Africa with coastline, and all over South and Central America.

There were seven crewmen aboard with him. It was low, even by the loose standards of that part of the shipping world his dilapidated, ugly old boat trafficked in. But seven was enough. He'd made more than a hundred transatlantic crossings in his career and knew what he needed. His men were known to him, handpicked, well-paid, trusted to do their jobs and keep quiet.

Earlier that day, Miguel had taken the helm through the Strait of Gibraltar, entrance to the

Mediterranean. It was clear enough to see—with the help of powerful binoculars—the Morocco Rock to the south. He could sense land, the smell of the earth, a salt aroma from the fishing ports. Now, at night, the lights of Spain were visible off the port side of the ship. Algeria was visible to the south, Tangier glowing orange in the far distance. Miguel loved the Mediterranean on nights like this. He'd experienced the same ocean at its worst, storms of seventy-knot winds and ocean swells twenty feet high. He had been across virtually every known shipping lane, and it was the Med that had given him the greatest highs and the worst lows. Tonight, the black water was like glass.

Part of him wished it was a rougher sea. It would've taken his mind off the job at hand. He hated the Middle East and especially Syrians. The fact that he was delivering the guns to ISIS made it a hundred times worse. They were evil. He'd seen it in their eyes on the two other occasions he'd brought cargo to them. He knew that it was only the fact that they might need him in the future that kept him alive. Now, it actually was the last shipment, according to Raditz. What if the people from ISIS knew this as well? It would mean he and his crew were expendable after the ship reached port. The terrorists would simply kill them all and unload the boat.

On the other hand, if he didn't make the delivery,

he'd never see his money. Raditz had made sure of that. As with Raditz's prior shipments, the anonymous banker needed confirmation, in this case a signature from Nazir himself, that the weapons had arrived.

Miguel cued the radio. "Sammy, come here."

A few minutes later, a short older man entered the bridge.

"Take the helm," Miguel said.

"Yes, boss."

Miguel walked out onto the bridge, beneath a cloudless sky. In front of him and behind him he could see the lights of other ships. He lit a cigarette and leaned on the railing.

His eyes moved to the water on the starboard side of the ship—then the gunnel. What he saw caused him to gasp. In one frightening, mesmerizing moment, a swarm of black figures appeared along the edge of the ship. In the dim light of the deck, he could see black rubber covering each man, glistening with water that shimmered in the low light. The cigarette dropped from his mouth as he turned and ran.

Miguel charged toward the bridge. Inside was his pistol. But as he neared the open door, he heard the click of a weapon. It was close by. Close enough to hear the friction of metal as a bullet was chambered.

"Don't move," came the voice.

American.

Hidden by the shadows, Miguel made out two men—commandos—dressed in all black tactical gear, dripping water on the deck. How long had they been there?

The man speaking held a short rifle with a silencer jutting from the muzzle, aimed at Miguel's head. The other man signaled silently to the others with his left hand as, with his right, he swept his weapon in a 270-degree arc behind the first commando.

Miguel raised his arms.

"Get down on the ground on your stomach, arms behind your back," the gunman said calmly.

Miguel got to his knees and dropped onto his stomach.

"Who are you?" he asked.

The gunman said nothing. Instead he pulled a pair of flex-cuffs from his belt and tied Miguel's hands together.

As Miguel felt the cold steel of the bridge against his cheek, he listened.

"Aegis Formation, this is Ryan, Lion Team One. We have the target secure. Repeat, we are on board the boat and have the CON. *Over.*"

31

On the ride back from Chantilly, Calibrisi briefed the president and the National Security Council on the Raditz interrogation. The meeting was already under way when he walked into the Oval Office.

President Dellenbaugh, seated on one of the sofas, had returned from Andrews Air Force Base, where he had been about to take off on a three-day campaign swing through New England, campaigning for various congressional and Senate candidates. Amy Dellenbaugh, in the middle of a doubles match at Bethesda Country Club, had hastily forfeited the match, then been choppered to Andrews in order to fill in for her husband.

Most presidents would've welcomed the change of plans. Three days on the campaign trail meant more speaking than a man was supposed to do, pastries, lobster rolls, hot dogs, cheeseburgers, donuts, every hour or two, in front of local photographers clamoring for a shot of the president doing the local shtick. It meant random harangues by angry citizens about this tax or that bill, most of which Dellenbaugh had as much to do with as they did. And yet, Dellenbaugh was disappointed. He loved the campaign trail the way a runner loves the course or the hunter the woods.

But there was no choice. Raditz and the arms-for-influence program—more than a billion and a half dollars and counting—threatened the very presidency. Whatever progress had been made in working with Islamic countries in the Middle East to stomp out Islamic terrorism would be gone if the information got out, which it would. But what weighed on Dellenbaugh's mind was not his job.

Calibrisi looked slightly ashen as he walked into the Oval Office. Seated on two large tan leather Chesterfield sofas were Dellenbaugh, Bill Polk, Secretary of State Tim Lindsay, Arden Mason, head of homeland security, National Security Advisor Josh Brubaker, White House Communications Director John Schmidt, and Harry Black, secretary of defense.

"Hi, everyone," said Calibrisi, sitting down in one of two red velvet wing chairs at the end of the Chesterfields. "Sorry I'm late."

Dellenbaugh looked at Calibrisi. "Where's Dewey?" he asked.

"I don't know."

"If he's dead, I will authorize the entire United States military to go in and retrieve his body," said Dellenbaugh. "And if he's alive, God forbid . . ."

Dellenbaugh paused, momentarily flummoxed with emotion.

"They're *not* cutting his head off, Hector," Dellenbaugh said. "We can't let that happen."

"A decorated Special Forces soldier, an American one, getting executed," said Schmidt, shaking his head. "That would be a fucking disaster."

Dellenbaugh shot Schmidt a hard look.

"I'm not talking about the goddam PR!" yelled Dellenbaugh, his face red, slamming his fist on the coffee table, causing his coffee cup to spill. "I'm talking about Dewey. He—of all people—doesn't deserve it! *Goddammit!* All I want to know right now is how the hell are we getting him out of there!"

Calibrisi nodded. He was silent for several moments, trying to rein in his own emotions. Slowly, he started to shake his head, but he didn't say anything.

The room went quiet for a long, pregnant pause.

Finally, it was Polk who spoke up.

"Dewey's a big boy," he said calmly. "If he could hear you all now, he'd be laughing. He'll be fine, trust me. Frankly, if they were smart they would've shot him already. In which case, he ain't gonna have his head chopped off. If they were stupid enough to keep him alive? Well, all I can say is, my money's on Dewey."

Calibrisi's eyes met Polk's.

"So basically let him fend for himself?" barked Dellenbaugh.

"No, of course not, Mr. President," said Polk.

"He was brought into Syria by the Israelis. I spoke with Menachem Dayan half an hour ago. He's mobilized a couple of teams from Shayetet 13 and Sayeret Metkal. Kohl Meir is running the operation."

Dellenbaugh looked at Harry Black. "Have we located the ship, Mr. Secretary?"

"Yes, sir," said Black. "Less than two hours ago, a team of SEALs took control of the ship in the Mediterranean. The ship is now in international waters and is under lockdown. We have an Aegis destroyer within sight line of the boat. In addition, the captain and crew are cooperating. They're not going anywhere, Mr. President."

"Harry," said the president, "what is the scale of the shipment in terms of the civil war?"

"I don't follow, sir."

"What would have happened if we hadn't caught the shipment? If it had been delivered."

Black let out a whistle and pulled his glasses from his head.

"This is almost nine hundred million dollars' worth of guns, bullets, and shoulder-fired missiles. Nothing fancy, just a ton of it. It's all Mexican, copies, and cheap. If it was American-made, we're talking about two billion dollars' worth of firepower."

Black paused.

"ISIS is already sweeping across Syria," he continued. "They control major parts of Iraq.

They have an unlimited supply of fresh soldiers. Mr. President, if this shipment were delivered, ISIS would have strategic advantage. They'd control all of Syria and about half of Iraq. They'd have a country."

Calibrisi spoke up.

"They would also control a petroleum supply sufficient to ensure long-term stability. Permanence. It would be the straw that broke the camel's back in that region, sir. If we thought the last decade was hard, with a madman like Nazir presiding over a well-resourced state, we would enter a new era. Once he stabilized Syria and Iraq, we would have to anticipate more aggression, more terror, and the possibility of a wider arc of jihadist influence. Israel, Jordan, Kuwait, even Iran. Just as Hitler did, Nazir would try to expand his reach—and quickly. It could be Jordan, Kuwait, Saudi Arabia—even Israel."

Josh Brubaker, the national security advisor, took a remote and aimed it at a bookshelf along the wall of the Oval Office. The bookshelf slid to the side, revealing a large plasma screen. He hit it again. Three photos of Nazir appeared.

"What few writings we have by Nazir are revealing," said Brubaker. "They're sober-minded, well-written, and thoughtful. He's studied every important political theorist since Thucydides. Machiavelli, Marx, Sun Tzu, even Thomas Paine. Deep down he's a political scientist. He believes in something called 'accretion and permanence.' Get control over resources and land—the rest will take care of itself. Nazir actually admires the United States' rise to power, which he calls the most successful example of accretion and permanence in human history. This might shock you, but I don't believe he's a terrorist, sir. He uses terror as a means to the achievement of political power—and it's working. In a way, he's worse than a terrorist. With control of a state he would be a very challenging adversary for a long time to come."

"But he isn't there yet," said Dellenbaugh.

"No, sir. Thank God for that."

"What are we doing with the ship?"

"It will be rerouted back to Virginia."

The door to the Oval Office opened. The president's assistant, Cecily Vincent, inserted her head.

"Mr. President, there's a call for you," said Cecily, glancing around the room, obviously aware of the importance of the meeting and yet still willing to interrupt it.

"I don't care who it is," said Dellenbaugh. "It needs to wait."

"The FBI ran it through a voice recognition program to confirm it," said Cecily. "It's Tristan Nazir, sir."

Dellenbaugh's mouth opened. He glanced to Calibrisi. The room was silent for several moments.

"He wants the guns," said Calibrisi.

"Why would I take the call?" asked Dellenbaugh.

Calibrisi paused, deep in thought, then looked at the president.

"If Nazir's calling, he's not admitting defeat," he said. "Which means he has leverage, or at least believes he does. If there's something deeper going on, it would be better to find that out sooner rather than later. We understand the risk of the weapons falling into his hands. We don't have to negotiate or do anything. He knows this and yet is still pursuing the guns. If he has something up his sleeve, he might reveal it."

Dellenbaugh nodded.

Calibrisi turned to Cecily.

"Have Langley CENCOM initiate the call back through DST," he told her. "Get DST to see if they can do anything in terms of Nazir's location. We also need a layer or two of encryption and protective jamming so he can't record it."

Cecily looked slightly confused.

"Ask for Tammy Krutchkoff and tell her what I told you. She'll understand what you mean."

"Got it."

The Oval Office was dead quiet for several seconds, then the speakerphone on the coffee table started ringing. Brubaker, who was closest to the phone, leaned in and hit the Speaker button. The phone clicked several times. Another few moments of silence, then a voice.

"President Dellenbaugh, this is Tristan Nazir."

"What do you want?" asked Dellenbaugh.

"I want to negotiate a deal."

Dellenbaugh paused. "The United States doesn't negotiate with terrorists."

"That is absurd and we both know it. You negotiate with terrorists all the time. I'm not here to debate you, President Dellenbaugh, but if I was, I would win."

"When have we negotiated with terrorists?"

"Well, Iran, for example. What, they aren't terrorists? Now that they will be nice to you a little?"

"Okay, you got me," said Dellenbaugh. "I guess I won't negotiate with people who cut the heads off of innocent people."

"How many American Indians do you think had their heads chopped off by Americans?" asked Nazir. "I am building a country, just as you built a country. And while we have different ideologies, the tactics are quite similar."

"You're a sick man," said Dellenbaugh. "And I'm done trying to have a conversation with you. I repeat, what do you want?"

"You know what I want: the shipment."

"That's not going to happen."

"If the world knew how many weapons America has already sent, Mr. President, I would think that would prove rather embarrassing."

"Not as embarrassing as that knowledge would

be to you," said Dellenbaugh. "Your loyal band of nutjobs would abandon you."

Nazir was quiet. Finally, he spoke. "Well, perhaps you're right," he said, resignation in his voice. "But you can't blame me for trying."

The Oval Office was silent. Dellenbaugh locked eyes with Calibrisi.

"The thing is," continued Nazir, "nutjobs can be very determined, and, as the leader of the nutjobs, I am the most determined."

"What the hell does that mean?"

"You leave me no choice," said Nazir. "Now something is going to happen that will make you reconsider your decision. It is something that you could prevent right this moment by simply letting the ship arrive in Syria. In twenty-four hours, you'll remember this moment. It was a moment you could have stopped things from escalating."

"I repeat, what are you talking about?"

"If I told you, then you would be able to stop it. So I'm not going to tell you, obviously. But it will upset some people. American people. Send the guns—or else."

32

PENN STATION
NEW YORK CITY

A white van with faded lettering—a logo for a Spanish bakery in Long Island—moved down a crowded Seventh Avenue in front of Madison Square Garden, then went right.

Several stories belowground, the 7:42 a.m. Amtrak Acela train from Washington, D.C., arrived on schedule. It was packed. Commuters, businessmen and -women, tourists, families, students, and, sprinkled about the train in random cars like poison, nine men, all in their late teens or early twenties, all of Middle Eastern descent.

Terrorists.

They moved through Penn Station, each man walking alone, blending into the morning commuter tumult. Two of the men headed for the subway, while two others took the crowded escalator to Eighth Avenue and got in line for the uptown bus.

Two moved through Penn Station and then Madison Square Garden, emerging separately from the building a few minutes apart, and walked in opposite directions.

A few minutes later, at approximately the same

time the uptown #1 train pulled out of Penn Station, and the bus shut its door and started to move, the slightly beat-up van pulled alongside one of the two men who'd chosen to walk. The man opened the passenger door and climbed in without saying anything. The van started moving, turning right on Thirty-sixth Street. Three-quarters of the way down the block, the van stopped and the second pedestrian climbed inside. The van started to move again. In a few blocks, it went left and headed uptown.

The last man to climb into the van, Sirhan, sat quietly staring out the front window. Behind him he heard movement. He recognized the sound of a magazine being slammed into a rifle. He could even tell the difference between the different assault rifles now being assembled, checked, and loaded—three Kalashnikov AK-47s and five AR-15s.

A few minutes later, Ali moved to the seat just behind Sirhan and the driver, Meuse. He said nothing. Instead, he looked in the rearview mirror, catching Meuse's eyes. Almost imperceptibly, Ali nodded.

The guns are ready.

Meuse registered the nod, then turned to Sirhan, in the passenger seat. He repeated the same silent, barely detectable nod.

"What about the IEDs?" asked Sirhan in a low voice.

Meuse nodded to the back.

Sirhan turned and saw a pile of duffel bags. Inside, he knew, were more than a dozen IEDs. Then he caught the sight of a long, black metal case tucked beneath the seats. Inside were two SA-24 surface-to-air missiles and a shoulder launcher.

The van moved up Broadway, through the Upper West Side. Meuse drove slowly; when he saw a yellow light, he stopped, drawing a horn from a taxi behind him. As he continued uptown, he remained well back from whatever car was in front of him.

By 105th Street, the neighborhood began to change. The sidewalks were less crowded and more youthful. Students. A glance above the rooflines of the low brick apartment buildings revealed the top of a majestic granite edifice some distance away.

Columbia University.

Each block now showed signs of students. Cars, minivans, SUVs parked illegally with hazard lights flashing; families arrayed nearby, carrying bags and boxes and furniture. The beginning of the school year.

At 114th Street, the van went right. On the left side of the street, a maroon minivan was parked behind a dark green Range Rover. Both vehicles had people around them; a father was helping his son remove a large flat-screen television from the back of the minivan as a woman looked on, sipping coffee. Another family, a father, daughter, and a young boy, pulled bags from the shiny SUV.

"God, I hate America," sneered Ali from the back of the van. "Look at the greed—"

"*Shut the hell up,*" snapped Sirhan. "Save your politics for someone who gives a shit."

Meuse drove slowly past the families to a quiet stretch down the block. Other than an old woman walking a small white poodle, there was no activity. He spotted an empty parking spot and backed the van in and shut off the engine. He and Sirhan climbed in back. They sat low, out of sight, and waited in silence.

Fifteen minutes later, the passenger door opened. It was Ramzee, from the subway. He climbed in the back. Mohammed joined him a minute later.

The terrorists sat in the van, parked on the side street next to Columbia, and waited without uttering a word. Half an hour later, both bus riders, Fahd and Omar, climbed in, Fahd getting in the driver's seat, Omar in the passenger's. They slouched down, out of view. Omar opened the glove compartment and removed two cans of black spray paint. He handed one to Fahd. They popped the tops off the cans. Fahd scanned the sidewalk and street. Other than a woman at the far end of the block, at least a hundred feet away, he saw nothing.

Over the next few minutes, Fahd and Omar spray-painted the interior windshield and side windows. Fahd handed his can back to Ali, who sprayed the rear windows.

The van was as dark as night. The chemical smell of paint was strong. The van was silent; no one said anything. Sirhan flicked a lighter, casting a campfire-like glow across the interior of the van.

He spoke in Arabic.

"We run a triangle formation. Tariq, Jabir, and I go first. Tariq, you carry the big case. Once we're out of sight, Mohammed, Ali, and Meuse, you need to move. Ramzee, Fahd, and Omar—you're the third group. The dormitory is over there."

Sirhan pointed with his thumb in the general direction behind the van and to the left, across the street.

"It's called Carman. There's a gate and then steps that lead to campus. Up the steps is the entrance to the dorm. We'll approach quietly and, hopefully, without any commotion. We'll take the lobby. You three come behind us and take point at the top of the triangle, after the steps. You need to be able to see the lobby and the gate at the same time. You'll give the signal for you three to move."

Sirhan pointed at the other men.

"This is very important. The first point is about getting inside the dorm and securing the lobby. The second point must establish the outer perimeter. This is the kill zone. We want to soften up the surrounding environment in order to buy time. So listen carefully: you shoot anything you see as you approach the dormitory. We won't, you will. Got it? Students, teachers, a man wandering around, dogs, cats, unicorns: *anything*. We want to clear out the area. Just as important, we need chaos. The few minutes after we enter the lobby are the most important. They determine if we succeed or fail."

"What if they haven't noticed us yet?" came a voice from the back.

Sirhan stretched his arm out, holding the lighter, trying to see who had asked the question.

"Tariq," said Sirhan, smiling ever so slightly, "good question. No such thing as a bad question."

Every eye in the van was trained on Sirhan.

"Our goal is to take the building, but we are but a part of a larger objective. That objective is unknown to me. The announcement of our arrival is essential. It must be done in blood, with maximum violence. Those are our orders. If we take over the dormitory quietly, we will have failed. Do you understand?"

The young man nodded.

"Approximately five hundred students live in the building," continued Sirhan. "I have no idea how many will be there, how many parents will be there today. It doesn't matter. There are only three ways to get into the building. We're going to secure those points of access. That is our duty. With so few ways inside, if we control them, we will have won. The only way for them to then get the building back is to attack. They will not want to attack, because that would mean dead students. It's the problem with hostages: in order to save them, one must risk killing them."

"What about security?" asked Mohammed.

"Columbia will have a lot of security. The dormitory will have security. They won't be as well-trained as you or even as police. But they'll be armed. This is the important part. They have lockdown procedures designed to stop attackers in the first two minutes and close off access. We're talking about steel gates that slam shut with the push of a button below the security desk. Alarms that call in the police, et cetera. If the police arrive before we establish a perimeter, then there will be a firefight and we will lose. Repeat, *we will lose.* We need to establish the line of control. This is the basement, first floor, roof. If we do that, then we have the students. Students are what we need. Students. Once we have control of the students, we control the building."

Sirhan let the lighter go off, then lit it again. He glanced across the faces of the men.

"You have the basement," he said to Tariq. "You'll need to take a few students with you to form a shield."

"Yes, Sirhan."

Tariq pulled on a tan full-length raincoat from a pile. He reached for an assault rifle.

"Please, be patient, Tariq," said Sirhan calmly. "I want to say something."

Sirhan again cast his eyes across the faces of the men.

"What we do today will create headlines. It will create history. We will be condemned. Hated. Reviled. *We will die today.* We will be a part of history that is called terrorism. But there is another history. It is the history of Allah, and it is within that history that we will be heroes. That is the only history that matters, my friends. Our actions will be celebrated for eternity. We are here because we are soldiers. One day, earth will be a caliphate, and ISIS will be a significant chapter in its creation on earth, and our actions, our success or our failure, will be written as part of that chapter. We're soldiers in the greatest war humankind has ever known. The war between two great enemies, and I'm not talking about America and ISIS or even about the West and the Middle East. The true battle is between *Allah and God!* Each one of you should feel humbled by the privilege of being called to serve in that war. I know I am. Today, we strike a blow deep into the very heart of God . . . into his children . . . into his corrupt world. Praise Allah."

33

ALEPPO HOSPITAL
SYRIA

Aleppo was a ruined city. Half its buildings were gone, destroyed in the sixteen-day battle for control of the city. The sky above Aleppo was still misty with smoke, dust, and the aroma of war. Every road into the city was closed off, controlled with checkpoints. On the main highway into the city, four armed gunmen stood across the road. They were dressed in the uniform of ISIS—black shirts and jeans, cloaks of black wrapped around their heads and hiding their faces.

A vehicle approached, a white Ford Explorer, filthy with reddish-brown dust, its windows tinted black.

Two of the gunmen stood directly in the vehicle's path; another moved behind the front two to provide backup in case the vehicle wasn't friendly.

A fourth gunman—a bearded man with dark skin, smoking a cigarette and clutching an AK-47—stepped to the window. He aimed his firearm at the driver, who lowered the window.

"Garotin," said the driver.

He nodded to the backseat, where Dewey was

sprawled out, shirtless, hands tied at the wrists in front of him. A piece of material—his own T-shirt, now torn up—was wrapped tightly across his mouth.

"The one from Damascus?"

The driver nodded. The gunman lifted the rifle and aimed it at the sky.

"Why didn't you kill him already?" asked the gunman.

"Shut up and do your job," said the driver, who raised the window and sped forward.

The streets of the city were cratered and pockmarked with the remnants of battle. Whole blocks of buildings had been turned to rubble. In certain places, sidewalks were littered with corpses, pools of black—blood, dried in the sun—surrounded the eerily still bodies in puddle-size splotches.

After two miles, a sign read DAR AL-SHIFA HOSPITAL.

Two men dragged Dewey from the vehicle and led him at gunpoint along a crowded, chaotic, filthy hospital corridor. Every door was open, every room filled with injured ISIS soldiers and the occasional doctor or nurse. The hallways were jammed with yet more injured soldiers, who sat against walls or lay on the floor, all waiting for treatment. Doctors and nurses appeared in the hall, then disappeared into the next room, their hospital garb covered in blood. There was total confusion, and the humidity and sweltering heat only made it worse. Yelling in Arabic filled the air. A din of low groans was punctuated every few minutes by a far-off scream of someone in acute pain. The smell was overwhelming—body odor mixed with antiseptic, along with dust and smoke still wafting in from the neighborhood outside.

Dewey was pushed into an elevator, which they took to the fifth floor. It was quieter and less chaotic there. Armed gunmen stood just outside the elevator doors, eyeing Dewey as he was pushed down the hallway.

Dewey heard a horrible scream from somewhere behind him.

He was led to a grimy-looking, unsanitary operating room and pushed down on top of a stainless steel table still wet with blood. A gunman stood watch as Dewey tried to shift his weight and get more comfortable. The gag in Dewey's mouth was tied so tight that the sides of his mouth were worn bare, the T-shirt dabbed with small stains where the blood had seeped. He was thirstier than he could ever remember being. He shut his eyes and tried to block out the realization that he would soon die.

Had Dewey been trapped inside a Chinese prison, or a Russian prison, or even an Iranian prison, he would have leverage in the fact that he was American. He would be a bargaining chip, someone whose death might draw a brutal reprisal from the long arm of the U.S. government. But here it meant absolutely nothing. In fact, it ensured he would die, and soon. He opened his eyes, and the first thing that came into view was a video camera mounted on a tripod. On either side of the video camera stood klieg lights.

They would videotape his death. A beheading. First, they would try to get his name out of him. There was value in that. Perhaps even a scripted confession about the terrible things America had done to the world.

Dewey felt neither calm or panic. Instead, he willed himself to feel nothing at all, except for the physical pain. He knew he couldn't be saved. There wasn't enough time. Even if someone tried—Shayeret 13, Force Recon, Navy SEALs—they had no idea where he was.

Pray for a meteor. He felt his mouth trying to smile beneath the tight gag.

Several minutes later, a young man in a light blue surgeon's gown entered the room. He reeked of cigarettes. One of the lightbulbs, dangling from the ceiling, flickered and made a buzzing noise. The doctor's gown was splattered in blood. He removed a pair of green rubber gloves, tossed them to the floor at his feet, then pulled on another pair. He stepped toward Dewey and examined the large scar beneath his left shoulder.

Suddenly, another man entered. Dewey recognized him immediately: Garotin.

ISIS's top military commander looked young, perhaps in his late twenties or early thirties. He had thick black hair, loosely parted in the middle, and a few days' worth of stubble. He stepped to Dewey's side and looked at him for several moments with a blank expression, then slammed his fist into Dewey's stomach. He punched him six or seven times, hard, which Dewey absorbed with pained grunts.

Garotin untied the cloth from around Dewey's head. He grabbed his hair and lifted it, inspecting his head.

"You killed seven men in Damascus," said Garotin, staring at him with hatred. "For what? Now you will die."

He let go of Dewey's head, which fell with a sharp thud onto the table.

"Who are you?" said Garotin.

Dewey ignored him. He stared at the wall, saying nothing.

"So Marwan gave you some information?" said Garotin. "Was it worth it?"

Dewey glanced up at him. "Fuck you."

"Who are you?" Garotin yelled, his voice rising.

"Go fuck yourself."

"What's your name?" asked Garotin. "Tell me and I'll give you a cigarette."

"Fuck off," mumbled Dewey.

Garotin pulled a pack of cigarettes from his

pocket, removed one, lit it, then extended it to Dewey.

Dewey ignored the gesture.

"Go on," said Garotin. "Trust me, you're not going to die of cancer."

Dewey pulled his bound hands toward him and took the cigarette, inhaling.

"What's your name?"

Dewey ignored the question, staring at Garotin with a cold expression on his face.

"What is your name?" Garotin said, louder now.

But Dewey said nothing. He took his time smoking the cigarette. When it was nearly to the filter, he put it between his thumb and middle finger then flicked it through the air. The smoking stub struck the gunman at the door squarely in the forehead.

"Bastard!" he yelled.

The gunman stepped forward and pummeled Dewey in the stomach, punching him with both hands, knocking the wind out of him. After several hard punches, Garotin pulled the man back.

"What's your name?" Garotin said again, calmer this time.

"It's confidential," Dewey said, coughing. "I could tell you, but then I'd have to kill you."

Garotin shook his head in frustration. He turned to the doctor.

"The wound needs to be cleaned before we cut his head off," he said in Arabic. "Nothing fancy, just clean it up. The video is much more effective if he looks healthy."

Garotin pulled a long KA-BAR knife from a sheath at his waist. He looked at Dewey.

"We're going to cut your head off," he said, reverting to English. "But first, you tell me who you are and who you work for. If I had to guess, the Central Intelligence Agency. Am I right?"

Dewey said nothing.

Garotin put the blade against Dewey's neck, pressing it against the skin.

"The knife we'll use on you," he said. "It will hurt, but look on the bright side: you're going to be famous."

Dewey stared up into Garotin's eyes, still silent. Garotin pressed harder.

"You used to be in the military," offered Garotin. "Special Forces. Combat Applications Group or Green Beret. Am I right?"

Dewey felt the blade pressing uncomfortably close.

Garotin smirked.

"It doesn't matter," Dewey said, straining.

Garotin pressed the knife, and Dewey felt the sharp blade cut into his skin.

"Why does it not matter?"

"Because I work for America. We're going to kill every single last one of you motherfuckers."

Garotin punched Dewey in the stomach, knocking the wind out of him. Dewey coughed several times, groaning in pain. He felt blood on his neck. Garotin punched him again.

Garotin removed the knife from Dewey's neck and slammed the steel hilt into Dewey's stomach. It took more than a minute for Dewey to catch his breath.

"You were wrong earlier," Dewey groaned, coughing up blood.

"Wrong?" said Garotin. "How was I wrong?"

"I killed at least twelve of you shitheads. I was counting."

Garotin turned and repeated his orders to the doctor, again in Arabic. He walked toward the door.

"Allah must be proud of you," said Dewey as Garotin reached the door.

Garotin turned. "Is that what you think this is about?" His expression grew savage. "This isn't about religion. This is about power."

"Cutting people's heads off?"

"Power derives from ownership," said Garotin. "Territory. Resources. Land. That's how you make a country. Look at Israel. Before you stole the land and gave it to the Jews, they were nothing, just a pathetic idea. Now they have a country. They have *power.*"

"Clever," said Dewey. "You're a bunch of fucking cowards. You can kill me and it doesn't matter because a hundred people just like me are going to take my place."

"That strategy doesn't seem to be working too well."

"You'll never have a country. We won't let it happen."

Garotin grabbed the rifle from the guard, moving it in front of Dewey. It was an M4 carbine, with no markings.

"This weapon, the bullets inside it, all of it was given by your government."

"I don't believe you."

"It's true. Why would I lie to you?"

Dewey stared for several moments at the rifle, then his eyes looked away.

The thoughts he'd pushed aside were now unavoidable—the terrible image of his mother and father seeing the video of his beheading.

"Shoot me," said Dewey, looking up at Garotin. "A soldier's death."

Garotin stared into Dewey's eyes. He paused, then trained the muzzle of the gun at Dewey's chest. He pulled the trigger back. Dewey's eyes remained open. A look of resignation was on his face.

Garotin moved the rifle away from Dewey, pointing it at the ceiling.

"No," he said.

"You don't have the balls."

"I have my orders. We cut your head off when the cameraman gets here."

34

CARMAN HALL
COLUMBIA UNIVERSITY

Across the street from the van, two car lengths back, Daisy grabbed a duffel bag as Andy lifted the last box from the back of the SUV.

Another girl had joined them. She had blond hair, was slightly chubby, and wore a pink-and-white Icelandic sweater. This was Charlotte, Andy's new roommate. After the last boxes were lifted out of the BMW, Charlotte shut the rear hatch, then looked at Andy and smiled.

"Are you sure you don't need some help?" Charlotte asked.

Andy shook her head. "It's okay."

At that very moment, on Andy's opposite arm, out of sight, Daisy elbowed her, then gave her a look, as if to say, *That's your roommate, and talk about nice, she's awesome! Let her help you!*

Andy rolled her eyes, then turned from Daisy to Charlotte. "Actually, this is sort of heavy."

"That's what I thought." Charlotte grabbed the side of the box.

Andy wasn't very good at small talk, but she took a shot.

"So, where are you from?"

"Charleston, South Carolina. How about you?"

"Baltimore."

"Baltimore? You're kidding. I absolutely *love* Baltimore. I had the biggest crush on a boy from Baltimore. Do you know Owen Shriver? I went to Andover with him. He was a senior when I was a . . ."

Daisy caught Andy's eye and smiled. She winked, then turned and stopped listening. Instead, she took a few seconds to think about how happy she was, how proud she felt of not only Andy but also of herself. She thought back to the first time she met Andy at Big Brothers & Big Sisters of Baltimore, so many years ago. Andy was still a small girl, but back then she was tiny and painfully shy. Getting her to say anything was like trying to get water out of rock. Daisy laughed at the memory. It was the first time she let herself feel pride for Andy's success, success that was always within the brilliant girl but that Daisy helped to bring out, driving up religiously—by her mother before she got her license, then alone—every other weekend to see the young black girl, father- and motherless, raised by a loving grandmother in a terrible part of a troubled city.

Daisy's thoughts were interrupted. She saw something. Ahead, parked across the street, was a van. A dark-skinned man was in the driver's seat, spray painting the inside of the windshield. A sense of dread came over her. Charlotte's loud laughter interrupted it. Daisy smiled and turned to Charlotte. Her mind dismissed what she'd seen. It was college, after all. Some sort of fraternity prank.

They traipsed in through the Columbia gate on 114th Street and walked to the dormitory entrance, saying hello to the uniformed security guard for the umpteenth time that morning. On the elevator, her mind flashed to the van. When the elevator stopped at the eighth floor, she felt her pocket for her cell phone, but it wasn't there.

They walked down the hallway, past students and parents unpacking their belongings. People were chatting in the hall and having a good time. Daisy walked ahead of Andy and Charlotte, arriving at the room before them, dropping the duffel on the ground. She saw her cell on the windowsill.

She started to dial her mother to tell her she would be leaving soon. As she dialed, she looked out the window, down to 114th Street. Her eyes caught the van. For several moments, she stared. Then an involuntary cry came from her mouth. She tried to speak, but her throat was choked with fear and emotion. The phone dropped to the floor before she could finish dialing.

She tried to say something, but no sound came out. She could only point as, eight floors down, five men—dark-skinned, Middle Eastern—charged from the back of the van, each man clutching an assault rifle.

The gunman at the front of the pack leveled the rifle and pointed it down the street. Her eyes followed the path of the gun. Several students were walking to Broadway, their backs turned.

"No!" said Daisy.

Gunfire cracked the air and echoed. The students were struck by the bullets. They tumbled awkwardly to the ground, contorted on the sidewalk, blood covering their backs, splattering the sidewalk, and quickly pooling.

Daisy's eyes shot right. Near the gate. Another gunman started firing.

Soon, gunfire was everywhere.

Each gunman wore a trench coat—navy or khaki or green so as to not stand out more than necessary—buttoned at the neck, arms empty so that the men's arms were beneath the coat, on the inside, where submachine guns and carbines were concealed, Uzis in front, in hand, carbines tethered across each man's back. Every firearm was loaded with ammunition, mags filled with Kevlar-tipped cartridges. The trench coats were packed with extra mags.

Tariq climbed slowly from the driver's door as, at the same time, Sirhan got out the passenger's side and Jabir climbed out the back of the van. Someone handed the long steel case to Tariq. He carried it with his left hand as he held an Uzi against his leg, finger on the trigger, hidden by his coat. They walked calmly toward the nearest gate into campus.

Sirhan walked in front. He stepped through the gate just as a man and a woman came in the opposite direction, followed by a small group of students. Sirhan passed them and went up a set of stairs. He glanced behind him, eyeing Tariq and Jabir, making sure the group of passersby hadn't somehow gotten suspicious.

Turning back around, Sirhan eyed the dorm entrance, now just several yards away. It was just like in the photos on the Columbia University Web site; one story tall, double doors of glass, slightly opaque, covered in stickers, placards, taped-on flyers announcing this and that.

There were people on the path to the entrance. He quickly counted twelve people in four tiny clusters. He passed the first two groups, which were made up of students, talking among themselves. The third group was a father and mother and their child, who was hugging his mother, saying goodbye.

He moved past them all, drawing no attention. Near the door, a tall man stood with his son, a student, Sirhan guessed. They were waiting for someone. The boy was looking past Sirhan at the group of girls who were chatting. But the father stared at Sirhan. He was white, bald, and wore a short-sleeve plaid button-down. Sirhan kept walking, pretending not to notice the man. The man was staring at him with a strange look on his face. His eyes seemed to be glued to the raincoat.

The entrance was now just a few feet away. As Sirhan came in front of them, the man held up his hand.

"Excuse me," he said.

"What?"

"Are you a student?"

Sirhan looked at him, attempting a smile.

"Yes." Sirhan pointed to the building. "I live in Carman."

"Dad," the boy said to his father. "There are lots of Middle Eastern—"

But the man ignored his son. He stepped forward to block Sirhan, reaching for Sirhan's raincoat.

Sirhan jagged left and raised the Uzi. The man lurched toward him, both arms out, but it was too late. Sirhan fired. Unmuted automatic weapon fire punctured the calm. Bullets ripped through the man's chest. The son turned, screaming, trying to get away. Sirhan triggered the gun again and sent another burst into the boy's head, killing him instantly.

Screams came from behind Sirhan, but he didn't turn. Instead, he ripped the coat from his neck and ran toward the entrance to the dorm. He saw movement through the glass and heard yelling and another pocket of screams.

Tariq, a few feet behind, pulled out his Uzi and started gunning down the fleeing people. He was joined by Jabir, who lifted an AR-15 and fired.

Tariq sprayed bullets at the small wave of panicked people, pumping a fusillade of bullets in a line, cutting most of them down. A girl near the back was hit in the arm but still managed to leap over a hedge and run toward the center of campus. Jabir charged to the hedge, leveled the gun, targeted the fleeing student, and fired. The first few slugs missed her, but he hit the back of her legs and she dropped, screaming. He finished her with a slug into her head.

Sirhan entered the dormitory with the muzzle out and his finger on the trigger. By the time his foot crossed the doorsill, the security guard was standing and pulling his gun from the holster. Sirhan sprayed him with a short burst of slugs, which struck his chest, washing the wall with blood and kicking the guard back and down behind the security desk.

Sirhan's eyes swept the room. There, to the left. Students. Five in all. Sirhan pointed the Uzi at them.

"Stand up," he said. "Now."

"Fuck you, Osama," said a male student, seated in the middle.

Sirhan moved the fire selector on the Uzi to

manual, then triggered the submachine gun. A single round exploded out. The slug struck the boy in the forehead, blowing out the back of his skull. One of the girls screamed.

The four remaining students climbed to their feet, arms up, cowering in fear.

Sirhan glanced to the entrance. He studied the sidewalk outside.

"Stand at the entrance," he told the four students. "If you attempt to run, the next thing you'll feel is a bullet in your back. Do you understand?"

Sirhan positioned the students in a line across the entrance, a shield in case someone in law enforcement arrived sooner than he expected and tried to shoot.

Sirhan studied the entrance for several seconds, noticing the steel security grate recessed along the ceiling.

Tariq came running into the lobby, followed by Jabir.

"Cover the entrance, Jabir, quickly," said Sirhan.

Tariq put the steel case on the ground and dropped his backpack. He removed a coil of chain and pulled out a handful of flex-cuffs. He noticed one of the students, a female with blond hair, turn her head. He leaned forward to see what she was looking at. At the corner of the building, a security guard was crouching and attempting to skirt along the building. Tariq dropped the flex-cuffs and lifted his carbine. He put the muzzle between the heads of the girl and another student, aimed, then yanked the trigger, sending a hurl of slugs into the man.

Sirhan moved behind the security desk, which was covered in papers and empty coffee cups. Two small black-and-white screens showed live footage of the front entrance, taken by a stationary camera outside the building. The other screen showed Carman's basement-level entrance.

Gunfire erupted from outside the building, at first a single weapon, then multiple weapons.

"Where are they?" Sirhan barked. "We don't have much time!"

A moment later, he saw Meuse round the corner, charging for the door, hurdling the corpses that littered the blood-drenched path in front. The rest of Sirhan's cell ran to the entrance behind Meuse, pushing past the students standing like targets.

Sirhan swept his free arm across the desk, shoving aside the papers and cups, searching. In a drawer he found a set of keys, which he pocketed. Along the underside of the desk he found a button. He pressed it and a steel gate rumbled down from the ceiling, blocking off access, sealing Carman Hall behind a wall of corrugated steel.

Sirhan moved around the security desk and found Tariq's backpack. He removed an industrial padlock and went to the entrance. He pushed aside a brass plate on the floor. Beneath it was a recessed area where a thick hook protruded, designed to attach to a similarly thick hook on the bottom of the steel security door. He padlocked the door to the hook.

Meanwhile, Tariq flex-cuffed the students' hands behind their backs. He wrapped flex-cuffs around their necks as well, then fastened each cuff to one of two chains, which he held across the back of their necks. He yanked each cuff tight, so that each student was now chained by the neck. If either end of the chain was pulled, it would tighten around their necks and choke them. He tested the chain, yanking hard, watching as the students, who were already hysterical with fear, struggled to breathe.

Tariq removed a black handheld device from the backpack. It looked like a controller to a video game. It was a cell phone detector, called a Wolfhound. He flipped the switch. A screen lit up and Tariq aimed it at the four students, waving it across each individual. When the Wolfhound made high-pitched beeping noises, Tariq reached out and removed the cell phones from their pockets, sticking the four phones in his backpack.

The other terrorists stood with rifles out, awaiting Sirhan's command.

He nodded at Tariq. "You know what to do," he said in Arabic. "Position the students in the basement. Wire the door. Then meet me on the roof with the explosives."

"Yes, Sirhan."

Sirhan looked at the others.

"It's thirteen floors, two sets of stairs," said Sirhan. "Jabir, you guard the lobby. Make sure no one comes in, and no one comes down from the stairs. The rest of you, start with the second floor, clear it out. One man per floor. Get everyone as quickly as possible up to the tenth floor. We want to be high enough so they won't jump, and we want a buffer if they approach from the roof. Move floor by floor. Use the east stairs." Sirhan pointed. "No students on the west stairs. Get everyone to the tenth floor as soon as possible. If someone argues, kill them."

The men grunted assents or nodded.

"Fahd, Omar, start wiring the stairs with explosives immediately," said Sirhan. "The first level you can do right away. We wire the stairs between one and two, three and four, five and six. Understood? Then meet us upstairs."

"Yes," said Fahd. Omar nodded his head, adjusting the large duffel he had slung over his shoulder.

"Fahd, after you finish wiring the stairs, remain on the sixth floor and cover the entrance. *Be careful.* Any minute they'll have snipers. If you stick your head up, it will get blown off."

Gripping the chain, Tariq went down the corridor past the elevators, pulling the four cuffed students along. He opened the door to a stairwell and descended.

Other than a lone hall light, the basement was dark. He tugged the students to the end of the dimly lit corridor, stopping at a green steel door. He examined it briefly, trying the doorknob, but it was bolted shut. A narrow glass window ran vertically down the side of the door. Behind the glass was an empty hallway.

Tariq locked one end of the chain to the door handle. He looked around the ceiling and walls for something to attach the other end of the chain to. A steel beam ran from floor to ceiling, built into the concrete. Tariq trained the rifle on the concrete and blew several slugs into it, creating a rapidly increasing crater until it recessed behind the beam. He repeated it on the opposite side of the beam until there was a channel through the concrete. He retrieved the end of the chain, tucked it through the hole and around the beam, pulling it tight, so that the chain was a taut line between the door handle and the beam. If someone tried to open the door, the students would die. The small window was a bonus. Before someone tried to enter through the door, he or she would see the students and know that entering would kill them by tightening the chain like a noose around their necks.

He removed a padlock from his backpack and locked the chain around the beam.

One of the students, a Korean girl, looked hatefully at him.

"If we sit down," she said, "we'll strangle to death."

Tariq nodded. "Yes, that's right."

After the students were tied up, Tariq removed a beat-up shoe box from his bag.

"What is that?" asked another student, fear in her voice.

"Shut the fuck up," Tariq snapped.

It was, in fact, an improvised explosive device, or IED, the creation of which Sirhan was an expert. The box contained a trigger, a fuse, a battery, and, most important, a large hunk of explosive material, in this case, Semtex. All of it was assembled inside the box. With duct tape, Tariq taped the box over the crack in the door, above the handle.

The IED would prevent the FBI from entering Carman from the building next door through the basement. If someone from the FBI opened the door, the IED would drop, the trigger would be struck, and the bomb would go off. Not only would the students die, but the basement would collapse beneath rubble.

"Is that a bomb?" asked one of the students, panic in her voice.

"Yes," said Tariq, double-checking the fuse and battery. Satisfied, he turned to leave. "If anyone attempts to come in through the door, you all die."

• • •

As gunfire echoed up from the street below, Andy and Charlotte ran toward Daisy. Andy had a look of panic on her face. Her eyes met Daisy's, then moved to the window. She gasped as she registered the corpses sprawled along the street and sidewalks below.

She turned and looked at Daisy. "What's happening?"

Daisy struggled to maintain her composure and hold back her emotions. She put her hand out and took Andy's hand.

"It's going to be all right," she said.

"Should we run?"

Daisy fumbled as she tried to dial her cell phone, tremors overtaking the movement of her fingers. She found the "1" and held it down.

As she waited for the phone to ring, her eyes went back to the street. Suddenly, one of the gunmen fired. The gunfire was loud and jarring. Daisy's eyes shot right. A young woman, a red patch spreading over her back where the bullet had entered, tried to limp away. The gunman fired again, hitting the back of her head.

"I need to call you back," said Daisy's father.

"Dad," she went to say, but the only sound was a hoarse whisper. *"Dad!"*

"I can't hear you, honey. I'll call you—"

"Dad!" she screamed, finally finding her voice. *"Whatever you do, do not hang up!"*

Calibrisi's voice went sharp. "Honey? Are you okay? What the hell is going on?"

"Terrorists. At Columbia. They're taking over the dorm. Andy's dorm . . ."

There was a long pause.

"Daisy, if this is some sort of . . ."

"Daddy," Daisy whispered, suddenly bursting out in sobs. "Oh, Daddy. I'm so scared. I love you. Tell Mom I love her."

35

OVAL OFFICE
THE WHITE HOUSE
WASHINGTON, D.C.

Calibrisi stood in front of one of the large French doors leading to the Rose Garden as he clutched the cell phone. He shut his eyes, trying to calm his frenzied breathing. A whirlwind flashed through his mind—

Run, sweetheart, run! Run to a low floor and jump! . . . It's ISIS . . .

He turned and looked at the president as his cell dropped from his hand. His face was creased with emotion. A severe pain abruptly struck his left leg, like electricity. The pain shot up to his neck and ricocheted like a spiderweb down his left arm.

He knew what was happening.

Dear God, not now . . .

He tried to wave his hand and get someone's attention. He was able to move it halfway around. President Dellenbaugh was listening to Kratovil, who was hypothesizing on what Nazir's ominous threats really meant.

Calibrisi's lips moved, but no sound came out.

Dellenbaugh looked at him. "Hector?"

Dellenbaugh stood up from his desk. A look of shock was on his face.

"Are you okay?"

Calibrisi reached for the door handle to prevent himself from falling. He registered the president's words in the same moment he felt a sudden stab in his arm, then a shot of warmth emanating from his chest, like a fever. A terrible, turbulent sensation followed as his heart started to spasm, beating a dozen times a second. Before he could say anything, the havoc that gripped his heart enveloped his whole body. Blackness followed . . .

"Get Terry!" yelled Dellenbaugh, referring to Terry O'Brien, the White House physician.

Dellenbaugh threw aside his chair and rushed around his desk. He charged toward Calibrisi, arms extended . . .

Calibrisi could see nothing. He could do nothing. He heard the voice again.

"Daddy, I'm so scared."

Somewhere in the recesses of his mind, he heard

Dellenbaugh's loud yell. He sensed the president's arrival in the light, the way it modulated, as he charged toward him. For a few moments, he regained his ability to see. Dellenbaugh was blurry, until his face came closer. A look of horror was on his face. His lips were moving as he reached for Calibrisi. Like being underwater, the words were faint, slow, rubbery.

Calibrisi tried to take a step, but it was like stepping into water. His ankle bent and his leg fell away. He stumbled and collapsed to the floor, landing with a reverberating crash on his side, then rolling onto his back. His eyes wavered inside their sockets as he searched the ceiling, trying to focus on something—a lightbulb, the president's face, a crack in the plaster, anything that might keep him in this moment, this room . . .

This world.

Calibrisi clutched his throat, attempting to stop what was coming, but it was pointless, which, on some level, he already knew . . .

36

ALEPPO HOSPITAL
SYRIA

Dewey awoke to a scream coming from somewhere down the hall. How long he'd been out, he didn't know, but it couldn't have been more than five or ten minutes. He smelled foul body odor; the doctor was next to the table, wiping blood from his forehead and neck, getting him cleaned up for his execution.

Dewey looked around the operating room. The cameraman had arrived. He looked like the others, except for a white T-shirt. He was standing next to the camera, adjusting it.

The gunman remained at the door. The rifle was in his right hand, its strap on his shoulder. In his left hand was a cell phone, which he was typing into.

A dull, throbbing ache came from Dewey's stomach.

Another scream echoed down the hallway.

Dewey stared at the cameraman, who was watching Dewey from behind the camera and making last-minute adjustments. The klieg lights remained off.

The doctor removed a small glass vial and a

syringe from a cabinet. He stuck the needle into the bottle and pulled back on the plunger, loading the syringe. When he finished, he stepped toward Dewey.

"Painkiller," he whispered in broken English. "It will make the pain less."

"Cut the rope," whispered Dewey, extending his hands.

The doctor shook his head ever so slightly.

"They kill me," he whispered back. "I have daughter and son. They're babies. My wife, she is dead. I'm all they have."

The doctor leaned toward Dewey, the needle out. He grabbed Dewey's arm and moved the needle closer.

Behind the doctor, Dewey watched the cameraman. He had the cord to the lights and was looking for an outlet.

The doctor placed the tip of the needle to Dewey's arm.

The cameraman found one and pulled the end of the cord toward it.

Near the door, the gunman put his arm in front of his face as he prepared for the lights to come on.

"Behind you," said Dewey as the cameraman jammed the plug into the wall.

The doctor turned just as the klieg lights flashed on, like two bright balls of halogen sunlight, bursting inside the room. He was blinded.

Dewey grabbed the doctor's wrist with his

hands, still bound. He stabbed the syringe into the doctor's neck, then sat up quickly and leapt from the table. He grabbed the doctor's neck and charged toward the door, pushing the frightened man in the direction of the gunman.

The gunman heard the doctor's muffled yelp and opened his eyes. He panicked at the sight of the doctor's back moving quickly toward him. The weapon was at his side and he reached for it. He swept it up and across the air as Dewey, clutching the doctor, barreled across the room directly at him. The gunman fired at the same moment Dewey reached him. The doctor's helpless body slammed into the gunman and pushed into the muzzle of the rifle just as the first shot was fired. The bullet struck him in the right side, blowing off a piece of his torso, barely missing Dewey. Dewey slammed the doctor, now screaming in pain, into the weapon with all his strength. The rifle was pushed to the side under the force of the doctor's frame. The gunman was knocked backward against the door, but he held on to the rifle and fought to free it.

Dewey let go of the doctor and pivoted, ducking just as the cameraman swung a knife across the air at him. As the blade whooshed inches above Dewey's head, Dewey kicked out with his foot, hitting the cameraman with a brutal strike to the side of his knee. The cameraman crashed awkwardly to the floor.

Dewey lurched toward the barrel of the rifle with his two bound hands, gripping it tightly just as the gunman kicked him in the leg. Dewey absorbed the kick. He leapt at the gunman with his shoulder, still clutching the barrel of the rifle, and slammed hard into the gunman's head, crushing him against the wall. Dewey kept the man pressed into the wall, backing into him and launching again, slamming him hard, preventing him from doing anything except struggle against Dewey's powerful frame. But the gunman still held onto the barrel of the rifle. It was at Dewey's side and the terrorist was trying desperately to aim it at the only part of Dewey he could, his feet. The gunman fired. The unmuted staccato of the bullets hammered into the floor a few inches from Dewey's right foot. Dewey slammed his elbow behind him. It hit the terrorist directly on the nose, crushing it. The gunman yelped in pain.

Dewey's bound hands tried to keep hold of the barrel of the rifle as he continued to grind the large man into the wall and prevent him from getting any room to move. The gunman, who held the gun in his right hand, finger on the trigger, yanked at the rifle, trying to free the barrel from Dewey's clutch and push Dewey far enough away so that he could shoot him.

Dewey's eyes swept left, where the cameraman was now standing. With a maniacal look on his face, he pulled a combat blade from his belt and charged at Dewey, who was doing everything he could just to keep hold of the rifle. As the cameraman sprinted forward, Dewey felt a vicious kick from the gunman behind him, a steel-toed boot striking his ankle, nearly collapsing him. He let out a low, pained grunt.

The cameraman raised the six-inch blade above his head and swung down, taking a ferocious cut at Dewey. Dewey pitched left, taking the gunman behind him with him, barely evading the cameraman's savage slash. Another kick to his ankle made Dewey groan, but it also enraged him. He maneuvered the barrel of the rifle up toward the cameraman as, in the pandemonium, the gunman triggered the carbine again. Bullets ripped into the cameraman's face.

In one fluid motion, Dewey let go of the barrel of the gun and raised both arms over his head. He reached over his head and back, wrapping his bound hands over the gunman's head. He pulled his hands down so that the rope at his wrists was now around the back of his neck. The gunman let out a pained gasp as he tried with all his might to free himself from Dewey's hold, but it was no use. Dewey pulled forward, bringing the terrorist's head closer, yanking his skull and neck down against his right shoulder.

The gunman was powerful and he fought back, but Dewey was stronger and his arms were longer. Slowly, Dewey tightened the hold; the terrorist's neck was soon noosed against Dewey's shoulder in a viselike grip. The gunman struggled to breathe as Dewey pulled down on his neck with all his strength. The gunman tried to swing the rifle across Dewey's chest as Dewey choked him, but he couldn't get the muzzle close enough to have any chance of hitting Dewey. The gunman panted desperately as Dewey continued to strangle him.

Suddenly, the gunman's other hand reached over Dewey's other shoulder and fumbled for the barrel of the carbine. When he managed to grasp it, he now had hold of both ends of the rifle, in front of Dewey. He heaved backward, slamming the rifle against Dewey's neck as Dewey maintained his clamp on the terrorist's neck, sealing off air. Dewey felt sharp pain from the strike to his neck. The gunman repeated the move, trying to choke Dewey with the rifle before he himself ran out of air.

The room was filled with the animal sounds of the two men struggling for their lives.

Dewey writhed as he tried to breathe, but the gunman was strong. Dewey staggered forward, still holding the terrorist against his shoulder, knowing that if he allowed him to get any air, it would all be over. The pressure from the rifle against Dewey's neck slackened. He lurched to his right in the same instant he ripped his wrists down with every ounce of strength he had. The abrupt motion took both men sideways and down. As they tumbled to the floor, Dewey heard the dull, rubberlike *thud* of the terrorist's spine snapping. For several seconds, Dewey lay there, catching his breath, the terrorist's lifeless face just inches away. Slowly, he raised his bound wrists over the dead man's head and let go.

Looking around, Dewey saw the knife on the floor and awkwardly cut away the rope that bound his wrists.

How had no one heard? It didn't matter now. Maybe gunfire was so common they'd all learned to ignore it.

Dewey picked up the rifle. He popped out the magazine, found a full one in the gunman's weapons vest, and slammed it into the carbine. He was breathing heavily and soaked with perspiration. He hurt all over. Breathing was painful. But he pushed the discomfort from his mind. He didn't have time to feel pain right now—not if he wanted to live.

Dewey stepped to the window, pulling aside the curtains. Sunlight entered the room. He looked down. It took his eyes a few seconds to comprehend what he was seeing. When he did, he recoiled.

A pile of corpses was stacked high atop a flat-bed truck, waiting to be moved to some sort of mass grave. Most of the bodies were in hospital garb.

He had to get out of there. He had to move. Garotin would be back soon.

Dewey set the fire selector on the gun to manual, allowing him to fire one bullet at a time. He clutched the gun as he stepped to the door, listening carefully for noise.

He pulled the door slowly in, peeking his head out of the room. The corridor was bright in green-hued fluorescent. A nurse's desk down the corridor was manned by two men, who were seated, smoking and talking to each other. The hallway was long, door after door of rooms, most closed. Beyond the desk, a line of beds on wheels lay empty.

The door across the hall opened. Dewey pulled back, shielded by the wall. He saw the head of a gunman. It wasn't Garotin. His front was covered in blood. Before the door could shut, he caught a glimpse into the operating room. Beneath bright overhead lights, a headless body lay strapped to the operating room table, blood still spilling from the freshly severed neck.

He'd long ago come to terms with the concept of torture, of being mortally wounded, handicapped, even dying. But the sight of the beheaded man sent a burst of terror through Dewey in a way he'd never experienced. It was pure terror, the feeling cold and empty, with no boundaries or hope. Dewey felt uncontrollably nauseous. He fought to regain himself, but liquid shot from his mouth, over his lips, onto the wall and floor. He vomited for several seconds, trying in vain to control the heaving noises.

The door opened. It was the gunman from across the hall. The man had short-cropped black hair and glasses. At the sight of Dewey, he was momentarily taken aback.

Dewey raised the rifle just as the gunman yelled, then fired. The slug struck the terrorist in the right eye, shattering the lens of his glasses, splattering blood and brain across the wall. He crumpled to the filthy linoleum floor.

He had no choice now. He moved the fire selector to auto-hail.

Dewey opened the door and moved, rifle out in front, finger on the trigger. He glanced right, seeing nothing; then left, swinging the muzzle around and aiming. The two guards at the nurse's desk stared at him, paralyzed in disbelief, but only for a half second. The far one threw himself down, diving for cover beneath the desk. Dewey marked the one still standing and fired. Slugs burst from the carbine, slamming him back, dropping him.

Dewey walked slowly toward the desk, waiting, muzzle trained. Then he stopped and waited. After a few seconds, the other man's head appeared at the side of the desk and Dewey fired. A hail of bullets pelted the desk and ripped into the terrorist's skull before he could pull back in.

The ominous drumbeat of steel-toed boots echoed from behind Dewey as terrorists ascended the stairs at the end of the hall.

Dewey charged across the hallway into the room of the decapitated man. The room was empty except for the dead man. Dewey saw the head, lying on the floor at the end of a wet trail of blood. He fought to not throw up again.

A siren blared, screeching menacingly through the hallway.

Dewey heard shouting in Arabic followed by a short blast of automatic gunfire. He went to a corner of the room, crouched down, and got ready.

Two gunmen charged into the room. They wore black T-shirts and nylon masks that covered their faces. Each man clutched a gun; the first a pistol, the second man a submachine gun. They scanned the room and one of them spied Dewey. Dewey's eyes locked with the terrorist's, who quickly registered the muzzle of the rifle. Dewey fired. Slugs slashed into the man's neck. He dropped, screaming, as the other guard froze, aware that Dewey now held him in the killing arc.

Dewey moved quickly and stuck the muzzle of the rifle beneath the remaining gunman's chin. With his left hand, he took the pistol. He held the barrel and hammered a crushing blow into the man's temple, dropping him to the ground.

More footsteps thundered from the corridor. The high-pitched siren continued to wail.

Dewey pulled the black shirt from the unconscious gunman and pulled it over his head.

Think.

He stared down at the dead terrorist. He knew what he needed to do.

37

**OVAL OFFICE
THE WHITE HOUSE
WASHINGTON, D.C.**

Less than thirty seconds later, Terry O'Brien, the White House physician, appeared at the end of the hallway, sprinting to the Oval Office. Behind him was a swarm of people from the medical unit, along with senior White House staff.

Calibrisi's eyes shut just as the full force of the coronary hit him and sent his 230-pound frame into a horrible spasm of seizures.

O'Brien stormed into the room, dropped to the floor by Calibrisi's side, ripped off his shirt, and pressed his fingertips into his neck, searching for a pulse.

A medical assistant attached Calibrisi to a portable heart monitor as O'Brien started performing CPR.

O'Brien looked up at Dellenbaugh.

"Tell them to get the Traumahawk ready, Mr. President," he said as he pumped his hands up and down on Calibrisi's chest in a timed rhythm. "We don't have much time."

The Oval Office was crowded with cabinet members, various high-level Pentagon officials, and senior national security staff. An eerie silence took over the room.

After two minutes of CPR, O'Brien again searched for a carotid artery pulse in Calibrisi's neck but felt nothing. The heart monitor told him the same thing.

"Lifepak!" he said.

He got higher on his knees and began an urgent, faster-paced, more violent form of CPR.

A few seconds later, a nurse moved a defibrillator to Calibrisi's side. She handed O'Brien a pair of paddles, which he placed against Calibrisi's chest. He waited for the tone, indicating the charge was set, then barked, "Clear!" ensuring no one was touching Calibrisi. He pressed the handle buttons and sent a searing two hundred joules of electric current into Calibrisi's body.

His eyes shot to the monitor. It blipped, then went steady, a green line laid out across the screen. After a few seconds, the defibrillator's high-pitched tone went steady again, and O'Brien repeated the blast of electric current to Calibrisi's heart, trying in vain to bring him back to life.

After a third attempt, a small green triangle appeared on the monitor, then another, and a third, all accompanied by a soft blip; he was alive.

"Let's go," said O'Brien.

They lifted Calibrisi onto a gurney. Someone opened the French doors. O'Brien and three others—two medical assistants and Dellenbaugh himself—sprinted as they wheeled the gurney, charging through the doors, across the Rose Garden, toward the South Lawn.

Calibrisi clung to life, his heart pumping in a weak, uneven pattern that O'Brien knew would last only a few minutes.

When they reached the South Lawn, a wall of wind hit them as they approached the bright red Sikorsky HC-60 Traumahawk. The chopper's rotors cut frantically through the air above their heads. They tucked the gurney into the chopper. O'Brien and one of his assistants, a physician named Lovvorn, climbed aboard. The chopper shot into the cloud-crossed Washington sky.

Lovvorn administered CPR as the chopper moved east, slashing the air as the pilots jacked the ferocious chopper to the max.

O'Brien leaned into the cockpit.

"Where to, sir?" asked the copilot, yelling above the loud engines.

"Bethesda!"

"I'll radio ahead!"

"Tell them to find Marc Gillinov!" yelled O'Brien above the noise of the chopper, referring to one of Walter Reed's heart surgeons. "Tell him we have an *advanced therapy situation! Use those exact words!*"

38

NEW YORK POLICE DEPARTMENT
PUBLIC SAFETY ANSWERING CENTER
METROTECH CENTER
BROOKLYN, NEW YORK

The first call came in at 1:18 p.m. Officer Manuela Vega of the NYPD took the call.

Vega was one of fifteen hundred emergency operators inside the sprawling Public Safety Answering Center.

"Nine-one-one, Operator Vega."

"Terrorists!" shouted the caller. Vega leaned forward, hearing what sounded like gunshots in the background. The caller continued, *"They're shooting people in the streets!"*

Vega's brown eyes flashed across the six computer screens in her cubicle. Her right hand reached out, touching one of the screens where a red light was flashing. This light was the location of the caller. She touched the screen and the view zoomed in, showing where the call had originated.

"I have you at 114th and Broadway, near Columbia."

"Yes."

Another screen brought up a grid of local, state, and federal agencies Vega could immediately inform of the incident, again by simply touching the screen. Every New York law enforcement agency, its individual branches, along with emergency medical and fire response, were integrated into MetroTech's extremely powerful technology infrastructure, making cross-department and interagency awareness and response immediate. State and federal law enforcement was also part of the MetroTech IT matrix, including the FBI, whose counterterrorism center Vega quickly searched for, found, and prepared to inform.

Vega linked the incident to the closest NYPD precinct, the 26th, along with emergency response.

Before she sounded a broader alarm, she wanted some sort of further confirmation. She tapped a third screen, one that could focus satellite feed in real time. She linked it to the caller's location. The picture was unfocused and hazy, but with each second it sharpened.

"Has anyone been hit?"

"*Yes!* Several people. They're dead. There are bodies in the street."

"How many gunmen?"

"Three or four, maybe more. I . . . I ran."

"That's okay. That's what you should've done."

Vega tried to get a better view from the video, but it was too unfocused.

She didn't wait any longer. She tapped several modules on the agency integration screen, sending the call to the emergency dispatch centers inside a multitude of NYPD, local, and federal entities, including NYPD Counterterrorism Bureau, NYPD Strategic Response Group, FDNY, and FBI CENTCOM.

"Should I do anything?" asked the panicked caller.

"No, you've already done something. Thank you."

Vega hung up and immediately pressed a red button on one of three phone consoles in her cubicle.

"Gutierrez."

"This is Operator two-two-six, Vega. I believe we have an active shooter scenario and what could be some sort of terror strike. I just uplinked it."

"Got it. My board is flashing here. We have multiple reports. I'm going to define the protocol and elevate. Thank you, Vega."

Suddenly, a low, emphatic emergency beacon sounded on the MetroTech intercom. This meant the active duty supervisor of the Public Safety Answering Center was establishing a protocol spelling out what all operators should advise citizens calling about what was happening at Columbia. This guidance flashed across the screens of all fifteen hundred operators.

In addition, the incident was being elevated. Jurisdiction was being officially passed up the food chain to the commissioner's office, with a cross-departmental "crisis patch" with active response guided by an intra-NYPD task force led by two departments: Emergency Services Unit and Counterterrorism.

Within three minutes of the first 911 call, several patrol cars from the NYPD's 26th Precinct were at the scene, along with a number of ambulances. The scene was chaotic. Working with Columbia University security, the first priority was evacuating the campus. A campuswide alarm system was activated—a piercing alarm sounded in every building, accompanied by a recording calling for all students, teachers, staff, and visitors to leave the campus immediately. Officers from the 26th quickly cordoned off the area. A security perimeter was established between Riverside Drive to the west and Morningside Drive to the east, and between 113th and 120th Streets. No vehicular traffic was allowed. Foot traffic was allowed up to the west side of Broadway and to the east side of Amsterdam Avenue for residents with proper identification. The campus itself was off-limits to everyone except law enforcement.

EMTs removed casualties from 114th Street and along the steps leading into the campus. Once police determined that the terrorists were not targeting the EMTs yet, corpses were quickly removed from the walk in front of Carman.

Within four minutes of the first 911 call, the commissioner of the NYPD, along with every deputy commissioner in the department, knew about the situation at Columbia.

In addition, the commanding officers of Emergency Services Unit and Counterterrorism were already together on the fourth floor of NYPD headquarters at 1 Police Plaza, in the Situation Center, a cavernous, windowless conference room that looked like Mission Control at NASA. Several dozen uniformed and plainclothes men and women populated the room, either at workstations, which filled the center of the room, or scrambling around to look at one of the fifty or so large plasma screens that lined the walls.

Henry Kaan, commanding officer of NYPD's Emergency Services Unit, stood before a conference table in the center of the room, a cup of coffee in his hand.

Across from him was Vince Blaisdell, commanding officer of the Counterterrorism Bureau.

A phone console was between them. Seated at the table were several officers, in front of them laptop computers enabling them to monitor the situation at Columbia and access various information.

"Patch him in," said Blaisdell, nodding to one of his deputies, who hit a button on the phone.

"Henry, Vince, what's the situation?"

The speaker was Temba Maqubela, who ran the FBI's Counterterrorism Division.

"We have reports of as few as six and as many as a dozen gunmen, all Middle Eastern, taking over a dorm at Columbia. So far, there are eleven confirmed casualties outside the building. We've received a number of calls from students inside, and it sounds like many more have been shot."

"How many people inside the building?"

"We estimate three to five hundred. We have students and we have some parents too. It's orientation day."

"I know it's early," said Maqubela, "but what are the options if we were to move now?"

"Option one, we enter with heavy weapons, explosives, armored vehicles, and a shit ton of SWAT via the ground floor. Option two, we drop a tight team onto the roof. Two or three choppers, a dozen men. Then we make it slightly more surgical."

"Have you modeled casualty counts?"

"Temba, it's five minutes old. It'll be high either way."

"What are chances for success?" asked Maqubela.

"We haven't even started the regression analysis. Again—"

"I know, I know, it's five minutes old."

"What do you think?" asked Blaisdell.

"We need to hold off," said Maqubela. "Don't fire until you're sure the guns are not aimed at your own head, as my father used to say to me."

"You guys are the ones preaching preemptivity."

"I know," said Maqubela, "but this feels different. We have a badly security-graphed structure, a large group of students, and unknown variables. This isn't an active shooter. I would worry about the ground assault. If we go hard with overwhelming force this early, they might simply blow up the whole building. I'm against doing anything other than getting a lot of snipers up there until we know a little more."

"Are you guys taking over?"

"Good question," said Maqubela. "Hold on."

Kaan looked at Blaisdell as they waited for Maqubela to get back on the line. They wanted to hold onto jurisdiction, but both men knew the Feds were about to take it. There was no question: it was a terrorist event. At the end of the day, it didn't matter much who had jurisdiction as far as they were concerned. It didn't mean they wouldn't be involved. They would do whatever was asked of them, by whoever asked.

The phone beeped as Maqubela came on the line.

"Hey, guys, sorry. Yeah, it's ours. We still need you. Doesn't change a thing. I'll get you the paperwork. In the meantime we've already assigned Damon Smith to it. He's en route from Quantico."

"Got it," said Kaan. "We'll get the baseline established up there."

"Sounds good."

The door to the Situation Center opened. A tall, attractive woman with shoulder-length brown hair entered the room. She was wearing black pants, high heels, a white blouse, and a red blazer. It was the commissioner of the NYPD, Judith Talkiewicz, trailed by several staff members.

Talkiewicz made a beeline for Blaisdell and Kaan. She stood at the head of the table, a stern, pissed-off look on her face.

"I want those choppers in the air right now," said Talkiewicz. "It'll take the goddam FBI two weeks to figure out what to do and I want to move now. Until the paper arrives, jurisdiction is still NYPD. Get them flying."

39

OVAL OFFICE
THE WHITE HOUSE
WASHINGTON, D.C.

The Oval Office was eerily quiet. Those who remained—Polk, Brubaker, Kratovil, Mason, and several other officials—were speechless. Many exchanged glances.

"Should we take a five-minute break?" asked Josh Brubaker, the national security advisor. "I think I need to take a break, if that's okay."

All eyes looked to Polk, Calibrisi's longtime deputy and closest confidant. It was an awkward situation. The Nazir call required thought and discussion. Perhaps even action. Yet the head of the CIA had just suffered a massive coronary. It was a moment that America's leaders must sometimes face, a moment out of view of most citizens, when the larger challenges of a violent, enemy-filled world are visited by mortal pain—by loss on a personal level, death not to faceless soldiers overseas but to individuals they know. Both hurt, but seeing Calibrisi down cut them all. They all knew they needed to go on. America needed them to go on. But they had shared a glimpse of mortality and fate, and it was a hard moment.

"Good idea," said Polk, standing up from the sofa. "By the way, he's going to be fine."

As Brubaker stood up, his eyes were drawn to the carpet near the president's desk. Lying on the ground was a cell phone. He picked it up. A red light indicated that whatever conversation had been going on was still live.

Was it Calibrisi's phone?

Brubaker couldn't remember if Calibrisi had been talking on the phone before he collapsed. It was all a blur.

"Hello?" he said. "Is anyone there?"

"Yes."

It was a soft female voice. She sounded like she was crying.

"This is Josh Brubaker," he said. "Is this . . . are you . . . were you talking with Hector Calibrisi?"

"Hector is my dad. Where is he? He just stopped talking. Is everything okay?"

Brubaker didn't know what to say. Suddenly, over the phone, he heard several gunshots in the background. A cold chill struck Brubaker in his spine and swept over him.

"*My God,* what was that?" he asked.

"My father didn't tell you? *Where is he?* Please tell me."

"He . . . wasn't feeling good."

"Is he okay?"

"Yes, yes, he's fine. But what is that? Was that gunfire?"

"I'm in a dorm at Columbia University. We're being attacked by terrorists! I think they're taking over the dorm."

"What?" Brubaker asked, incredulous.

More gunshots. A girl screaming. Calibrisi's daughter was sobbing into the phone.

"Listen, it's going to be okay," Brubaker said in a soothing voice. With his free hand, he snapped his fingers, getting Polk's attention. Dellenbaugh, returning from the South Lawn, appeared at the door. Brubaker held up his finger, letting Dellenbaugh and Polk know that something was going on. "I'm Josh Brubaker. What's your name?"

"Daisy."

"That's a nice name, Daisy. Forgive me, I didn't know Hector had a daughter at Columbia."

"I'm not a student. I was bringing my Little Sister here. She's a freshman."

"I was a Big Brother where I grew up, in Chicago," said Brubaker. "Now tell me what's happening."

"Terrorists," she sobbed. "I counted eight. They're shooting everyone. We're trapped in a dorm."

"Daisy, hold on for one second, will you?"

Brubaker covered the phone and looked at Polk, then Dellenbaugh, then the others, all of whom were waiting for him to explain what was going on.

"It's Hector's daughter," said Brubaker. "She's

at Columbia University. She says they're under attack. Terrorists are taking over the dorm. I heard gunfire."

"ISIS," said Dellenbaugh. He looked at Kratovil. "George, get some people up there."

"Whatever you do, Josh," said Polk, stepping closer to Brubaker, "do *not* tell Daisy about her dad. Not right now. Not yet."

"What *do* I tell her?"

"Tell her to remain strong and do what they say."

Just then, the FBI director's phone made a loud beeping noise. A moment later, the Homeland Security chief's did as well. Soon it seemed every phone in the Oval Office was ringing.

Brubaker took his hand off the phone.

"Daisy, we're all over this. We're moving people to Columbia as we speak. FBI, New York Police, everything we have. We're going to get you and everyone else out of there. But I need you to do something for me."

Daisy didn't answer. All he could hear was her sobbing.

"Daisy?"

"Yeah."

"I need you to remain strong. Can you do that?"

"He had another heart attack, didn't he?" whispered Daisy in between sobs.

Brubaker glanced at Polk, who was on his phone.

"Yes, he did. But he's going to be fine. He's at the hospital."

"Thank you for telling me, Mr. Brubaker. In a strange way, I feel better."

"You do?"

"When he wakes up, if he wakes up, he's going to need me. I'll stay strong. I'll stay more than strong. For my dad."

40

ALEPPO, SYRIA

Dewey removed the unconscious gunman's ski mask and pulled it over his own head. Then he stood up, placed his foot on the man's chin, and stomped down, snapping his neck. He took the terrorist's .45 and stuck it between his belt and back.

He remembered the words from training: *When the shadows are gone, when the night has turned to day, when all around you is the enemy, you must hide in plain sight.*

Dewey moved into the corridor, now crowded with gunmen, all looking for him. Doors were kicked in as soldiers searched. Shouting in Arabic added to the sense of bedlam and confusion.

Dewey counted six men, none of them Garotin. Like him, all had on black T-shirts and black face masks.

Dewey followed the line of gunmen, keeping the rifle trained out in front of him. He went past them, taking his turn at the next room in the line, kicking in a hospital-room door, staring for a few moments at a pair of men strapped to beds. Both had light skin; they looked French. Dewey pretended to scan the room, then left.

Dewey was last in line when the group reached the stairs at the end of the corridor. He followed the men to the door, then held back for a brief moment. By the time he entered the windowless stairwell, he heard footsteps below and followed. From a half flight up, he watched as the last of the gunmen stepped through the door onto the fourth floor.

Dewey charged down the empty stairwell, leaping three steps at a time. Every second mattered now. Every moment was a lifetime.

At the first floor, he glanced through a small window in the door. The place was in a state of pandemonium. In the middle of the floor he saw Garotin. He appeared calm, standing with his elbow on top of the nurses' station, leaning over and studying a laptop computer. Garotin was distracted. There were bigger fish to fry—or else his men had yet to tell him of Dewey's escape.

Suddenly, Garotin looked up. His face had a look of urgency, then he started yelling.

Dewey charged down the stairs to the basement, assuming Garotin was yelling about his escape.

But his ears caught the high-pitched buzz of a missile—the noise Garotin had heard a second before. Then an explosion rocked the ground. He was thrown forward, down the stairs, landing on his arm, rolling and slamming into the wall. The missile took out the stairwell lights. Silence came, followed by shouting and a few muted screams.

It was a Hellfire or Tomahawk or something Russian, if he had to guess. A direct hit somewhere up above him, at the other end of the building.

Move. Get up.

The opportunity for escape was *now.*

Dewey got to his feet. He continued down the pitch-black stairs, navigating with his hands, feeling the concrete walls. He came to a door and opened it.

Another corridor. Ambient light came from somewhere. The corridor was dank and gray. His eyes adjusted as he skulked down the hallway. Suddenly, he spied three bodies on the floor. There were two terrorists, both lying awkwardly after being thrown by the explosion. Next to them was a corpse.

Dewey aimed the rifle down as he moved toward the men. One was trying to get up. He noticed Dewey and said something in Arabic. Dewey fired, striking him in the head. He swept the rifle to the right and fired again, placing a slug in the second terrorist's chest.

In the shadowy light, he followed a trail of blood leading down the corridor to a pair of swinging doors. Dewey went through. It was a large storage room. Wooden pallets were lined up in rows, with boxes of medical supplies stacked high. At the far side of the room, the ceiling was freshly collapsed. Dust from the rubble created a cloud. He heard voices and pained moaning drifting down from above.

He moved quickly through the large room toward the light. Past the stacks of boxes were loading docks. Parked at the first loading dock, backed up to the large opening, was a flatbed semitruck. A cold, nauseating feeling came over Dewey as he stared at corpses, dozens of them, thrown haphazardly onto the truck and piled so high he could make out only the top foot of the truck's cab.

Dewey retraced his steps. He searched the pockets of one of the men in the hallway and found a pistol and a pack of cigarettes. He took the pistol. The other man had a cell phone and the keys to the truck. He grabbed both.

Dewey picked up the corpse they'd been lugging. He dragged it down the hall and through the storage room. Through another loading dock he could see a black-clad soldier standing in the parking lot. He was pointing up at the hospital and speaking to someone. He noticed Dewey but said nothing. The missile strike had created a world of confusion. Whatever search had been going on for the escaped American was superseded by the disaster.

Dewey threw the dead man onto the stack of corpses. He jumped down from the loading dock and moved to the front of the flatbed trailer, releasing the fifth-wheel locking handle, which cradled the trailer's kingpin and kept it attached to the cab of the truck. He lifted the ends of a pair of chains connecting the trailer and cab, letting them drop to the ground. Dewey climbed into the cab of the semi and started the engine. He released the air brakes, put the truck in gear, and drove forward. When he felt the air and electrical lines holding the trailer to the cab, he stomped down on the gas, ripping away from the flatbed. He glanced right just as the trailer slammed to the tar, collapsing onto its front. The guard in the lot looked over. Dewey raised his gun and fired before the man could react. The slug tore the top of his head off.

Dewey maneuvered the cab through a badly damaged parking lot, watching to see if anyone was following, seeing no one. At the edge of the parking lot, a gunman came running toward him. Dewey pulled the pistol from his back and clutched it as the man charged, motioning with his hand as he gave Dewey an order in Arabic, no doubt telling him to return to the hospital.

In the side mirror, Dewey eyed the hospital. The missile had struck the side of the building, causing a massive gash in the concrete. Other than a few steel beams that stood in the free air, one entire end of the hospital was destroyed. Thick smoke and dust rose in a steady cloud from the crater.

The gunman moved in front of the truck, raising his hand to stop it. As Dewey came closer, he suddenly accelerated. A scream preceded the sound of the truck slamming into the terrorist, followed by a noticeable bump as the front tires squashed him like roadkill.

Dewey steered calmly onto an empty road that led away from the hospital as, with his right hand, he dialed a six-digit number. It was a number that could be dialed from anywhere in the world. After a few seconds of silence, he heard a high-pitched beeping noise. Dewey punched in a ccode. A man's voice came on the line.

"Commencing voice recog. Go."

"Andreas, Dewey."

"File?"

"NOC 2294-6."

"Zone?"

"Scorpio," said Dewey as he maneuvered between the burned-out skeletons of vehicles littering the roadway.

"Go."

"Tracker lock my location."

There was a momentary pause followed by a beep.

"You're locked. What's the situation?"

"I need an immediate bridge to IDF Sector Alpha in this order: Kohl Meir, Menachem Dayan, Fritz Lavine, Benjamin Cooperman. This is Code Black. Repeat, *Code Black.* And stay on the line."

"Yes, sir. Hold on."

He listened to a series of clicks as his call was put through. A half ring was followed by a familiar voice.

"Who is this?" asked Meir.

"It's Dewey. I'm in—"

"Trouble," interrupted Meir. "Satellites picked up the scene in Damascus. What happened?"

"I don't have time right now, Kohl. I need an extraction."

"Where are you?"

"I have no fucking idea."

CENCOM Control interrupted. "We have you," said the operator. "Commander Meir, I'm live wiring the tracker feed."

"Okay," said Meir. "I have you on screen. You're in Aleppo. Jesus, how the hell did you end up there?"

"Kohl—"

"Okay, okay. It looks like you're headed west. Take your next right. That will take you north. It's Highway Sixty-two. It'll be the first big road you see."

"Isn't Damascus south?" asked Dewey.

"Yes, but if anyone's looking for you it will be toward the south. We're going to come over the water and penetrate up there somewhere where e don't have to worry quite so much about being shot down."

"How far on Sixty-two?"

"Drive for an hour, then get off somewhere that looks remote. It will be dark in a few hours. Find a place to sit tight. A barn or something. We'll need room to land."

41

WALTER REED NATIONAL MILITARY MEDICAL CENTER BETHESDA, MARYLAND

The Traumahawk flew north, rushing above a calm landscape of buildings, monuments, cars, and people.

At some point en route to the hospital, the heart monitor attached to Calibrisi went monotone.

"Flatline!" Lovvorn barked above the din.

Lovvorn studied the monitor. He held up five fingers. It meant that Calibrisi's heart had revived for five minutes before stopping.

"Hit him!" ordered O'Brien.

Lovvorn repeated the defibrillator as the chopper descended toward the rooftop of the hospital. He stared anxiously at the portable monitor, watching the straight line that ran across the screen, indicating that Calibrisi was dead.

The chopper bounced violently down on the helipad at Walter Reed. Four men, all dressed in military uniforms, grabbed the stretcher and sprinted for the open door atop the hospital's roof, held open by a fifth man.

Inside, the four men dropped the stretcher on top of a gurney and charged amid a cacophony of shouts and activity, as the Level One Trauma unit prepared to attempt the impossible. They sprinted down the corridor as doctors, nurses, and a variety of others watched. The CIA director was whisked down the hallway toward the operating room for what everyone knew would be one last chance at saving the life of a man considered by many to be the second most important man in Washington, behind only the president.

The operating room was a cavernous, brightly lit high-tech theater of lights, machinery, flat screens, and devices. In the center, alone, stood a simple, shiny stainless steel operating table. Above it was a high-tech chandelier of powerful lights. At least a dozen doctors and nurses moved about the room, getting ready.

Calibrisi was lifted onto the table, then was swarmed by doctors and nurses, who hooked him up to a variety of life monitors, IVs, and blood bags, attaching them to his appendages, away from his chest.

The door of the operating room swung open,

and in stepped Dr. Marc Gillinov, all six foot six of him. He moved to the side of the operating table. Without hesitating, he pulled the blue sheet back from Calibrisi's body, throwing it to the ground, revealing his slightly obese chest, covered in dark hair.

A pair of bullet scars sat like pieces of chewed gum just above Calibrisi's navel. A scar from a knife wound at the neck looked like a small pink ribbon.

Gillinov studied the monitor for a few brief seconds. He put his stethoscope to the center of Calibrisi's chest.

"This is going to get a little messy," said Gillinov calmly, his Australian accent thick.

Gillinov's eyes darted to one of the nurses.

"Kara, I want an ACLS protocol, stat."

"Got it, Doctor."

He nodded at one of the doctors. "Steve, I want the cameras turned off."

Gillinov had a laid-back manner, insisting that everyone call him by his first name, even—and especially—during surgery. He stepped to one of the flat screens and scanned it.

"When did he suffer the event, Terry?" asked Gillinov.

O'Brien, who stood along the wall, looked at his watch. "Eighteen minutes ago."

"How many times did you hit him?"

"Two rounds, seven hits."

Gillinov took the defibrillator paddles from one of the nurses and placed them against Calibrisi's chest.

"Any drugs?"

"No."

"Okay, that's good. Let's see if we can get one last pick at him. Charge to a hundred fifty joules."

Gillinov waited for the tone, and when he got it, he pressed the handle buttons and sent a bolt of electric current into Calibrisi's body.

The monitor blipped, then went flatline again. Gillinov nodded to the nurse, putting his three fingers up, indicating he wanted a higher charge, this time to three hundred joules. She typed, readying the paddles for a second, more powerful charge. The defibrillator's high-pitched tone went steady again, and he repeated the fierce blast to Calibrisi's heart. Nothing. Gillinov tried once more, but it was no use. The monitor did not even tick up this time.

Gillinov handed the paddles to one of the nurses.

"Get the body tight to the table," he said as he took two steps back, then ripped off his purple surgical gloves and tossed them to the ground. "As tight as you can."

Two surgical assistants wrapped straps across Calibrisi's chest, torso, neck, and waist, anchoring him to the steel table.

"Get the blood moving," said Gillinov. "Charlie, I want a large-bore IV line run in through the femoral. Get some antibiotics in the backflow along with anticoagulant. We're going to be giving him a little infection, I'm afraid, and we don't want pneumonia."

"Got it," he said, prepping the area near Calibrisi's groin as he prepared to puncture the femoral vein.

"Once I go in, we need to stem the flow of blood as quickly as possible," said Gillinov. "We don't want to get his heart beating again only to bleed him out."

Gillinov pulled off his mask and surgical cap. His blond hair fell out, dropping nearly to his shoulders. He had several days' worth of stubble. He appeared to be in his midtwenties, though in truth he was thirty-three. Technically, Gillinov was about to violate a stunning array of medical rules and protocols; he could've been fired and decertified for it. But they all knew the rules didn't matter anymore. Technically, the patient was already dead. What Gillinov was about to attempt required warmth in his hands and a sense of touch and feel that the gloves would prevent.

This would be the fifth time he had attempted what he was about to do. Thus far, it had worked twice.

As for the mask and cap, only Gillinov knew why he took those off too. Only Gillinov knew that by removing it all, he imagined himself back at his family's station in Australia, where he'd learned it all from his father—the art of heart massage, saving the life of the young foals born prematurely, too weak to live.

"Scalpel," he said calmly, stepping forward to Calibrisi. "Ten blade. Get ready with the epinephrine, ten milligrams."

A nurse handed Gillinov a long silver scalpel. He felt quickly with the fingertips on his left hand for a spot on Calibrisi's chest, then inserted the knife forcefully, cutting away Calibrisi's skin. He cut in a straight line down the center of Calibrisi's breastplate all the way to the sternal bone.

Blood coursed out in a dark crimson gusher.

"Sternal saw."

Gillinov handed the scalpel back to the nurse and she handed him the saw, similar to an electric drill. He inserted the saw at the top of the sternum, forcing it through the bone and cutting all the way down toward Calibrisi's navel.

He placed the fingers of his right hand down into the wound, along the cut line, gripping the underside of the bone. He pulled up slightly, clearing the space in front of the heart.

"Here we go," Gillinov said to the room, not looking up from Calibrisi's blood-soaked chest.

Gillinov took two quick, deep breaths. He felt the underside of Calibrisi's sternum with his fingertips. He inserted all four fingers in the cut line. With every ounce of strength the big man had, he tore the edges of Calibrisi's sternum to the sides. The fierce yanking motion was accompanied by a loud, deep grunt. A thunderous cacophony followed: the crack and stretching of Calibrisi's bones as Gillinov pulled them away from the chest cavity, revealing Calibrisi's bright purple heart, which lay still.

"Scaffold," said Gillinov.

Another surgeon placed a small retractor beneath the cut sternal edges, keeping the bones spread apart and elevated so that Gillinov could go to work.

"Get the blood circulating," said Gillinov. "Anesthesia, load him with amiodarone and milrinone."

Gillinov's face was now spattered with blood, though he didn't seem to mind. His arms were also drenched. He stared at the chest cavity, then he gently placed his hands around Calibrisi's heart, cupping it as if it were a bird. Steadying himself, he began contracting motions with his hands, replicating the pressure of the heart.

For several moments, it was as if everyone in the room was frozen in time, watching Gillinov as he worked. Except for the sound of monitors, there was utter silence. There was no movement in the OR other than Gillinov's hands gently squeezing Calibrisi's heart. To a person, they were mesmerized by the sight, temporarily forgetting their roles, their professions, everything.

"Okay, Jenny," Gillinov whispered, continuing

to pump the heart, speaking to one of the nurses, who now held a small, thin syringe filled with epinephrine. "We have one last shot here. I want you to put it right there"—he nodded—"between my left index finger and my thumb. Can you do that for me, Jenny?"

She leaned in with the small needle. Her hands shook.

"Calm down," said Gillinov. "Nice and easy now."

Carefully, Jenny moved in closer and inserted the tip of the needle into Calibrisi's heart as Gillinov continued to gently pump it with his hands. Blood shot from the heart as the needle took, spurting across Gillinov's neck and shirt, which were already drenched in red.

Gillinov felt an odd sensation, a faint, rubbery tremor, then the steady uneven movement between his fingers as the heart began to pump on its own, as life regained itself, as the heart fought to return . . .

As Calibrisi came back to life . . .

He felt it first in his fingers, then in the palms of his hands. Gillinov wanted to say something, but he did not. He could not.

A moment later, the heart monitor's dull monotone was interrupted. A faint blip. One heartbeat. Then the monitor began to show a weak but steady pattern. The green EKG line bounced up and began a jagged rhythm.

"Where's orthopedics?" Gillinov whispered, his eyes focused on the beating heart in his hands.

"Right behind you, Doctor," said another surgeon. "How long?"

Gillinov glanced around the OR for the first time, registering the looks in the eyes of his colleagues. He had a blank, stony expression on his handsome, rugged, blood-spattered face. He saw Jenny wipe tears from her eyes.

"Ten minutes," he said, continuing his steady pressure on Calibrisi's heart. "Then we'll put him back together."

42

CARMAN HALL
COLUMBIA UNIVERSITY

Sirhan entered one of the two elevators. He took a hammer from his bag and put the claw beneath the edge of the steel plate on the control panel and pushed, loosening the small screws that held it to the wall. He went around the edge, pulling the panel away from the wall, then yanked it off, letting it fall to the floor. He stuck a small piece of C-4 in the spaghetti-like cluster of wires that controlled the elevator, then inserted a detonator.

Sirhan repeated it on the other elevator, down the hall. When he was done, he moved away from the elevators and hit the detonators. A low boom shook the air, rattling the ground ever so slightly. He waited a minute, then stepped back to the elevators. The interiors were scorched black. A few small flames were visible through the smoke as the plastic casing on the wires burned. The flames would be gone soon, so too the smoke. But neither of the elevators would ever work again.

He walked quickly to the west stairs and headed for the roof.

Because the first floor was occupied by the lobby and cafeteria, the second floor was the lowest residential floor in the building. Mohammed was in front as the gunmen charged up the stairs, and he signaled to the others that he was going to the second floor.

He waited half a minute for the others to catch up with him. Then he burst through the door and fired. It was meant to be a warning shot, but his slug hit a young student, a black male, in the head.

Screams filled the hallway. The gunfire, followed by the blood and sprawling corpse, sent shrieks through the air.

"Get to the stairs," Mohammed yelled. He fired again, this time into the ceiling. "Now! No talking. Tenth floor! Run!"

Two students—both male—suddenly turned and charged at Mohammed. He leveled the gun and fired, hitting them both, one in the chest, the other in the head. Hysteria ensued, then muted sobs. Nobody said anything as they filed down the hall toward the stairs.

Fahd took up position on the first floor, at the bottom of the west stairwell, just off the lobby. From this vantage point he could cover the lobby as well as anyone attempting to escape from upstairs. Omar did the same at the east stairs.

The others charged quietly past Fahd and headed upstairs.

Fahd dropped his duffel. Keeping an eye on the stairwell above, he removed a large spool of thin tungsten wire from his bag. He tied an end around the lowest banister on the right, then moved to the opposite banister and wrapped the wire around it.

Fahd heard gunfire coming from the second floor, then cries of panic. He raised his rifle just as the first students entered the stairwell. A few of them noticed him, staring down at him, eyeing his rifle. They quickly looked away and moved up the stairs. Soon, the stairs above the second floor were crowded with students and parents making their way to the tenth floor.

Fahd continued to weave the wire back and forth across the stairs, working his way up, moving the duffel with each step so that it was above him. Halfway up, he stopped and put down the spool of wire. He looked up. The second floor was clear.

No more students were coming from that floor. Not that it mattered. He reached into the duffel and removed an IED.

The device was the size of a loaf of bread. Three-quarters of the device was made up of rectangular blocks of black material, taped together with blue duct tape: Semtex 10, designed for the destruction of concrete and metal. A cluster of objects was taped or wired to the end of the Semtex, including the detonator, a battery, and a trigger—in this case a firing button which, when pressed, would set off the bomb.

Fahd gingerly attached a green wire to the battery. This meant that the IED was live. If somehow the firing button—sticking out from the side of the device—was pressed, the block of Semtex would explode. Very gently, Fahd placed the IED on top of a section of wire so that it was elevated above the stairs. He picked up the spool of tungsten wire and continued weaving a web across the stairs. When he reached the landing at the top, he stopped and looked down. The IED was sitting on top of the silvery web, half-way down. If anyone cut the wire, at any place in the wire, the IED would fall to the stairs and explode.

Over the next hour, Fahd set IEDs in the first-, third-, and fifth-floor stairwells, all utilizing the same tungsten web. Omar did the same on the opposite side of Carman. If any one of the IEDs went off, the concussive power of the explosion would almost certainly cause the other bombs to detonate.

With the elevators destroyed and both stairwells wired for massive explosions, there was no way to get up to the tenth floor.

There was also no way to get down.

On the third floor, Ramzee stepped out of the stairwell a few seconds after Mohammed had moved on the second floor. Ramzee moved down the hallway, AK-47 in both hands, pointed in front of him.

Doors to student rooms lined both walls, and people poured into the hall, alarmed by the gunfire from below.

Soon, the hall was filled with panic-stricken students and parents. Ramzee stood at the end of the hall as if studying the scene. No one noticed him for at least a dozen seconds. Then a girl sensed Ramzee behind her and turned. A dazed moment of shock followed, then she screamed.

Ramzee fired. The bullet ripped into her neck and kicked her back and down.

Gunshots sounded somewhere above.

As the girl tumbled to the carpet, the third floor erupted in hysteria. A woman fainted.

A male student was kneeling and had his cell phone aimed at Ramzee, taking a video. Ramzee fired a bullet at him. The slug hit the cell phone before it ripped into the young man's head.

"No cell phones! No videos! That's what happens!"

Ramzee fired again—a short burst of slugs into the ceiling. For good measure, he dropped the muzzle and let one more volley fly at the crowd, injuring several people and killing several more. A boy with glasses and curly hair was still alive; the slug had hit him in the shoulder. He was on his stomach, moaning in pain, trying to crawl forward. Ramzee fired again, spraying the student's back with bullets, putting him out of his misery.

"Go! The other stairs. If you want to live, go right now," Ramzee warned loudly. "No talking! No phone calls! Up to the tenth floor. *Now!*"

The remaining students and parents didn't hesitate. Amid soft sobs, they filed down the hallway toward the stairs. Ramzee followed, looking in the rooms to see if anyone was trying to hide, listening as, somewhere above, more gunfire mixed with muffled cries.

Ramzee heard footsteps behind him. He turned, but it was too late. A middle-aged man was charging. Ramzee tried to swing the rifle around, but the assailant caught the muzzle. The man dived at Ramzee, the barrel of the gun in one hand, his other hand finding Ramzee's hand on the stock. He was a big man. His hands were larger than Ramzee's and he was powerful.

He pushed Ramzee backward and tackled him, then slammed the rifle across his neck.

Ramzee punched the man, just as steel slammed against his neck. He tried to look up and see. He was American, with short brown hair and a savage look. Ramzee swung wildly, kicking whatever he could, but the pressure on his neck was unremitting. Students ran to help. Ramzee felt hands on his arms and legs, holding them down. He couldn't do anything.

Ramzee felt as if he was watching TV. It all happened so abruptly, and he was barely a participant.

The man grunted and Ramzee heard a dull snap, which, in the moment before he went black, he realized was his own neck.

On the fourth floor, Ali waited for several minutes. He watched his floor through the window in the stairwell door as screaming and gunfire came from both above and below. It was an eerie sight. With each howling cry from another part of the building, students poured into the hallway. Many were crying, hugging each other. Many were on cell phones, calling for help. For a brief moment, Ali imagined what it must be like to be a student under attack. Or to be a student at all. To live in such a building and not have to fight, hate, kill. His father had attended university in Toronto. He remembered his father telling him stories of what it was like. The dances. The dormitory. Teachers. The papers he wrote.

The memory flashed through his mind over a pregnant moment, then was gone.

He pulled his ski mask down and opened the door.

"Move to the stairs at the other end," he said calmly, the rifle in his right arm, aimed at the ground, pointing with his left hand. "No talking."

A tall man with neatly combed gray hair pushed through the students. He was angry.

"Who are you?"

Ali pointed again with his left index finger.

"If you want to live, turn around and start moving."

The man came a little closer to Ali. He stopped when he was just ten feet away.

"This is a *dorm,* for God's sake," the man said, trying to remain calm. "They're *kids!* Let them go. You can keep me. Keep the parents. They're *children.* They have their whole lives in front of them!"

Behind the man, the throng remained still.

Ali moved his left hand to the rifle, raised it, and pulled the trigger.

Bullets flew down the hall. The crack of automatic weapon fire was joined by screams and by the sound of footsteps, yelling, and desperate cries as the people fought to get away from the fusillade.

Ali held the trigger until the mag was empty. He popped it out and stepped over the dead man, whose chest was a riot of crimson.

"I warned you," said Ali to the dead man. He threw the empty mag at the man's head and pulled another from his vest, slamming it in.

The hallway was littered with bodies. Ali counted seventeen dead as he made his way to the far stairs.

Jack Sullivan looked at Ramzee for several moments. He picked up the dead terrorist's gun.

The floor was silent. All eyes were on him. To reinforce the silence, Sullivan held his finger to his mouth. He waved everyone toward the middle of the hall.

"Daddy," came the whisper of his daughter, sobbing as she stepped toward him.

"It's going to be okay, sweetie," he said. "Go in the bedroom. Everyone, get in these two bedrooms. Hurry. We only have a minute or two."

He continued to wave his arm, calling everyone in. He clutched the carbine, watching both ends of the hall, his head swiveling back and forth, looking for more terrorists. He waved everyone into a room.

"Hurry!" he whispered impatiently. "We don't have a lot of time."

They crowded into two rooms as Sullivan stood in the hallway, guarding the doors. When everyone had packed into the rooms, he spoke.

"Look out the window," he said. "Is anyone out there?"

"Some people who look like soldiers. SWAT."

"How far away? Are they moving in?"

"No."

Sullivan looked at his daughter.

"Now everyone, listen. I don't need to tell you these men are terrorists. They're going to kill everyone. But you are all going to escape."

"How?" asked someone.

"It won't be easy," said Sullivan. "We're on the third floor. That's low enough to jump and not die."

"We'll break our legs."

"You might, but staying here is not an option. You have a better chance of living if you jump. A broken leg will heal."

A low rumble of whispers and sobbing spread over the crowd of students.

His daughter hugged him. "I love you, Daddy."

She pushed through the crowded room. At the window, she looked out, then unlatched and opened it. The entire room watched.

She looked down. The street was empty. Directly beneath her was concrete.

"Let your legs absorb the landing," said her father. "Go, sweetheart. For me. I love you."

Tears streamed down her face. She looked at her father one last time, turned, and jumped.

• • •

Daisy took Andy and Charlotte each by the hand and pulled them to the corner of a room. They were both hysterical. Charlotte was on her cell phone, sobbing to someone. Daisy put her hand over the speaker.

"Come with me."

"Dad, can you hold on?"

"You need to hang up."

"Why?"

"Because he doesn't have any answers and right now you need to focus on staying alive, not talking on the phone."

Charlotte nodded as tears flowed. "I love you, Dad," she said.

In the corner, against the wall, they huddled together and held hands.

"We're going to be rescued," Daisy whispered. "You have to keep thinking that. But until then, we need to stay strong. That means no eye contact, no crying, no talking, pretend you're invisible. We're going to do what they say. Okay?"

"What are they going to do to us?" asked Andy.

"It doesn't matter," said Daisy. "They obviously want something. To get it, they're going to kill people. It's not going to be you."

Andy sobbed louder.

"Be thankful they're after something," said Daisy. "If they weren't, they would've blown up the whole building. Come on. I can't do this without you two."

Charlotte looked up.

"I can't do it without you either," she said. She grabbed Andy's hand. "Or you. We can do this."

Gunfire ruptured the din of crying and whispers on the floor. Daisy squeezed harder. She looked at them with a fierce look.

"We can do it," she said calmly, forcing a smile. "I know I'm going to die someday, but I'll be damned if it's because of some fucking terrorist."

43

NEAR IRHAB, SYRIA

Dewey kept the ski mask on as he drove away from Aleppo. He kept the rifle and the handgun on the seat next to him. For several miles, his breathing was fast and nervous, his heart racing. He expected to see ISIS gunmen guarding the road at the outskirts of the city. But he saw no one except a few teenagers wandering in the road, climbing over collapsed buildings, staring at him as he drove the truck slowly by.

Soon the destruction of Aleppo—blocks of rubble where homes used to be, roads pockmarked with craters, bodies still lying on the ground weeks after being killed, a visible, acrid-smelling haze of dust—disappeared. The air grew clear. He took off the ski mask and put it on the seat next to him.

The highway was little more than a two-lane paved road. It cut straight through vistas of brown flatland and clusters of small homes and dilapidated buildings. Soon there was nothing except empty brown land in both directions, with the occasional swath of green where a farm was. Broken-down cars sat just off the road by the dozens. After an hour of driving, Dewey had seen only three vehicles, all of them cars that passed him heading north, away from Aleppo.

After an hour or so, Dewey slowed and took a left onto a dirt road. He checked to make sure he still had cell coverage so that the Israelis could track him. Every so often another small dirt road cut off from the one he was on, leading to farms and homes in the distance, barely visible. He drove for twenty minutes. When he had gone for several miles without seeing any roads, homes, or signs of life, he stopped, turned the truck around, and drove back for a mile, then went right, rumbling off the dirt road onto the open land.

After a hundred feet, he stopped the truck and climbed out.

He ran back to the road. He inspected the tire tracks. They weren't deep, but they were clearly visible.

Dewey took off the T-shirt and whipped it down at the tracks, sweeping the lines away from the dusty dirt. He waved the T-shirt left and right, swatting the land, brushing away the evidence of his departure from the dirt road. He walked all the way to the truck, erasing the tracks. When he was done, he scanned the horizon in every direction, seeing nothing. He climbed back into the truck and drove.

After a half mile, he turned off the engine.

The cell phone showed one bar.

He climbed down from the cab of the truck, taking the mask and guns with him. Looking around, Dewey couldn't see anything other than flatland and, far in the distance, a low ridge of hills.

He was thirsty. He searched the truck from the passenger's side door to see if there was anything to drink, coming up empty. He walked toward where, in the distance, the sun was close to setting, always checking the phone to ensure that there was coverage. After more than a mile, he sat down. As thirsty as he was, his mind flashed to the pack of cigarettes in the pocket of the dead gunman in the basement of the hospital.

He lay down and put his left arm beneath his head, the rifle next to him, the handgun tucked inside his belt in front.

Soon the sun was gone and the orange sky turned purple and deep blue. He relaxed as a wall of clouds swept in from the west, darkening the sky. His eyelids were heavy and he let them fall shut. He fell into a deep sleep, lying there in the middle of nowhere.

He awoke and sat up quickly, grabbing the gun.

He'd been dreaming.

Much of the time, his dreams were vague and terrible. Images from his past he couldn't remember. Feelings of terror as he ran from something, or unbelievable guilt because of what he'd done. But now he felt only warmth as he sat there in the cold dark. It had been a dream about someone, and he tried to claw his way back into the dream to find out who she was. But he couldn't find it. Nevertheless, he let the warmth inhabit him for a little while.

And then he saw what had stirred him.

Far in the distance, headlights twinkled across the blackness. Dewey watched as the vehicle moved right to left. It was obviously on the dirt road. More than likely, it was just some random Syrian, out for a drive, yet he couldn't help feeling anxious.

They couldn't have tracked him. It was impossible. The route he'd chosen was in the opposite direction of what Garotin would expect. His exit onto the dirt road was random, not to mention his cut into the open plain.

Still, he watched with a sense of foreboding. As the vehicle continued to move, its lights grew larger and more defined. It was still on the dirt road and coming closer. For the first time, he noticed bright lights separate from the headlights.

Searchlights.

Dewey was grateful that he'd wiped away the tire tracks. But what if they had night optics? They would be able to see the truck.

He looked up at the sky. There were no stars. It meant the detection range of the optics would be limited.

"Keep driving," he whispered.

Where the hell is Kohl?

He listened for the sound of helicopters.

"Son of a bitch," he muttered as he hit the cell.

He dialed Meir. The signal went from one bar to none and back again. For more than a minute, the phone tried to dial . . . but it didn't go through. A moment later, the cell shut off, its battery dead.

In the light, he could see his footprints.

Dewey cursed himself, recalling the tracking abilities of various groups indigenous to the Middle East, including Syrians. He'd fucked up. Dusting the tracks was irrelevant if they could see the truck and his footprints. He should've dusted the ground between the truck and where he was now.

The truck stopped.

Dewey dropped to his hands and knees and started frantically to dig. The earth was gravelly and his fingertips were soon raw. He stopped after less than a minute, realizing that he wouldn't have time. The headlights were now aimed in his direction and getting bigger.

He should've kept going. He could've made it to Turkey.

Stop thinking about what you should've done. It's irrelevant. What are you going *to do?*

The oncoming vehicle went dark as they killed the lights.

Dewey took the handgun from his waist and put it on the ground. He got down on his stomach, placing the AK-47 in front of him. The moon-shaped magazine was the lowest point to the earth and it made the gun, in this firing position, unstable and hard to keep still. He dug a small hole that allowed him to stick a few inches of the mag down into it, then got comfortable, putting his cheek against the buttstock. With his right index finger, he moved the fire selector to semi-automatic. He reached for the muzzle, feeling for the sight. A small piece of the sight flipped up. This was a luminous dot for improved night fighting.

The rifle had a thirty-round mag, but Dewey had already fired off several rounds. More important, he didn't know how many rounds the terrorist he took it from had already spent. The biggest problem was the gun's range. At most, it was effective to around four hundred yards. In the dark, with no night optics or scope, Dewey assumed his effective range would be half of that at most.

Dewey remained on the ground, waiting, his finger on the trigger. He couldn't see or hear anything. He would get few opportunities to target the killers—and perhaps none.

If they opened the cab door of his truck, or the door to their vehicle, he would be able to target around the light. In addition, once they reached his truck, they would need to find his foot tracks, something that likely required a light source, unless they could do it with night optics. But that would be hard for the trackers to do. The one thing he was sure of was that he would have their muzzle flash to aim at.

After several minutes, he heard the squeak of a door opening. He scanned for the light of a vehicle but saw nothing.

Then a light went on. A flashlight. It went on and off briefly. He swept the rifle left, trying to put the luminous dot of the sight where he thought he'd seen the light. But he needed another flash. A few seconds later, it came again. It was just a fraction of an inch off the sight. He moved it and locked on just as the light went off. Then he triggered the gun, holding the trigger down. Three loud explosions cracked the air as slugs ripped through the darkness. He heard the clang of a cartridge hitting steel of the truck. He fired again and heard a sharp groan. Then the terrorists started firing.

Dewey focused on the orange-red flashes, trying

not to think about the incoming bullets. He ducked low against the ground, trying to ignore the noise, listening for the helicopter. Every few moments, he raised up and fired in single rounds, trying to conserve what ammo he had left. He hit another man, who screamed and continued to moan.

He waited for what seemed like forever, listening and watching. Suddenly, the gunfire started again. It was coming from two different points. He found the red flash and fired, hitting steel. Gunfire started once more and he triggered the gun, only to hear his bullets hit his truck. The gunmen were using it as cover, firing intermittently. He waited and aimed again. When he triggered the gun, all he heard was the dull thwack of an empty round. He was out of ammo.

He ducked low and twisted the AK-47 sideways, rotating the mag in the dirt, creating a little cover. He felt the ground for the pistol and took aim but didn't fire. He waited. He was sweating and breathing fast. More shots rang out. One of the slugs hit the rifle, making a loud *ding*. Dewey let out a sharp cry, hoping they heard it. He rolled left just as both gunmen focused everything on the area surrounding the rifle. He rolled several times, clutching the handgun and trying to stay as low as he could. He stopped. Propped low on his elbows, he gripped the pistol with both hands and waited as bullets peppered the ground to his right. Then the shooting stopped.

For more than a minute, Dewey waited, gun out. Then he heard an engine.

They were coming to make sure he was dead. But they kept the lights off. It meant they weren't sure. He knew they were scanning with the night optic. If he tried to run, they'd mow him down with ease. Yet it was clear that the detection range of the optic was poor.

If he was going to move, now was the time.

They'll see you.

It was an impossible situation.

You need to run.

The vehicle's lights shot on. He was illuminated in one of the floodlights. It was a pickup truck, moving quickly. The headlights were aimed to his right. He fired. All he heard was a *click*. The chamber was empty.

He lay his head on the dirt, left cheek against the ground, and remained still. There were two men— the driver and a black-clad gunman in the back, a carbine in his hands, searching for him.

Dewey's mind traced the dozen things he should've done. He felt self-loathing for his laziness.

Why didn't you switch vehicles? Hide in an abandoned shack?

Worse, the thought struck him that whatever he'd gone to Damascus to retrieve had been worthless. A ruse by al-Jaheishi. He had so many things to live for. The thought that it had all been a waste was a bitter tonic; he felt anger and regret. The lights came closer and the gunman searched . . .

Peltz watched the video on the screen in front of him as Walls piloted the chopper. The screen showed a video feed, taken by satellite somewhere in the sky above. Beneath thin digital grid lines was a black-and-gray landscape, a holographic view of a remote area in Syria called Irhab—location of the last captured signal of Andreas's cell phone. But cloud cover made the feed grainy and illegible.

The chopper's lights were off as it moved north along the Mediterranean coast.

"Get ready, guys," said Walls over his headset. His voice went over the intercom in back. "We have a safe corridor inland. Swinging right."

Peltz typed into a keyboard, trying to adjust the screen and get a sharper view. Andreas's location was locked into the chopper's NAV system, but that was all.

Another voice came over Peltz and Walls's headsets. It was Abramowitz in operations command back at Ramat David Airbase.

"South clearing in five, four, three, two, one," said Abramowitz. "Zebra Ninety, you have a vector inland to the target zone."

"Roger, mission leader," said Peltz, swinging the Panther AS565 MA sharply right. "Heading southeast at one-three-zero, over."

Walls looked at Peltz. "Ten minutes out."

Peltz didn't look up or acknowledge Walls. His eyes were glued to the screen. A break in the clouds had allowed him to focus in on Andreas. He saw the ghostlike holograph a few yards from the point where the cell phone had been locked. But there were two other figures and a vehicle on the screen. Then the telltale bright white sparks of gunfire.

"Oh, shit!"

"What is it?" asked Walls.

"Trouble."

Peltz turned to the cabin and made eye contact with Meir, nodding, telling him he wanted to show him something. He hit a button on the chopper dash and pulled down a black digital screen from the top of his helmet, then grabbed the joystick in front of him. This controlled the weapons aboard the Panther, which included Nexter M621 20mm guns and AS-15TT antisurface missiles.

"What?" asked Kohl Meir.

"The clouds broke." Peltz pointed at the screen with his left hand as, with his right, he adjusted the joystick. On the screen, a red square target box appeared imposed over the holographic feed of the ground. Then the screen went black again as clouds covered the view. Peltz dialed in the ordnance, preparing to fire one of the AS-15TTs. He heard the electronic hum of the targeting architecture beneath the chopper.

"Jonathan," said Meir. "Tell me."

"He's in trouble."

Meir, dressed in black tactical gear, face painted black as well, leaned toward the screen to get a better view.

"How close are they?"

"Twenty meters. If I miss—"

"Fire!" barked Meir. "If you don't it won't matter!"

As the pickup came closer, Dewey felt the light on him. He shut his eyes. He heard shouting in Arabic. The truck stopped. Squinting, he saw the gunman in back move to the side of the truck and point at him. Dewey didn't move.

A loud noise came from the sky—electric, high-pitched, something moving blisteringly fast. The shriek of an incoming missile, too fast to react to. In a fraction of a second, as the noise became unbearable, there was a deafening explosion. The pickup burst into a cloud of smoke and fire. The sky lit up in a massive fireball and the ground shook. Dewey was catapulted up, pummeled backward, where he landed several feet away and tumbled, his face scraping dirt, until finally he came to rest. All he could hear was a high-pitched ringing noise in his ears. A few moments later came the sound of smoldering metal. Dewey lay still, eyes shut, waiting for the shock to dissipate so that he could determine if he was injured. He didn't move for several minutes. He felt numb.

At some point he heard helicopter rotors above the din of the flaming truck. Slowly, he sat up, shielding his eyes as the wind picked up and sent dirt and sand flying over him. He didn't see or hear the chopper land.

He felt hands on both sides of him, lifting him up by his arms.

It was Meir who awakened him from his shock. "You okay, Dewey?"

Meir was standing beside him, holding one of his arms. Dewey stumbled, wrapping his arms around Meir and another commando. They moved to the open door of the dark chopper, its rotors slashing the air.

"What took you so fucking long?" groaned Dewey.

"Traffic."

44

CARMAN HALL
COLUMBIA UNIVERSITY

The tenth floor was soon fetid with heat and so many people in such a tight space. The initial hysteria had dissipated into quiet disbelief and sorrow.

Ali dumped out a large cardboard box from one

of the bedrooms. He and Mohammed stood just inside the entrance to the tenth floor, each man holding a cell phone detector, which they waved over every person as he or she entered, confiscating cell phones.

As his men corralled the students onto the tenth floor, Sirhan climbed the empty east stairs to the roof. It was imperative to secure the roof before the FBI or NYPD had time to mobilize an assault team and drop it down on top of the building by chopper.

He clutched an AK-47, safety off, finger on the trigger, and slowly pushed the door open. The urgent scream of sirens came from several directions at street level below. He crouched low and glanced cautiously around, his rifle sweeping the air along with his eyes. He surveyed the surrounding buildings and distant skyline. Seeing no movement, he placed his canvas rucksack on the ground and pulled out binoculars, again searching for movement. He saw none—but he knew snipers were coming soon. Perhaps they were already in position but waiting for the order to shoot. The FBI might attempt to negotiate before staging any counterassault or attempting to kill anyone, though he doubted it, especially after the trail of blood they'd left in the street.

The roof was empty and unfinished. A waist-high brick parapet ran around the edge. A few beer bottles, a broken lawn chair, and cigarette butts were evidence of its occasional use by students.

Looking up, Sirhan again scanned the buildings in proximity to Carman. None were as tall. Across 114th Street, several floors below, he eyed a few people at windows, looking down on the street, checking out the dead bodies and watching as police and ambulances arrived on the scene. They were oblivious of him.

Tariq stepped onto the roof. He was perspiring.

"Where is the case?" asked Sirhan.

"Behind me," said Tariq. "Just inside."

Sirhan nodded.

"Is it ready if we need them?"

"Yes."

"Good. Now let's hurry up and get the roof wired. They're going to be here any minute. If they take the roof, they'll be able to stop us."

Sirhan knelt next to his rucksack and removed a large spool of tungsten wire, the same kind that Fahd and Omar were using on the stairs. He fastened one end to a steel post near a corner of the roof, at waist level. He walked diagonally across to the opposite corner. He pulled the wire around a piece of steel roof support and drew it tight. He moved to the middle of the roof, looking for another structure strong enough to hold the line. He found a thick pipe and wrapped the wire around it, and moved in the opposite direction, quickly building a latticework of tightly knit wire, a web that soon crisscrossed every section of the roof.

Meanwhile, Tariq removed six IEDs from the rucksack. They were exact copies of the ones on the stairs—Semtex 10 with firing buttons sticking out. On each device, Tariq attached the wires to the batteries, getting them ready. Gently, he handed each live IED to Sirhan, who set them on top of the tungsten web. If any part of the wiring was cut, the latticework would collapse, the IEDs would drop to the ground, their firing buttons would strike the hard surface, and they would explode. It was now impossible for the dorm to be infiltrated from above.

Each IED had enough explosive force to level whatever was on the roof and destroy part of the floor below. If they all blew at the same time, the building would likely lose several floors in the blast.

Tariq was near the edge of the roof. Looking down the smooth side of the dorm, he saw a figure. It was a student, a male, standing on a windowsill of the third floor. Suddenly, the boy jumped. He landed on the sidewalk next to the building and tumbled, clutching his leg.

"Sirhan."

Sirhan was near the opposite side of the roof. He'd crawled along the edge with an IED and was setting it on top of the wire.

"What is it?" he asked. Sirhan turned and looked

at the sky to the south. Then he heard it: the distant whirr of helicopters.

Sirhan put the IED gently atop the wire. He shimmied backward until he was in the corner. He had one more IED to set, but he was exposed, crawling along the brick precipice of the roof, the wires laden with IEDs on one side, open air to the other.

Sirhan's eyes shot to Tariq. He nodded toward the door. "Go."

Tariq went inside the building as Sirhan crawled along the edge of the roof and set the fifth IED.

Tariq undid the latches on the long case. He removed the SAM and the battery-cooling unit, a round canister that powered up the missile while it was still in the launcher as well as kept it cool. He placed the weapon on his right shoulder. With his left hand, he stuck the battery-cooling unit into an opening in the underside of the SAM. He flipped up a square metal slat, enabling him to target the missile. He placed his left hand on the uncage button at the front of the launcher, then gripped the trigger with his right hand. He used his thumb to press down on the safety-and-actuator switch behind the trigger and prepared to fire.

At the open doorway, Tariq eyed a pair of choppers cutting over the skyline to his right.

He put his right eye against the sight and activated the missile's guidance system on the blue sky all around the approaching choppers, then focused in on the nearest one, rushing toward them. He listened for the hum that would signal the target's acquisition.

"Sirhan," he said, as he held the SAM steady and prepared to let it rip. "They're getting close."

Sirhan was along the near edge of the rooftop, holding the final IED in his left hand. He set it on top of the wire.

Tariq heard the hum as the first boom came from the approaching chopper. Bullets ripped the roof just behind Sirhan. He didn't have time to crawl backward.

Tariq fired. The missile tore from the end of the launcher. A low hiss mixed with the sound of the chopper's guns. A trail of smoke followed the missile, which weaved in the air, then straightened out. The chopper abruptly swerved left and up, accelerating to avoid the incoming missile. But it was too close. It took just seconds for the missile to slam into the right side of the helicopter. A moment later, it exploded—orange, black, and red flames shot out in a cataclysm of smoke and fire. Then a cloud of thick smoke plumed outward. The chopper broke into parts, plummeting to earth several blocks away. Distant screams could be heard from the streets below.

Sirhan, who was on his stomach, clutching the precipice of the roof, turned his head. He said nothing. He inched backward as the other chopper cut high and away.

Sirhan crawled to the door, where Tariq was waiting.

"Thank you, brother."

45

IN THE AIR

He was asleep. Then he felt it. A hand on his shoulder. He was back in the hospital. He felt the knife on his neck. He lurched up from the chair.

"Dewey, hey, it's me!"

Dewey was standing, his right arm around her neck. It was the female copilot. His mind raced. Then he remembered. He let go.

"I'm sorry," he said. "Instinct."

He looked down. In the pilot's right hand was a small knife that was now pressed against Dewey's torso. He looked up as she pulled it back.

"Sorry," she said, a small grin on her face. "Instinct."

Dewey laughed.

"Is that how you usually greet a girl when she wakes you up?" she asked.

Dewey shook his head.

He reached absentmindedly for his neck, feeling the spot where Garotin had pressed the KA-BAR knife. There was a small scab. It didn't hurt, yet he couldn't stop thinking about it. The thought of being beheaded had never crossed his mind. He realized now that having his head cut off was infinitely more horrifying to him than being shot. Perhaps it was because he'd been shot—on multiple occasions—and knew he could handle it. Or maybe it was how close he'd just come to death. He removed his hand from his neck and forced himself to banish the thought from his mind.

"Only the pretty ones," he said to the female pilot.

"You should put a Band-Aid on that," she said.

"How long have I been out?"

"We left Israel four hours ago."

"How long until Andrews?"

"They're not letting us land at Andrews. There's been some sort of attack in New York City. The FBI has it under control, but Homeland is rerouting all inbound flights along the eastern seaboard. We're trying to get clearance, but it isn't working. Everyone is panicking."

"I need a SAT phone."

"Sure." She went to the cabin and returned with a phone. Dewey extended the antenna and dialed Calibrisi. The call went to voice mail. He tried several times, leaving a message after the fourth attempt.

"Hey, it's me. I'm on the plane. Call if you get this."

Dewey dialed a six-digit number he knew by heart. The phone clicked several times, then a female voice came on.

"Identify."

"NOC 2294 dash six."

"Hold."

A series of beeps followed, then a male voice came on.

"Control, please hold for voice RECOG. Go."

"Andreas, Dewey."

Again a series of beeps, then another voice.

"Control, who do you need, Dewey?"

"Hector."

There was a slight pause. "He's not available."

"Tell him I need him. It's urgent."

Another pause.

"Hold on."

Several seconds later, the phone started ringing.

"Dewey?"

It was Polk.

"Hi, Bill. Where is he?"

"Where are you?"

"In the air. I'll be back in an hour, but they're not letting us land at Andrews."

"I'll get you clearance."

"Where's Hector? Was the information actionable?"

"Very," said Polk. "But we have a situation."

"I heard. Where in New York? What happened?"

"At Columbia. A dormitory was taken over. It's

a hostage situation. But that's not what I'm talking about. Dewey, Hector is at GW Hospital. He had a massive heart attack."

Dewey was silent.

"They . . ." Polk started, then paused. Dewey could hear him trying to control his emotions. "They don't know if he's going to make it."

Dewey shut his eyes. He reached out and put his hand against the seat back, steadying himself.

"I'm here right now," said Polk. "They put him into a coma. Even if he does make it, they're not sure how long he went without oxygen."

Dewey cleared his throat. "Has someone told Vivian?"

"Yes. She's on her way."

"Bill, can you make sure there's a chopper waiting for me at Andrews?"

"Yes, of course. By the way, how are you doing?"

"Fine. See you in a few."

46

CARMAN HALL
COLUMBIA UNIVERSITY

By the time Mohammed stepped onto the eleventh floor, gunfire and screams had repeated themselves so many times the students and parents were terrified into silent acquiescence. Mohammed cleared the floor without incident, just a few gun-shots into the ceiling to get people to hurry up.

The problem was, the stairs were overcrowded as everyone moved ineluctably to the tenth floor. The doorway itself was a logjam. The floor was getting filled to capacity.

Many of the hostages had watched in horror as the helicopter was shot down. Everyone heard it. If any resistance had existed, the sight and sound of the chopper being blown up in midair shut up even the boldest of the crowd.

Meuse was responsible for the twelfth floor. He stepped inside, but before he even raised his gun, a young woman in a hijab stepped from the hushed crowd and held up a hand, then spoke to him in Arabic.

"You don't need to shoot," she said. "We'll do what you say."

"Go to the tenth floor," he said. "Praise Allah."

At Meuse's words, the girl's face grew angry, but she held her tongue. She turned.

"Tenth floor, everyone," she said.

Sullivan was crouching on one knee, pivoting almost constantly between the ends of the third-floor hallway, moving the gun back and forth. He could feel his heart racing.

Had someone told him that morning that he would kill someone—by snapping his neck—as dozens of people looked on, including his daughter, Sullivan would've spat out his coffee. The most violent thing he'd ever done to another living creature was during a fistfight in college, when he'd been reluctantly dragged into a barroom brawl in Brunswick, Maine. Sullivan had beaten the crap out of two locals after they picked a fight with him and his roommate. Sullivan's roommate had gotten knocked out with a beer bottle. Even then, he'd tried to avoid the fight, pleading with the two drunk bikers to let him walk away and take his unconscious roommate to the hospital. But they were having none of it. Sullivan had broken one of the thug's arms and the other man's nose on the way to beating them both senseless. To this day, he didn't know where it had come from.

His mind flashed to that memory and a slight grin came over his face. He was still batting a thousand.

As for handling a firearm, he was completely inexperienced. He clutched the terrorist's assault rifle and tried to familiarize himself with it, though other than the trigger he wasn't quite sure what most of the various switches, latches, and knobs were for.

He glanced behind him. The dorm room was half-empty as students and parents did what he'd asked them to do, and what his daughter showed them was possible—leaping two floors to the hard ground below.

They're going too slow, he thought.

His mind raced with worry. The terrorists were obviously distracted as they tried to secure the building. The minute one of them saw someone jump, all hell would break loose. They'd know something was wrong—that their man was dead—and they would come looking.

He noticed an older woman, someone's grandmother, sitting in the corner of the room. She looked terrified.

Sullivan stood, cased both ends of the hallway, and went to her, training the rifle at the floor.

"What's your name?" he asked.

The woman stared at him.

"All right, why don't I start," he said. "I'm Jack Sullivan."

He put his hand out to shake the woman's hand, but she didn't move. Rather than pull it back, he placed it on her shoulder.

"Where you from?" he asked.

"Toronto."

Sullivan nodded.

"I'm from Philadelphia," he said.

"My name is Ruth."

"Are you here dropping off a grandchild?"

"Yes, my grandson."

Sullivan nodded toward the window.

"You're scared, aren't you?"

"I have two artificial hips. I have a mechanical valve in my heart. My body will break into a hundred pieces if I jump."

"Ruth, these men aren't here to make friends. They're going to kill everyone. They're terrorists. If they find you, they'll kill you."

"I know."

Sullivan led her to the window, moving in between people preparing to jump. A male student leapt, fell quickly, and landed on his legs, a muffled scream echoing up as he struck concrete.

Ruth moved her hand to her mouth. She let out a low yelp.

"I can't," she pleaded, looking at Sullivan.

He was silent for a few seconds.

"I need to go back to the hall," he said. "If you stay, I want you to hide. Get under a bed somewhere. If you have a cell phone, turn off the ringer."

After wiring the first-, third-, and fifth-floor stairs with IEDs, Omar joined the rest of the cell upstairs.

Fahd, as instructed, had taken up position on the sixth floor, above the highest of the wired stairwells. As he descended the stairs, he removed a suppressor from his coat pocket. It was an FA556, black, four inches long. He attached it to the muzzle of the rifle. When he walked onto the sixth floor, he fired off a round, testing it. A low, metallic *thwack* echoed quietly in the air as the round struck a distant wall.

He knew the snipers would be positioning themselves soon, if they hadn't already. He needed to be careful. Fahd knew he was going to die, but he couldn't die yet. None of them could. The size of the cell was a function of mathematical necessity based on the operation. Each one of them had a job to do. Right now, his was to kill anyone who tried to come inside the building through the main entrance.

He found a bedroom halfway down the hall. Fahd crawled along the floor of the room, pressing himself against the wall.

When he reached the waist-high windowsill, he got to his knees. Very slowly, he raised his head and looked out.

The sidewalk in front of the dorm was empty. The campus looked abandoned. Blood stained the tan-colored surface where people had been gunned down. He tried to see the front of the building, but it was difficult. He would have to lean out the window if he wanted to see the area immediately in front of the entrance.

He took a monocular from his vest and studied the rooftops, looking for movement. *There:* straight ahead he marked two men in tactical gear. They were crouching on the roof of a brick building nearby. One of the men had binoculars and was scanning the dorm. The other was speaking on a cell phone. They were visible from their shoulders up, partially blocked by decorative iron.

Fahd studied the six-story building, looking into each window for signs of law enforcement. He went floor by floor. On the third floor, he noticed an open window and, behind it, movement. The room's lights were off. Though he couldn't see in, he assumed they were establishing a sniper nest inside.

Fahd lowered the blinds and adjusted them so they were cracked just a bit, enough to see through. Enough to fit the muzzle of his gun. He pushed a bed against the wall, near the window. The bed was the height of the sill and would allow him to sit and keep watch for what he knew would be long hours of waiting. He repeated the setup in a room across the hall.

Fahd had one huge advantage over the snipers. How would they be able to tell if he was a sniper or a student? Even if he was spotted, would they shoot and risk killing an innocent student?

Fahd returned to the bedroom above the entrance. With the monocular, he looked through a seam in the blinds at the men on the roof. They were both looking up into the sky above the dorm. Fahd craned his neck, trying to see, but couldn't. Then he heard helicopters.

Carrying his AR-15, Fahd moved again to the other side of the building, searching until he found the two black objects whistling across the sky. He watched as the helicopters moved closer and started to descend toward the roof. Suddenly, gunfire erupted from the front helicopter, a furious spray of bullets shot from the machine gun mounted to the copter's underbelly.

Was Sirhan still on the roof? What if they hadn't wired the roof yet and the FBI attacked and killed him?

Stop thinking so much.

But he couldn't. The sound was loud and unrelenting.

Then his ears picked up the telltale hiss of a missile. A moment later, he saw it screech across the sky and hit the chopper. His heart jumped as the fiery debris dropped from the sky.

A moment later, he heard a scream. It was somehow different from the others.

He ran back to the other side of the building and looked out. The scream had come from this side, but he saw nothing. He climbed onto the bed, then the sill, wedging his body against the window frame, though still behind the blinds. He knew they would be distracted right now. He pulled the slats apart and looked down. This was where the scream had come from—and there it was. A woman was lying on the ground next to the side of the building. She was crawling. Then another individual appeared in the window above her. He was standing on the windowsill. He jumped.

Fahd felt the anger rising inside him. They were escaping! Whose floor was it?

He now counted four people, all crawling along the very edge of the building to safety.

He swept the muzzle of the AR-15 to the open window, then aimed it down along the brick face of the building. With the monocular, he looked quickly through the slats, first at the roof of the neighboring building, then the third-floor window. The men on the rooftop were gone. In the window, he didn't see any signs of activity.

They're distracted.

Fahd convinced himself that the explosion of the helicopter had caused them to leave. He moved the silenced rifle to the open window, preparing to fire.

Sirhan stepped onto the tenth floor. It was packed. Students and parents filled the hallway and dorm rooms. He strolled casually down the length of the hall, his rifle out in front of him, brushing the muzzle just inches from people's heads.

Sirhan was a short man—five foot five—though he projected a sense of strength that made those around him not think about his height. His head was large. He was bald, with an overgrown mustache and beard, olive skin, and a sharp, long nose. His eyes were calm, confident, and he rarely looked people in the eye. This aloofness gave him a measure of strength. Sirhan had spent much of his youth lifting free weights at the gym inside the Cairo juvenile hall he'd been sent to at age ten.

His arms were defined, the biceps rippled, even grotesque and out of proportion. He wore a tight black T-shirt that showed off his thick chest muscles. He was bowlegged and walked with a limp due to a broken leg that didn't heal properly after jumping from a window during one of his many escape attempts from the youth prison.

At age twenty-three, Sirhan was the youngest man in the cell. Yet Nazir had put him in charge. Several members of the group had initially been angry, but they all came to understand the wisdom of Nazir's selection. Sirhan was a masterful operator—highly organized, disciplined, open to opposing thoughts and new ideas. He was intensely loyal. He gave each man a sense of belonging and mission. At the same time, he made each one of them feel that he cared about him. Because he did. Of course, he also had a ruthless side bordering on evil. Sirhan had single-handedly figured out how to get each man into the United States. He'd created cover stories. He'd kept them together, patiently planning for this day. Some believed that being a terrorist was about the ultimate moment of violence, the planes flying into the Twin Towers, suicide vests being detonated. But it was the quiet times, the waiting, the planning, the kindnesses given to those whom you would see dead—these were the parts of terrorism that were far more difficult. Sirhan had understood that and had somehow succeeded in building as close to a family as most of the eight jihadists would ever know.

Many were crouched on the floor in mute horror. He walked the length of the hall in silence. If a space was too tightly packed with people, he waited for someone to move. He wasn't vicious about it. He got to the end of the hallway. Mohammed and Omar stood in front of the door, rifles out, aimed at the floor. Sirhan made eye contact with both men, turned, and walked back to Tariq, Ali, Meuse.

Fahd, he knew, was on the sixth floor. Jabir was in the lobby.

"Where is Ramzee?" he asked Ali in Arabic.

Ali looked at Sirhan with a concerned look, a hint of guilt on his face.

"I don't know, Sirhan."

"Something happened," he said. "Did any of you see him?"

"I did," said Ali. "I cleared the fourth floor. He was in front of me, on three."

"Did anyone see him after that?"

They all shook their heads.

"One of you has to go down there," said Sirhan.

"The stairs are wired, Sirhan," said Omar. "Between five and six and between three and four. It's not possible to access them any longer."

"What about climbing on top of the banister?"

"No," said Omar. "It would take a high-wire artist, and even then, the banisters are wired. Even

391

a slight touch to the wire could break it. And if you slipped, it would be all over."

"What do you think happened?" asked Tariq.

"He's dead. He must be. Perhaps one of the students knows self-defense or had a weapon."

"Or a parent," said Ali.

Sirhan nodded, deep in thought.

"If we can't get down, whoever is there can't get up," said Tariq. "They're trapped too."

"With Ramzee's gun," whispered Sirhan, an agitated look on his face.

If there was somebody down there, they were trapped, thought Sirhan. Still, the possibility that Ramzee was dead, and that the killer might still be out there, worried him.

Sirhan walked to the gathered students and parents. He stopped in the center of the hallway.

"Welcome to Columbia," he said in English with a harsh Middle Eastern accent. "We wanted to begin the school year with some festivities."

There was silence. Then a girl yelled, *"What the fuck is wrong with you?"*

The girl stepped forward. "What have we done to deserve this?"

She was young, plain-looking, and had short brown hair.

"What did those people in the helicopter do?"

"What is wrong with *me*?" asked Sirhan, grinning.

He fired. The bullet hit the girl in the chest. She fell to the floor as people around her screamed.

"In case any of you don't get it," he said, looking around savagely, "we're not fucking around."

He paused, continuing to make eye contact.

"If you want to live, do exactly as I say. Rule number one: keep your mouth shut unless I tell you to talk. Rule number two: we're not afraid to kill you. Bullets hurt, and we have a lot of them."

Sirhan glanced at Tariq, who was standing guard near the end of the hallway. Tariq nodded at him. Sirhan walked to the end of the hall and took him aside.

"You're sure there's no one on the top two floors?" he asked in Arabic.

"Yes, I'm sure."

"Go to the sixth floor with Fahd. Keep watch, especially the hallway. If someone killed Ramzee, he has Ramzee's weapon. We have to be careful."

Sirhan pushed past him and took the stairs to the eleventh floor. The hall was eerily quiet. He walked with his assault rifle in his right hand, finger on the trigger, trained in front of him, sweeping it methodically back and forth between rooms.

A few doors down, he stepped into a dorm room. It had a pair of desks, bunk beds, a pile of boxes. He slunk slowly along the wall. It was early in the assault, but if the Americans—the university, the FBI, the police—were prepared, they would already have snipers in place. He inched delicately along the wall until he was a few feet from the window, and looked down on 114th

Street and, in the distance, Broadway. Other than cars, 114th Street was empty. Broadway too was abandoned, except for a line of armored vehicles at the corner of 114th.

He looked up. He counted three helicopters, hovering in the sky. But they were far away. The missile strike had done its trick.

Sirhan moved back to the hallway. He pulled out his cell phone and hit Speed Dial. The phone rang a few times, then Nazir picked up.

"Sirhan?" asked Nazir. "Is everything okay?"

"Yes, Tristan. We're inside. We've sealed off the building and established strategic advantage."

"Very good. It's all over the news. You shot down a helicopter."

"Yes. They were coming in close, perhaps to try and take the roof. It's wired now."

"Are there any reporters there yet?"

"I don't know. The area is cordoned off. They have a perimeter. I saw armored vehicles. It's hard to see beyond the other buildings."

"Don't use your cell phone unless it's an emergency," said Nazir. "They'll be picking up the signals soon, if they haven't already. I'm surprised they haven't jammed everything yet. Then again, maybe I'm not surprised. The Americans are slow. Remember what to do if you lose cell coverage."

"Yes, I know what to do," said Sirhan. "When should we start throwing students from the building?"

"As soon as possible."

"Every hour?"

"Yes, every hour."

"What if they agree to your demands?" asked Sirhan.

"Until the weapons arrive, the executions must continue. It is the only way."

"And if they somehow—"

"They won't, brother," said Nazir. "The trap is too perfect."

"But if they do—"

"You must make the ultimate sacrifice in the name of ISIS and of Allah. It will only make us stronger. The next time, there will be no negotiation! If the dormitory is destroyed, our power will only grow!"

"Of course, Tristan. I will not let you down."

47

LATAKIA, SYRIA

Nazir put down the phone. It was nearly midnight. He was alone.

There were many questions in his mind. What had happened to Allawi? Had Raditz killed him? More likely, the information from al-Jaheishi had enabled America to find them both. It didn't matter now. In a way, the ship that held the weapons was a metaphor for his own fate. Everything he had worked for and planned on was now beyond his ability to control. Like a ship, the entire operation was under way, at sea, and whether it floated or sank was now in the hands of others. His work was largely done. Selecting Sirhan, choosing a college dormitory versus a mall, even the choice of explosives. It was all set. Nazir felt neither good nor bad about it.

He knew he needed sleep, but instead he made tea and sat down at his desk. He would write for a few hours. He had learned much in the past twenty-four hours. His journal was filled. He would start a new one. He placed the old one on the bookshelf; there were now hundreds. Some-day soon, very soon, he would have them all printed. Nazir understood how famous he was, but it was for acts of terror and barbarism. What the world didn't yet comprehend was that a larger philosophy was beneath it all. His name would be remembered, like Marx, Stalin, Khomeini, Hitler.

He reached up and grabbed an old journal from many years ago, a random choice. It was from Oxford. He stared at the cover for many moments, paralyzed in thought. Then he opened it and started reading.

The Diary of Anne Frank is admired by millions of readers, and justifiably so. On one level, it is a deeply moving book about one individual's strength of character in the face of evil. Perseverance, hope, resiliency, adaptation, and survival—or the desire to, anyway. These are the lessons, among others. The presence of a family that is not a target of the Nazis but is nevertheless willing to risk their lives for one that is hints at a deeper human strength and bond that is more powerful than that of government.

—T. Nazir, 22 Nov.

A pained look came over Nazir's face. It was the date—November 22. It was to be his last day at Oxford. Like all great lessons, it was a day that taught him so much, a night that opened his eyes every bit as much as it closed his heart.

He put the journal down and walked into the bathroom. He lifted up the eye patch and stared at the hollowed-out cavity where his eye had once been. He touched the edges, imagining it was still there, picturing what it looked like—remembering the cruelty that had seared evil into his being for eternity . . .

Nazir heard a knock at the door.

"Tristan?"

It was Clive, who lived down the hall from Nazir. The voice was aristocratic and smooth, like almost everyone at Oxford.

"May I come in?"

Nazir said nothing. He was lying on his bed. His face was buried in a book.

"Oh, Tristan," Clive cooed laughingly. "I know you're in there."

"Tristan isn't here," said Nazir, continuing to read. He took a pencil from behind his ear and made a mark on the page.

"The race begins at midnight," said Clive, "followed by a party. We were both invited. We can't be late."

"I don't want to go," said Nazir. "I told you that. Ask someone else."

"Entering in three, two, one—"

The door opened and Clive came in. He was dressed in a striped maroon sweater and khakis. He was tall, with tousled brown hair. He walked to the side of Nazir's bed. Nazir still did not look up.

"*The Diary of Anne Frank*?" asked Clive. "Humanities? Did I miss an assignment?"

Nazir finally looked up. "No, I'm reading for pleasure."

"Anne Frank? I thought you guys despised the Jews?"

Nazir shook his head.

"What have they ever done to me to justify my having any feelings whatsoever about them?" Nazir said. "I've met a total of three Jewish people in my life. One was an accountant who worked for my father. One was the mother of my friend. And then there is Murray, upstairs. He seems nice."

Clive nodded. "Point taken. I just meant, for pleasure? Really? Anne Frank?"

Nazir put the book away and sat up.

"It's about the desire to live versus the power of fear," he said. "Perseverance against paranoia."

"Yes, I suppose that's true." Clive changed subjects. "So what about tonight?"

"Why would I go? To be the token Muslim in Bullingdon?"

"Oh, bollocks," said Clive, "don't be silly. I went to Eton and you're my best friend. As difficult as you are, people do actually enjoy your company. Maybe it's because you despise everyone equally?"

Nazir let a barely susceptible grin come to his lips.

"How did you get us invited?" asked Nazir. "I thought it was the 'hardest ticket to get in five hundred years' and all that, blah, blah, blah."

"I did what you were unwilling to do," said Clive.

"Which is what?"

"Ask your brother."

Nazir turned. "I told you not to," he snapped. "And he's *not* my brother."

"I forgot. *Step*brother," said Clive.

Nazir stood at the window, looking down into the courtyard.

"What did he say when you told him one was for me?"

Clive looked at Nazir, a blank expression on his face, then shook his head.

"Who cares?"

Francis Leopold Dorchester Highgate III, or Franny, as everyone referred to him, was Nazir's stepbrother. Nazir's father, considered by many to be the most brilliant currency trader in the history of the London Stock Exchange, had, after the death of his first wife, Nazir's mother, married Barbara Highgate, a stage actress who had never been married but who had a son with James Rensallear, Earl Cadogan. Franny was an infamous character on the Oxford campus. He cut a wide swath. He looked down upon Nazir's father and, by extension, Nazir, despite the fact that his entire life, a life of utter luxury and proper British accoutrements, was paid for by Nazir's father.

Franny Highgate had become Nazir's step-brother when Nazir was six and he was eight. Since then, Franny had been withering in his treatment of Nazir, a combination of racism and physical cruelty that his father thought healthy for Nazir.

Nazir didn't care about money. The fact that his father had so much meant little to him. Truth be told, it didn't mean anything to his father either.

He enjoyed the thrill of properly executing upon a theory. The fact that being good at it equated to massive wealth was, to Nazir's father, irrelevant.

Over Easter holiday, Nazir found his father's will. Half of everything was left to Barbara, the other half shared equally between Franny and himself. But attached at the back of the will was a codicil, registered that very week. Instead of splitting half between him and Franny, Franny was now to receive the entire half, other than a few trinkets and artifacts that were his mother's, such as her favorite gold brooch.

Nazir was deeply offended by the first will. The codicil practically made flames come out of his ears.

Despite the fact that he'd been snooping in his father's office, he stormed upstairs, where his father and Barbara were sleeping. His father awoke and looked up, startled.

Nazir's father stood up and put on a silk robe, then grabbed a cigarette. "Come with me."

Nazir followed his father out onto the terrace off the master suite. Workers were unlocking the gates of Kensington Park, across the street.

"So you found the will?" asked his father as he lit the cigarette.

"Yes."

"I'm going to explain something to you, Tristan."

He took several puffs, exhaling into the cool breeze.

"You, like me, Tristan, are meant for great things," said his father. "In fact, I believe you are meant to change the world. I don't know how, but I do know it. Money is not a gift. It's a curse. Francis is a worthless human being. But he is my son. My adopted son, but nevertheless my son. Without money—money left to him, because he will never earn a shilling—Franny would end up bankrupt and in all likelihood embroiled in various legal difficulties. In other words, he needs it."

"So clearly my mistake was being the top of my class," said Nazir sarcastically, "instead of a drunkard."

Nazir's father flicked the stub off the terrace. He turned to Nazir.

"With you, it is the opposite. If I leave you that money, it will be a curse. Whatever you're meant for will not be achieved, because necessity, hunger, even desperation, these are the roots of greatness. And you are destined for greatness."

Nazir was silent. He stared down at the park, watching the first few early morning joggers cutting in through the majestic iron gates.

After more than a minute of silence, his father leaned down, trying to get Nazir to acknowledge him.

"I just said you were destined for greatness. Have you no response?"

Nazir shot his father a contemptuous look.

"At some point you became infatuated with

being white, father," said Nazir. "It clouded your mind. This is proof. You might believe what you say. But believing it doesn't mean it's right—or even sane."

Nazir's father grinned appreciatively.

"I can't argue with your reasoning, but none of that is true. I don't see things in terms of skin color. It was your mother who taught me that. When we were poor in Cairo, she taught me that I had a destiny having to do with numbers. You have a destiny having to do with something much bigger."

"What are you talking about?" said Nazir with hatred in his voice.

"I don't know. That is what you need to figure out."

Nazir began to walk toward the French doors that led inside.

"Have a good trip back to school."

"Imagine what they will say someday," said Nazir, back turned to his father. " 'Nazir was hated by his father. He cut him out of the will.' "

"But you will always know why I did it. Because I love you."

Nazir stared straight ahead, saying nothing, and continued to walk toward the doors.

"Look at me, Tristan."

Nazir took the small brass doorknob in his hand. He paused, not looking back, then opened the door and walked away.

• • •

There were at least fifty students assembled on the massive brick back patio of Bullingdon. One of the members was moving through the crowd of eager first-years with a rolling silver tea service, making first-years drink either vodka or whiskey.

The initiation into Bullingdon was a drunken run across the grass of the club, through Marsh Park to the large, striking hedge out beyond the rugby fields and around the pond, followed by a ritual skinny dip in the pond. Those first-years invited to the races were being considered for membership in Bullingdon. It was Oxford's most exclusive club, though nobody was really sure what its members actually did other than drink and destroy things.

The challenge of the races, other than the run and the swim in and of themselves, had to do with the fact that drinking was integral to every stage of the race.

Nazir was standing next to Clive. He took a few gulps of vodka. He watched Franny out of the corner of his eye. Other than the occasional coincidental sighting around campus, it was the first time Nazir had seen his stepbrother since arriving at Oxford.

Someone leapt onto the low wall at the back of the terrace and proceeded to let his pants drop to his ankles, then urinated as he sang a song.

"By the way," said Nazir sarcastically to Clive

as they both averted their eyes in disgust, "thanks for getting me a ticket. What a wonderful cultural event."

"Oh, lighten up, will you?"

At some point, Franny came over.

"Clive," said Franny, then looked at Nazir. "And you must be . . . ?"

Everyone laughed.

"Hi, Tristan," said Franny. "How do you like it? I hear you have Ogilvy."

"Good," said Nazir, barely glancing at his stepbrother.

"Well, as we both know, you probably are smarter than most of the professors here," said Franny.

"And how are you?" asked Nazir.

"I'm good. Graduation in six months. Believe it or not, Tristan, I'm going to try for SAS."

"Really?"

"Yes. Do my part, as they say, for England. Crazy, I know—"

Clive interrupted. "What happens next?" he asked.

"Yes, of course. So listen, there will be a call for a members challenge. Each member asks one of you blokes to race, and off you go. All in good fun. I believe Wilson was going to ask for you. He's harmless."

The drinking, smoking, and partying continued for several hours; then one of the members, an obese, dandily attired blond-haired boy, climbed onto a table and blew a whistle.

"Welcome, all you sick bastards and future masters of the universe! Welcome to the four thousand eight hundred and twenty-sixth running of the hedge, wherein we learn what it means to be a Bullingdon gentleman. Now drink up. When you get tapped on your shoulder, that is how you know who your challenger is. You must not only triumph over your challenger, you also are expected to bring along adequate supplies, and by supplies, I, of course, mean alcohol, so that the entire process might be more enjoyable. Now most of us can't run more than a few hundred feet without throwing up, so it shouldn't be that big a deal, really."

A tall, handsome student with black hair approached Nazir.

"Tristan? Patrick Wilson. Let's go."

"Should I grab something?"

"Yes, grab that bottle of champagne, will you? We'll take it easy, nice trot, yes? Then a swim. You're sort of a legacy, even though technically Franny isn't blood."

Approximately fifty students moved down across the massive field in a whooping, shouting cabal of inebriation. The field grew dark as they jogged across the grass, the sky was clouded over. Various students formed small packs, stopping for a few swigs of alcohol or a cigarette. In the distance, Nazir watched as one of the upper-classmen tackled Clive to the ground, playfully wrestling with him.

At some point, Nazir lost track of Wilson but kept running. As he came to the end of the field, he saw the massive hedge, rounding the corner. A light was coming out of the ground. It was a small door to a root cellar. Franny was standing near the door, as if expecting him. A strange, cold shivering feeling came over Nazir then. He stopped and turned, but Wilson was there to grab him. Then there were others and soon they were on him.

Nazir could have screamed, but he didn't. For some reason, he remembered Anne Frank. He remembered the way she remained always convinced that she would live, despite the over-whelming odds against her. He also remembered the inhuman brutality that would've seen her killed for no reason. *Why?* was the question he couldn't figure out the answer to. Why would someone want to kill someone like Anne Frank?

As they dragged him down the rickety steps of the cellar and started beating him mercilessly, Nazir understood the answer.

They threw him on the ground and kicked him everywhere, punched his face, poured alcohol on him, all the while laughing cruelly, until they were so winded they couldn't laugh anymore. The front of someone's pointed shoe—perhaps a wingtip—

struck him in the right eye. He screamed. Other than involuntary grunts and moans, it was the first display of weakness and defeat Nazir showed that day.

"My eye," he mumbled. "Stop. Please."

But they kept beating Nazir until he was nearly dead. He saw Franny's sweat-covered face through the dim light.

"Don't ever talk to your father about my inheritance, or my mother's," said Franny, holding Nazir by the hair and lifting his limp head a few inches off the dirt. "And by the way, that's how an empire rules, you ungrateful nigger."

"My eye," sobbed Nazir, clutching his face. "Please, Franny . . ."

He didn't wake up until the next day, when an old man, one of the groundskeepers, found him and brought him to the hospital. His right eye was ruptured beyond repair.

In the hospital where Nazir slowly recovered, he refused to speak with anyone, not his father, not Clive, not the police, not even the doctors and nurses who took care of him.

On his tenth day of silence, he looked at one of the nurses as she took his breakfast tray away.

"My belongings," he whispered.

"Yes, Tristan. They are over here." She pointed to some cardboard boxes.

"Is there a journal?"

The nurse looked through the boxes, finding it near the bottom of one.

"Is this it?"

Nazir nodded.

"Could I have a pencil?"

After the nurse retrieved him a pencil, Nazir started to write:

The Diary of Anne Frank (continued) I would like to reflect on this book from a different perspective, that is, what it shows about the weakness and imperfection of the Third Reich. While the book shows what we all know to be true, namely, that the Nazis were evil, it also exposes failures of planning and implementation of the Nazi system of government. The Nazis permitted families who were agnostic to the Third Reich to live, thus enabling situations such as that of the Frank family, who were able to hide. In retrospect, Hitler should have exterminated not just Jews but anyone who had ever associated with them, such as hiring them or being friends. While venal, this broader cleansing—from a purely political perspective—would have done more to prevent Jews from continuing to live, and engaging in such things as writing books, for it was works like this book that elicited the righteous anger that resulted in America joining the battle against the Third Reich and defeating them.

Thus, it works as such: when consolidating power, one must exert control on behalf of whatever agenda is that of the consolidator, and administer control with widespread and unfathomable violence, fear, and bloodshed. The Nazis, in summary, were not evil enough if their goal was permanence and political legitimacy—and power. The point is not that Nazism is good or bad. It has nothing to do with Nazism or, for that matter, with Anne Frank. The point is, when one has an objective, whether a government or an individual, one must bring to bear unbridled, unvarnished terror and pain in the pursuit of that objective. Anything less leads to defeat.

—T. Nazir, 1 Jan.

Nazir finished reading the passage. He flipped the page. Taped to the next page was a newspaper clipping.

Oxford Student Drowns

Francis Highgate III, an undergraduate student at Brasenose College, Oxford University, drowned two days before he was to graduate, it has been reported. Highgate, twenty-one years of age and the son of Vaughan Nazir and Barbara Highgate, was a resident of Kensington, London. According to Oxford police, Mr. Highgate was found floating in the Thames near the lower acres of Port Meadow. No further information has been released in the matter. A memorial service is to be performed this Saturday, 17th May, 12:30 P.M., in the Brasenose College Chapel.

48

WASHINGTON, D.C.

Dewey stared out the window as the chopper took him from Andrews Air Force Base across Washington, D.C. He was alone. When the chopper landed on the helipad at GW Hospital, he was greeted by a pair of plainclothes CIA paramilitary.

They stepped onto a waiting elevator, which descended to the second floor. When the doors opened, Dewey's first sight was the expressionless face of J. P. Dellenbaugh, standing next to Amy Dellenbaugh, both consoling Vivian Calibrisi.

A cadre of other officials, staff members, Secret Service agents, and a medical team was also in the corridor. The tone was hushed.

On the wall above the nurses' station, a television displayed live coverage of the hostage crisis at Columbia.

Behind him, on his cell phone, stood Polk. His normally friendly face was ashen, even haunted.

It was Vivian who saw Dewey first. Tears streamed down her face. Dewey wrapped his arms around her.

"Dewey," she whispered, sobbing.

"He's going to be all right, Vivian," he said. "He's the toughest son of a bitch I know."

Dewey felt his own tears begin to moisten his eyes, but he fought to hold them back.

Dewey stepped to Dellenbaugh and extended his hand, but the president instead reached his arms out and hugged him.

"I need to talk to you," Dellenbaugh whispered. "Go see him first."

A nurse accompanied Dewey to the room. A sliding door—like a barn door—was moved aside by a nurse. It was a large, modern operating room. Dewey registered three nurses and four doctors. The walls were lined with plasma screens displaying digital readouts. The steady monotone of the heart machine seemed familiar.

In the center of the room, on a large, elevated

steel table, covered in light blue blankets, was Calibrisi. His eyes were closed. An oxygen tube protruded from his mouth, running down his throat. Three separate IVs were attached to his arms. His skin was the color of parchment.

Dewey placed his hand on Calibrisi's hand, clutching it. As hard as he tried to not cry, he felt tears on his cheeks.

"You're not leaving yet," said Dewey, squeezing his hand. "This is not how it ends."

One of the doctors stepped forward. He placed his hand on Dewey's shoulder.

"Are you family?" he asked.

Dewey looked at him but didn't answer.

"It's okay," said the doctor.

"How bad is it?" Dewey asked. "People recover from heart attacks all the time."

The doctor nodded. "Yes, they do. He's alive. For now, that's all that matters. We're going to do everything in our power to bring him back."

Dewey gripped Calibrisi's hand as tears now rolled down his cheeks. He held onto his hand for more than a minute, until he felt a hand on his shoulder. He turned to see J. P. Dellenbaugh.

"He's going to be fine, Dewey," said Dellenbaugh, forcing a smile. "You know it and I know it."

Dewey walked back into the hall. Polk stood near the elevator, still speaking on the cell phone.

It was then that Dewey felt a cold, terrible emptiness, a chemical feeling of silent terror.

He looked around the corridor, searching for her.

"Where's Daisy?" he asked, his voice a little too loud.

Dellenbaugh motioned for Dewey to follow him. They walked to an empty room.

"Daisy is in the dormitory at Columbia," he said. "The one taken over by ISIS. We haven't told Vivian. I'm not sure if you agree, but she's in a tough state."

Dewey stared blankly into Dellenbaugh's eyes.

"How did she end up in a Columbia dorm?"

"She was bringing a girl there. Her Little Sister, a precocious kid from inner-city Baltimore she's mentored since the girl was eight."

Dellenbaugh was choked with emotion.

"The information you got out of Syria detailed a massive illegal arms program involving the deputy secretary of defense," Dellenbaugh said. "We supplied ISIS with everything. More than a billion dollars' worth of guns and missiles. We made them. We created ISIS." Dellenbaugh looked angry.

"Who did it?"

"Mark Raditz."

Dewey was quiet. He knew who Raditz was. In fact, Dewey had a high opinion of him. Raditz was a key player in the discovery of the plot to detonate a nuclear device on American soil just a few months ago.

"A ship left Mexico four days ago loaded with

another shipment of weapons," Dellenbaugh continued. "We stopped the ship in the Mediterranean. That's when Nazir's men took over the dorm. They want the guns and ammo. They *need* the guns and ammo."

When Dewey climbed aboard the jet earlier that day, he thought he would enjoy a calm ride home followed by a few weeks off. He felt battered and bruised. Not to mention the horrible feeling he could not shake, the feeling of having a knife against his throat.

The knowledge that he had asked Garotin to kill him.

Shoot me. A soldier's death.

He was planning to head up to Castine and see his family. He needed some time. He figured Calibrisi would start looking for him in late October. He was going to avoid his calls for a few weeks, spend Thanksgiving in Castine, then head back to Langley. But when he found out Calibrisi had had a heart attack, everything changed. By the time he landed at Andrews, he was prepared for the worst. Calibrisi might die. Now he understood the gravity of it all. And as much as he wanted to think about the hundreds of people who were now hostages, who, if he knew ISIS, were slated to die, he could only picture Daisy. He could only ask, *Why? Why, Daisy?* Why did you need to be there, this day, that college, that dorm?

"No wonder he had a heart attack," whispered Dewey.

"What?" asked Dellenbaugh.

But Dewey remained silent. Only someone who's lost a child can understand. He reached out and grasped Dellenbaugh's arm, trying to ease the anguish that now coursed through him.

Dewey shut his eyes for several moments, steadying himself. He knew what needed to happen. He knew what he needed to do. He alone could change it all. He could never bring Robbie back, but he could save the hundreds of Robbies who at that moment were slated for death. He could save Daisy. But he would need to strip away the feeling of helplessness. Replace it with anger.

He thought of the knife at his throat and let the memory course through him. He pictured the moment in the basement of the hospital, the two men dragging the corpse, the feeling of the trigger beneath his finger as he sent slugs into the terrorists. The sound of blood hitting the wall behind them. The look in their eyes as they understood, these monsters who pretended to not value life, that they were slated for death. That he would be the one. It was a look of pure human fear. Cowardice. For him, a feeling of superiority and victory, a feeling that nothing else on earth had ever given him.

Dewey grabbed that anger then, in that moment. He took it and didn't let it go. Whatever sadness, guilt, and sorrow caused him to reach for Dellenbaugh slipped away. He stood tall, spreading his legs, and a look came over his face that caused Dellenbaugh to flinch.

"Who's running Columbia?" he asked.

"The FBI has command authority," said Dellenbaugh. "Domestic terrorism."

"I want to be involved, Mr. President."

"You work for the Central Intelligence Agency. Technically, it's illegal."

Dewey stared into Dellenbaugh's eyes. The president, a former professional hockey player, was the same height. He was also built similarly to Dewey—wide and stocky, his legs, arms, shoulders, chest, everything packed with muscles.

"The FBI has a lot of experience with this sort of thing," said Dellenbaugh. "Obviously, their top CT team is on it. Half the guys in the group are former Special Forces or CIA."

"You're probably right," said Dewey.

Dellenbaugh grinned. "Then again," he said, "I'm not a lawyer. Plus I hate lawyers."

Dewey nodded and turned.

"I'll call George Kratovil," Dellenbaugh said. "Dewey, keep me in the loop. You have my personal cell."

"I'm not looking to make problems, sir. If they know what they're doing, I'll back away."

"And if they don't?"

Dewey stared at Dellenbaugh with a cold, blank

expression. He said nothing. Then he walked down the empty corridor, away from the crowd of nurses and doctors and medical staff, away from Polk, away from Vivian. He found the stairs, climbing at a fast run to the roof. On the helipad were two choppers, including the CIA Traumahawk. He opened the cabin door and climbed in.

"Get this thing in the air," said Dewey.

Both pilots looked back as Dewey took a seat.

"This is an assigned—"

"I don't care what it is," said Dewey. "Get it in the air now. Head for New York City."

Dewey pulled out his cell and hit Speed Dial. He heard the low, groaning rumble of the chopper engine beginning to move the rotors.

A familiar voice came on the line.

"Hey," said Rob Tacoma.

"Are you in the United States?"

"Yeah."

"New York City?"

"Maybe."

"What does 'maybe' mean?"

"It means," said Tacoma, whispering, "that I'm at the Four Seasons with Ilian Gateeva. She's in the bathtub."

"Who?"

"She's a *Sports Illustrated* model."

"Congratulations. I'll call someone who hasn't turned into a douche bag."

"Fuck you. What do you need?"

"I need a place to land a helicopter and I need you to meet me there."

"West Thirtieth Street has a heliport."

"Better get Katie. Tell Igor while you're at it."

"What are we doing, if you don't mind my asking?"

"I need your help with something."

" 'Something'?"

"Remember the bomb in the harbor?"

"Yeah, sort of."

"That kind of something."

"Oh. Why didn't you say that in the first place?"

49

CARMAN HALL
COLUMBIA UNIVERSITY

Sullivan heard a noise coming from one of the stairwells. He walked slowly to the door, his rifle extended, finger on the trigger. At the end of the hallway he leaned carefully out and looked up. What he saw made him gasp. The stairs were covered in a latticework of wire. Near the center, a large object with a flashing red light was perched.

Sullivan quietly inched over to the stairs. A thin gap along the banister allowed him to see up and down. His heart racing fast, he leaned into the opening and looked up. The floor above appeared normal, but two floors up, wire was wrapped around the banister, the same way as on the stairs directly in front of him. He looked down. Though it was dark, he could make out more wires two floors below.

"Oh, my God," he whispered as he tiptoed back to the door.

He took his cell phone from his pocket and dialed 911.

"Nine-one-one," came a female voice. "What is the emergency?"

"My name is Jack Sullivan. I'm inside the dormitory at Columbia."

There was a brief pause, which Sullivan guessed was disbelief.

"We're aware of the situation. Are you all right?"

"Yes, but I need to speak to someone who is managing things," said Sullivan.

"Mr. Sullivan—"

"Please listen to me. I'm not a student. I'm a parent. I killed one of the terrorists. I need to speak to someone. There's a bomb. The building is wired."

"Hold on, sir."

As Sullivan waited, he ran to the stairs on the other side of the building. He saw the identical wire lattice and bomb. The floors two up and two down were also wired to blow.

He let out a deep breath, trying to calm down.

"This is Andrew Ronik with the Federal Bureau of Investigation. Who am I speaking with, please?"

The voice on his cell phone awakened Sullivan from his shock.

"Hello?"

"The . . . the building is wired," whispered Sullivan.

"When you say wired—"

"There are bombs on the stairs. I counted six. There could be more. They're balanced on some sort of wire netting above the stairs."

"Let's take a step back," said Ronik. "Who is this?"

"My name is Sullivan. Jack Sullivan."

"Who are you?"

"A parent. My daughter is a freshman. I was dropping her off. I'm inside the dorm. I hid. I killed one of their men."

"Where are you, Mr. Sullivan?"

"On the third floor."

"Are you alone?"

"Yes. Well, actually, no. There's an elderly woman. She was too old to jump. She's hiding."

"I'm going to ask you to hold for a sec."

"Okay."

More than a minute passed, then someone else came on the line.

"This is Dave McNaughton with the FBI. Mr. Sullivan?"

"Yes. Jack Sullivan."

"Okay, Jack. I need you to do something for me."

"What?"

"Can you take some photos of one of the bombs? Try to get a close-up. There will be an area with a bunch of wires, maybe a light. I'm especially interested in that. Also, you told Agent Ronik it's on wires?"

"Yes."

"Please try to get a close-up."

"What should I do with them?"

"Text them to me. I'll give you my cell."

As Sirhan started for the stairs, he heard suppressed gunfire.

Fahd.

He ran into a room facing the campus. This time, he was careless, sprinting to the window and looking out. It appeared empty. Green lawn spread in neat rectangles between large, majestic buildings and sidewalks punctuated by statues. He saw a cluster of SWAT-clad law enforcement officers at the top of wide granite stairs in the center of campus, way in the distance. Looking left, in front of a building on the other side of campus, he saw a similar cluster of men in tactical gear.

He heard another suppressed gunshot. It seemed to be coming from directly below him.

He leaned closer to the window, trying to get a better view down the side of the building.

He saw movement below. He pressed his face against the glass.

"Oh, my God," he said aloud.

Someone was crawling along the side of the building on the sidewalk, dragging a leg. Then he eyed several others, moving away, a few crawling, some walking, all clinging to the brick façade of the dormitory.

He pressed his face tight to the glass. Then he saw it: third floor. Students were jumping from the window.

Fahd, you stupid idiot!

Sirhan sprinted down the hallway and up the stairs. When he reached the tenth floor, he motioned for Tariq. Another round of gunshots echoed. They scrambled down the stairs toward the sound.

Sullivan went back to the stairs. He listened for several minutes, making sure no one was on the stairs. He stepped to the area below the bottom stair, a few inches from the beginning of the wires. He took several photos. Back in the third-floor hallway, he texted them to McNaughton.

Sullivan heard gunfire coming from above. Then he heard screaming from the bedroom where the students were jumping.

He ran down the hall and charged into the room. A male student was standing on the ledge.

"Back inside!" Sullivan screamed.

It was too late.

The slug hit the boy's shoulder. Blood splattered down his front and across the window as the boy screamed.

Sullivan lurched for him, but he fell just as Sullivan reached him. He watched, helplessly, as the boy tumbled out, somersaulting to the ground, landing on his head.

The sniper, Kulka, was on his stomach on the roof of the School of Journalism, several hundred feet away. His rifle was an FN SPR A3G, the standard-issue sniper rifle of the FBI, manufactured by a Belgian company, and deadly accurate.

The rifle was on a ceramic bipod. He stared through a Millet Designated Marksman Scope, searching for the gunman he knew was somewhere hiding behind one of the hundreds of windows.

For the past minute and a half, Kulka had listened as the gunman fired suppressed shots at the ground below, trying to hit the students. But the angle was too tight. The gunman couldn't get the correct downward angle unless he leaned the entire weapon out the window. Thus far, he'd remained just inside.

Or had he? The sun splashing off the glass was wreaking havoc on his ability to see.

The spotters were equally perplexed.

"Are you sure there's someone shooting?"

"Yes," said Kulka.

"Why hasn't he hit anything?"

"He doesn't have the angle. Now stop fucking talking."

Thud thud.

There it was again. Desperately, he scanned the building. For some reason, his eyes shot to the seventh floor. Nothing. Was it the eighth?

Then he saw the boy step to the windowsill on three—and above it, on six, the black appurtenance.

Thud thud.

He listened to the scream without looking, knowing that the student had been hit. Kulka remained focused, tilting the rifle ever so slightly. He acquired the outline of the gunman just as the suppressor was pulled back in, disappearing.

Kulka pulled the trigger and fired.

A loud, dull boom exploded across the cavern between the two buildings, combining with the sound of shattering glass as the slug obliterated the window and, behind it, the gunman.

Kulka fired another slug into the room, in case someone else was there, then another.

"Man down," he said into his commo. "I got that little motherfucker."

As Sirhan reached the sixth floor, he heard the boom of the gunshot he knew had come from a sniper rifle, then the shattering glass and a pained grunt he knew was Fahd.

He got to the hallway outside the room, kneeling. When Tariq caught up, he held up his hand, making him wait. Several more gunshots echoed from the distant sniper. Glass shattered, and the wall above Fahd was gutted with big holes.

Sirhan looked at Fahd. The bullet had hit him squarely in the chest. Blood flooded down onto the floor of the bedroom. Fahd's eyes were open, staring up at the ceiling, but life was gone.

"You stupid son of a bitch," Sirhan said.

He looked at Tariq, Fahd's older brother.

"I'm sorry."

Tariq was quiet. He stared at his brother for several seconds, then looked at Sirhan.

"We are all going to die today," said Tariq.

"Yes," said Sirhan, his eyes glued to Fahd's destroyed chest. "Now it's their turn."

50

CARMAN HALL
COLUMBIA UNIVERSITY

Daisy sat upright, against the wall. Andy and Charlotte both had their heads on her lap.

The room was packed with people. There were many students who were alone. There were also family members. For a long time, Daisy stared at a man who wore a light blue baseball cap with the Columbia logo on it, his arms around his son, who sat in front of him, leaning against him, as if he was just a child. For some reason, the image gave her strength.

It also distracted her, and she needed that.

As horrible as her own predicament was, thinking about it was preferable to thinking about her father. Every time her mind flashed to the phone call—and then Josh Brubaker's words— she felt as if the ground might open up and swallow her. It was a feeling of helplessness and futility. How could she be with someone one day and then have it all disappear the next?

Please, God, please protect him.

A smile creased her lips. For whatever reason, she pictured her father from some Christmas morning, so many years ago, and a Barbie dollhouse. It was all she wanted. She and he had spent the day carefully putting it together. Three floors, purple and pink, with a miniature hair dryer that sounded like a hair dryer and, if you pressed the doorbell, the most annoying but, at age eight, wonderful song ever.

Andy suddenly looked up.

"Are you okay?" she asked.

"Yeah, I am," said Daisy. "I have a good feeling about this."

51

Damon Smith, the FBI's in-theater commander, stood inside a large room on the first floor of John Jay, another Columbia dormitory on 114th Street, with Butler Library, Columbia's main library, in between it and Carman. The room Smith had commandeered was the dormitory's common room on the ground floor. It now served as crisis command center.

Tables in the room were occupied by young FBI and NYPD analysts with laptop computers, tied into Homeland Security's mainframe. The walls were lit up by high-definition plasma screens. There were eleven in all, displaying a variety of real-time activity in and around Carman Hall. Every side of the building was displayed by cameras that had been put in place since the hostages were taken. The roof was shown from a chopper overhead. Cameras also displayed the entrances to the dormitory, now mostly empty and quiet. Other screens displayed coverage of the scene as it happened on the various local, national, and international news channels.

The room was crowded with law enforcement:

428

FBI agents, Homeland officers, and NYPD's anti-terrorism group were everywhere. So too were high-level staffers from the Pentagon and White House. The governor of New York and the mayor of New York City, as well as several members of their staffs, were also present.

Smith stood at a table on the far side of the room, near an unused fireplace, behind a set of glass French doors. Four other agents were with him: Moore, Calder, Francisco, and McNaughton. Each had a specific category of responsibility. Each had a wireless headset on, with live connection to a CENCOM operator, whose job it was to make calls, receive calls, and patch the men into real-time commo from on-the-ground operators.

Moore was in charge of perimeter security, including the management of all street-level access points and security teams, along with the establishment and, if necessary, amendment of rules of engagement. He was also in charge of air rights—making sure non-law-enforcement helicopters didn't get too close.

Calder was in charge of external affairs, which was mainly managing the press corps, keeping them in line and not in the way, answering their questions, and utilizing them for the purpose of managing whatever message the FBI wanted out there.

Francisco's job was managing the various non-operational constituencies—families, university officials, politicians and staff, and other VIPs—and keeping them happy.

McNaughton was Smith's in-theater strike force commander. It was Dave McNaughton who, along with Smith, had handpicked the team on the ground near Carman, manned them with communications and weapons, and who would now implement whatever tactical design Smith came up with for freeing the students.

Smith knew the key to successful management of the hostage crisis was being able to think and react to events as they occurred. The chaos would quickly overwhelm his ability to act and react, to take advantage of potential mistakes made by the terrorists, and, at some point, to attempt to free the students. Moore, Calder, and Francisco were there to free Smith from the time-consuming and ultimately purposeless aspects of dealing with what had become a major crisis, not only in the United States but also abroad. Of the five hundred students inside Carman, more than one hundred were from foreign countries.

Calder, Moore, and Francisco did the things Smith didn't need to do, so that he, with McNaughton's help, could somehow figure out a way to save the students, whether through negotiation or violence.

Smith was a veteran, the FBI's top on-the-dirt crisis manager. He took a disciplined approach to everything he did and it showed. Usually, he was a picture of calm. But right now he was livid. He rarely showed emotion, but he couldn't hide his anger.

The reason why he was so angry appeared at the entrance to the room, surrounded by several aides. Judith Talkiewicz, the NYPD commissioner, who had sent in an NYPD helicopter which the terrorists had shot from the sky. Talkiewicz entered the room. When her aides started to join her, Smith held up his hand, signaling them to stay out.

"I want them with me," said Talkiewicz.

"Tough," said Smith as Calder shut the door. "Let me explain something to you, Commissioner: that was a bullshit stunt you pulled. There are five hundred hostages in that building. This is not PR time. You cost the lives of seven people, including a twelve-year-old girl who got hit by part of that fucking chopper. Six men in the chopper, employees of yours."

"I'm aware of the situation, Lieutenant," said Talkiewicz. "Obviously we didn't expect them to have MANPADs."

"You didn't? Then you're a bigger fucking idiot than I thought."

"Is that why you brought me here?" asked Talkiewicz, taking a step toward Smith, unafraid. "To ream me out?"

"Partially, yes. But the main reason is that I want

to make something crystal fucking clear. This is an FBI operation, got it? I expect full cooperation from your officers, access to any and all NYPD assets and information, and I expect your people to do exactly as I say. Am I clear?"

"We're both after the same thing."

"The difference is, I know how to do it. You're a politician."

"I heard you were a megalomaniac," said Talkiewicz.

"I don't care what you heard," said Smith. "I implement strategies, that's all. Someone much higher than me is going to make the call on what we do here. But I can't do that if I have a police commissioner making unsanctioned operational moves that haven't been vetted, discussed, or approved. Got it?"

Talkiewicz stormed out.

Smith glanced at McNaughton. "Was I too harsh, Dave?" he asked.

"No," said McNaughton quietly. "I will say this: that chopper did force them to waste one of their SAMs. I can't imagine they have many more. Also, we broke down the video from the chopper. The roof is wired. Looks like they have five or six IEDs. Munitions thinks it's Semtex. They're exactly the same as the ones on the stairs."

"What about the tunnel in the basement from the library?" asked Smith.

"They wired it," said McNaughton. "It's

identical. Semtex. They've also tied up four students just behind the door. Even if there wasn't a bomb, opening the door into Carman would kill all of them."

"What kind of detonators?"

"Trigger buttons. The ones on the stairs, like the ones on the roof, are balanced on some sort of wire web. Unless they're fake, we're talking about a very dangerous situation. Frankly, we're lucky the NYPD minigun didn't hit the wire. If that thing breaks, they all fall. One of 'em is bound to explode. And when one explodes, all the others will too. It cuts off any penetration opportunities from above."

"And if the stairs are set—" Smith didn't need to finish the sentence.

"It's a big suicide bomb," said Francisco, seated in front of one of the plasmas. "Whatever they want, whoever is behind this, they have the leverage. It's scary how asymmetrical the situation is. They have five hundred hostages, an impenetrable fortress, and a pack of suicide bombers. We're looking at the next nine-eleven. I don't mean to be so dark, but that's what we're looking at."

Smith stared at Francisco. He was his closest friend in the FBI. He couldn't remember all the times they had been together at the beginning of a tough operation, but Smith knew that Francisco was usually right about these things.

A low beeping noise sounded in Smith's ear,

over a Tic Tac–size earbud connected live to CENCOM.

"CENCOM one four one, Commander Smith, please hold for Director Kratovil."

Smith put his hand to his ear. He looked around the table, holding up a finger, indicating he needed to take the call. He stepped to the corner.

"Hi, Damon."

"Mr. Director."

"What's the status?"

"It's the same as last hour. Everything is stabilized. We've seen no activity."

"What about your perimeters?"

"Perimeters, manpower, tactical control are now live and functional. Team communication protocols are aligned. We're ready to implement any directives from CENCOM."

"Well, it sounds like an improvement over an hour ago."

"An hour ago one of my snipers killed one of the terrorists," said Smith. "I'm not sure how you improve on that, sir."

"You know what I meant," snapped Kratovil.

Smith was silent. He knew what Kratovil meant. He didn't appreciate it.

"Director, are we negotiating with these guys?"

Kratovil paused. "That's still being worked out."

"What's the delay? Every minute that passes cuts off opportunities. If we're negotiating, it doesn't matter. But if we're not, the sooner we design and stage an assault, the better our odds for minimizing casualties."

"This thing is not simply a hostage crisis. There are a number of parties at the table: Langley, the Pentagon, the White House. We're trying to keep it from becoming a turf war, but the president wants to make sure we have the . . . well . . . the team that will give us the best chance of limiting casualties and saving those kids."

"Of course," said Smith. "I understand. But until that happens, I'm flying a little blind here. What if our best shot to take the dorm is right now?"

"They have five hundred hostages in there," said Kratovil. "They have strategic advantage. They're also jihadists. If they're willing to die, no assault is going to matter. They'll simply blow the building. Whoever is behind this wants something. That negotiation is under way."

"What do they want?"

"This is top secret, Damon, FYEO. No one in that room is authorized to know."

Smith was quiet.

"We stopped a shipment of arms to Syria in the Med. They want it. That's what this thing is all about."

"And the president doesn't want to do it?"

"Of course not. But the alternative is worse. If he lets it go, ISIS will have enough guns, ammo, and missiles to finish the job in Syria and possibly

Iraq. We're talking about a container ship. Almost a billion dollars' worth of weapons."

"Billion with a *b?*"

"Yes. The president is in an impossible situation. Damon, you need to assume you're going to be asked to design and execute a plan to take over the dorm in a way that minimizes casualties and allows the president to stop the shipment."

"What time frame are we talking about here, George?"

"Hours. This needs to happen soon. I have a feeling they're not just going to sit and wait for a response."

"You mean—"

"Polk thinks they're going to start executing students," said Kratovil.

"Jesus," said Smith. "Okay. I'll get to work. Do I need official approvals and whatnot?"

"Yes. But obviously everyone including the president is standing by."

"I understand."

"Listen," said Kratovil, "the main reason I called is to see how you're holding up."

"I'm all right," said Smith. "But my men are spending half their time entertaining fucking VIPs. The governor, the mayor, senators, you name it. It's getting in the way."

"Delegate it."

"I did. But you try to tell the governor to stay the hell away. These assholes are interfering with my ability to calm things down so that we can properly watch, analyze, and make clear tactical decisions."

Kratovil cleared his throat. "Then you're not going to like what I'm about to tell you."

"What do you mean?"

"There's someone coming to see you," said the FBI director.

"Who?"

"He's a former Ranger, like yourself, Damon."

"There's lots of former Rangers."

"He also spent some time in Combat Applications Group. He's high level. He was part of the team that stopped the nuclear bomb a few months ago."

"Why?" asked Smith. "Am I being taken off this?"

"Chill the fuck out," said Kratovil, "or you *will* be taken off it. I'm not the one sending him in. The president of the United States is the one sending him. Got it? You might consider having an open mind. He's there to help. I know him. He's not a talker. If he can't do anything, he'll tell you."

"Fine. What's his name?"

"Dewey Andreas."

There was a momentary pause.

"I know who he is," said Smith, calming down. "That's fine. Look, that's more than fine. You're right, he might have some ideas. I hope he does."

Smith tapped his ear, cutting off the call. He looked at McNaughton.

"I want three scenarios. You have fifteen minutes."

McNaughton nodded and walked into the next room.

Andreas.

Smith stared at the table, thinking back.

Winter School. Rangers. Smith was in the same class. He knew Dewey, or knew of him at least. Andreas didn't talk much. He didn't have any friends. All business. But Smith used to watch him. He shocked everyone when he won the boxing championship. But it was more than that. It was as if he wasn't meant to be there, confined by the uniform and the rules and the need to rely on others. He was different. Everyone knew it. He wouldn't have won a popularity contest, but every Ranger in that class feared him. He was the real deal.

Smith got Francisco's attention. "We have a visitor coming."

"Who is it?"

"His name's Andreas. When he gets here, bring him in."

"You got it."

52

An hour later, after a smooth flight from D.C., the CIA-owned Sikorsky S-76C landed on the small helipad at West Thirtieth Street, Manhattan.

"Thanks for the ride," said Dewey, leaning into the cockpit.

"No worries," said the man on the left. "SPEC OPS Group briefed us on the way up. We're gonna refuel and stay here, in case you need us."

Dewey opened the cabin door and stepped quickly down. He took the stairs from the helipad and walked to the street. A black Suburban was idling.

The front passenger window slid down.

"Hey, asshole," came a voice.

Dewey grinned. He opened the back door and climbed inside.

"You working for Uber now?" he asked.

Seated in the back was a striking blond-haired woman, dressed in a stylish tight-fitting dress.

"Jesus," said Dewey as he sat down next to Katie.

"Sorry," she said. "I was on a date."

"Lucky guy."

The SUV peeled out.

"Is Hector alive?" Tacoma asked.

"Yes," said Dewey.

"What are you not telling us?" asked Katie.

"We know the reason Hector had a heart attack," he said. "Daisy called him. She's inside the dorm at Columbia."

Dewey stared at Katie for a few seconds, then looked out the window.

Katie Foxx and Rob Tacoma were, next to Hector, Dewey's closest friends. The truth is, he didn't have many friends. For too long, he'd lived the kind of life that didn't lend itself well to establishing relationships. Since Boston College, Dewey had been a soldier, a roughneck on a succession of offshore oil platforms off the coasts of the UK, Africa, and South America, a ranch hand, a CIA agent, and, for a brief time, an accused murderer, rotting away in a Georgia jail cell. Not the kind of places for making friends. Dewey didn't talk much, hated fakes and idiots, and preferred the solitude of the outdoors and the satisfaction of manual labor to socializing.

But Katie and Tacoma were different. It was a relationship based on a shared profession. They could talk without breaking the law. Katie was thirty-three years old and had already served as deputy director of the National Clandestine Service before leaving Langley to start her own consulting business with Tacoma. Tacoma, a twenty-nine-year-old former Navy SEAL, had been recruited by Katie into Special Operations Group. Now their firm, RISCON, was the most exclusive for-hire security and intelligence firm in the world. Hiring Katie and Tacoma was like hiring the cream-of-the-crop from CIA paramilitary. They worked all over the world, primarily for a handful of large multinational corporations. RISCON had broken many laws in many countries, but one thing about the firm was sacrosanct: they viewed themselves as an extension of the U.S. government. They refused any client that Calibrisi didn't like and they turned down assignments from clients they felt weren't in the country's best interest. That was why their biggest client was the CIA.

Katie and Tacoma had been instrumental in a series of successful operations going back four years, when Dewey needed help infiltrating Iran in order to steal Iran's first completed nuclear device and free Kohl Meir from Evin Prison. When agents from Chinese Intelligence killed Dewey's fiancée in a failed attempt at Dewey, Katie and Tacoma had helped plan and orchestrate the violent counterstrike against China. And the summer before, the pair had helped thwart an attempted nuclear strike on New York City.

Tacoma was handsome, rugged, disorganized, and had the maturity, at times, of a fraternity brother. He was also a phenomenal athlete who'd risen meteorically within the SEALs and then NCS. Katie, on the other hand, was elegant, shrewd, highly organized, strategic, and sometimes seemed like a scolding parent to Tacoma. She was also gorgeous, sinewy, with a girl-next-door smile and look that implied the potential for being a troublemaker.

They were an odd pair, like brother and sister, but it worked. They'd grown close to Dewey based on some very hairy times together. But there was something more. In Dewey, Katie and Tacoma saw someone who shared a similar approach to America's enemies, a willingness to take big risks, advanced combat skills, and a religious-like belief in the critical importance of taking no prisoners.

The Suburban's special plates allowed it to move quickly up Broadway toward Columbia, past roadblock after roadblock.

Dewey was seated in the backseat, alongside Katie. Tacoma was in the front next to an FBI agent who was tasked with taking them to the scene.

Broadway was virtually empty. Starting thirty blocks away, National Guard trucks sat across the road, blocking any traffic that might've contemplated getting through. Every block, another tan camo truck sat across the street, forcing the Suburban to run up onto the sidewalk. They came to a halt at 100th Street—almost a mile from the campus.

"What's going on?" Dewey asked.

The driver pointed.

Dewey looked through the front window. The street was clogged with satellite trucks and reporters.

"It goes for ten blocks," said the driver. "That's the perimeter."

"And how are we supposed to get through?"

The driver looked in the rearview mirror.

"I'm not in charge. I was told to pick you up and take you up here."

"Well, the bad guys are that way," said Dewey, a touch of anger in his voice. He pointed toward the campus. "Start fucking driving. Honk your horn if you have to."

The tenth floor was crowded with hostages and reeked of sweat.

Sirhan had a wild look, anger at losing Fahd. With the AK-47 raised, he pushed his way down the crowded hallway, past silent, terrified students and parents seated along the walls, many crying, holding hands, only a few daring to even look at him. He entered a dorm room four stories above the room Fahd had been killed in. The room was crowded with people, perhaps twenty in all. They were seated on the ground, families grouped together, cowering in fear.

Sirhan walked quickly to the window. He glanced out, looking for the sniper on a nearby roof. In the distance, he saw a pair of helicopters, hovering. They were news choppers, no doubt broadcasting live to America—to the world.

"You want some news?" he whispered. "I'll give you some news."

Near the opposite end of Columbia's campus, he saw a line of armored vehicles.

You think you're in charge? I will show you who's in charge.

Sirhan retreated from the window and looked around the room. A family of four was against the wall, huddled up together. None of them returned his gaze. They stared at the floor, as if it might cause Sirhan to somehow not notice them. It was a mother, father, and two sisters, one no more than ten, the other an incoming Columbia freshman. They were Korean.

Sirhan stepped in front of the older sister. He trained the muzzle of his rifle on her.

"Get up," he said.

The Suburban maneuvered through crowds of onlookers on Broadway, then the small armada of media trucks parked closer to the campus. The sidewalks were filled with dozens of reporters, some lined up one after the other along the block, all doing live dispatches from the scene. Bright halogen lights on stanchions shone down on those reporters closest to the scene. These were the network news channels—ABC, CBS, NBC, CNN, and Fox, and the local NY1. Cameramen jostled for position, yelling at anyone who stepped between their talent and the camera.

At 113th Street, a line of steel barriers was staged across the road and sidewalks. Uniformed police officers along with a horde of FBI agent in SWAT gear stood guard behind the barriers, many clutching carbines or submachine guns.

The Suburban stopped at the barrier. Dewey and Tacoma climbed out. When Katie started to get out, he leaned against the door, indicating he didn't want her to come. He spoke quietly.

"I need you to do something."

"What?"

"Go find Igor. We'll meet you at his apartment." Katie gave him a quizzical look. "Igor?"

"Brief him," said Dewey. "Have him start analyzing this thing."

"Why?"

"Because."

"Because why?" she asked, smiling.

"God, you're a pain in the ass. Just because. See you in a little while. Tell him to look in the basement. He'll know what I mean."

Dewey had on khakis and a short-sleeve light blue button-down shirt. In front of the barriers, several dozen people milled about: curious onlookers, journalists, friends of the hostages.

Dewey pushed his way through the throngs of people. He stepped to a break between sections of the barrier, where several police officers and FBI agents stood.

The streets and sidewalks were in a state of total bedlam. Broadway was filled with people. It was noisy, hot, and chaotic: reporters doing live feeds, conversations in front of the barriers, the occasional horn or siren coming from a side street nearby, and, loudest of all, the steady electric whirr of helicopters overhead—law enforcement as well as news channels.

Dewey knew the area near Columbia would be pandemonium. It wasn't necessarily a bad thing.

For the first time, he looked at the dormitory.

On a campus of majestic brick buildings and classical architecture, Carman Hall looked very out of place. It was just plain ugly, as if it had been designed by an architect from the Soviet Union. Almost unnoticeable, partially hidden by Lerner Hall, Carman was—in tactical terms—a fortress. As a place to stage a hostage strike, it was ideal.

The sidewalks and streets immediately surrounding the building were empty except for armed gunmen, who stood at each corner of the building, behind portable steel barricades brought in to shield them from bullets. Sunlight splashed off the windows, making it impossible to see into the rooms. If the terrorists' choice of the building was intentional, it was a good choice: stand-alone, limited number of windows. It was like a medieval fortress: ugly but built for defense.

"At least one good thing might come out of this," said Tacoma.

"What's that?"

"If these guys blow themselves up, maybe they'll take down that ugly fuckin' building."

"Good one," said Dewey.

At the barrier, a tall man in SWAT gear, clutching a carbine, blocked his path. Dewey pushed his way through.

"I'm here to see Damon Smith," said Dewey.

The guard eyed Dewey, then glanced at Tacoma, who had on jeans, a T-shirt, and running shoes.

"The perimeter's shut down."

"He's expecting me."

The man eyed Dewey an extra moment, looked at Tacoma again, then turned. A pair of FBI agents stood off behind the line of men keeping watch. The guard motioned to one of the agents, who nodded. He had on jeans and a blue coat with FBI in bright yellow emblazoned across the chest. He looked young, no more than thirty years old. He stepped toward the barrier.

"What is it?" he said, looking at the guard, who nodded at Dewey.

"I'm here to see Smith."

"Are you Dewey?"

Dewey nodded.

"Come with me. He's expecting you."

"I said, get up!" screamed Sirhan.

The Korean girl burst out crying. Sirhan grabbed her arm and lifted her violently from the floor. Amid a low chorus of sobs from many in the room, Sirhan dragged the girl to the window ledge. He pumped a spray of slugs at the window, shattering it. Screams came from the girl's sister. Sirhan lifted the girl to the ledge and pushed her toward the opening. She let out a low moan as, behind her, her mother cried out in Korean.

"Ani, nae agi, nal delyeoga!"

Not my baby, take me.

The girl faced the wind, inches from the precipice, the only thing holding her back was Sirhan, who had one hand on the back of her shirt.

Sirhan's eyes pored over the roofline of the buildings nearby. This time, he found the sniper. He was on his stomach, partially blocked by a copper balustrade on the roof. His legs were exposed, along with part of the rifle. The sniper had his weapon trained at the building. Indeed, it seemed to be aimed directly at the room.

Sirhan put the muzzle of his rifle between the girl's legs. He moved the fire selector to full-auto. He framed the sniper in the sight. Then he fired. A fusillade of bullets rained down at the FBI gunman. Dust and mortar arose from the roof as the sniper scrambled to get all the way behind the balustrade. Across the chasm between the two buildings, he heard a pained yelp. He stopped firing, staring down through the scope. A large splash of blood covered the place where the sniper's legs had been.

Dewey and Tacoma were led in a circuitous route, along 113th Street to Amsterdam Avenue, then up a block to 114th Street, out of the way of snipers. They entered the John Jay common room and followed the agent through the crowded central area, filled with VIPs, including the governor of New York, the mayor, both U.S. senators, a posse of congressmen, and various staff, past tables filled with people on laptops, as well as others standing before one of the many plasma screens now alight.

At the back of the room, glass-paned French doors were shut. Behind them were five individuals, a few seated, the others poring over a document on the table, which, along with the blueprints, was covered in paper, coffee cups, and a charging device with several cell phones and other devices attached to it.

The room was uncrowded. This was the nerve center.

The young agent led Dewey and Tacoma in, then departed, shutting the doors behind him. Two plasma screens, volume down, hung on the wall behind Smith. One showed live visual of Carman Hall, separated into four sections. The other displayed an aerial view of the roof of the building.

Smith was dressed in jeans and a blue polo shirt, tucked in neatly. Smith scanned Dewey from head to toe, then Tacoma.

"Dewey?" said Smith, reaching out his hand. "I'm Damon Smith."

"Thanks for seeing me. This is Rob Tacoma."

"Hi, Rob."

"Commander," said Tacoma, shaking his hand.

Smith introduced Dewey and Tacoma to the other men in the room: Francisco, Calder, Moore, and McNaughton.

"I'm supposed to give you a briefing," said Smith, "but if you'll forgive me, I don't have the time. Knowing a little bit about your background, however, I don't think you need a briefing. Ask me anything you want. I'll try and answer."

Dewey got right to the point. "What's the penetration shell?"

Smith pointed at the blueprints on his desk. The sheet was large, three feet by two feet. It looked like an architectural drawing of Carman, with the building laid out by floor. Pencil notes were scribbled at various points on the architectural rendering.

Dewey and Tacoma moved closer.

Smith picked up a pencil and placed it on the roof.

"The roof is wired," he said, scratching an X on

the paper. "Six IEDs the size of shoe boxes. Same with the stairs and the basement. They have four students tied up there; if we force in the door they all die. I'd be okay with that, by the way, if it was our only option, but I'm not sure it is. That bomb is just one story below the one on the stairs. It would probably collapse that whole side of the building." He drew a zigzag line down each stairwell, then put a big X in the basement. "We analyzed electrical inputs, and it appears all elevators have been destroyed." Smith made large slash marks on the drawing over the elevator shafts. "All the students are on the tenth floor. High enough so they won't jump."

Dewey nodded, thinking to himself.

"Any outbound commo?"

"They confiscated the cell phones. But there's a citizen in there, father of one of the students." Smith circled the third floor. "Hid when the terrorists came, killed one of 'em."

"Ex-military?"

"No, a general contractor from Philadelphia. After he killed the guy, he made everyone on the floor jump, including his own daughter."

"Smart," said Dewey.

"Real smart. Other than some broken bones, he saved a lot of lives."

Smith pulled out a stack of photos. They showed up-close views of the bomb and wire.

"He took these."

Dewey flipped through the photos.

"Semtex. That's enough to blow a pretty big hole in the building."

"There are thirteen of them, including the one in the basement. They're sitting on wires and the detonators are trigger buttons. If any of them falls from the wires, it'll go off. If one goes off, they all go off. It's like dominoes."

"So moving in through the ground floor with some sort of armored vehicle would set off the bombs on the stairs, is that what you're saying?"

"Yeah."

"How many men do they have?"

"Hard to say. In looking at video of the event taken by several people, we believe eight or nine, but we don't know for sure. One of my snipers took out one of them. Sullivan did too. So maybe seven left."

"How many snipers do you have?"

"Nine."

"What are the rules of engagement?"

"At will. The snipers can shoot what they want. I trust them all."

Dewey glanced at Tacoma, then back to Smith.

"What do you think?" asked Smith.

Dewey shrugged. "I think it's a clusterfuck. They designed it well. They have leverage. What are you thinking?"

"I'm thinking, why are you here?" said Smith.

"I want to help," said Dewey. "I don't like these

"No. It's about image. If he let them live, it would be construed as soft. Nazir's image is his strength. It's more important than any weapons."

"Would you lead it?" asked the president.

"Yeah."

"What about the FBI? The last thing we need is two operations going on at the same time."

"The man running the FBI's on-the-ground operation is aware of it. He supports it. To the extent we're able to get in there, they could be very helpful at creating some distraction."

"And you trust the FBI to not leak it?"

"I trust this guy."

"I had a feeling you'd be going in no matter what."

Dewey was silent.

"If you didn't, I'd be disappointed. It's what you should be doing. Of course you have my support. Good luck in there."

54

THE PIERRE HOTEL
FIFTH AVENUE
NEW YORK CITY

Dewey and Tacoma walked through the elegant art deco lobby of the Pierre to the tower elevators. At the thirty-eighth floor, they stepped along the patterned maroon carpet to a door that was already ajar.

The apartment was sprawling and modern and, above all, lavish.

Dewey cut through the entrance foyer to a library, which looked as if it belonged in a British country house. Books filled the shelves—though not in a uniform manner; some were vertical, others horizontal—surrounding the paned windows that showed Fifth Avenue and Central Park. The lights were dim.

In the middle of the room sat three long sofas, two made of leather, one corduroy, the kind of deep-backed couches a person could spend a day or two on, reading. Katie was seated on one of the leather ones, reading her iPhone.

A pair of leather club chairs, beat-up and inviting, stood at the side of a large fireplace. A glass table in the middle of the room was stacked with more books. In the corner, out of the way, was a desk. On it were two large, brightly lit computer screens. A man was seated in a chair, facing the screens. He had long dirty-blond hair. The faint din of music—coming from earbuds in the man's ears—permeated the quiet room. The Grateful Dead.

Dewey stood and waited. After a few moments, the man turned. A large smile creased his lips. He removed his earbuds.

"Dewey," Igor said in a thick Russian accent, "it's good to see you."

"Have you had time to break down the dorm?"

"I have learned a little in the thirty-four minutes since being told I was needed."

"What do you got?"

They took seats on the sofas, facing each other. Igor and Tacoma sat on one of the leather couches, Dewey and Katie across from them.

Igor pressed a button on a remote. A ceiling vent opened and a large screen descended. He pressed another button; a live video feed of the front of Carman Hall appeared on the screen.

He clicked again and the screen went black. Then the building appeared in brightly lit lime-green digital lines, viewed from the side. Each floor was demarcated in bright green lines. Several floors were completely black, but small red lights stood out high in the building. Two lights were visible on the third floor. Four lights were visible in the basement. The tenth floor was a blurry wall of red lights.

"This is the situation," Igor said. "Each of these lights is a person in the building. The terrorists have almost everyone on the tenth floor."

"If they jump, they die," said Katie.

"Precisely," said Igor.

Dewey stood to move closer to the screen. He pointed at the third floor.

"These two are on our side. One's a grandparent, the other's the father of a student. Apparently he killed one of the terrorists." Dewey pointed to the basement. "These four are students. They're chained to the only door in, along with a big bomb."

"So who's the guy on the first floor?" asked Katie. "Are you able to do anything more advanced?"

"Like what?" asked Igor.

"Like determine who's a terrorist and who's not? Other than the ones Dewey pointed out, we're going to be flying blind."

"That would be pretty sophisticated stuff," said Igor, giving Katie a sly grin. "Then again, I'm a pretty sophisticated guy."

Igor clicked the remote. A handful of red lights turned blue. He clicked again and the blue lights flashed into a tile of photos. All were young, some bald, others with dark hair—terrorists. A few said UNKNOWN. Others had names and biographical data.

"How did you . . . ?" Katie asked, dumbfounded.

"Don't ask."

"I'm asking."

"I hacked into the university system. I got the security tape. I waited until there were only a few cell phones, after they confiscated them from the students. I pushed the facial data into certain databases containing the identities of certain individuals. Then I tracked the numbers and matched them. After that I was able to map out thermal indicators. By cross-referencing the heat being emitted by the various bodies with the other data, I was able to complete a fairly robust tool for constant visualization. We can see what everyone is doing, at all times."

"We need to understand the structure of the building," said Dewey.

"Well, it's architecturally a piece of shit. What the fuck? I thought Columbia was Ivy League?"

Dewey, Katie, and Tacoma looked at Igor.

"Sorry," he said. "I hate bad architecture."

He clicked the remote. The digital outline of the dormitory moved to the basement and then below, to a series of orange and yellow lines that were illuminated in bright white. The screen displayed a chaotic crosshatch of lines in varying directions, sizes, and colors.

"What is it?" asked Dewey.

"It's the underground below the dormitory. Way below. Various sewer and plumbing lines are in white. Water mains are the large orange ones. Electricity and other utility tunnels are green. The big purple lines are subway tunnels. The city belowground is in many ways more highly constructed than aboveground. It's a spiderweb down there."

Dewey studied the screen.

"Interesting."

Igor clicked the remote several times. Most of the lines faded except for a single line that he lit up in bright red.

"You were right, Dewey," said Igor. "There might be something here. This is an old water main I found when I started poking around in the city water department archives. As you can see, it leads directly beneath the dormitory to a utility tunnel. The tunnel leads directly to the basement of the dormitory. The water main connects to that tunnel and should be empty. There's only one problem."

"Only one?"

"We need to get to the water main. I don't know how."

Dewey reached for his cell.

Out on the terrace, Dewey scrolled through his contacts until he came across a long international number with many digits. Dewey dialed and listened to a series of static clicks. Then he heard a ring. The phone rang a half dozen times, then went to voice mail. Dewey hung up and tried again, again getting voice mail. He dialed a third time. After three rings, someone picked up.

"Who the hell is this?" came a Russian accent. Loud music pulsated in the background.

"Dewey."

"Dewey?" said Malnikov. "How are you?"

"I need your help, Alexei."

Alexei Malnikov was the thirty-four-year-old head of the Russian mob. For three years running, Malnikov had occupied a prime spot on the FBI's Most Wanted list.

Malnikov's criminal enterprise now controlled organized crime in Russia, parts of Europe, and the United Kingdom, and was vying for leadership in Tokyo, Shanghai, and several Asian capitals. In the United States, organized crime in most cities was controlled by Malnikov, who built the tightly disciplined, ruthless network after being sent to the United States by his father at age seventeen.

Dewey liked Malnikov. The Russian had helped prevent a nuclear bomb from being detonated in New York City. He was ruthless and sold more heroin than any other criminal enterprise in the world. But he was also a good person.

And he was resourceful. It was a long shot, but the man who controlled organized crime in New York City might know someone with knowledge of the underground.

"Where are you?" asked Malnikov.

"New York City."

"Columbia?"

"Yes."

"Of course. They send you to clean that shit up because they know how incompetent those idiots at the FBI are."

Dewey ignored him.

"You know New York pretty well."

"Are you kidding? Yeah, of course. I lived there for ten years."

"Do you guys ever move product through the underground?"

"I'm hanging up now, Dewey," said Malnikov.

"Why?"

"Are you recording this?"

"No, I'm not recording it, asshole," said Dewey. "Trust me, if I ever want to get you, I won't do it with a fucking cell phone. The dormitory is wired with bombs. The only way in is through the basement. There's an old water main that runs beneath the dorm. From that water main we can climb up a utility tunnel that leads to the basement. The problem is getting to the old water main. We need to follow it in. It's so old it's not on any of the maps and surveys."

Malnikov laughed.

"Forgive me for being so paranoid," said Malnikov. "I do know someone. He grew up with my father. He came to New York when he was sixteen. He worked for the city in the water department. They fired him because he was too old. Now he helps us move certain . . . items into the city. He knows every fucking sewage pipe, air tunnel, and water main in New York City better than I know my own ass."

"Lovely image," said Dewey. "What's his name?"

"He's called *Vodoprovodchik*," said Malnikov. "The Plumber."

Ten minutes later, Igor whistled loudly, calling them all back into the library.

"What is it?" asked Dewey.

Igor was seated at his desk, typing into a computer. Without looking up, he reached to his right and grabbed a small wooden box. He threw it back over his shoulder, saying "Don't drop it" as it sailed through the air. Tacoma caught it. He opened it and removed four individual plastic cases containing small roundish objects the size of Tic Tacs. These were earbuds for communications.

"The battle link platform is done," said Igor. "We now have ubiquitous voice and data inter-connectivity for a safer and better world. By the way, I had to borrow a few things from the Rockwell Corporation."

"Including their advertising copy?" said Dewey.

"Yes, well, that was by far the least of what I borrowed. I'm assuming they won't mind and that if they do, someone will be able to explain to them why we needed it."

"What does 'borrow' mean, Igor?" asked Katie.

"I had to hack into one of their systems and appropriate some functionality," he said, waving his hand through the air, then continuing to type. "The problem, of course, was that we don't need most of their various bells and whistles, just certain algorithms from their TruNet system having to do with signals latency as well as multi-hop technology, which, as you know, we can't achieve without advanced IP waveforms."

"Totally agree," said Tacoma.

"Thank you, Rob." Igor continued, "I had to hack through several Janus crypto engines. I'm glad someone can appreciate how hard this was. Those Rockwell guys," he added, shaking his head, "talk about eating your own dog food, huh?"

Dewey, Tacoma, and Katie were staring at Igor as if he was insane.

"I'm not sure what you just said," said Dewey, "but if you keep talking I'm going to stick a crypto engine up your ass."

"Sorry," said Igor, looking around at their faces. "Basically, our frequencies can't get jammed. We'll be able to communicate and I'll be able to manage your positioning in real time, with no confusion as to location vis-à-vis the terrorists. In addition, if needed, I'll be able to easily integrate into relevant systems, such as Langley or Quantico."

Dewey moved to the plasma screen that showed Carman in a three-dimensional digital form. He stared for several moments at the screen, studying the blue lights that enabled Igor to track the terrorists and differentiate them from the students and parents. There was now one terrorist on the twelfth floor, three on ten, one on eight, one on seven, and one on the first floor. Other than the men on ten, they all moved around constantly.

"Can you tell how they're communicating?"

"Walkie-talkies. They also, obviously, have cell phones."

"Why doesn't the FBI set up a jamming device?"

"How? My guess is, anything the FBI has wouldn't be effective unless they somehow got it to a high floor."

"Can you jam them remotely?" asked Dewey.

"No, but you could bring something in."

"It'll need to be there before we get there."

"They could climb up," said Tacoma. "Won't be easy."

"If a jammer was in place, our stuff would still work, is that what you said?" asked Dewey.

"Yes."

"What about your ability to track them? If we're using some military frequency you stole, we'll be able to circumvent a jamming device, but it'll knock out their cells. We'll be blind. It's a Catch-22."

"Very perceptive, Dewey," said Igor, grinning. "Basically, if I'm tracking their cells and suddenly their cell signals get scrambled, how can I track them? Alternatively, if they don't get jammed and can still communicate, they have tactical strength that could result in your death."

"Exactly."

"And because I don't want anything stuck up my ass, I'm not going to explain what I did. But suffice it to say, I anticipated this conundrum. Get the FBI to put a jammer somewhere high up in or around that building. I won't lose them."

Dewey nodded. He looked at Tacoma.

"Rucks packed?" asked Dewey.

"No. What do we need? Guns, ammo, suppressors?"

"Yeah, climbing equipment too," added Dewey.

Katie studied the digital screen. She looked at Dewey with a slightly concerned look.

"They have seven guys. We have three."

"So?"

"So, we need one more gun."

"We'll be fine," said Dewey.

"We're doing a single-stage, multilevel move," she said. "We need another gun."

"We'll kill the guy on one," said Dewey, "then move in a single wave on different floors. Right now they're on three floors: twelve, ten, eight—"

"And seven," said Katie. "Putting aside the possibility of one of us getting hurt *before* we get

468

there, just look at the schematic. Two of us need to hit ten at the same time. Even if one of us can take three guys, that still leaves a nonacquired target."

"We'll need to move quick," said Dewey.

"Dewey, the building is wired with enough Semtex to take it all down," she said. "This is a suicide bomb. As soon as they know we're there, the one guy who's not targeted is going to set it off. One extra guy gives us tremendous flexibility."

Dewey stared at the screen, nodding, then glanced at his watch, wondering when the next student would be thrown from the building.

"We don't have time," said Dewey calmly. "I'm not going to take some guy off the street we haven't worked with. There are too many things that can go wrong. Now let's finish packing the rucks and get down there."

55

CARMAN HALL
COLUMBIA UNIVERSITY

Sirhan, Tariq, and Ali gathered on the twelfth floor while the other three men kept guard on ten.

In one of the bathrooms, they took turns washing their hands and splashing water on their faces. They dried themselves with paper towels.

In the hallway, they stood, looking in the direction of Mecca, and shut their eyes.

It was time for *Salah*, their daily prayers. Like most Muslims, they prayed five times a day, at specific times. Now it was time for the midday prayer, called the *zuhr*.

The other three had just finished the *zuhr*.

"*Allāhu 'akbar*," Sirhan said, closing his eyes, raising his hands, then bowing. Tariq and Ali repeated the incantation, then all three began a low prayer, the *rakāt*, as they bowed in subjugation.

Ten minutes later, Sirhan walked the entire length of the tenth floor hallway, saying nothing and constantly checking his watch. At precisely 12:25, he entered one of the bedrooms facing campus. Omar was in the room, looking out at the campus with binoculars. Four students stood at the window, shielding Omar from snipers.

Sirhan studied each of the students from behind. A dark-skinned female was closest to the wall. He stepped closer and looked at her face from the side. She was Middle Eastern.

"*Ma hu aismak, fatat latifa?*" asked Sirhan.

What is your name, kind girl?

The girl pretended to not understand.

"What is your name?" he repeated, an edge in his voice.

She started to cry.

"Aimal," she whispered.

"*Hal 'ant Sunni 'aw Shayei?*"

Are you Sunni or Shia?

She was sobbing now.

"Sunni or Shia?" he screamed.

The student next to her on the windowsill grabbed her hand, holding it.

Sirhan looked at his watch: 12:29.

He aimed the rifle at the window and fired. The glass shattered and fell into the open air, a moment later hitting the concrete ten floors below.

He looked at his wrist: 12:30.

"Just so you know, it wouldn't have mattered," whispered Sirhan. He placed his hand against the girl's back, then he pushed her out the window. The soft, high pitch of her sobs was the only noise for several moments until she hit the ground.

56

THE PIERRE HOTEL
FIFTH AVENUE
NEW YORK CITY

Dewey and Tacoma were in a room off the kitchen that had been turned into a weapons room. They were packing rifles, submachine guns, pistols, ammo, and knives.

Katie suddenly screamed from a room down the hall.

Dewey jogged past the library and into the den, followed by Tacoma, then Igor.

A large flat-screen television showed live news coverage of the dormitory. The CNN logo was in the upper left-hand corner. Scrolled across the bottom was a news ticker: CRISIS AT COLUMBIA.

The screen showed a grainy, distant view of the dormitory, focused in on a tenth-floor window.

Katie was alone, watching the TV with a hand across her mouth in silent horror. She had tears in her eyes.

. . . I repeat, the glass was just apparently shot or kicked out of the window you are looking at right now. This is on the tenth floor where the hostages are being held. Please, if there are children in the house . . .

Standing in the window was a female student. It was hard to see the details of her face, but she had long black hair, brown skin, and glasses. She looked Middle Eastern. Her hands were raised and out to the side.

. . . What you're seeing right now is live aerial footage from the CNN news helicopter of what appears to be a Columbia student standing on the tenth floor of the dormitory—Carman Hall— taken over by terrorists less than six hours ago. This is the first sighting of anyone in the building since about an hour ago, when another female student was pushed to her death . . . Oh, my God!

The girl fell from the window, kicking her legs in the air, wrenching her body in a desperate spasm, as if she might somehow fly away. She dropped quickly in a straight line as, offscreen, the voice of a CNN producer could be heard: "Cut the shot!"

She struck the concrete just before the screen went black.

A few moments later, a different view appeared on the screen. It was live footage of the reporter, standing a few blocks away, holding his earpiece to his ear and a microphone to his mouth. He was surrounded by mayhem, as crowds of onlookers tried to push their way into the media area and get a look at live feeds on display. Muted screams and yelling erupted nearby as the footage of the fallen student, and the knowledge of what had happened, spread through the media area and beyond to the crowds of friends, families, and other onlookers.

The reporter's face was red. His eyes revealed panic and emotion; he struggled to cough out words to fill the silence.

. . . I . . . I don't know what to say. Terror has come to our shores . . . My God . . .

Dewey glanced at Katie. She didn't move. Tacoma and Igor were standing just inside the door, both silent.

"We can't wait any longer," said Dewey, looking at all three of them. "We go in now."

57

DAMASCUS, SYRIA

Nazir clutched the remote as he watched, for the third time, footage on Al Jazeera of the girl falling to her death.

He looked at his watch. It was 7:30 in the evening, exactly one hour after the first body Sirhan pushed from the dormitory. It meant Sirhan was now on a specific schedule.

He picked up his cell phone and dialed. After nearly a minute of clicks and beeps, the phone started ringing.

"Good afternoon," came a female voice, "the White House. How may I direct your call?"

"The president's office, please."

"Is he expecting your call?"

"I don't think so."

"I'm afraid the president doesn't accept unsolicited or non-prearranged calls," she said politely. "Is it something I can help you with?"

"Perhaps," said Nazir. "My name is Tristan Nazir. I am the leader of ISIS."

The phone was quiet for several seconds.

"Please hold."

A half minute later, a male voice came on the line.

"I am running your voice through a program to determine if you're who you say you are. Please repeat your name."

"Tristan Nazir."

"What is today's date and time?"

"September fourteen, seven thirty p.m."

"Hold."

A minute later, the phone clicked.

"This is Josh Brubaker. I'm the president's national security advisor. What do you want?"

"You know what I want."

"The weapons shipment. So let's talk about that."

"What is there to talk about?" asked Nazir. "You stopped the boat. Until those weapons are delivered to Syria, one student dies every hour."

"Mr. Nazir," said Brubaker, "if we were going to allow that shipment to go through, we would need guarantees on those students and family members. In other words, we're not going to deliver anything until we understand precisely how the ones you haven't murdered yet get out alive."

"They walk out the front door," said Nazir, "after we have the guns."

"What's to stop you from simply blowing up the building?"

"None of my men want to die. As I see it, the ship arrives, I send word to my men, and the students get released."

"What happens to your men?"

"I assume you arrest them and they go to one of your little torture camps."

"I have a feeling they wouldn't like knowing their leader sold them down the river."

"They volunteered for it, Mr. Brubaker."

"I'll take it to the president," said Brubaker, "but you need to stop throwing students from the building. It's a nonstarter."

"I'm sorry, no," said Nazir. "Every hour, at approximately half past the hour, a student drops. If you try to put up a net or something like that, we will simply shoot them and then throw them. We stop when the weapons arrive and we've been able to inspect the contents."

"That's insane," said Brubaker, barely above a whisper. "You're a—"

"Monster?" interjected Nazir. "Maniac? Barbarian? Yes, all three."

"I was going to say coward," said Brubaker. "That boat is twelve hours out. That's twelve more kids."

"Then I suggest you speak with your president as soon as possible and get the ship moving. We stop executing the students only when the shipment arrives."

58

RIVERSIDE PARK
NEAR NINETY-EIGHTH STREET
NEW YORK CITY

As Tacoma steered Igor's navy blue Range Rover along Riverside Drive, Dewey picked up his cell and hit Speed Dial.

"CENCOM."

"Task Force one six," said Dewey. "Damon Smith. Tell him it's Andreas."

A few moments later, Smith picked up. "Hey, what do you got?"

"We're getting ready to move," said Dewey. "I'll be out of range for I don't know how long. I'll call you when we surface. In the meantime, the operation is going to be run from a remote location. Our eyes and ears is a guy named Igor. To the extent he needs any information, I've given him your number."

"You have a way in?"

"Yes."

"What do you need from me?"

"Have you been able to disrupt their communication?"

"We tried jammers along the base of the building, but we're still picking up spectrum coming off the upper floors. The problem is, the terrorists are too high up. We thought about somehow firing one through an upper-floor window. Problem is, even if we pack it in protective packaging and it still functions, they're just going to throw it back out."

"We need one, Damon," said Dewey. "One that blocks cell and walkie-talkie transmissions. We'll be using Pentagon spectrum. Just make sure your COMMS people don't use a military-grade jammer."

"We'll figure it out."

"Thanks."

"That it?"

Dewey glanced at Katie.

"Actually, no. There's one more thing."

"Whatever you need," said Smith.

"We could use another body," said Dewey. "We need a fourth man."

"I have plenty of agents. I can also send one of the Navy guys upstairs. What's the SPEC?"

"Number one, he needs to be able to climb. We're going to be moving quickly up through the elevator shafts, and whoever it is has to keep up. Ideally, a Ranger."

"White thread?" said Smith.

"Yeah. Winter School."

"What else?"

"He needs to be calm. Someone with combat experience. Also, I'll have in-theater command authority. If it's one of your SWAT leaders, he needs to understand that."

Smith was quiet for several moments.

"Let me find someone. When do you leave?"

"We're leaving now," said Dewey. "I should've called you earlier. If you have someone, get him to Riverside Park. There's a lot beneath the Henry Hudson Parkway at Ninety-ninth Street."

By the time Dewey hung up, Tacoma had parked the Range Rover along Riverside Drive.

It was two o'clock in the afternoon. The sky was cloudless, the temperature in the eighties. Moving now was not ideal; night would be better, but Dewey didn't want to wait.

Always, a thought lurked in the recesses of his mind. A single word, but it kept sounding, like a chant from a distant room.

Daisy.

He saw her eyes looking at him as they stood in the driveway. That moment, just before it happened, and then the moment itself, as he leaned toward her. He remembered the softness of her lips against his. Then came the sight, the memory, of the student falling from the dorm . . .

He pushed it away. He had to.

He pressed his earbud.

"Commo check," he said. "Igor?"

"I'm here."

"Check one," said Katie.

"Two," said Rob.

"You're all coming through loud and clear."

"What about GPS?"

"I have you. Stamford, Connecticut, right?"

"That's not funny, asshole."

"Okay, okay, Jesus. Ninety-eighth and Riverside, right?"

"Yeah," said Tacoma.

Dewey, Tacoma, and Katie climbed from the SUV. From the back, they each lifted duffel bags; Dewey and Tacoma's were filled with weapons and ammo, Katie's with a variety of explosives, thermal optical equipment, and powerful sound equipment for eavesdropping. Most were purposed for close-quarters combat: small, powerful, light, highly lethal. Handguns, submachine guns, and an anti-materiel rifle, capable of firing through concrete.

Dewey removed a canister the size of a tennis ball can from his jacket. This was an incendiary device whose main purpose was to sound loud and discharge high volumes of harmless smoke. He moved the lid of the device a quarter turn, and a small red light flashed. It could now be set off remotely. He placed it on the sidewalk, at the base of a tree.

They walked across Riverside Drive, each scanning the street and sidewalks that bordered the road. Several blocks to the north, flashing lights from police cruisers were visible. The cars were parked across Riverside at 103rd, preventing access.

A faint hum came from helicopters above Columbia, fifteen blocks to the north. Dewey counted five in the air, all in a circle outside a no-fly zone the FBI had imposed on the area.

The sidewalk along the park had a few pedestrians on it, seemingly oblivious of the situation at Columbia and the helicopters overhead. An older woman walking a small dog looked up as Dewey stepped from the street onto the sidewalk. She jerked back, as if in fear, then looked away and kept walking. The neighborhood, the city, was on edge, her reaction the first indication of a general mood of quiet fright that permeated the air.

They walked south for a block, Katie in the lead. They entered Riverside Park at Ninety-seventh Street. A long, gradually sloping set of stairs led into the park. A central paved lane for bikers and pedestrians ran down the center of the park, with built-in benches every hundred feet or so on each side, along with big, pretty, well-manicured trees—elm, apple, dogwood, maple. Sweeping lawns of fresh-cut grass sat on both sides of the park. To the east and the city, the grass swept up toward a denser grove of trees to the stone wall that bordered Riverside Drive in the distance. On the other side of the park, the grass ended at another stone wall. The Hudson River was visible beyond the wall.

There were a few bike riders, joggers, many people out for a walk, a few children playing in the park. Dewey entered first and walked along the center path at a casual pace. Katie and Tacoma waited a minute, then followed, holding hands, pretending to be a couple out for a walk. The duffel bags looked out of place and slightly suspicious, but only an experienced officer would've noticed.

At some point, Dewey looked back to see Katie and Rob, several hundred feet behind him. He nodded almost imperceptibly, then cut left, strolling casually to an empty bench on the Hudson River side of the park. He passed the bench, not looking back, and kept walking toward the far wall of the park. Between the river and the wall was Henry Hudson Parkway. Usually the highway was jammed. It now sat empty, closed to traffic. The park wall dropped forty feet to the ground below. It was an empty lot, strewn with garbage, which ran beneath the highway.

Dewey turned. He scanned the park. A young man, sitting on a bench, was watching him. When he saw Dewey looking at him, he looked back at his book.

Dewey looked right. Katie and Tacoma were now also standing next to the wall, still several hundred feet away. Tacoma faced the wall, where he was hammering something into the mortar as Katie stood in front of him, shielding him from view.

What Dewey worried about most was the unknown. The friend of a reporter who sees them, calls the friend, who then reports it on the news, which the terrorists see, causing them to try to figure out why a group of people are entering an old sewer on the Upper West Side. Low probability, but worth the effort of avoiding.

Unspoken was the real fear: that someone working with, or sentimental to, the jihadists would see them and tip the terrorists off.

Dewey removed a small black device shaped like a pack of cigarettes. He flipped open the top. A red switch was hidden beneath. Then he flipped the switch on the detonator. A second later, a low, loud boom came from Riverside Drive. Every head turned to look. The man on the bench jumped up, trying to get a better view. Smoke filled the air—black and sooty, mixed with red, creating a rapidly growing mushroom cloud that had the appearance of chaos.

Several people, including the man, started running south, away from the explosion.

Dewey removed a small piton and hammer from his coat. He quickly pounded the piton into the wall. He pulled a coil of thick black rope from the bag and pushed it through the piton. He put on a pair of climbing gloves, then strapped the weapons duffel across his back. He tied a knot at one end of the rope, creating a handle.

He glanced at the park. Other than the small, receding figures of people moving away from the smoke, it was empty in both directions.

Sirens pealed from Riverside Drive.

He glanced at Katie, who nodded. Dewey waited a few extra moments, then climbed over the wall, clutching the knot with his right hand as, with his left, he let the rope slide slowly through. The rope went through his left hand, up through the piton, then lengthened in his right hand as he descended. He moved quickly, feet bouncing against the wall of granite. Even through the thick Kevlar-and-steel-mesh-palmed gloves, he could feel the burn of the rope. When he hit the ground, he pulled the rope through the piton up above until it dropped to the ground. He re-coiled it and stuck it back in the duffel, looking right, along the base of the wall. Katie was on the ground, watching Tacoma finish the last few feet of his descent.

The wall loomed overhead. He saw no one. He scanned the abandoned lot beneath the highway. It was empty and lifeless. The tar was cracked, with weeds growing in crooked lines, and garbage, thrown from the park or highway, was strewn about, blown by the wind. At the far side of the lot was a steel fence, which spread all the way from the ground to the lower edge of the overhanging steel rebar of the highway several floors above, preventing access.

"You have company," said Igor over commo. "Two blocks up, other side of the highway."

Dewey walked to Katie and Tacoma just as a black sedan appeared to the north, at a gate in the chain-link fence. The sedan was late model, windows tinted dark. Law enforcement.

"Igor, can you run any diagnostics on that car?" asked Tacoma.

"Not the car itself without knowing the VIN, but I have an algorithm running against FBI, Homeland, and NYPD. It's none of them."

"It's the Plumber," said Dewey.

A short man climbed from the sedan and stepped to a gate in the fence, unlocking the padlock and pulling the gate open. The sedan pulled in, then the man closed the gate and relocked the padlock.

The sedan charged forward, toward them, accelerating.

"He's going pretty fast," said Tacoma quietly. "You sure it's him?"

The sedan barreled closer.

"It's him," said Dewey.

The sedan came within fifty feet, then forty, thirty, not slowing or hesitating. A second later, the sedan jacked abruptly right, brakes screeching, the back tires sweeping over the concrete. It came to a smooth, surgical stop a few feet away.

A moment later, the driver's door opened. A head emerged, followed by a short, stooped man.

He was, at most, five feet tall. He was bald, with a scar along his forehead that looked like the letter *L*. His skin was pale and colorless, almost gray. His ears stuck out.

A smile creased his lips, revealing a mouth half-filled with brown teeth.

He had a high-pitched voice.

"My name is Vladimir Leonid Roestelkolnov. But you may call me the Plumber."

59

FBI TASK FORCE 16
JOHN JAY HALL
COLUMBIA UNIVERSITY

Smith looked at Dave McNaughton.

"We need to get a cell jammer up high," said Smith.

McNaughton nodded. "I can get one on the side of the building," he said. "Front or back's gonna be tough."

"Why?"

"Because my climber will get shot."

"It needs to be on one of the faces of the building," said Smith. "As close to a window as we can. The stairwells have a fire barrier. Just slapping it on the end of the dorm won't work."

"Not that simple. We can't just shoot an anchor up to the roof and hitch up. Way too risky with those bombs. And I sure as shit don't trust any suction device, at least none I've seen, and certainly not on that brick."

"Keep it simple. Pitons or bolts and a drill with masonry bits, or a hammer," said Smith. "Have someone belay from the ground. Lead up the side then move around when he gets to ten, snipers at the ready. He won't be exposed for more than a minute or two."

"If someone starts drilling or hammering into that brick, it'll alert them," said McNaughton.

"Use some sort of manual screw kit. Set the anchors, let someone belay your lead guy from below."

McNaughton nodded, thinking.

"I'll get one of my climbers moving. How much time do I have?"

Smith checked his watch, a distracted look on his face.

"Just figure it out. Make sure you coordinate with the snipers. Also, tell Ray not to use a military-grade device."

McNaughton had worked with Smith now for fourteen years. McNaughton, an ex-Marine, was all business. He was born into a military family and whether it was the FBI or the Marines, all he cared about was managing assaults and other military-style operations. Still, he sensed something.

"You okay, Damon?" he asked.

Smith looked at him.

"There's something else," said Smith. "I need you to do something."

McNaughton was silent.

"Andreas needs another man," said Smith.

"You want me to go?" asked McNaughton. "I'll do whatever is necessary, you know that."

"No, these guys need you a lot more than they need me. I'm going to go. I need you to take over tactical command."

60

RIVERSIDE PARK
NEW YORK CITY

The Plumber glanced at Dewey, saying nothing, then looked at Tacoma. When he noticed Katie, his eyes seemed to open an extra half inch.

Dewey stepped forward and extended his hand. "I'm Dewey."

The Plumber nodded enthusiastically, saying nothing.

Tacoma stepped forward and shook his hand.

The Plumber looked straight ahead at Katie. His slightly mischievous expression flashed into a full-on smile as he took in her tanned, freckled, beautiful face. His eyes scanned down her body, the grin not going away at any point.

Katie glanced at Dewey, one eyebrow raised.

They trailed the Plumber along the granite wall for several minutes, then cut right and moved to a massive concrete abutment beneath the Henry Hudson Parkway. The Plumber stopped before a pile of empty cans and broken glass.

"*Chertovy panki,*" he muttered to himself as he kicked the garbage aside.

Beneath was a rusted manhole cover. The Plumber knelt, removing a small tool from his coat that resembled a screwdriver with a hook on the end. He stuck it near the edge of the manhole and lifted the cover. Dewey leaned forward and helped pull it to the side.

Beneath was total darkness. The tunnel dropped into a black void.

Suddenly, the sound of an approaching helicopter made all of them look up to the sky. The all-black Bell 206L4 LongRanger IV dropped recklessly from above. There was no place to land. The chopper stopped a hundred feet up and hovered, its rotors slashing the air in a furious roar of sound and wind. A coil of rope flew from the open back compartment, followed by a figure clad in tactical gear, who leapt out and rappelled to the ground a few feet from them.

It was Damon Smith.

"You still need an extra hand?"

Dewey nodded. "Yeah."

Dewey's eye caught Smith's weapons vest. A small old Ranger tab was visible, stitched to the vest with white thread, indicating that Smith had graduated from Ranger School during winter.

Dewey grinned. "I didn't know."

"You were in my class," said Smith.

"That was a fun time," said Dewey. "Remember Captain Hardy?"

"Lucifer?" said Smith, laughing. "I can't tell you the number of times I've thought about sending a few of my guys to his house."

Dewey laughed, along with Smith. Then he looked at him with a more serious expression.

"Let's go. Katie, this is Damon Smith."

"Hi," said Katie.

"Who's that?" asked Smith, looking at the short man who was waiting near the tunnel.

"The Plumber."

Katie removed four Petzl headlamps from her pack, handing them around. She offered one to the Plumber, but he shook his head.

"We go," said the Plumber. "Last one, move back," he added, pointing to the manhole cover.

As the Plumber started to climb down into the tunnel, a pair of medium-size rats scurried into a pile of garbage a few feet away. A horrified look came over Katie's face. She looked at the Plumber.

"Are there rats in there?" she said.

"Are there rats?" said the Plumber, disappearing into the darkness. "Are you kidding? They have their own government. Just ignore them."

Tacoma followed the Plumber.

"You like dogs?" asked Dewey.

"Sure," Katie said.

"Think of them as little dogs. That's how big they get."

Katie looked as if she might throw up.

Dewey tapped his ear.

"Igor, we're going in," he said.

"You'll be dark in there," said Igor. "No signal."

Dewey waved Katie to the tunnel. Smith followed her down.

"I'll come back on when we're in the building."

"Got it. I'll be waiting."

"As soon as we get there, I want to move."

"I'll be ready, Dewey."

Dewey removed his earbud and put it in a watertight ziplock bag. He pulled the headlamp over his head, turned it on, climbed into the tunnel, and dragged the manhole cover back until it dropped with a loud clank above his head, sealing off the tunnel.

Dewey glanced down. The three headlamps below trailed off into oblivion. Eerie shadows played against the blackness.

"Let's go," he whispered to no one.

61

CARMAN HALL
COLUMBIA UNIVERSITY

Sirhan considered the situation as he paced down the twelfth-floor hallway, empty now.

The dormitory was secure—as secure as it could be.

The entrance was sealed off behind a steel wall—ironic, for it had been built for the opposite purpose: to keep the bad guys on the outside and the students safe. Now it was a barrier that prevented anything other than a blunt-force intrusion, such as a tank or shoulder-fired missile, from penetrating the hostage zone. So far, the FBI had been unwilling to use either, perhaps fearing what would happen if they forced the terrorists into a corner. Even if they did get through, the elevators were trashed and the stairs were impassable. If they attempted it, by the time they figured out how to disarm or get around the IEDs, every student and parent in the dormitory would be dead.

The roof was wired with explosives that would detonate if anyone attempted to land. Even a single commando dropped from a chopper would be unable to penetrate the web of thin wire. If any part of the web broke, all six of the high-powered Semtex-laden IEDs would drop to the ground and detonate. Anything above the roof would be immolated; below, several floors would be destroyed and, with them, hundreds of the hostages.

The basement was sealed off by a locked, triple-bolted fire door with a massive block of Semtex attached to it. It was the largest IED the terrorists had brought. If any law enforcement officer attempted to open the door, the bomb would drop to the ground and explode. Even if the FBI employed robotic bomb removal technology, the IED would potentially set off other IEDs in the dorm, ultimately taking down most if not all of the structure. In addition, just behind the thick steel door was the line of four students, chained together. Any attempt to blow the door in would kill them all, either from the detonation or by pushing them back against the tight chains around their necks, choking them. Granted, it was their weakest link, but if they were willing to sacrifice the four hostages in the basement, the FBI would have to face the stairs.

Sirhan had turned two rooms on the twelfth floor into an ad hoc operations center. A table sat in the middle of each room. The rooms were across the hall from each other. Sirhan wanted to keep an eye on both sides of the building.

On one of the walls, he'd drawn a detailed

elevation plan, showing each floor, highlighting key access points, as well as showing where students were. He also made small X marks on the sixth floor, where Fahd was killed, and on the third floor, where Sirhan believed Ramzee lay dead.

They had passed the period of highest vulnerability. They now had clear strategic advantage. It would be extremely difficult for the Americans to dislodge them now, unless they were willing to lose hundreds of students and parents. Still, the loss of Fahd and Ramzee gnawed at him. It made him angry.

He checked his watch: 1:07. Twenty-three minutes until the next execution.

He went to one of the bathrooms and looked around. There was something strangely peaceful about being alone on the floor of the dormitory. The bathroom was empty and clean. The shower reminded him of home, back in Karachi, with the blue tiles. He looked in the mirror, then heard a faint sound. Or perhaps he felt it.

Sirhan cued the mike on his walkie-talkie. All he heard was silence.

"Tariq," he said. "Meuse. Anyone?"

There was no response.

He turned on his cell and tried to call Tariq's cell. The call did not go out. At the top of the phone screen, he saw NO SIGNAL.

To the south, on the far side of the building, across the hall. Yes, he felt it.

Sirhan threw the bathroom door aside and charged through the room, grabbing his AK-47 from the ground, in stride, then sprinting across the hall. He came at the window from the right, out of the sight line of snipers. He was shielded by the wall next to the window.

He swept the rifle in front of him, raised it, then skulked toward the window.

His eyes scanned the side of the brick wall, looking for what he thought he'd heard. He saw nothing. The walls to the left and above were empty. He leaned toward the glass, despite the risk, and looked down. He didn't see a thing. Sirhan dropped to his knees and crawled below the windows. Then he stood and looked to the right, to the one wall he couldn't see from the other angles. He jerked backward.

They're here.

A man was tight to the building, held there by a rope, moving sideways, gloved hands on brick, clutched against the building, leaning as close as a spider. Commando: black-clad, helmeted, carbine strapped across his back. He was holding a rectangular plastic box to the side of the building, a few feet from the window, affixing it somehow.

How long has he been here? Where did he come from?

It didn't matter. What mattered was not letting him get any nearer to the window.

Sirhan pressed the mike button on his walkie-talkie.

"We have a visitor," he said, swinging his rifle around.

Then he realized: the commando had attached a jamming device to the side of the building. He hurled the walkie-talkie against the wall, where it smashed into pieces.

Sirhan scanned the roofs of a row of low brownstones across 114th Street. He looked for snipers. He saw one—in the window of one of the houses. The only thing visible was the muzzle, its metal refracting light in the dark rectangle of the window. It was targeted below the commando.

Sirhan opened the window. There he was. A black swatch of material that momentarily blocked the light. A flash of dark. It was the top of his helmeted head.

Slowly, Sirhan switched hands, taking the rifle into his left hand and holding the stock with his right, positioning the weapon. He eased the tip of the gun into the open window, aiming along the plane of the building. Sirhan put his right index finger on the trigger. He glanced one last time at the window where the sniper was. Then he pulled back on the trigger. A staccato of weapon fire rattled the air as a burst of slugs sprayed out, shattering glass—he'd aimed too close to the side of the building—then the air, missing the climber, who lurched sideways, toward the window. Sirhan fired again. This time the hail of bullets ripped the man's legs, then up, across his chest, then his neck. Blood sprayed out into the air along with a low, painful groan. The commando's flak jacket had stopped some of the slugs, but not all. He was dead. The man slumped; tethered by his climbing rope, dangling upside down from the side of the building like a Christmas ornament.

Sirhan dived to the floor just as a *thwack* echoed from across the way. The window above him shattered and a dull thud came from the wall. Broken glass fell to the sill and across his back. As he'd expected, the sniper had found him, but not in time.

Another slug, then a hail of rifle fire rained across the destroyed windows as gunmen searched in vain for Sirhan. The gunfire lasted a dozen seconds, then stopped. Still, he waited another minute, catching his breath, feeling the warmth of adrenaline pumping into his veins.

Carefully, he crawled out of the room, dragging his gun. In the hall, he stood and brushed off the glass. He sprinted to the room closest to the dead commando. He slunk along the wall, weapon raised, and spied out the window. The commando was directly in front of him. Blood was dripping from his boots, the wounds drenching his clothing and gear.

Sirhan quickly inspected the side of the building. He couldn't see any other agents trying to scale the walls. He ran out of the room, down the empty hall, and descended the stairs to the tenth floor. He saw Meuse, guarding the door, rifle in hand. Sirhan stepped past him, a look of fury in his eyes.

He checked his watch: 1:24.

The floor was crowded with hostages.

Sirhan had a wild look, fury at how close they'd gotten.

How sloppy his men were.

With the AK-47 raised, he pushed his way past silent, terrified students and parents, seated along the walls, many crying, holding hands, only a few daring to even look up at him. He entered the first dorm room, just below where the dead agent now dangled in the open air.

The room was crowded, hot, and fetid with sweat. Everyone was seated on the floor. Families were grouped together, cowering in fear.

Standing in the windows, spread like shields across them, were four students.

Sirhan walked quickly to the window. He leaned forward—between a student's legs—and looked right. The dead agent was still hanging just a few feet away.

He looked to the room. In the far corner, a male student was seated, arms crossed, eyes down. He wore a blue shirt and brightly colored plaid shorts. He was white, with dirty-blond hair.

Sirhan stared at the student.

"You," he said, hatred in his voice.

The boy kept staring at the ground, pretending not to hear him.

Sirhan walked over and kicked him in the ribs. The boy grunted in pain.

"Stand up!"

The student looked desperately around the room, as if searching for help, but the others avoided his look.

Sirhan dragged him along the floor to the windows.

Sirhan aimed his rifle at one of the students already positioned in the window, a black male. He fired—a fusillade of slugs—which pulverized the student. The boy was kicked by the bullets. He tumbled out the window and disappeared.

"Get up!" shouted Sirhan to the student in the plaid shorts.

"Fuck you."

Sirhan stared at the boy. Then, without looking, he turned the rifle to the right and fired indiscriminately along the wall. Screams and pained cries created a cacophony as bullets hit several people.

"Get up," Sirhan said quietly, "or I will kill every other person in this room, and then you."

The student climbed to the windowsill, inches from the precipice. The wind blew his long hair back from his face.

Sirhan reached to his waist and pulled out a long fixed-blade combat knife.

"Here," he said to the boy in heavily accented English. "Cut him down."

He handed him the knife.

The boy's trembling hand reached out and took the knife. He turned back toward the window. He started to reach for the rope, then abruptly pivoted, slashing the blade down toward Sirhan.

It was a ferocious swing—quick, unexpected, deadly. The blade just missed the side of Sirhan's skull.

But Sirhan had anticipated it.

He ducked at the same moment he caught the boy's forearm, stopping the lethal swing.

"You lifted your leg. I knew you were coming."

He grabbed the blade from his hand. He turned, took a step toward a middle-aged woman seated with her son on the floor, then nonchalantly stabbed the woman in the neck. Blood spilled out as her son—and several others—screamed. Sirhan pulled the blade out and handed it back to the white student.

"Do you think you could cut him down now?" Sirhan asked.

The student faced the open air. He reached to his right and put the blade against the rope holding the dead commando. He sawed back and forth several times.

Sirhan held the back of his shirt as his eyes pored over the roofline of the brownstones across from the dormitory. He saw another sniper, this time more clearly. His head and upper body were exposed; the muzzle of the rifle was trained at the room. Sirhan put the muzzle of his rifle next to the boy's thigh as he continued to cut. He aimed at the sniper, protected by the boy, then fired. A slug slammed into the sniper's head, kicking him backward. Dust and mortar rose from the building.

The rope ripped and the dead agent dropped. A low thud could be heard as he hit the pavement ten floors below.

Sirhan grabbed the hilt of the knife from the boy's hand. Then he gave him a slight push. He fell from the open window, silent as he dropped to his death.

He glanced at his wrist: 1:32.

62

SOMEWHERE BENEATH NINETY-FOURTH STREET AND BROADWAY NEW YORK CITY

The descent was slow and difficult, the concrete seemed to grow tighter and tighter. The air was wet, clammy, and permeated with a dank, moldy odor. A steel ladder ran down one side, with thin rungs dripping with condensation.

Looking down, Dewey could see Katie far below, the top of her blond hair and her Petzl shining up, illuminating the aging concrete.

They climbed down for twenty minutes. Dewey counted 340 rungs by the time his foot hit hard ground. He looked around. The space was no bigger than a bathroom stall. Katie and Rob were pressed against one wall. The Plumber was crouching, looking at a hand-drawn piece of paper with his flashlight. Smith was next to him, watching over his shoulder.

Dewey looked at Katie.

I hate you, she mouthed.

Tacoma was smiling.

After more than a minute, the Plumber looked up. "Let's keep going."

"Are we almost there?" asked Katie.

The Plumber shook his head.

"No, I'm afraid not. It's a little bit of a maze. In order to get from point A to point B we first have to go to point Z."

A low vibration arose from the ground, becoming more intense, though there was no sound, only the feeling of the earth moving. It became violent, knocking everyone.

"What the hell was that?" asked Tacoma.

"To be honest, I don't know," said the Plumber. "It happens."

The Plumber aimed his flashlight at the ground.

Dewey looked at Katie.

It happens? she mouthed, shaking her head, incredulous and slightly indignant.

The Plumber reached down and lifted a steel loop, pulling aside a square piece of steel. He aimed the flashlight into the dark. He stared down for several moments, then looked at Smith, Dewey, Tacoma, and Katie. He had a morose look on his face.

"I haven't been in here for many years," he said. "That being said, I don't think I will ever forget it. The tunnel goes down at a forty-five-degree angle for approximately fifty feet, then sideways."

"Forty-five degrees?" said Tacoma. "If you fall at that angle for fifty feet you'll break your neck."

The Plumber grinned, flashing his teeth.

"That won't be a problem, my friend. It's a very tight space."

"How tight?"

"Tighter than when you came out of your mother. You'll need to crawl, drag the bags." He studied Dewey. "You're going to be *very* tight. Very tight indeed. Maybe too tight."

"Too tight?" asked Katie.

"Unless I'm mistaken, you're too big," he said to Dewey. "You're going to get stuck."

"I'll be fine. We need to move."

"After the first part, the tunnel bends into a straight line. The bend is the tightest part of the tunnel." He looked at Dewey again. "It is extremely tight. After that, another thirty or forty

503

feet, then we'll be at the end. That's the old water main."

The Plumber looked into the tunnel and climbed in headfirst. He soon disappeared.

"You're next," said Dewey to Katie.

"Why me?"

"If I get stuck, would you rather be behind me or ahead of me?"

"Good point."

Dewey pointed at the opening.

Katie started to climb in, then turned.

"On a serious note, what if you do get stuck?"

"I won't. Now get moving."

Katie plunged in, disappearing.

"I'll go next," said Tacoma, "then Dewey. I'll go feetfirst, in case I need to pull you. Damon can push from behind."

Tacoma threw the weapons ruck into the darkness and slipped down into the tunnel. Dewey followed, headfirst, fastening the weapons bag to his ankle so that he could pull it with his legs. Smith lifted it and tossed it in after Dewey.

Within only a few feet, Dewey knew the tunnel was going to be a problem. Seemingly every inch of his upper body was touching the cold concrete. It was difficult to even get a full breath of air without pressing hard into the tunnel wall.

"Pull the bag out," said Dewey, calling to Smith, behind him.

He could barely breathe.

"Why?"

"Just do it."

A minute later, after Smith had backed out of the tunnel, Dewey felt a tug at his ankle as Smith pulled up on the weapons duffel. Dewey pushed with his hands, using all his strength, as Smith tugged mightily. After several minutes, he felt the relatively fresher air of the room. He climbed out.

"Is it that tight?"

"Yeah."

Dewey pulled off his coat, shirt, pants, shoes, and socks. He was standing in skintight red sports briefs. He stuffed everything into the bag.

"You go first," said Dewey. "Take the bag."

Smith looked at Dewey, then pointed at the large scar on his shoulder.

"What's that from?"

"Kalashnikov," said Dewey. "Why don't you go before me."

"What if I need to push?"

Dewey shook his head.

"I'm not going to get stuck. If I do, eventually I'll be able to get out. You three can still run the assault. Katie knows what to do. She ran Special Operations Group for five years. Rob's also good to go. Best gunman I've ever met. Commo will link you guys into Igor, who's managing the protocols. You'll be fine."

Smith nodded and climbed into the tunnel. Dewey followed.

With no clothing except his briefs, the walls scraped his skin mercilessly. He held both arms above his head, using his fingertips to nudge his body on, synchronizing each pull with his fingers with a push from his toes. But the tunnel held him in its grip, and he had to fight for every inch. By removing everything, he'd reduced his profile a little. He felt the difference, but barely. He felt as if he was buried under tremendous weight. He could not take in a full breath of air; there simply wasn't enough room for his lungs to fully expand. At some point, his back scraped across a sharp, jagged object, like a rusty screw. There was nothing he could do. He pulled himself over it, as it ripped into his back and scraped down until finally he passed it by.

Dewey reminded himself why he was there. By focusing on the goal, on the dormitory, on Daisy, he was able to occupy his mind long enough to ignore the stale air, the cold walls, and the paranoia of thinking the tunnel was growing thinner, tighter, and that there would be no way ever to get him out if he didn't make it through.

Then his fingers hit a wall. His eyes had been shut and he opened them. He looked ahead.

"No," he said aloud.

He saw the end of the tunnel, and then, to the right, a round opening. It was a little bigger, Dewey guessed, than a basketball.

"There's no fucking way."

Dewey closed his eyes and tried to calm down. Then he looked up and pushed himself toward the hole. He inserted his hands, then his head, and shimmied in. With every inch, it felt as if a vise was tightening around his head. His shoulders would never make it. Painfully, he backed out, using his right hand in front of him and his left down by his side. He tried to relax so that he could depress his lungs as much as possible.

A thought flashed in Dewey's mind. What if he really *couldn't* get through? There was no way on earth he could go back up through the tunnel, backward. Even with the downhill slope, he'd barely made it. Uphill would be next to impossible.

He pushed against the sides of the tunnel wall with his feet as hard as he could while, with his hands out in front of him, he tried to pull himself through. His shoulders became tighter and tighter against his head as he continued to push with his feet, until he felt he might break his skull open. He struggled to catch his breath. He couldn't make it through—and now he was stuck. He shut his eyes, trying to relax. For the first time, he felt like he might suffocate. He tried to inch his way backward to the comparatively wider part of the tunnel before the turn. He couldn't move.

"Oh, God," he said.

"Dewey!" The distant voice of Katie at the end of the tunnel.

His heart racing.

Panic.

"Yeah."

"Are you at the turn?"

Dewey could barely breathe. He imagined this was what it felt like to drown, in the moments just before unconsciousness, knowing what was about to come.

He closed his eyes. Then he blacked out.

He heard yelling, at the edge of consciousness, coming from somewhere, like in a dream or being underwater. He awoke to the feeling of someone touching him, pulling at his arm. He looked up. It was Katie. Her mouth was moving, and for a brief few seconds he couldn't hear her; then he could, and she was yelling.

"Wake up, Dewey."

She was just inches from him. She was holding a rope in one hand and a green plastic bottle in the other. When she saw his face, her mouth opened in shock.

"You're turning blue."

"I can't breathe."

"Oh, Dewey."

She reached out and gently took his hand. She rubbed it, trying to calm him down.

"Sorry," he whispered.

"Are you kidding?" said Katie, her face smudged in dirt. "Best fun I've had in years."

"Promise me something."

"No."

"What?"

"No, I won't promise you something. I know what you're gonna say."

"Which is?"

"'If I can't get through, shoot me.' Am I right?"

"No," said Dewey. "Have Rob shoot me."

Katie took the end of the rope and moved it toward Dewey's hands.

"We're going to get you through."

Katie wrapped the rope around both of Dewey's wrists. She tied a series of knots. Then she opened the plastic bottle and poured its contents on the concrete, splashing it around. It was dark black and thick—oil. She dipped her hand in it and reached out, rubbing Dewey's upper arms and any other part of him she could reach.

"Oil?" he asked.

"It was the Plumber's idea."

"It's a good idea."

"Relax," said Katie. "Try to relax. I'm going back out. Then we'll pull."

"Katie?"

"Yeah."

"Thanks."

"You're welcome."

Several minutes later, Dewey felt pressure on his wrists, then the rope tightened.

"Dewey," yelled Tacoma, "here we go."

The rope went tighter. He clutched it as they pulled, trying to squirm. For half a minute, they pulled. His arms felt like they might rip off at the shoulders. Dewey made a low, guttural groan. The pressure ceased for a few moments, then started again. He felt his shoulders move, no more than an inch, then another. Then his shoulders reached the part of the tunnel that Katie had covered in oil. Slowly, Smith, Tacoma, Katie, and the Plumber pulled Dewey through. It took them twenty minutes to get through the final feet.

Dewey's hands emerged first, covered in oil, then his arms, and finally his head. He was filthy, most of his face wet black. He panted in rapid, desperate gasps.

Katie was in front, climbing gloves on. Tacoma was behind her. Smith had the back of the rope. The Plumber was seated on the ground, studying a diagram. All of them were filthy, but compared to Dewey they looked clean.

Dewey climbed out of the opening, his body mostly covered in oil. He found his duffel and pulled his pants back on, not bothering to wipe off the oil; it would've been pointless. Then his socks and shoes.

Dewey reached around to the cut at his back and touched it gingerly. He looked at his fingers. Intermingled with oil was blood. He couldn't tell if he would need stitches, but it didn't matter now. That was a question for later. He pulled on his shirt.

The Plumber held a portable lantern, dimly lighting the old water main. It was massive; concrete, fourteen feet high, large structural cracks and hunks of concrete dangling in places. A small pool of stagnant water covered the floor. There were rats, hundreds of them, on either side, remaining away from the group, but visible, scurrying around in the water like fish.

Dewey wiped his face and looked at Smith, who couldn't hide his shit-eating grin at the sight of Dewey, head to toe in oil.

"Tell me we're close," said Dewey, glancing at the Plumber, who looked up from a piece of paper—a copy of an old map—that he was studying.

"We're close," he said.

"Why do you look worried?" said Dewey.

"There is a small problem," said the Plumber, sweeping his eyes across their faces.

63

CARMAN HALL
COLUMBIA UNIVERSITY

Sirhan was on the twelfth floor, standing just inside one of the bedrooms, the campus visible in the distance. He powered up his cell phone.

He remembered Nazir's words as he explained the operation to him. It had been two years now. *"They will shut off all your communications devices. But you already know what to do. Every hour, a student must die, until they are all dead, or you are dead. There is nothing I can tell you, Sirhan, that you don't already know. In the moments just before victory, fear, intimidation, violence, brutality must be doubled, tripled, quadrupled. It is not because you are evil. It is because this is how countries are born."*

Munich.

As he waited, he looked around. He saw a menu for a Chinese restaurant. He dialed the number for the restaurant and hit Send. He waited for more than a minute, but the call didn't go through. He wasn't surprised, and he shouldn't have been angry, but he hurled the phone at the wall, smashing it to pieces.

• • •

Daisy was asleep when the gunman entered the room. She didn't mean to fall asleep, but it happened. What awoke her was Andy, stiffening. Daisy glanced at her. Andy was staring at the terrorist.

"Stop staring," she whispered, elbowing her.

But the gunman had already noticed. He stopped his perfunctory scan of the dorm room and stepped toward Andy. He aimed the rifle at her.

He was tall, with black hair that looked wet with sweat or because he hadn't washed. He looked like anyone. In a different shirt and pants, he could've been a student.

"Do as he says," whispered Daisy.

The terrorist leaned forward and grabbed Andy by the hair. He yanked it sideways and she screamed. He lifted her up, dragging her from the wall.

Daisy lurched for his leg. "No!" she pleaded.

But the gunman held her.

Andy was screaming.

Daisy stood up. She followed the gunman. Near the window, she pushed herself between the terrorist and Andy.

"Take me," she said.

The gunman ignored her as he continued dragging Andy, who was hysterical now.

Daisy wrapped her arms around the terrorist's neck, trying to stop him.

"Take me!"

64

"What do you mean, 'problem'?" asked Dewey.

"Not everything is easy, you know. There was bound to be at least one problem."

"So crawling through a fucking hole that's tighter than a nun's ass wasn't a problem?"

"That was a minor inconvenience," said the Plumber. "This is slightly bigger. In any event, we don't reach it until we're closer to the building. We need to move."

They followed the Plumber down the tunnel. They moved at a fast clip, jogging through the pool of foul-smelling water, sloshing fetid, muddy, rat-infested sludge as they pushed on. In places, the filthy water came all the way up to their thighs.

Everyone except the Plumber had on a head-lamp. The Plumber gripped the portable lantern. Shadowy silhouettes danced along the walls as they moved. After twenty minutes, the Plumber stopped and held up his lamp. A few feet ahead, the tunnel stopped at a large steel door. It looked like a bank vault, covered in rust, with a round wheel for opening it.

The Plumber removed a stethoscope, which had

been wrapped around his neck and tucked inside his shirt. He stepped to the steel door and listened.

"Just as I thought," he said.

"Where are we?" asked Dewey.

"Directly beneath the building."

"So what's the problem?"

"When they built the dormitory, they upgraded the university's electrical grid, how they connect and what they connect to. In order to do that, they also needed a tunnel for maintenance. A way for the workers to move up and down as they constructed the new infrastructure—cables, circuitry, diagnostic equipment, redundancies, et cetera. That tunnel provided access to the smaller electrical tunnel. The workers could work on the wiring through side hatches. That tunnel is right behind that steel door. It leads up into the basement of the building. It's big, with ladders on both sides, and, I'm guessing, still has some lights that work."

"Sounds perfect. What's the problem?"

"The problem is, access to that tunnel is on the other side of the door."

Dewey stepped toward the steel latch. He put both hands on the wheel and started to turn.

"I wouldn't do that."

"Why not?"

"It's filled with water. That's why there's a big steel door there. It's why there's a little water in here. It leaks through."

"So we get a little wet."

"It's a lot of water."

"How much?"

"At any one time, we're talking about several *thousand* tons of pressure," said the Plumber. "Imagine being hit by a tidal wave, then multiply that by about a hundred. Like a freight train made of water."

Dewey stared daggers at the Plumber.

"So why the fuck did we bother going through all this?" he asked. "What's the point? You said we could get into the building."

"Oh, we can," said the Plumber. "You see, the tunnel on the other side of the door is what we call a switch pipe. It's one of about twenty places where the water department alternates among the reservoirs that feed into the city's water supply. It's automated. Like clockwork. At precisely fifteen minutes after the hour, one supply main gets shut off and the other gets turned on. During the switchover, the pipe is empty. That's when we can open the door, go to the worker tunnel, and climb up without getting killed."

Dewey looked at his watch. It was ten after four.

"How much time do we have?" asked Smith.

"To open the door, move through, close the door, go about ten feet, open the hatch to the worker tunnel, climb up, then shut the hatch behind us," said the Plumber, "we have exactly one minute."

"One min—" Tacoma started, eyes bulging, incredulous.

Dewey glanced again at his watch.

"What time do you have?" he asked the Plumber.

"Four thirteen."

"How close is that to the clock the water department is on?"

"Down to the second."

Dewey tightened the weapons ruck on his back and stepped to the steel hatch. He gripped the wheel and turned to Smith, Katie, and Tacoma.

"I'm going. If you don't want to, I understand. You need to decide on your own. But it needs to happen right now."

"I'm in," said Katie.

Smith and Tacoma nodded without saying anything.

"You stay here and close the door after we're through," Dewey told the Plumber. "That'll buy us a few seconds."

"I want to help," said the Plumber, though a nervous grin belied his words.

"You already have. But unless you have close-quarters combat experience, you'll get in the way."

The Plumber looked relieved. He nodded and looked at his watch.

"You have fifteen seconds."

Dewey looked at Tacoma, who was tightening his duffel to his back.

"I'll open this door. You go first. Get the hatch open—"

"Ten seconds," said the Plumber, who moved to the side of the door and listened through his stethoscope.

". . . and climb like a motherfucker," continued Dewey. "Katie, you go next—"

"Five."

". . . then you, Damon."

"Three, two, one," barked the Plumber. *"Go!"*

Dewey tugged with all his might on the wheel that secured the door, but it didn't move. Smith joined him, then Tacoma. A high-pitched squeaking noise followed a few seconds later. The wheel moved imperceptibly.

"You need to hurry!"

The three men struggled harder. The squeaking grew louder and steadier.

"You only have forty-five seconds," said the Plumber. "Forty. *Wait until next hour!* If the hatch door doesn't open—"

Dewey ignored him, and like peer pressure on the playground, his continued struggle with the door made Tacoma and Smith continue turning. Suddenly, the wheel turned more quickly, then spun. The steel hatch burst open. A small wave of water followed, waist high, which splashed across the five as the door opened fully.

"Thirty seconds," screamed the Plumber as Tacoma charged through the water and into the tunnel. "I'll keep the door open until ten seconds. You must hurry!"

Katie followed, then Smith, then Dewey.

"Twenty-five seconds," said the Plumber. *"Hurry!"*

Tacoma searched the ceiling of the tunnel with his headlamp, trying to find the hatch.

"To the left!" yelled the Plumber *"Lower!* You have twenty seconds! *Come back! You'll never make it!"*

Tacoma searched desperately, scanning the ceiling.

"Lower!"

He finally found the hatch; it was at ten o'clock, a round section of the tunnel with a smaller latch, which also opened and closed with a wheel.

"That's it! Turn it! Quickly! You only have ten—"

Dewey turned, watching as the big steel door closed.

"Hurry, Rob!" said Katie.

Tacoma, grunting loudly, turned the hatch wheel.

Then they heard it—in unison, all four heads turned: a low rumble echoed from somewhere up the tunnel.

"Oh, my God!" screamed Katie.

The rumble grew louder. A horrifying sound, like thunder, and the ground shook beneath them.

Tacoma loosened the wheel, spun it, pushed up

the hatch, and leapt up into the open compartment. Katie jumped immediately after him as the echo of water—massive amounts of water—grew louder and more ominous, like the seconds after lightning strikes and the explosion of thunder is about to occur. A drumroll with deathly power.

The ground kicked and thrashed violently.

Smith and Dewey looked down the tunnel as the first wave of water splashed a dozen feet away. Smith pulled himself up just as the front wave of the water barreled down the tunnel at Dewey. It was a black wall, moving fast, the water level rising. Just as Smith climbed through the hatch, the front part of the wave hit Dewey. The pressure struck his legs first, like being tackled. He leaned forward, arms reaching out to the hatch. Across the knees was where the first crest hit, then the torso, and soon he felt himself being thrown backward, down the tunnel, as the water hit his head . . .

Something prevented him from being thrown back. Above him, he saw only darkness and the blurry yellow of halogen. Hands gripped his wrists—strong hands, like vises—and then his feet left the ground and he was being pulled. His head suddenly breached the water; he was inside the hatch. Above, Katie was looking down from higher in the tunnel. Tacoma was standing, legs spread across the tunnel, feet on steel rungs, and in his arms were Smith's legs from the knees down. Smith was upside down, and Tacoma was clutching him at the knees so he could dangle down into the oncoming deluge and grab hold of Dewey.

Dewey coughed water, then registered Smith, directly in front of his face, still holding his wrists, panting, his face beet red and drenched.

"Grab the ladder!" Smith yelled.

Dewey reached for the wall, feeling for the steel as rushing water tried to yank him back down into the main. He climbed onto the ladder. Smith pushed the hatch down and twisted it shut. Tacoma lowered him slowly to the ground.

All four remained silent for almost a minute, Dewey and Smith trying to catch their breath.

It was Katie who broke the silence, in between rushed gasps for air. She looked at Dewey in the light from her Petzl, then smiled. "You okay?" she asked.

Dewey started coughing. It became slightly uncontrollable. Finally, he stopped.

"Yeah."

65

Back at his apartment, Igor went to work.

On his desk, five big plasma screens were spread in an arc. The largest screen, on his left, showed Carman Hall in a three-dimensional grid, with the precise architecture of the entire building. This was the "master" screen. Small holographs of the building's occupants were lit up. These digital representations of the students, parents, and terrorists were like tiny lights. Igor had created a state-of-the-art, real-time tracking tool, capable of monitoring the dormitory floor by floor, to see the individuals on each floor and to monitor their movements. With a click, Igor could zero in on a particular floor or individual, then put that magnified view up on one of the other screens, enabling him to manage the team's movements, including multiple simultaneous actions, while at the same time, through the master screen, maintaining a more holistic picture of what was going on.

The screen to Igor's far right was a tile of live video of the building from different angles.

The feeds mirrored what the FBI was looking at.

The underlying technological platform Igor had built was a relational database capable of integrating multiple diagnostic inputs from various external applications. A dynamic GPS module was one of more than two dozen programs feeding into the database, which could synchronize multiple streams of information around particular individuals; an individual marked as a probable terrorist by Igor could thus be tracked, monitored, and dimensionalized by the appliance.

Igor had also figured out a creative way to hitch a ride on the dormitory's wireless network infrastructure and install a custom-built thermal-imaging scanner that worked in conjunction with the GPS, thus creating very accurate representations of the exact locations and movements of everyone inside the building.

What's more, a powerful air quality module—also run via the dorm's wireless routers—could read an assortment of chemical, electronic, and environmental emissions. Igor customized the underlying algorithm to focus in on a tighter framework of objects. By targeting microwave emissions, radio frequency waves, and non-ionizing radiation, for example, he'd been able to isolate all cell phones in the building, including those turned off. Because the terrorists had collected all cell phones and placed them in a room on the eighth floor, Igor was able to locate those few still in use.

Another flourish Igor had coded on was a simple time-elapse replay module. He was thus able to watch and replay certain events and mark the actions of specific individuals against those events.

The goal was to look at the past not in order to know what had happened; it was to know what had happened in order to mark the terrorists with confidence so that Dewey and his team could kill them.

Igor was the conductor. He watched the unfolding events in real time so as to direct Dewey and the team as they made their assault on the building.

Igor had marked all nine terrorists, including the two dead men, whose corpses lay on three and six. He also had a tracking protocol on Sullivan, who was on three. But there was a slight discrepancy.

A low beeping noise came from the computer. He double-clicked on a star-shaped icon. The view of the building shifted lower, focusing on the underground floors. Thermal images, four in all, came into sharper relief as the figures came into range. The first climber was small and thin, with a female form: Katie. She moved quickly, trailed by three larger figures.

Moving the mouse and hovering, he quickly clicked on each one, making them a bright fluorescent green and labeling each holograph with initials: *D, K, T, S.*

Daisy held the gunman around his neck, trying to pull him down as he swung violently. People in the room were screaming. She didn't care anymore if she lived or died. A low, guttural moan came from the terrorist. Suddenly, he let go of Andy's hair. But then Daisy was being lifted— an arm on her hip, another squeezing her armpit— and she was hurled through the air. Her back slammed into the wall, and she dropped to the floor.

Daisy looked up. She felt woozy. She saw Andy. She slashed her eyes left, toward the door, signaling to Andy: *Move. Get out of the room.*

The gunman had his rifle trained on Daisy's head.

A loud voice echoed down the hallway, shouting in Arabic. The gunman stared at Daisy for a little longer, then his eyes shot to Andy. He looked panicked, as if he might just kill everyone in the room. He took the rifle in both hands, moved toward Daisy, and slammed the butt into her face.

Gasps of horror mingled with sobs.

The steel struck Daisy below the eye, kicking her into the wall. Blood soon covered her face as she lay crumpled on the floor.

The terrorist ran to the door.

Andy crawled toward her, grabbing her head

and cradling it. She took off her sweatshirt and pressed it against the wound.

"Is there a doctor?" Andy asked, looking around the room at the terrified faces. "Anyone?"

66

CARMAN HALL
COLUMBIA UNIVERSITY

Sirhan moved to the tenth floor. The smell had become overwhelming. That he didn't mind. The thing he did worry about was the possibility of a rebellion. If anyone in the group understood basic guerrilla tactics, they would know that even with weapons, the sheer number of students and parents gave them an advantage—if they were willing to use it. It would entail rushing against Sirhan and his men and sacrificing themselves to the bullets, but five hundred people working together could do it—and most would survive.

He found Ali standing just inside the hallway entrance.

"Move half the people to eleven," he said. "There are too many in one place."

"Yes, Sirhan."

Tariq approached from the stairs.

"We're splitting the students up," said Sirhan.

"Get Omar and Mohammed up here. They will guard eleven. You and Meuse guard ten."

Tariq nodded.

Sirhan glanced at his watch. It was nearly half past the hour.

"And throw someone out a window," he added.

They moved up through the tunnel toward the basement of Carman. As the Plumber predicted, a few lights were still on—old fluorescent bulbs that somehow hadn't burnt out over the years—and they cast grainy, bluish light.

They scrambled up the steel ladders. Katie set a blistering pace. Dewey panted hard, still coughing water. His legs and arms burned. To distract himself from the pain, he again counted rungs on the ladder. By the time Katie stopped climbing and signaled with her hand that she was at the top, Dewey had counted out 296 rungs.

Katie aimed her headlamp at the steel plate above.

"You guys ready?"

"Hold on," said Dewey. He removed a small airtight canister from a side pocket and put his earbud in his left ear. He tapped his ear several times. The others followed suit. Katie had an extra bud, which she handed to Smith.

"Igor," said Dewey.

"I'm here," came Igor's voice. "I need a COMMS check."

"Commo one," said Katie.

"Two," said Tacoma.

Katie looked down the tunnel at Smith, pointing to her ear, instructing him how to trigger the device.

"Smith," he said.

"You're all coming through loud and clear," said Igor. "You're in the building. Katie is just below the entrance to the subbasement. Rob is next, then Damon. Then you."

"Give us the lay of the land," said Dewey.

"We have three-dimensional, real-time multilateral views of the interior of the building. Katie, push up the plate. There's nobody in the room or, for that matter, within two floors. You're safe."

Katie pushed open the plate and climbed into the room, followed quickly by Tacoma, Smith, and Dewey. The room was cavernous, dimly lit, and loud—a utility room, with several large boilers on one side and a mess of pipes crossing the other.

They set down the duffels and unzipped them. Dewey nodded to Tacoma, pointing to the duffels, indicating he wanted him to get the four geared up as soon as possible.

"I've isolated the terrorists," said Igor.

"Are the students still on the tenth floor?"

"Yes."

"What about the terrorists?" asked Dewey.

"They're spread out. A few roam between

floors. Right now, I have one on six, one on seven, one on nine, three on ten, one on twelve."

"Are they still throwing people out of the building?"

"Every hour."

Dewey swallowed, momentarily silent. In the dim light, he glanced at Katie.

"Have they . . ."

"There have only been two females," said Igor, anticipating Dewey's question. "One was Middle Eastern, the other was Japanese or Korean."

Dewey felt guilty for even asking, and even guiltier for the peace of mind that washed over him when he realized Daisy was still alive.

"What is the news saying?" asked Dewey. "Are we negotiating?"

"They don't know. They're speculating that some sort of negotiation is going on, but they don't know."

"*We* need to know," said Katie.

"I know someone who will know," said Dewey. "Igor, patch in the following number."

Dewey read off Dellenbaugh's cell number.

"Will do. Hold on."

A few seconds later, Dellenbaugh's calm, deep voice came over commo.

"Hi, Dewey."

"Mr. President," said Dewey, "we're inside the building and preparing to move. I'm on commo with a few other people. Before we go in, can you give us a status on what's happening? Are we negotiating?"

"Yes, but it's going nowhere. We're trying to get them to stop the killing before we'll discuss terms. It's not working. They won't stop throwing people until the shipment arrives."

"What's the ask?"

"ISIS gets the weapons, the students go free. The problem is, those weapons will kill a lot more than five hundred Americans if the shipment is delivered. The bigger problem is that Nazir is a pathological liar. Doing any deal requires him to keep his word. If these guys are suicide bombers, they'll wait for the shipment to arrive, then blow up themselves and the building."

"Thank you, sir."

"Good luck."

Dewey tapped his ear. He looked at Smith.

"Should we check in with your guys?"

"Good idea. Igor, can you patch me into McNaughton?"

"Sure."

A few moments later, Dave McNaughton from the FBI came on.

Smith tapped his ear. "Hey, it's me."

"Are you in?"

"Yes. You're on a party line. We made it into the basement and are getting ready to move. Is there anything we need to know?"

"We managed to place a jamming device up

high," said McNaughton. "It was Robbins. They shot him, but he managed to set it before that."

"I'm sorry to hear that," said Smith.

Dewey spoke up. "Getting that jammer up high was critical. Their interoperability is now shut off, not to mention being able to communicate with Nazir."

"I think now is the time to start pre-positioning for the different scenarios our assault is going to create," said Smith. "Hopefully, we're successful, but you'll need munitions people before you can even get to anyone upstairs. After that, it's medical."

"Already on it," said McNaughton.

"I figured," said Smith. "Now, if we aren't successful, it's because of one of two things. Either they stopped us and held the building, in which case I believe you'll have to look at one of your assault scenarios. I'm not sure which one, but getting half these kids out of there is better than none. If somehow they manage to detonate all or part of the building, well, we don't need to talk about that one. You know what to do."

"It won't be that one," said McNaughton. "Good luck in there."

Tacoma stood up. On the floor was a neatly lined-up array of submachine guns, handguns, and a variety of more firearms, as well as knives and piles of mags.

"We need to move right now," he said.

Tariq entered the tenth floor and fired an unmuted shot into the wall. Except for a few grief-filled moans and cries, the gunfire no longer caused the pandemonium it once had.

"Everyone on the right side of the dorm," he barked, "up to eleven. Now!"

He looked into a room on his right, realizing that, depending on which direction he was walking, either side could be the right-hand side of the building.

"That's everyone in here!" he shouted, firing a round into the ceiling.

"What about those of us in the window?" asked someone who was shielding the room from snipers.

Tariq suddenly remembered: Sirhan had told him to push another one out. He was quietly grateful to the student who reminded him.

"Good question." Tariq moved behind the boy who had asked the question, pumping a round next to his head, which shattered the glass. "If you're in the window, remain standing in the window."

Tariq pushed the boy out. He tumbled forward, screaming as he fell.

Two students were running toward him. Both were male. One was tall, with long, curly blond hair. The other was shorter and stockier.

Tariq triggered the gun just as they leapt, aiming at the short boy, who was closer, at the same time lurching to his right, away from the tall one, whom he knew he would not have time to hit. Then a set of arms grabbed him from behind, just as his first shots ripped the short student's chest and sent him spiraling to the floor amid screaming and confusion.

The tall one reached Tariq just as the muzzle crossed the last inches of air, then was ripped upward, out of his hands, by another student.

They beat Tariq as rabid screams came from their mouths, which mixed with the high-pitched, metallic, bee-sting noise of an Uzi, firing from the door, and they all looked, including Tariq, bleeding and trapped.

It was Meuse. He held two guns, a rifle, aimed at the door in case anyone dared to enter, the other an Uzi, which he fired with calm efficiency at the students surrounding Tariq and then along the walls. He looked at the windows, where four students still stood. He swept the submachine gun across them. All four fell out, their horrible screams mixed with the sound of breaking glass. Then they hit the ground and the screams ceased.

Meuse went to Tariq, whose nose and mouth were bleeding.

"Come," he said, holding out his hand.

Dewey climbed the stairs from the subbasement to the basement, entering a low-ceilinged, brightly lit corridor.

"Hold on," said Igor over commo. "Looks like there's movement."

"What do you mean?" asked Dewey.

"They're moving students from ten to eleven."

"Why?"

"I don't know."

Dewey stopped and removed a black Sharpie from his pants pocket. He looked around at everyone, then started writing on his forearm.

"Let's have the terrorists again, Igor, by floor."

"One on the first floor, one on six, two on ten, and now it looks like two on eleven. One on twelve."

As Igor dictated, Dewey wrote down a sequence of numbers: 11, 61, 102, 112, 121. Each number showed the floor where the terrorists were and the number of terrorists on that floor.

He handed the pen around. Tacoma, Smith, and Katie all wrote down the same numbers.

"Igor, if that changes—"

"I'll let you know if any of them move. Don't forget the four students down the hall."

"Thanks."

Dewey shook his head, not knowing what to do. If they released them, they would have to stay put. People could be very irrational, especially teenagers, and especially terrified teenagers.

"What would we do with them?" asked Tacoma.

Dewey thought for several seconds. He looked at Smith.

"If we get the bomb down, your guys can get in there, right?"

"Yeah."

Dewey looked at Tacoma.

"I have an idea."

Dewey moved down the basement corridor toward the door. The students were behind it.

The stench of urine was strong, even through the door.

He opened it. The students were chained across the room from the far door, which led into a tunnel that connected to the next building. There were three girls and a boy. One of the girls looked okay, if tired. The boy looked unconscious, as did one of the other girls. The last girl, Chinese, was sobbing. They were all standing. They had to, otherwise they would all be strangled by the chain that gripped their necks. The floor was covered in wetness from urine. There was also blood. Studying the students, he saw that the calm-looking girl had tried to pull her head through the chain. Her neck was cut almost completely around. Blood still trickled.

The ones who were awake did not even register Dewey's entrance, so deep was their shock and trauma.

He moved to the door and studied the shoe box. It was set lengthwise, parallel to the door. If the detonator was a trigger button, Dewey assumed it was on the bottom of the device, designed to detonate if the box fell. Dewey held the box firm to the door and removed his combat blade, inserting the tip into the seam and slashing down, tearing a neat cut along one side of the bomb.

"No!" screamed one of the students.

It was a horrendous yell, full of terror.

"I'm here to save you," said Dewey. "You've all been extremely brave. It's going to be okay."

He slashed the blade along the other side of the IED. Holding the device gently, he moved the blade to his mouth and clenched it in his teeth as he lifted the IED and moved it away.

Dewey flipped open the three dead bolts, then pulled the door in. The chain slackened. All four students collapsed to the floor.

"Please help us," said the calm one.

The boy woke up, as did the sleeping female.

"Who are you?" said the male student.

The sobbing girl, who'd just screamed, continued to wail and sob.

"I'm American," said Dewey. "You're being rescued. The FBI will be here to cut that chain in a few minutes. Can you hold on just a little longer?"

Dewey moved past them, down the corridor, shutting the interior door behind him in case any of the students screamed. At the end of the hallway, he opened a door. It was a janitor's closet. He placed the bomb gingerly at the bottom of a large utility sink, making a mental note to make McNaughton aware of it.

Dewey hit his earbud.

"Igor, patch in McNaughton."

Katie, Tacoma, and Smith were waiting at the bottom of the stairs that led up to the first floor.

"McNaughton. What do you got?"

"The basement bomb is down," Dewey said. "Those kids are a mess. Commander, the bomb is down the hallway, in a utility closet, trigger down. Looks like a shoe box. Careful."

"How soon until I can get them out?"

"As long as your guys go in and recon the four, immediately. But they need to be quick, quiet, and they can't hang around. I don't want any men trying to come in beyond there. Even the slightest noise echoing up those stairs could lead to more casualties."

"Understood."

"Of course, as soon as we're clear upstairs, that can be the primary egress for your munitions people and first responders."

Dewey studied his arm again: 11, 61, 102, 112, 121.

Designing an effective assault was a challenge. Ideally, they would all move at the same time, in unison, on different floors. But the terrorists were too spread out to do that. This meant that if the terrorists had some form of internal communications, anything—a grunt, a scream, even the mere absence of one of the men from their commo—would tell everyone else they were there.

Dewey hit commo. "Igor, is that guy still on one?"

"Yes."

"Okay, listen up."

He gestured for Tacoma, Katie, and Smith to come in closer. He trained a light on his forearm: 11, 61, 102, 112, 121.

"Our only way up is the elevator shafts. We can do it from this floor, and try to avoid the guy on one, but I think that's risky. If he hears anything, we're screwed. Besides, I kinda want to kill him."

"Me too," said Smith.

"The problem is, even though we jammed their walkie-talkies and cells, they probably have some sort of periodic check-in. A yell up the stairs or something. Once we kill this guy, we're in a race against time. Which means we climb hard and fast, got it?"

"Yeah," said Tacoma. "What about up top? Who hits what?"

"We climb to seven and move in," said Dewey. "Except Katie. You get off on six and take that guy. Then meet us on seven. Igor, we're going to need real precise movements here."

"I'll do my best."

"Why not hit him from seven?" asked Tacoma.

"If he hears anything, he's going to go to the sound. I'd rather have him run down the sixth-floor hallway than up to seven. He's likely to yell if he does that."

"Got it. I agree."

"I'll take the stairs to one and take that guy," said Dewey, signaling and walking down the corridor, giving the design over commo. "You guys follow me up."

"Yeah, got it."

"We do a commo check to make sure we're all in position. Nobody moves until I give the go. No one. Let's go."

Dewey felt a surge of adrenaline in his arms, then all over. He pulled his Colt M1911A1 from his shoulder holster, a black suppressor jutting ominously from the end.

"Igor, you ready?"

"Yes, I'm good."

At the entrance to the stairs, Dewey glanced at the others, then pulled the door open and stepped in total silence up the concrete steps. He rounded the landing and kept climbing.

"Where is he?" Dewey whispered.

He reached the top of the stairs. The door to the first floor was directly in front of him. He stepped lightly to it, trying not to make any sound.

"Directly in front of the door," whispered Igor. "Be *very* quiet. You are only a few inches away."

The doorknob was on the left-hand side of the door. He would need to open the door with his right hand and fire with his off hand.

Slowly, he moved the gun to his left hand and reached for the doorknob. Carefully, quietly, he turned the knob as far as it would go.

"His head moved a little," whispered Igor. "He may have heard something."

Dewey raised the suppressed .45 and trained it on the seam of the closed door. He pulled the door slowly open, every inch taking endless moments, his heart racing, until he had the first glimpse of the black hair on the back of his skull, then his entire frame, until at last the door was fully open and the terrorist was standing in front of him, back turned, a submachine gun in his hands. He wore jeans and a black T-shirt. He had black hair down to his shoulders. Dewey trained the gun at the man's head and moved it closer until it was less than an inch away. The suppressor tremored just a bit, as if blown by a peaceful wind. He felt the ceramic trigger against his finger as he pulled it back . . .

A scream from somewhere up above. Arabic. A signal. The check-in?

The terrorist looked at his watch.

Dewey's mind raced. The terrorist had heard the call, but the door had been open. His ears would've sensed it. He had to know the door was open.

Can he see me? Did he turn enough to catch a glimpse?

Yet Dewey didn't shoot. He needed the man to give the signal back. Otherwise . . .

Instinct.

The gunman sensed something.

It happens now.

"Dewey," said Igor, so softly Dewey thought his mind was playing tricks.

The terrorist wheeled around, murder in his eyes. He found Dewey.

Instinct, fear, hatred—they all disappeared in that fraction of a second. It came back then, the moment he'd grown to know so well, a crucible in time, a passage that, once made, one could never return. Dewey felt himself transported to the place of his innermost desire, a primal state. Timeless, ageless, a place without borders. It was the place of the hunter, the assassin, the soldier.

He fired the Colt—three quick taps—three telltale *thwacks* from the suppressor. The first bullet struck the terrorist in the center of his neck, the throat, the larynx. The second went straight through his mouth, blowing out the back of his skull. The third ripped into his left eye. He tumbled awkwardly, silently, falling in the path of the blood and skull that rained a crimson shadow across the lobby floor.

Dewey paused, catching his breath.

"One down," he whispered.

Smith, Tacoma, and Katie moved silently to the first-floor landing. Katie stepped toward the stairs. She removed a small flashlight and aimed it up. A massive web of thin wire covered the entire flight of stairs. Set on top of the web near the centermost point was an IED. Any movement—*any movement*—of the wires and the bomb would fall and detonate.

"That's a lot of Semtex," she said matter-of-factly.

She leaned into the middle of the stairwell and peered up, aiming the light. She removed a powerful night optic to get a better view. She counted two more flights with banisters wrapped in wire.

"That's enough Semtex to take out half the floor," said Katie. "Not to mention what would happen to the ones above it after the first explodes. This side of the building would collapse."

Dewey glanced at the bomb. He understood even more clearly that the terrorists had no intention of leaving the building—or letting the students live. Every exit point was gone; the elevators were destroyed; both stairwells were wired with enough Semtex to take down half the building—and likely trip the IEDs on the other side of the building as well.

But Dewey didn't say anything.

They cut across the lobby, past several dead bodies. Tacoma pried open the first elevator door.

He pulled a portable electric screwdriver from his jacket and reached up, as did Dewey a moment later. They removed the top panel of the elevator car, handing it to Smith, who put it in the hallway. A small steel door was visible at the roof of the elevator. Tacoma reached up and pushed it open. Beyond was pitch-black.

Tacoma turned, pointing at his eyes, indicating they would need night optics.

Dewey took climbing gloves and night optics from the duffel and handed them out. He looked down at his forearm. He pulled out the Sharpie and crossed off the first number:

~~11~~, 61, 102, 112, 121.

Dewey pulled on his optics and left them on top of his head. He reached into the weapons ruck and removed a silenced M4, then strapped it to his back. He popped the mag from the Colt pistol and slammed in a new one. He grabbed an extra mag for the carbine.

The others performed a similar ritual, all in silence.

Dewey climbed up through the roof. He pulled the optics down over his eyes and flipped the switch. The lower level of the elevator shaft came into view in shades of fluorescent orange. It was vast, dark, and eerily quiet. The elevator car was like a square block of steel dangling from thick steel cables. Looking over the side of the car, he could see the ground two stories below.

Dewey stared up into the shaft. The only lights were small tendrils of yellow cutting through seams at the doors to each floor.

Dewey turned to Smith, Katie, and Tacoma.

"Igor, any movement?"

"No."

Dewey felt each of the steel cables. One was loose enough to use a modified "break-and-squat" climbing method, which he'd mastered in Rangers. He jumped, grabbed the cable, and let it lie to the outside of his right leg. He stepped on the cable with his right foot and brought his left beneath the cable and pulled up. The combination of the cable across the top of his left foot and stepping on it with his right locked the cable in place.

He looked down at Smith, even releasing his hands from the cable for a moment to demonstrate the strength of the lock he'd made with his feet.

Smith grinned.

"Break and squat?"

Smith grabbed the cable on the third car, jumped up, pulled his legs up, locked, then reached up again.

Tacoma, meanwhile, was already halfway up to the sixth floor. There was no climbing science to his ascension, just brute force. He pulled himself up with his hands, barely using his legs. Katie was below him, but was quickly at his heels.

Daisy opened her eyes. For a moment or two, she couldn't remember anything. All she saw was Andy's adorable face.

"Are you ready to go over the calculus again?" she asked groggily.

Andy started laughing. "Sure."

Then the pain hit her. "What happened?"

"Sssshhhh," said Andy, forcing Daisy's head back to her lap.

Charlotte walked quietly from the bathroom and handed Andy another damp towel. When she saw Daisy, she smiled.

"He hit you with his gun," Andy explained.

"Who?"

"The terrorist."

Daisy looked crestfallen. She closed her eyes again as Andy dabbed the contusion on her cheek.

"Oh," she said. "Oh, yeah."

As Katie clung to the tiny precipice with her left hand, she reached to her belt and removed a combat blade. She inserted it into the crack between the two elevator doors.

"Igor, is there anyone on the other side of the door?" she asked.

"All clear. Open it, then move left. He's in the second to last room, near the window. He's a lookout. He has a sniper rifle. He hasn't moved in several minutes."

Katie looked up at Tacoma, who was holding steady outside the elevator doors on seven, waiting for her to go in. He smiled at her.

Katie stuck out her tongue, then pushed the blade between the doors and slowly twisted, creating a crack. She stuck her other hand in, and as she held herself steady, she put the blade between her teeth and moved her other hand to the opening. She moved the elevator doors apart. A series of mechanical clicks followed, loud enough for them all to hear. It was now halfway open; she stepped forward, blocking the two doors that wanted to close.

"He's moving," said Igor. "Could be nothing."

She paused, resheathing the knife, then removed her silenced pistol: SIG Sauer P226 with an Osprey suppressor screwed to the muzzle.

"Katie, he heard you."

"Do I have time—"

"No! He's almost to the hallway. *He's coming to the elevators! Close the doors!"*

Katie felt with her left hand for something to hold. She found a piece of the door mechanism.

"He's in the hallway. *He's running! Close them!"*

Holding the piece of thin steel, she removed her foot from between the doors, which slid shut, though not before she inserted the suppressor of her gun, chest level, inching it back so that the tip aligned with the plane of the doors.

"Is he searching rooms?" she asked.

"No. He heard the elevator. He's two rooms away. He's moving."

Katie pulled herself closer to the inch-wide gap in the doors and reached down with her off hand, finding a different piece of the door to hold onto, this one at waist level.

"He's nearly there," whispered Igor.

Katie knelt, sliding the gun down, the suppressor dropping to knee level. She tilted it up, then leaned forward, breathing quickly, until her forehead was pressed against the door. She looked with her right eye.

"He's there."

The light in the hallway flickered with shadow as the gunman paced in front of the bank of elevators. Then she saw him, his legs first, running shoes, black pants, black T-shirt. He was inspecting the first door.

He was tall, with a bushy mustache and beard, olive skin, clutching a submachine gun. He studied the door at eye level, realizing something was amiss: a slight seam. He looked up; his eyes seemed to say, *Why?*

He pulled the gun to his right, reaching out with his left and stepping forward.

Katie didn't move. Except her index finger, which she pressed to the trigger, tightened. She had no ability to move the gun to the left or right. He stepped closer, arm out. Then she fired. A dull thud echoed from the suppressed round. The bullet smashed into the center of the terrorist's chest, a pained groan, and he stumbled back.

But as the bullet ripped out of the gun, the small kick pushed the suppressor from between the elevator doors. Now the pistol was the only thing she held. When it moved back, she felt her body being pulled down by gravity. She reached for the side of the elevator as the sound of automatic weapon fire erupted from the terrorist.

"Oh, God," she moaned, suddenly helpless to prevent the fall that was about to come.

Katie fell backward, trying to grab the steel cable and slow her descent through the dark shaft, but she was moving too quickly.

"Katie!" yelled Tacoma, looking in horror from the seventh-floor ledge.

And then she remembered her father's words: *Cover your head.* Advice at the summit of Cannon Mountain in New Hampshire before every race.

"If you fall, cover your head. The rest of you can be fixed. Your brain can't."

She threw her hands behind her head and twisted just as she slammed onto the roof of the elevator car. The point of impact was her left hip, left leg, and ribs, all of which shattered in an excruciating moment. The pain was blinding, worse than anything she'd ever experienced. Her optics, earbud, and most of what she'd been

548

carrying was tossed upon impact and she lay in the dark, unable to move.

"Katie!" said Igor.

Tacoma looked over at Dewey, but he was gone.

As much as Dewey cared about Katie, he knew he didn't have time to think about her. If the man on six alerted the others, all would be lost. Including a very badly injured Katie.

He jammed his knife blade in the elevator doors the moment he heard her cry, "Oh, God."

He pulled the elevator doors open and charged down the hallway toward the stairs.

Dewey's mind was in chaos. He didn't ask Igor which stairwell the gunman was headed for. He should've, but he didn't think of it, and by the time he reached the stairs, he knew he'd gone to the wrong one. There was no one there. He was on the other side of the building.

Then he heard him. He was below, running down the stairs.

The terrorist wasn't trying to alert the others. He was running for the bombs!

"He's going downstairs," said Igor, suddenly realizing what Dewey had done. *"He's going for the bomb!"*

Dewey pulled the carbine from over his head and charged down the stairs. He wasn't there. The concrete landing was drenched in blood; the terrorist was bleeding out but still moving. Dewey moved to the railing and looked down. To the right, he saw the terrorist's gun lying on the stairs. He'd abandoned it! He had but one purpose now. Dewey heard labored breathing, but he was out of view.

"He's below you! Against the wall! He's halfway down! You can't reach him! Get out of there! Run!"

Dewey leaned over the banister, putting his finger to the trigger of his carbine.

Below, diagonally to the right, he could see the IED nestled on top of the spiderweb of wires. But his view of the top part of the stairwell was blocked by the ceiling. The terrorist would be able to reach the top of the wires before Dewey could even *see* him. He'd be able to set off the IED and not only kill him but also set off a chain reaction, as the other bombs would fall and explode, a domino effect that likely would take down most of the building.

He didn't have time to descend. It was too late.

"Five steps! Four! Dewey, get out of there!"

He lifted the butt of the gun to his shoulder. He trained it at the banister that ran along the half flight of stairs just *above* the wires, the flight where the terrorist now skulked like a wounded rat, clinging to life long enough so that he could kill himself and take everyone else with him.

The handrail was thick steel, round, atop thin

rungs. His only hope was a ricochet. He fired once, the bullet clanging. He fired again. He moved the fire selector to full-auto and pulled the trigger. A furious din of clanging steel filled the air until he heard the mag click. It was empty.

Dewey dropped the gun and charged down. Dark, wet blood streaked the wall and stairs where the terrorist had been crawling. He took the first flight in two enormous leaps. He stopped at the top of the third flight. The wires were visible below. The terrorist lay on the stairs, arms outstretched toward the wires. One of the slugs had hit him. A trail of blood covered the concrete behind him. He was inches from the first wire, lying motionless.

And yet, Dewey continued his descent, pulling his knife from his belt. He came alongside the terrorist, who appeared to be dead. His eyes were closed, he didn't move. Dewey knelt and reached out his left hand, putting it just above the man's arm, waiting. He didn't touch the terrorist, but he waited. In his right hand was the blade, a fearsome-looking object with a black blade, double-serrated, well-worn.

A second became two, then five. Then the man's arm shot out toward the wire. Dewey grabbed it, twisted it back behind him, and yanked up, snapping it. The man grunted in pain. His eyes opened, black and bloodshot, filled with hatred and defiance.

Dewey ripped the blade across the terrorist's throat, nearly severing his head, then plunged it into his chest, once, twice, then once more.

"Igor," said Dewey, slowly standing up.

"What?"

"Tell McNaughton to get some medics in." He started sprinting up the stairs. "Damon, Rob, meet me on nine."

Tacoma and Smith were standing in the empty ninth-floor hallway when Dewey got there, drenched in perspiration.

"We should save her first, then go back," Tacoma said.

"No," said Dewey. "We don't have time. I love her too, but her best chance of surviving is us killing those fuckers. It needs to end *right now.*"

"Medics are moving," said Igor.

"Dewey," said Tacoma.

Dewey paused. His eyes met Tacoma's. He looked at the floor, then to Smith.

Dewey tapped his ear.

"How are they positioned on ten and eleven?"

"They're at opposite ends of the floor," said Igor.

He looked at Smith. "How's your marksman-ship?"

"Meaning?"

"Can you take two guys on the same floor? One

point-blank, the other three hundred feet or so away, under three seconds?"

"I'm a good shot, Dewey," said Smith. "I'm a better climber."

"All right, you go take care of Katie."

Dewey signaled to Tacoma.

"You have ten. I'll take eleven. On my go. When you hear screaming, move."

"What about twelve?" asked Tacoma.

"We're going to have to run fast."

"What if he runs for the roof?" asked Tacoma.

Dewey nodded.

"Igor, patch in McNaughton real quick."

A few seconds later, McNaughton came on.

"Hey, guys."

"Dave, we're almost done, but we have a guy on twelve. He might run for the roof and attempt to detonate the bombs."

"I'll bring a chopper in tight."

"Bring in a couple," said Dewey. "They need to expect the man on twelve to run for the bombs on the roof. They can't miss."

"Got it," said McNaughton. "Hold on."

Dewey moved to the west stairs as Tacoma sprinted down the hallway to the east stairwell.

"What's the setup on each floor?" asked Dewey, climbing in silence, just behind Smith.

"The last two bedrooms on each side are empty. They're using them as lookouts. They're pacing back and forth between the rooms. They look out the window for a few seconds on one side, then walk back across the hall. The students are packed into the rooms in the middle of the floor, hallways too."

"Are they coordinating movements?" asked Dewey.

"It doesn't appear so."

Dewey reached the tenth-floor landing and kept climbing.

Tacoma stopped at ten and held up next to the door.

He suddenly became aware of the sound of rotors, as the choppers swept closer to the building.

Dewey took off his optics and left them on the floor. He stuck a fresh mag into the MP7. He unfolded the butt, then flipped up the weapon's infrared scope. He moved the fire selector to semiauto and walked to the door, just out of the way of the narrow window.

Sweat poured down every inch of his body. His mind raced with thoughts of Katie, of Daisy, of Hector. But he knew he needed to push them all aside now.

"Igor, we need precise timing here," said Dewey, removing the silenced Colt from his shoulder holster and holding it in his left hand as, with his right, he held the MP7. He put the butt of the handgun against the doorknob, grasping the knob with the tips of the same fingers that clutched the .45. "I need you to tell me when the gunman at the *far end* of eleven is moving from the window toward the hallway."

Quietly, he turned the knob but didn't open the door yet.

"He's moving from the window, Dewey."

"Where's the near guy?"

"Directly in front of you, moving left. Get ready. Far gunman is almost there. He's at the door in three, two, one . . ."

"Rob, go when you hear screams. Your guys will probably flood into the area directly in front of you."

He turned the knob.

"Now, Dewey!" said Igor.

Dewey ripped open the door, swinging the pistol up in the air just as the terrorist heard the door open, turned, and leveled his Uzi, firing; the slugs from the terrorist were unmuted. The first screams pierced the quiet. A deadly slash of bullets ripped across the door and wall, closing in on Dewey. Dewey lurched right and down, then fired the Colt with his left hand. The first bullet nicked the terrorist in the cheek, and he stumbled. Dewey fired again, the slug hitting him dead center in the forehead, splattering brains and blood.

As screams erupted, Dewey moved calmly—dropping the Colt, kneeling on his right knee, lifting the MP7 to his shoulder, aiming down the corridor, looking through the scope at the far end.

"Everybody, *get down now!*" he barked to the fear-stricken students.

The screams turned desperate: pandemonium. But Dewey remained calm. Several people were standing, despite his order, but there was no time to warn them again. He looked through the powerful scope. Four or five people were running down the hallway, away from Dewey.

Somewhere below, from the tenth floor, Dewey heard gunfire.

Another terrorist came into view, a lone figure at the far end of the corridor. He screamed something in Arabic. Dewey studied him through the scope. He was bald, dressed in black, and he emerged from the bedroom on the left with his weapon raised, turning down the hallway. Dewey locked him in just as he raised his rifle. The sound of the gunman's unmuted carbine echoed down the hall, and the muzzle flash made the scope momentarily light up. Pandemonium turned into terror.

Dewey fired.

Thwack! Thwack! Thwack!

Three dull metallic thuds which, though suppressed, seemed somehow to cut through the screams and the chaos and the terrorist's unmuted rifle fire. Dewey watched through the scope as the wall behind the terrorist went abruptly red in the same instant the slug caught the man in the forehead, blowing off the top of his skull.

"Twelve is moving," said Igor.

• • •

Sullivan was seated in the hallway when he heard the noise. It was a loud thud followed by a female voice. She was crying.

Had they thrown another?

He went to the window and looked down. The sidewalk in front of Carman was covered in blood, but no bodies. The last student thrown had been removed. That was twenty minutes ago.

He looked for the grandmother, finding her in a bedroom down the hall. She was hidden beneath an unmade bed. When he tried to ask her how she was doing, she said, *"Sssshhhh,"* and waved him away.

Sullivan went through every room, searching for the source of the crying. She wasn't anywhere on the floor. Rifle in hand, he went to the stairs. He made sure no one was there and moved quietly down to the second floor. He went through every room.

He heard her again, more clearly this time.

He walked to the elevators and stopped. He listened for at least a minute. Then he heard the woman's soft cry once more.

Sullivan put the gun against the wall. He scanned the floor for something to pry open the doors. He ran into the nearest bedroom and threw open a box. Inside were books, framed photographs, bedding. He found a small plastic case near the bottom and opened it. Inside was a glass pipe, several lighters, and a bottle opener.

He took the bottle opener and ran to the elevator, jamming it in the seam between the doors and twisting until he could get his fingers in between. He pulled the doors apart with all of his strength, his face turning red with effort. Finally, as if giving up, the doors slid open.

The elevator shaft was dark. But still, he could see a figure. There, on the roof of the elevator car, was a woman. She had blond hair and was dressed in some sort of black paramilitary gear.

"Help," she whispered.

"I'm right here," said Sullivan. "I'm going to get you. Don't you worry. Can you move?"

The woman didn't answer.

Sullivan ran back to the room and grabbed a lighter from the box. He lit it and held it out into the shaft. Below the elevator cars, he could make out the basement floor twenty-five or thirty feet below.

He could easily step onto the roof of the car, but the woman was perched precariously. Her head and chest were dangling over the edge. The slightest jostle and she'd drop several floors to the concrete floor of the basement.

Suddenly, the elevator car shook.

Sullivan held the lighter out and flicked it, illuminating the shaft above. He saw a vague silhouette several floors above.

"*Stop!*" Sullivan said. "Who are you?"

"FBI."

"Don't move any closer!" Sullivan implored in a loud whisper. "She's going to fall if you do!"

"Okay," said the FBI agent. "I got it."

Then the words, in a whisper from above, "Are you Sullivan?"

Sullivan nodded. "Yeah."

"I'm Damon Smith. Okay, I can see what you mean. She's barely on there."

"I know," said Sullivan.

"Do you still have the rifle?"

"Yes."

"Does it have a strap?"

"Yes."

"Okay, that's good. I want you to remove the strap and get to the roof of the car to your right. Then hook the strap to her vest. She's wearing a tactical vest that has various places you can attach it. Go ahead."

"What do I do with the other end?"

"You hold it. Then I can come down."

"Got it."

Sullivan removed the strap from the rifle, then went back to the elevator doors. The car the woman was perched on was directly in front of him. He didn't want to so much as look at it. He looked at the wall immediately to his right and then the roof of the next car. He leapt out and landed on that car. Then he got to his hands and knees and crawled to the far corner, near Katie. She was at the very edge, her hand wrapped like a vise around a carriage bolt on the roof. Gently, he ran his hands along her back until he found a loop. He fastened the metal clasp on the rifle strap to the loop. He then wrapped the other end of the strap tightly around his wrist and pulled slowly but firmly back.

"Okay," he said, looking up. "She's secure."

Smith rappelled swiftly down from above.

He felt her neck for a pulse. Then he shone a light into her eyes, pulling back each eyelid.

"She's alive. Good pulse. Looks like she has brain activity too."

He waved the light down her body. The positioning looked awkward.

"Her legs are fractured," Smith continued. "Let's hope not her neck."

He removed carabiners and ropes from his backpack and quickly built a system that would allow them to lower her to the bottommost level of the elevator shaft. He started by securing her in three places: at her feet, her waist, and her upper torso, using rope and tension to replicate the stabilizing effects of a stretcher. Each section had steel heavy-duty carabiners, which Smith put ropes through. The ropes were wrapped around the cable housing on top of the elevator car; this would provide the counterweight as they lowered themselves and her to the ground.

Smith removed his gloves and handed them to Sullivan.

"What are these for?"

"Climbing. You're going to climb down there and we're going to lower her down together."

With a separate rope, Smith improvised a harness around Sullivan's legs and torso, then wrapped the rope around the cable housing atop the car. He handed the rope to Sullivan.

"Hold this end. Let the rope out as you go. Don't let go and don't go too fast."

"What about the gun?" asked Sullivan.

Smith grinned. "You don't need it. If you do, I'll give you one."

"Okay."

"Is that what you killed the guy with?"

"Yeah."

"If we get out of here alive, I'm going to have it gold-plated for you."

Sullivan descended slowly, aided by Smith, who governed the flow of the rope. When he was on the floor at the very bottom of the elevator shaft, Smith lowered Katie's body down through the dim light, using the ropes and the leverage of his body weight against hers, with the steel cable housing as a sort of down-and-dirty pulley, to bring her down gently. When she was down, Smith tied off the top of one of the ropes and quickly rappelled down.

Smith looked for a door and found it. He and

Sullivan lifted her and walked toward the subbasement, then up one flight. As they got to the top of the stairs, they heard voices. A team of FBI EMTs was charging toward them, wheeling a gurney. Behind them, another crew was cutting apart the students, freeing them.

After Katie was secure, the EMTs moved quickly toward the tunnel beyond the students.

"Coming through!"

Smith turned to Sullivan. "Contractor?"

"Yeah."

"What kind of stuff?"

"Mostly kitchens."

Smith nodded. He put his hand on Sullivan's shoulder.

"I'm going back in. I want you to walk through that tunnel. I'll tell them you're coming. You can get a cup of coffee, see how your kid's doing. What do you have, daughter or son?"

"Daughter."

"Go see how your daughter's doing."

"Thanks."

"No, Jack. Thank you."

"Mr. Smith," said Sullivan, "there's a woman on the third floor. She's in the last room on the right, hiding beneath the bed."

"I'll make sure we get her out safely."

Tacoma stood at the east stairwell, back against the steel door. He was breathing quickly and drenched in sweat. His left side was pressed against the door, left hand on the knob. In his right hand was a SIG Sauer P226 .45 caliber semi-automatic, silver silencer threaded to the muzzle.

He waited, listening.

Strapped across his back was an HK MP7A1, the same submachine gun as Dewey's. The retractable butt was folded, the fire selector set to full-auto: Tacoma didn't like to fuck around.

"Rob, go when you hear screams."

Tacoma turned the knob but didn't open the door.

He heard Igor. *"Now, Dewey!"*

Dewey was moving.

Tacoma took a deep breath, turned the knob a little farther, and spoke: "Give me positioning, Igor."

Screams from the floor above.

"Rob, you have a guy in the room immediately to your right. The terrorist at the far end of the hallway is on the left side. Both men are moving to the hallway."

Tacoma pulled the door open and stepped in, back against the wall, SIG P226 clutched in his right hand, aimed at the door to the right.

Several gasps came from students in the hallway. Tacoma put his left index finger to his mouth, telling the students to be quiet as he slid silently along the wall until he was in the corner, parallel to the door.

Tacoma saw the short steel end of the Uzi first as the terrorist charged into the hall. The terrorist didn't notice him. Tacoma triggered the gun. The slug spat from the pistol, ripping the terrorist in the temple. A red cloud of bloody mist sprayed the door as students screamed. The terrorist crumpled, his face turned toward Tacoma, lifeless.

Tacoma holstered the SIG as he stepped into the hall. In one fluid motion, he swept the MP7 from across his back, unfolded it, raised it, and looked quickly through the optic.

Contingency.

Plan for the worst.

But what he saw startled him, even causing him to momentarily lower the gun and lose the target.

The terrorist was in the hallway. He held a young female student in one hand and had his gun pressed to her skull. The hall was silent. Slowly, the terrorist looked at Tacoma.

Tacoma fired without aiming—a three-burst spray of slugs that flew down the hallway just as the terrorist pressed his trigger. The man kicked violently as slugs ripped his back, neck, and skull. He dropped in a contorted heap, facefirst.

The girl screamed as she held her bloody cheek, nicked by the gunman's bullet.

"I'm clear on ten," he said.

Tacoma pointed the MP7 at the ceiling. He stepped toward the first cluster of students, seated several feet away.

"Stay where you are," he said. "I'm American. We're here to rescue you. But we're not out of this yet. I repeat: *Stay where you are!*"

Sirhan heard the screams from below. He ran to the stairs and started to charge down. Halfway to eleven, he heard the deep baritone of a foreign voice. American.

He sprinted back up the stairs and down the hallway. His eyes were drawn right, to the south side of the building. He saw the two black specters in the same moment he heard the deep whirr of the helicopters slashing the air.

Sirhan stopped.

The din of the FBI choppers grew louder.

Dewey picked up his .45 from the carpet and was already moving when Igor came over commo, urgency—even panic—in his voice.

"He heard something," yelled Igor. *"He's running to the stairs!"*

Screams from the tenth floor suddenly echoed up from below.

"Which side of the building?" Dewey asked as he charged toward the stairs that would deliver him up to the twelfth floor.

"East side. He's coming to see—no wait, he's going up! *He's going for the roof!*"

A female voice startled him: *"Dewey!"*

He stopped and looked down the hallway,

scanning the swarm of students and parents now looking at him. Standing in a doorway was Daisy. He paused for several moments, looking at her. He didn't speak.

Igor: *"He's on the thirteenth floor! Run, Dewey! You can cut him off!"*

"I'll be right back," he finally said to Daisy.

"No," she said, shaking her head.

"Tell everyone to stay where they are," he said. "It's not over."

Daisy nodded, putting her hand to her mouth, trying not to cry.

He charged up the stairs three steps at a time. He passed the entrance to the twelfth floor and kept moving.

"He's almost there!"

When he got to the thirteenth floor, he found the door to the hallway open, pushed by the wind. The choppers sounded as if they were only a few feet away. Dewey held for a half second, then slunk into the hallway, looking around but seeing nothing.

"...he's...!"

Igor was saying something, but Dewey couldn't hear him. Was the terrorist on the roof already? He had to be.

As much as he tried to not think about it, Dewey found his mind imagining the moment when the terrorist ripped the wire and sent the bombs tumbling to the ground—the detonation and destruction.

You won't feel it.

He ran up the stairs to the roof. There was a darkened alcove next to the door, and he swung the pistol. His eyes adjusted and he saw a shoulder-fired missile, already in its launcher.

The sound of the choppers was deafening. He glanced out to the roof. Both helicopters hovered just feet above the roofline and the surreal web of wire, saddled atop with IEDs.

Where is he?

It was pandemonium. Igor was yelling. Dewey held his .45 out in front of him, guessing the last terrorist was outside, just around the corner.

". . . Dewey!"

Dewey covered his ear with his left hand, trying to hear Igor.

". . . behind you!"

The next thing he knew, a knife plunged into his back. It entered below his right shoulder blade and moved deep and quickly.

Dewey let out an anguished groan as he slammed into the floor, then another as the blade was pushed farther in.

Igor's warning had been too late to avoid the knife, but it had saved his life. If Dewey hadn't turned at the last moment, the knife would've gone into his back and straight through his heart.

He couldn't breathe. Blood spat from his mouth and nose as ferocious pain savaged every part of him.

The pain from the blade handle underneath his back, banging against hard concrete, and the blunt steel now goring his chest was otherworldly, the kind of moment that can never be forgotten, a moment just before death. A moment instead of death.

Gun.

Instinct, desperation, fear, above all, an animal need to keep living made Dewey reflexively lurch, still clinging to the handgun—somehow managing to stand—and fire at the dark blur that was now above him. Dewey fought to keep his eyes open and he searched within the fading light for the terrorist, firing again and again, the dull spit of the slugs lost in the gale until he heard the scream.

Dewey kept firing, emptying the mag into the black-clad figure, until there was only the click of the chamber on empty and the watery cough of blood, choking him now. Blindness swept his eyes, and all he could hear was a low, horrible groan, as an animal makes whose leg has been torn off by the steel teeth of a hunter's trap—and he realized the sound was coming from him. He wanted to lie down, but he knew he needed to move. Not because he could do anything more. He needed to move because he knew if he didn't get to a hospital immediately, he would die.

But he tumbled to the ground.

A few moments later, he heard footsteps, then Tacoma.

"Dewey!"

He felt Tacoma's hand turning him over on his side so that the blade wasn't pushed by the concrete.

"Holy shit," Tacoma said. "Igor, tell McNaughton to move the choppers back. Twelve is dead. The wind is going to knock the bombs down. Then get a mobile surgical unit up here. Dewey's been stabbed and I'm not sure he can be moved. They need to hurry. He's going to bleed out."

Tacoma sat down next to Dewey. He inspected the knife that jutted from both sides of Dewey's body. Tacoma lifted Dewey's head so that he didn't drown in his own blood. Blood was everywhere.

"Dewey!"

Dewey heaved involuntarily. The spasm was like a convulsion, and Tacoma knew he was drowning.

"Igor," said Tacoma, "change that. We need one of the choppers to lower a line down *now.* Dewey's about to go cardiac. If he doesn't get to a hospital in the next minute or two, he's going to die."

67

SITUATION ROOM
THE WHITE HOUSE
WASHINGTON, D.C.

The Situation Room was crowded with people: White House senior staff, National Security, CIA, NSA, Pentagon, Homeland, FBI, and State Department.

The walls were covered in plasma screens—sixteen in all—and all were in use. A screen in the middle of the room had flashing, bright yellow letters and numbers:

CENCOM
00:00:00
EST ARR TARGET=01:27:44

Four screens showed live video of Columbia University, the dormitory seen from different angles.

Another six screens displayed various iconographies of the Mexican container ship, now loaded with nearly a billion dollars' worth of guns, ammunition, and shoulder-fired missiles. Four were delivering a real-time video stream of action on the ship. Another provided an aerial view from a drone overhead. One more displayed the section of the Mediterranean, with a large flashing red X that was the ship and a green circle representing the Syrian Port of al-Bayda.

President Dellenbaugh sat at the head of the table. He was quiet. Bill Polk was speaking, presenting an ad hoc operation that required immediate action.

The ship had been moved closer to the Syrian coast in case the decision was a go. They would need to execute the plan quickly, before Nazir realized or found out the dorm had been lost.

"Nazir doesn't know the dorm has been taken back," said Polk. "He doesn't know his men are dead. So why tell him? We shut down all live coverage from Columbia. Move the students out through the basement. Pretend the terrorists are still in control. We cave in and let the ship go. We have eleven Navy SEALs on board that boat. Send the ship in, then lay waste to whoever comes to meet it. Trojan horse."

Harry Black, the secretary of defense, was Polk's main opponent.

"If it works, great," said Black, his voice deep and gruff. "But if it backfires, ISIS might somehow still end up with the weapons. There are enough arms on that ship to finish the job in Syria and Iraq. Why create that sort of intolerable risk? Without the shipment, ISIS has serious, possibly fatal, problems."

"They'll figure out another way to get weapons," said Brubaker, the national security advisor. "This operation shows how resourceful Nazir is. It's worth the risk. We can always drop bombs on the ship if what you're saying happens."

"And kill a team of SEALs?"

"Mr. Secretary, if what you're saying could happen does happen, they'll already be dead."

Stacy Conneely, Langley's top ISIS analyst, chimed in. "I believe Nazir might even show up to inspect the boat," she said.

"Ego?" asked the president.

"No, Mr. President. Symbolism. It's the image, like MacArthur walking ashore at Leyte. Actually, now that I think about it, I'd bet anything."

"You willing to bet your life?" asked Black, pointing at the twenty-nine-year-old. "Because that's what we'll be doing with the lives of those men."

"Yes, I would," said Conneely. "But Bill's right. It only works as long as the illusion of Columbia is still real. We need to hurry."

Black was mildly irate. He turned to Dellenbaugh.

"Let's quit while we're ahead, Mr. President."

"We're not ahead, Mr. Secretary," said Dellenbaugh. "We're behind. We created this monster. We'll be ahead when he's dead. Send the ship."

68

CARMAN HALL
COLUMBIA UNIVERSITY

Tacoma dragged Dewey as gently as possible to the edge of the roof. There was just enough space to lift him through, but it would be awfully tricky. The wires crisscrossed the entire roof like a web. He couldn't even imagine how FBI munitions would remove the wires without detonating the bombs.

He was patched into the pilot of the FBI helicopter that now hovered above the roof.

"You ready?" asked the pilot.

"Yeah, let it down. Real slow. We can't let it touch the wires."

"Roger, guide us down."

Tacoma glanced at Dewey. His big frame looked relaxed. He was unconscious. Tacoma realized he might never gain consciousness again.

"Fuck that!"

"Come again, Rob?"

"Nothing. Just talking to myself."

A steel cable descended from the side of the chopper. The wind was furious. At the end of the cable, a large, heavy steel hook dangled. Still, the wind played with the cable, jostling it back and forth, until its swing was too wide. It was impossible to catch.

"No," said Tacoma. "Bring it back up, then down."

The same thing happened three more times. On the next attempt, something changed and the shear wasn't as powerful. The hook moved lower and lower. Tacoma—his hip pressing gently against the outermost piece of wire—grabbed it.

"Got it!" yelled Tacoma. "Steady now! I need two more feet."

He pulled the cable down toward Dewey, lying at his feet, until the hook was just above him. Tacoma latched the hook to a steel loop on Dewey's vest.

Now came the hard part. Working with the chopper winch, Tacoma would have to help lift Dewey so that all parts of his body avoided the wire on the way up.

"Okay, guys," said Tacoma. "Real slow. Can you see me?"

"Yeah, we got you. Here we go."

The cable tightened and Dewey's slack body climbed up into the air. His head was beneath the outermost edge of wire. Tacoma grabbed Dewey and—just as his head was about to bump into the underside of the wire—heaved Dewey away from the roof. Tacoma gritted his teeth as he held Dewey away from the wire as the helicopter lifted him up. When he was above the plane of the wire, he held another few seconds, then slowly let the pendulum of Dewey's large frame move back above the wire, directly underneath the chopper.

"Lift him!" yelled Tacoma.

"Roger," said the pilot.

Two men pulled Dewey's bloody body inside the hovering chopper. One of them saluted Tacoma, who nodded back. The door shut and the chopper lifted, then slashed nearly horizontal as it bolted away from Carman.

69

NEAR AL-BAYDA
SYRIA

The container ship moved slowly toward a deserted promontory of land near al-Bayda, a windswept, out-of-the-way coastal town just south of the Turkish border.

The ship was guided by a single tugboat, manned by Syrian fishermen loyal to ISIS.

Al-Bayda was remote, which was precisely the point. Remoteness was what was called for under the circumstances. A deep hole lay along the promontory's northern edge, the result of being dredged more than fifty years ago when someone in the Syrian government had decreed that al-Bayda have its own deepwater pier. But the pier was never built. Only the trench remained, along with a large flatland just next to it.

Miguel counted at least a dozen flatbed trucks, all waiting for the cargo. Several pickup trucks and three SUVs were parked nearby, in view of the ship but not in the way of the gantry crane that would be used to off-load the boxes of weapons.

Two men stood on the bridge of the 662-foot ship: Miguel, the vessel's Mexican captain, and another man, much younger, who wore a black nylon mask over his face. He also had on a black short-sleeve button-down shirt, black pants, and boots. He clutched an AK-47, which he trained at the ground, only a few feet away from Miguel.

Miguel's eyes moved right. A black pickup truck appeared along the rocky shore, its headlights on.

Miguel watched the ship's speed relative to the unfinished jetty, knowing they were going too fast, but he knew the hull of his ship was of no consequence to the pigs of ISIS. A few moments later, he felt a slight kick from somewhere near the bow. The tugboat had delivered them hard into the dredged-out trench near the ugly, empty shore.

Crewmen anchored the ship and extended the gangway to the rocks below.

It was 2:48 a.m.

Miguel flipped on the vessel's lights, illuminating everything in bright yellow. He left the bridge and took the stairs to the deck of the ship.

He walked to the starboard side and stood

looking down on the dock. Two men emerged from the pickup truck, both ISIS. One wore jeans and a gray T-shirt. The other had on black khakis and a short-sleeve shirt. Both men had on black ski masks.

"They all look the fucking same," he muttered. "Why bother with the masks?"

They stepped to the edge of the rocky coastline.

"Start unloading," ordered one of the men, pointing to the containers.

"I need a signature first," said Miguel.

The two men conferred. "Bring it down here."

"You come up here."

"No," said the man on the right. "Bring it down!"

Miguel shook his head.

"No. These are my orders from the United States government. These do not belong to you until I deliver them."

Again, the two men conferred. After more than a minute, both men moved to the walkway and climbed aboard the ship.

Miguel met them near the top of the gangway.

"Which one of you is Nazir?"

The two men looked at Miguel, then at each other.

They conversed in Arabic for more than a minute.

The tall Arab spoke. *"Give us the fucking containers,"* he seethed.

"No," said Miguel. "I was told that under no circumstance am I to deliver anything without his signature."

"Fine, I'm Nazir. Give me the form."

Miguel pulled the clipboard away.

"He has an eye patch. Even I know that."

"Are you out of your mind?"

"I do what I'm told. The Americans want their hostages back. You want your weapons. 'You' means Nazir."

"What happens if he doesn't sign for it? He could be traveling."

"I'll wait," said Miguel.

The short man reached behind his back and pulled out a gun.

"There's one man who knows how to operate the crane on that ship," said Miguel, "and it's not you, Mohammed. And if you think you can do it yourself, go ahead and try. But the man from the U.S. government told me that if you hurt me or any of my men, they will know it's a trap, which they said wouldn't be the first time for you people, and they will destroy everything within a square mile of this place. Got it? You'll get your weapons, America will get its hostages, and I will get to see my family again. Go get Nazir."

He holstered the pistol, shaking his head in anger.

"He's hours away from here. This is ridiculous. I will see if I can get him on the phone."

"Signature. Nothing less."

"It could take days."

"I have days. How many days do you think I've been at sea?"

"How do we know it's not a trap?"

"I'm a ship captain," said Miguel, shrugging. "What do I know? Wouldn't the Americans lose all the students if they did something to him?"

The men turned and walked down the gangplank. They climbed into the truck. The truck sped quickly down the pier and out of sight.

Suddenly, the doors of the three SUVs opened. The drivers all had weapons, which they trained in Miguel's direction.

Then two men emerged from one of them. One was Nazir. The other man, in jeans and a white button-down, was taking video of Nazir.

Nazir walked slowly behind the vehicles, flanked on either side by gunmen. The photographer walked backward, in front of Nazir, filming his every move.

He'd been there the entire time, no doubt waiting for the containers to start getting offloaded so he could have a photo op.

"Un-fucking-believable," said Miguel under his breath.

Nazir was tall. His hair was slightly long and combed to the side, where it feathered above the eye patch. He walked with a regal bearing, his posture straight. His presence was unmistakable.

Everyone around him either stared at him in awe, or swept their weapons toward the shadows, as if protecting a god. He wore a white shirt and dark slacks. He looked clean-shaven. But the eye patch gave him a malevolent air. Or perhaps it was simply Miguel's knowledge of everything he had done. The lives he'd taken and the way he'd taken them. The children pushed from high floors, the beheadings of innocent citizens.

Even Miguel felt his own adrenaline spike as the terrorist approached the ship.

When Nazir reached the end of the gangway, he allowed the photographer to go before him and take up position on the ship. The man gave him a slight nod, and Nazir stepped forward and climbed. When he reached the deck, he approached Miguel, who was standing in front of one of the containers.

The ISIS leader was calm. He glanced once up at the sky, then looked at Miguel.

"I'm Tristan Nazir."

Miguel looked at him for an extra moment, then extended the clipboard. Nazir took it and signed it, then handed it back.

"Is there anything else?" asked Nazir.

"No. We will move the containers to the parking area."

Nazir, for the first time, surveyed the deck of the ship. Nearly every square foot was covered in containers, stacked five and ten high.

He walked back to the gangway and started to climb down.

Suddenly, the photographer said something in Arabic:

"*Alsyd alrrayiys, madha ean surat mae al'asliha?*"

Mr. President, what about a picture with the weapons, as we discussed?

Nazir paused, then shrugged and turned.

Miguel walked toward the base of the crane.

"Excuse me," said the photographer. "Open one of the containers. We want video."

Miguel looked at the man with annoyance. "Fine. Stand back. One of these doors would crush you."

Then he added, barely above a whisper, "Not that I would mind."

Miguel removed a large round steel spike inserted at the juncture of the end of the container and the side. He repeated it on the other corner. He looked in front of the container to make sure no one was standing there. Finally, he eyed the photographer, who held a camera and was waiting. He nodded to Miguel.

Miguel reached up and yanked one of the spikes, thrusting the heavy end piece outward. It slowly eased away, the rusted hinges creaking. Then he removed the other spike. As the massive piece of steel swung down toward the deck, the dull *thwack! thwack! thwack!* of suppressed

581

automatic weapon fire punctured the air. The bullets took down every man on the deck before the gunmen arched their weapons and sprayed the ISIS guards along the rocky coast in lead.

By the time the steel slammed onto the deck, two black-clad commandos had emerged from the container, killing almost everything in sight, and burning through the oversized mags of 7.62mm cartridges clutched in the gut of their carbines. As they jutted left, a second pair of commandos charged out, filling in the gap between the first two, who quickly dropped their mags and slammed in new ones. From the instant the container door was halfway to the ground, not a moment had gone by in which the sound of Navy SEAL gunfire hadn't tuned the air.

And yet still more men emerged.

The next pair held MANPADs atop their shoulders. They stepped to the deck as, all around them, their teammates continued to rip steel into the ISIS SUVs and other vehicles on land. They let their missiles fly. They slammed into the posse of vehicles, causing a large explosion as gasoline ignited under the intense heat of the blasts.

The few gunshots from Nazir's guards stopped just seconds into the attack.

Still, the Navy commandos moved carefully down the gangway, with multiple layers of cover. They methodically swept through the destroyed remnants of SUVs, pickups, and flatbed semitrucks, looking for anyone hiding. They inspected each ISIS guard, making sure they all were dead. Twice, quick blasts from one of the commandos indicated that a pulse had been found.

Ryan, the team leader, who'd been one of the first two commandos to emerge—the most vulnerable—walked over to Nazir.

Nazir stood still, surveying the carnage. In the silence that followed, Ryan reached to his waist and removed a SIG Sauer P226 from his holster. He aimed it at Nazir.

"Not your lucky day," said Ryan.

"Who are you?"

"The dormitory failed," said Ryan. "We killed all your men."

"I don't believe you."

"It's true. All of them."

Nazir surveyed Ryan. He looked down at the ground, struggling for words.

"So this was all . . . a subterfuge?"

Ryan said nothing. He kept the gun aimed at Nazir's head.

"You have no intention of killing me. I know too much."

"Should I cut off your head," asked Ryan, ignoring Nazir, anger in his voice, "or burn you?"

"I could be extremely valuable to the United States," said Nazir. "Even in a prison cell."

Ryan shook his head. "There might be some

guys in my government who think that way, but I'm not one of them."

"You're making a mistake. I can help your country. I demand you ask your superiors!"

Ryan glared at Nazir. His eyes moved to the burning vehicles onshore. He took a step toward the side of the ship, nodding at one of his men to keep Nazir under the muzzle.

Ryan tapped his ear three times.

"Centurion to Tower Three, over."

"Roger, Centurion. What do you got, Billy?"

"I want to make sure as to the ROE, sir," said Ryan, glancing at Nazir, who stood at the far side of the deck.

"You know the answer to that."

"Do we need to run it by Langley, sir?"

"I already did," said Bosse, Ryan's SEAL team commander. "Also ran it by the White House. Kill 'em."

Ryan tapped his ear. He glanced at Nazir, adopting a slightly chastened look. Slowly, reluctantly, Ryan ambled back toward Nazir.

"Well, Mr. Nazir, you were right," said Ryan, holstering his gun beneath his armpit. "Apparently you are to be escorted to the United States and offered immunity in exchange for your help."

Nazir straightened, his posture becoming erect and dignified.

"I told you."

Ryan moved in front of Nazir. He stared at him for several seconds.

"Just kidding," said Ryan, pulling his gun from his holster and sweeping it to Nazir's head.

Ryan fired. The bullet hit Nazir in his good eye, a nickel-shaped hole that sprouted as the slug fragmented and the lead pellets became heated physics inside the trajectory of the casing, expanding the path of the bullet, grabbing at tender flesh, so that, by the time it reached the back of Nazir's skull, it was avocado size. The back of Nazir's head, accompanied by a meaningful handful of brains and skull, went flying, followed soon after by Nazir, who fell awkwardly.

Ryan holstered his gun. He stepped forward and lifted Nazir with one hand, grabbing the front of his shirt. He carried Nazir to the side of the ship and unceremoniously threw the corpse overboard. He heard the dull *thunk* as the body landed on some rocks next to the ship.

Ryan put two fingers in his mouth and blew a short, sharp whistle to his men.

We're moving.

He looked at Miguel.

"Let's get out of here."

70

Summer Dellenbaugh walked out of her bedroom and down the long, high-ceilinged hall to the large living room that was the centerpiece of the private residence for the first family. Summer had on orange corduroy pants and a dark blue sweater. It was 6 a.m. on a Saturday morning.

Her father, President J. P. Dellenbaugh, was seated on a large armchair, one leg draped over the arm. He was sipping coffee. There was no newspaper, iPad, cell phone, magazine, briefing paper, or anything else. Dellenbaugh was simply sitting and thinking.

When you're president, what most people don't understand is that you are the same person you were before you were president. In fact, you are the same person you've always been, deep down. Much of Dellenbaugh's thoughts were in fact preoccupied with this. He never wanted to lose that thing that made him real. The kid who helped his dad build the backyard hockey rink back in Michigan. The Detroit Red Wing who had his nose broken in a fight after scoring the game-

586

tying goal in game three of the Stanley Cup Playoffs. The man people always seemed to like, and who somehow ended up becoming president. It astonished him. It was what confirmed his belief in God, and it was what made him the most popular president in a generation.

"Hi, Dad," Summer said.

"Hey, cutie. What are you all dressed up for?"

"I thought I would go with you today," she said.

"Really?" he asked, smiling, impressed. "Did your mother tell you to do this?"

"No. I just want to go."

"Oh, okay," said Dellenbaugh, sipping from his mug. "And why is that?"

"I want to thank them."

Dellenbaugh reached out his arms, motioning for his daughter to come close. She walked to him and he gave her a hug.

"I'm proud of you," said Dellenbaugh.

"Thanks, Dad. I'm proud of you too."

"Summer, what you're going to see isn't pretty. All three of them were severely injured. They might not be able to even see us. I just want you to understand that."

"Dad, I'm almost twelve. I think I can handle it."

The motorcade was long, extended, and highly secure. There were eight vehicles in the staff section, all bulletproof and flexed-out with a variety of accoutrements such as run-flat tires and supplemental oxygen. The presidential state car was in the middle of the motorcade. It was a customized Cadillac DTS limousine, with a shell of armor capable of withstanding most armaments below missile as well as protecting against biochemical attacks. A switch in back sealed the interior as tight as a supersonic jet. Another switch kicked a five-hour supply of oxygen into the limo. In the trunk was a container of the president's blood type.

Multiple Chevy Suburbans and vans were intermixed with the sedans. They carried a variety of FBI and Secret Service agents with enough firepower to start a small war. A half dozen police cars were also in the motorcade. All of it formed a long line that moved quickly north up the Rock Creek Parkway. A missile-laden helicopter glided overhead, high enough to be unobtrusive, low enough to react to any airborne intrusions or on-the-ground situations that the police, FBI, and Secret Service couldn't manage.

Dellenbaugh was seated at the back of the presidential limousine. Summer was on his left. Holden Weese, his personal aide, was across from him. Dellenbaugh was reading a briefing sheet.

Weese dialed a number into a phone and then handed it to the president.

"Haley and Barbara Lancaster," said Weese. "From Rochester, New York."

Dellenbaugh took the phone. He glanced at Summer, then looked at Weese.

"Stephen," said Weese.

Dellenbaugh put the phone to his head.

"I'm here."

"White House Control, they are on."

"Thank you." Then came a click.

"Hello?"

"Haley?"

"Yes, sir."

"This is J. P. Dellenbaugh."

"I know, sir."

"Is Barbara on too?"

"No, she's not. Don't get me wrong. She supports you, Mr. President. But she hasn't been well."

"It would have destroyed me," said Dellenbaugh. "I can't imagine. I'm so sorry."

Dellenbaugh heard the beginning of a low, painful series of sobs on the line.

"I'm sorry . . . Mr. President," he whispered in between sobs.

"It's okay," said Dellenbaugh. "Go ahead. I'd be doing the same thing."

Dellenbaugh let him cry for almost twenty seconds, occasionally saying something like, "It's okay. You go ahead."

Finally, Haley Lancaster, father of Stephen Lancaster, a freshman at Columbia, stopped crying.

589

"He was such a smart kid, Mr. President," Lancaster said proudly.

Dellenbaugh reached out and grabbed Summer's hand.

"Valedictorian from School of the Arts," said Dellenbaugh, referring to Rochester's premier high school. "I hear he also got into Harvard, Stanford, Princeton, and Bowdoin."

"But he chose Columbia," said Lancaster.

"I'm guessing he would've been a professor someday."

"That's exactly what he would've been."

"I spoke with Lee Bollinger yesterday," said Dellenbaugh, referring to Columbia's president. "Columbia is going to create endowed chairs for every student who died. I was thinking that the Stephen J. Lancaster Chair for Civil Engineering had a nice ring to it. What do you think?"

"I think he'd be very proud, Mr. President."

The motorcade swept into Bethesda Medical Center a few minutes before 7 a.m.

On the fourth floor, Dellenbaugh, his daughter, and a trio of armed Secret Service agents stepped off the elevator where doctors, physician assistants, and nurses were gathered.

"Hi, everyone," he said enthusiastically.

"Hi, Mr. President," said one of the nurses. Several other people said hello, while others waved. They all smiled.

"Everyone, this is my daughter, Summer," said Dellenbaugh.

One of the doctors stepped forward. It was Marc Gillinov, the surgeon who'd performed the surgery on Calibrisi.

"Hi, Mr. President," said Gillinov, his Australian accent sharp. He glanced at Summer Dellenbaugh, smiling and nodding. "And you must be the vice president?" he said, extending his hand to her.

She blushed and giggled.

Gillinov looked back at the president,

"Someone said you wanted to see me, sir."

"I heard about the operation," said the president. "That was a gutsy, amazing thing you did. You saved the life of a good man. A good friend. I wanted to thank you."

"You're welcome, sir."

"How is he?" asked Dellenbaugh in a low voice, leaning away from Summer.

"Which 'he' are you talking about?"

"Hector."

"Well, he—"

Gillinov began speaking, but Dellenbaugh interrupted him. "Actually, Dewey," he said.

The surgeon paused, waiting to see if Dellenbaugh was done speaking.

"Dewey is—"

"Katie," interjected Dellenbaugh. "I mean, I know those two are going to be fine. She's the one I should be asking about."

Gillinov let out an exasperated laugh. Dellenbaugh joined him.

"Sorry," he said. "I'm a pain in the ass."

"Not at all, Mr. President. Other than the broken legs, the rotator cuff tear, and the four broken ribs, Katie's in good shape. She's probably in the most pain of all three, but she's also the most out of danger. All I can say is thank God she landed the way she landed. Dewey is continuing to bleed. We went back in today and repaired a small internal hemorrhage caused by the knife. It was tiny, too small for even the human eye to see, but it was growing."

"And Hector?"

Gillinov shrugged. "The heart is continuing to perform. He's damn lucky to be alive."

"Did stress contribute to the heart attack?" asked Dellenbaugh.

"Without question. Forgive my bluntness, but if you want Hector Calibrisi to live a long life, make him retire. Make him ambassador some-where. One more of those, and no fancy surgery is going to save him."

Dellenbaugh patted Gillinov on the back.

"Thanks again, Doctor," said the president.

If only our country could afford to have him retire, he thought.

"So can we go say hi?"

"I suppose so. They're in three adjoining rooms. All I ask is that you not get them too worked up, particularly Hector. No loud noises, movement, anything like that. Same with the other two. Last time I checked, which was an hour ago, all three were resting. Please, if they're still asleep—"

"Of course," said Dellenbaugh. "We'll let them sleep."

They walked down the hallway with Gillinov and a group of other doctors and nurses trailing behind. Near the end of the hall, they stopped at a door.

"This is Dewey's room," said Gillinov. "Go ahead in. *Quietly.*"

Dellenbaugh nodded and looked at Summer.

"Go ahead," he said, encouraging her to knock and go in first.

Summer knocked quietly, then a little louder, but there was no answer. Finally, she pushed the door. All three stepped inside. Of the three, it was Gillinov who had the most shocked look on his face.

He turned to a nurse. "Where is he?" he demanded.

The room was empty. Even the bed was missing.

Gillinov looked at the president with a mildly concerned look on his face.

"Mr. President," said Gillinov, "I have no idea where he is."

A loud yell came from down the hall.

Gillinov—with Dellenbaugh half a step behind

him—ran to the room next door, where the yell had come from. It was empty.

"Get security!" barked Gillinov just as, a moment later, another yell came from somewhere farther along the corridor.

Soon the hallway was mobbed with people, led by Gillinov and Dellenbaugh, with security just behind.

"No!" came a loud female shriek from the next room.

They charged into the room—Gillinov, Dellenbaugh, then a pair of gunmen.

Dewey, Katie, and Hector all looked up. All were in hospital beds, attached to various IVs and life monitors. They were set up in a sort of triangle, in the middle of which a garbage can was propped up on a chair. Dewey had a tennis ball in his left hand, his right being covered in bandages. He was about to throw the ball and try to land it. An impressionable-looking male orderly was standing off to the side, watching and waiting in case the ball missed.

"Jones," said Dewey, talking to the orderly. "What's the score?"

The orderly looked as if he was going to faint. He made eye contact with the president, then gulped. Then he found Gillinov.

"Um, it's Hector five, Katie seven, and you, um . . . well, you don't have any yet, Dewey."

"None? I'm glad you're not the one who

operated on me," said Dewey. "You're obviously blind. I've sunk like twenty in a row."

Dewey lofted the ball. It bounced off the far rim of the trash can and ricocheted. It landed front and center on the blanket on top of Calibrisi.

Several people gasped.

"Asshole," coughed Calibrisi in a raspy voice. He noticed Summer Dellenbaugh. "Ah, excuse me, sir. It's just that . . . well, it's the third time he's hit me."

"That was interference," said Dewey. "I should get another shot."

Dellenbaugh shook his head. "To think I was actually worried about you assholes."

"Dad," said Summer.

"Sorry, honey. Don't tell your mom."

Dellenbaugh signaled to the orderly, who paused for a moment, then tossed the president a ball. Dellenbaugh stood near the door. With the ball in his right hand, he made a few practice motions toward the garbage can, which was in the middle of the room.

Summer looked at Katie and rolled her eyes.

Katie glanced at Dewey.

"I thought only you and Rob were this immature," she muttered to Dewey.

"We're all this immature," whispered Dewey. Then he spoke louder: "Now don't miss, Mr. President." Dewey waved his left arm through the air, trying to distract Dellenbaugh. "Just relax and realize that if you don't sink that shot, World War Three is probably going to break out. Maybe a stock market crash too, followed by a major recession."

Dellenbaugh grinned midtoss said, "Dewey, this is how it's done," then hurled the ball. It sank dead center inside the garbage can. He glanced arrogantly around the room, just as the ball bounced out and landed a foot away, then rolled toward the corner.

Everyone laughed uproariously.

Dellenbaugh looked at Dewey. He had a pissed-off look on his face, the look of a friend who just missed a shot. It melted away. He stepped to him.

"Hi, Dewey," he said, leaning down and hugging him. "Thank you."

Dewey said nothing. After Dellenbaugh stood back up, he looked at Summer.

"This is Summer."

"Hi," said Dewey.

Summer blushed. She stepped forward and extended her hand. Dewey grabbed it with his left hand and gently shook it.

"Hi, Mr. Andreas."

"How old are you? Wait, let me guess."

Dewey scanned Summer from head to toe, then nodded knowingly. "Sixteen," he said.

Her mouth went agape, but before she could say anything, he spoke: "No, wait. Seventeen?"

Summer giggled and shook her head.

"Twenty-two? Oh, my God, you do not look twenty-two years old. Don't take this the wrong way, but you're kind of short."

Summer burst out laughing.

"So you made your daughter come along, huh, Mr. President?" said Calibrisi struggling slightly.

"Actually, he didn't make me," Summer said. She had not let go of Dewey's hand. "I wanted to come and thank you, all of you."

Calibrisi smiled, as did Katie.

"I know I'm only twelve, but everyone knows about what happened. My whole school was talking about it. They were asking me what my dad was going to do and I didn't know what to say. And then you stopped them. It was so amazing. I was so proud. They announced it over the intercom. We all went into the gym and the headmistress, Mrs. Boynton, told everyone. It was very brave of you to climb into that building like that. I'm sorry you got hurt. I just wanted to say thank you, just as a person. Not as my dad's daughter but as an American citizen."

For several seconds, the room was quiet.

Dewey, whose face had remained cool, with a blank expression, suddenly smiled. He reached out and handed the tennis ball to Summer.

"I bet you're a better shot than your dad," he said.

Bashfully, Summer took the ball. She glanced at the garbage can, then looked at her father.

"Sorry, Dad," she said as she tossed the ball. It struck the outer rim of the can, bounced to the other side, and then was thrust up into the air above, where it seemed to hover, as if suspended. A moment later, it dropped into the can.

EPILOGUE

BANGOR ACRES
HERMON, MAINE
THANKSGIVING DAY

"Two passes, please," said Dewey.

The man behind the counter was doing a crossword puzzle. He looked to be in his seventies, with deep creases on his face, thick glasses held together with green duct tape, and a baseball hat whose logo was illegible due to the layers of dirt and oil. He finished penciling in a word and then, with a look of mild annoyance, glanced up at Dewey.

"Eighteen holes or nine?"

"I thought there were only nine holes," said Dewey.

"No, there's eighteen all right."

"When did you guys put in another nine holes?"

"We didn't. You just play the same ones over again."

Dewey glanced at Daisy.

"We'll play nine," he said.

"It's the same price either way," said the man.

"What's the point in—" Dewey started to say, then stopped. "We'll play nine."

"Okey dokey." The man leaned a little to his left so he could see Daisy, who was standing just behind Dewey.

"One adult and one child," he said with a thick accent and a shit-eating grin. "That'll be twelve dollars."

Dewey threw down a twenty as Daisy laughed.

Dewey leaned forward and whispered, "Keep the change. Get yourself some breath mints."

"Why would I do that?" he asked, pushing eight dollars back to Dewey. "Last girl I kissed was in 1978. That jackass peanut farmer was president. Enjoy it while you can, hotshot."

Dewey escorted Daisy to the rack of putters near the first tee, a sorry-looking collection of dented, rusty, bent, duct-taped clubs all of which had seen better days.

"Any advice?" she asked, looking at the row of putters.

"Personally, I like to go with something with advanced perimeter weighting and a solid, forgiving feel," said Dewey.

"Has anyone ever told you you're a jackass?"

Dewey ignored her and picked up a dilapidated putter with a crust of rust and a torn handle.

"As for you, you're new to this. An amateur, so to speak."

Dewey eyed the putters and removed one that had, at some point, been a woman's putter, a pinkish handle still visible. It appeared to be in pretty good shape, except that it was bent in the middle at an almost ninety-degree angle. With a little effort, he bent it back.

"This has a nice balance between length and loft," said Dewey, handing it to her. "I think you'll do well with it. If I'm not mistaken, Hobey's the one who originally bent it after he and I had a slight scoring dispute a few years ago."

Daisy was shaking her head and laughing.

Dewey and Daisy were the only ones on the course, which, like the putters, and like the old man behind the ticket counter, had perhaps passed the zenith of its splendor. A few of the holes still had plastic carpeting, though it was well-worn and had tears, stains, and missing sections. Most of the holes were plywood with a coat of paint on top. As for the obstacles—a sadistic-looking clown with a tunnel through its left shoe, a replica of a Mississippi River steamboat with a ramp that led to a mazelike curving ball chute on top, a hole with mirrors on both sides intended to create some sort of visual challenge—they too looked like the only thing keeping them from the local landfill was the lack of someone willing to bring them there.

At the second-to-last hole, Daisy stared at the obstacle, nothing more than a two-by-four painted brown that led to a pile of wood.

She looked at Dewey with a quizzical look on her face, as if to say, *What is it?*

Dewey shrugged.

"Last time I played there was a plastic pig lying there," he said. "You had to hit the ball into its mouth, then it came out its—the other side. Someone must've stolen the pig."

"Maybe we should skip this one?"

Dewey nodded. "Sure, but you sort of need it. I'm beating you by a fairly hefty margin."

"Beating me? I didn't know we're keeping score."

"Of course we are. Bangor Acres. You gotta keep score."

"And where have you been keeping score, Dewey?" she asked. "I don't see any scoring sheet."

Dewey tapped his temple. "Up here."

"Right," she said, laughing. "Like I would ever trust you to keep score."

"You don't trust me? I'm offended."

"Dewey, first of all, you're terrible. I can't believe I believed you were this great golfer. Then I find out it's miniature golf, which is a joke, and you're not even good. It took you five shots to get it around that red squirrel thing back there."

"That was a lobster. And that was my mulligan."

"Oh."

They came to the last hole. After a short straightaway, a beat-up windmill spanned the end of a plywood straightaway. The mildew-covered shingles of the windmill were covered in seagull excrement.

"This is the windmill?"

"Yeah. It's kind of pretty, isn't it?"

"Very picturesque."

A small opening was visible in the middle. The big wheel that should have been spinning around and blocking the hole every few seconds sat stationary.

Dewey stared at it for a few seconds. He looked mildly peeved.

"For chrissakes," he said. "Twelve bucks, you'd think the one thing they could do was keep the windmill working."

Daisy handed him her putter and walked to the windmill. She climbed around it, inspecting it, leaning close to the dollhouse-size window near the top.

"At least the squirrels like it," she said.

She looked at Dewey and then cast her eyes toward the old man at the ticket booth, whose back was turned. Suddenly, she leaned back and kicked the windmill as hard as she could. A cacophonous *bang* rattled the air. The old man didn't so much as budge.

"What are you doing?" asked Dewey.

Daisy kicked again, harder this time. The windmill miraculously started spinning slowly around.

She walked triumphantly back to the tee.

"Fo shizzle my nizzle," she said, taking her putter from Dewey and setting up her ball on the broken tee.

"I'm not going to ask you what that means."

"Good, because I don't know. Now, it seems to me the fixing of your precious little windmill by yours truly means we're even. So what say we make this last little hole interesting, Andreas. Or are you . . . scared?"

Dewey leaned close to Daisy, his nose almost touching hers.

"Nobody has ever beaten me at the windmill," he said. "Name your price."

"Okay, fine. If I win, you have to kiss me. A real kiss."

Dewey looked at her with a blank expression. Slowly, he started to nod.

"I suppose that wouldn't be the worst thing in the world," he said. "What about if I win?"

"Name *your* price."

"You have to kiss the old man."

"Ewww."

Dewey thought for a few seconds. "I win, we skinny-dip off the town dock."

Daisy's smile vanished.

"It's late November," she said. "Thanksgiving. Remember? We'll freeze to death. Plus you still have about a kajillion stitches and a bandage."

"Salt water won't hurt it."

"It's like forty-eight degrees outside!"

"Then you better make sure you sink that ball."

Daisy shook her head and moved over the ball. She studied the windmill as it circled around and around, lifted the putter far too high, as if she was going to drive it, then hit. The ball went sailing hard to the left, banging off a board, then ricocheted and bounced wildly toward the windmill, somehow screeching into the hole below. A series of loud bangs echoed from the inside followed by a few moments of quiet and then a distinctive clinking noise.

Daisy looked at Dewey, her face beaming. She ran around the windmill and looked in.

"Hole in one!" she shouted as she jumped up and down.

"Okay, hot stuff, stand back."

Dewey put his ball on the tee. He glanced at the spinning wheel, then hit. The ball rolled slowly toward the hole just as the windmill spun around and closed the hole. The ball escaped in just as the hole opened back up. Dewey walked casually around the windmill just as the ball struck a board at the far side, bounced back, and rolled painfully slowly toward the cup, where it stopped at the lip for a moment just as Dewey got there.

He jumped in the air and came down hard. The ground shook a tiny bit. The ball trickled in.

"That was unfair," Daisy said.

"Life is unfair."

"Well, it looks like it's a tie," she said. "What should we do?"

The table was set. The bottles of wine were open. The keg of Pumpkinhead Ale was on ice. The lamps were lit. The laughter was loud.

Reagan and Sam Andreas had built an eighteen-foot-long harvest table out of old barn boards, then hauled it out to the middle of the big lawn in front of the Andreas farmhouse. Tiki lamps surrounded the table, sending smoky orange flames up into the starry evening as the Andreas family and their friends gathered for Thanksgiving.

It was originally planned for inside the house, but this year's weather had been crazy. Tonight, the temperature in Castine was fifty-two degrees.

Just in case, a bonfire crackled the air near Margaret Andreas's garden, now put away for winter. Chairs surrounded the burning wood, each one filled with an Andreas family member or close friend. Laughter mixed with the sound of the fire, and the orange flames twisted up into a sky that was star-filled and cloudless.

The mood was that magical one, when a family and their closest friends are together, and the air is warm but not hot, and something special is about to happen, something everyone knows is going to happen, but hasn't happened yet. The anticipation of a simple thing that is to come.

There were supposed to be twenty-two people in all, but at some point during the day the size of the Thanksgiving dinner had climbed to more than fifty.

Hobey had smoked a pair of turkeys on the Big Green Egg, with assistance from Sam. Margaret had, as usual, roasted a turkey indoors.

Grey Terry, from up the road, hauled over his old wooden cider press and, with some assistance from the youngsters, made several gallons of apple cider. He'd also been kind enough to supply some rum—cheap stuff, but better than no stuff.

The ocean was visible from the hilltop perch they called Margaret Hill. It may not have been the fanciest of Castine addresses, but, as everyone knew, it was the prettiest.

Then that thing occurred, that simple thing they were all waiting for.

A blue pickup truck, a Ford F-250, with dried mud on its tires and sides, rolled slowly along the meandering dirt driveway that skirted the edge of the farm's peeling white picket fence.

It was not an exaggeration to say that every person gathered that evening turned at the same moment to see the guests who had arrived an hour and a half late.

The driver's door opened and a woman stepped

down. She wore a simple white sweater and red pants. On her head was a Boston Bruins cap. Her hair was wet.

Even from 150 yards away, she stood out—sensual, elegant, above all, beautiful. She stepped to the passenger door and opened it. Slowly, a man stepped down. He was dressed in cutoff khaki shorts, flip-flops, and a striped, long-sleeve Lacoste shirt. His hair was also sopping wet.

Daisy looked at Dewey. "That was insane."

"Yeah, but it was fun."

She stepped closer and very gingerly touched his chest on the left side.

"Is it okay?"

"It's fine," he said, smiling.

"So this is your home?"

"Yeah. I know it's not fancy or anything."

"It's just what I imagined," she said. "It's charming."

He blushed.

"Why is everyone staring at us?" she asked, nodding across the field, where the entire table, along with everyone by the bonfire, was looking in their direction.

"They're Mainers," said Dewey. "They like to stare. It's easier than talking."

Daisy laughed.

"So they don't talk very much?"

"No."

"You're kidding?" Daisy said. "A relative of

yours who doesn't talk very much? I can't imagine."

Daisy took his arm and wrapped it around her neck. Dewey grinned. It was barely perceptible, but she noticed.

"I got you," she said.

They started walking toward the feast.

"Just find yourself a drink," said Dewey, "and please don't steal the silverware."

They walked slowly across the field, toward the gathering of family and friends.

Dewey's father and mother stepped across the lawn to greet them.

"Hi, Mom, Dad," Dewey said.

John and Margaret Andreas both reached for Dewey and wrapped their arms around him. They had seen him several times since the events at Columbia, visiting him during the month he was in the ICU at Columbia-Presbyterian Hospital after barely surviving the knife wound inflicted on him by a man who was now, though dead, a household name: Sirhan el-Khan. Still, they held him as if they hadn't seen him in a decade.

"This is Daisy," Dewey said, gently pushing his parents away.

John gave Daisy a hug, followed by Margaret.

"It's so nice to meet you, Daisy," said Dewey's mom. "We've met your father many times. A wonderful man. I heard that he's starting to walk again."

"Yes. He's doing great. Thanks for asking, Mrs. Andreas."

"John and Margaret, dear," said Dewey's father.

"We're delighted to have you," said Margaret. "Dewey has told us a great deal about you."

Daisy looked at Dewey and smiled.

"Oh he has, has he?" she asked.

"Yes," said John. "He said you have a law degree. Hobey has a law degree too."

"He also said you're beautiful," added Margaret.

Daisy looked down, blushed, and smiled at Dewey.

"That was nice of you," said Daisy.

"He also said you two have become friends," said John.

This time it was Dewey who turned a little red as Daisy laughed.

"Yes, we have," she said. "Did your son tell you how he saved my life?"

Margaret looked at Dewey, then back to Daisy. She smiled with unabashed pride.

"He did?" said Margaret. She took a step closer to Daisy. "He's a very special person."

"I know."

Dewey rolled his eyes. "Mom."

"She's just a friend," Dewey had warned his father and mother over the phone when he called them the week before from Washington. "In fact, I'm not even sure she's a friend. She's Hector's daughter, that's all. She wanted to see Maine. She's never been. I had nothing to do so I figured I'd take her. So no comments, looks, winks. I'm not getting involved with anyone. Tell Hobey too. Same with Sam and Reagan. No shit giving. We're friends."

"So why's she coming?" his father asked.

There was a long pause on the phone.

"I guess she wants to see Castine," answered Dewey.

A female voice came on the line; someone had been eavesdropping.

"Why does she need *you* to do that?" asked his mother, who'd been listening in on the upstairs extension.

"When did you get on the phone?" asked John.

"Oh, hush," said Margaret. "Dewey, I can show her around."

Dewey was silent for several moments, trying to come up with an answer.

"I guess maybe I thought she might need a tour guide or something," he said.

"You don't need to come all the way up here, honey, just to show someone's daughter around," said his mother teasingly. "Especially someone you're not sure is even a friend."

"Okay," said Dewey, ignoring his mother, "see you next week. Maybe Hobey can make one of those smoked turkeys again?"

"I'll ask him," said Margaret Andreas, "although

610

he really doesn't like to go through all that effort just for someone who *might not even be a friend*."

"Stop riding the boy, Margie," said John Andreas. "Dewey, we'd love to have you two. We'll put you in separate bedrooms, of course. And I'm positive that Hobey would be delighted to smoke a turkey for Thanksgiving."

"Thanks, Pop."

"You're welcome," he said. "And tell your girlfriend to bring a few sweaters. It's starting to get a little chilly at night."

Dewey and Daisy walked to the long harvest table. Everyone stood up as they moved around the perimeter of the table, saying hello, giving hugs, meeting Dewey's guest.

Before sitting down, Dewey stood at his assigned seat, in the middle of the table, between Sam and Reagan.

"Why on God's green earth is your hair wet?" asked Aunt Boo, John Andreas's sister. "For chrissakes, it's almost winter."

"We, ah, went swimming," said Dewey, glancing at Daisy, who was already laughing.

"Wasn't you supposed to be here yesterday, Uncle Dewey?" asked Sam.

"Weren't," said Dewey, correcting him.

"Weren't what?" asked Sam.

"Weren't, as in, *weren't* you supposed to be here yesterday."

"Oh, man, not you too," said Sam. "Why's everyone always nitpicking what I say. It's not like I'm gonna be a encyclopedia writer when I grow up."

"So first of all, everyone," said Dewey, "I want to apologize for being late. I think you all wouldn't believe me if I told you we ran out of gas, but it's the truth, we did."

"It's okay, Dewey," someone yelled. "I got plenty of gas if you need it."

The table erupted in laughter.

"I should've filled the tank when we left Camden."

"What were you doing in Camden?" Dewey's mother asked.

"Nothing," said Dewey, immediately regretting mentioning Camden.

"Did you two spend the night?"

"Mom, that's not the point of the story. The point is, sorry for being late."

"We went antiquing," interrupted Daisy, grinning at Dewey.

"*Antiquing?*" said Uncle Burt, from the far end of the table. "*Fancy shmancy,* Dewey. I'm impressed. Those antiques can get mighty expensive."

"They certainly can," piped up Doris Russell, Margaret's sister and Dewey's aunt, also the mayor of Castine. "Bought an old dresser one time, down in Massachusetts. Goddam thing fell apart."

"That's what you do with a *lady*," yelled Grey Terry, lifting his rum and cider in a mock toast of respect to Dewey. "Did you buy any of them little doilies, Dewey?"

Laughter, hooting, and hollering accompanied each rip on Dewey, to Daisy's great delight.

Dewey stared straight at Daisy with a look of resignation. She returned his look with a playful smile.

Finally, when everyone at the table had given their own particular opinion on antiquing, the town of Camden, and running out of gas, Dewey again took the floor.

"Second, you all met Daisy by now," he said. "If you didn't, everyone, this is Daisy. She's kind of visiting Maine for a little while. I guess maybe we're also coordinating schedules a little bit. Anyway."

" 'Coordinating schedules'?" said Reagan. "How *romantic*."

"Seriously," said Daisy, laughing. "As I recall, *you* were the one who asked me to come."

Nods washed over the crowd.

"Well, I . . . um. You know. I was just . . . Yeah."

More laughter as Dewey's face turned red.

"Second," said Dewey.

"You just did second," said John Andreas, from the end of the table.

Dewey glared at him, but John didn't budge.

"Third," said Dewey, "Daisy isn't interested

in stories about me when I was a kid. They bore her."

"What are you talking about?" asked Daisy. "Why else do you think I'm here?"

"I just—well, I just figured they'd probably bore you. You're a busy person. I didn't want you to get overloaded with information."

"Hobey," yelled Nat Morse from the far end of the table, "tell that one about the time Dewey sank Dr. Wetherbee's sailboat."

"No," said Bill Andreas, another of Dewey's uncles, "you gotta tell her about the cow."

"The cow?" asked Hobey.

"The time he rode the cow and got arrested."

"Oh, yeah."

"I didn't get arrested, Uncle Bill."

"You got thrown in jail," said John. "Lucky for you, you were only twelve."

"He was eleven," said Margaret. "Same year he kissed what's his name's daughter, the girl with the buck teeth."

Dewey sat down, sinking slowly into a resigned, silent slouch. He looked across the table at Daisy, who was listening to someone start in on Kat Higgins, the girl from up the road whom Dewey, in point of fact, had not kissed, but who had kissed him after tackling him on the snow-covered fairway of the second hole at Castine Golf Club, then told the entire school it had been Dewey who'd tackled her. Nobody had ever believed

Dewey's version of the story, and to attempt to argue now would have been, well, pointless.

The table was practically erupting in laughter at every word, from one end to the other, and no one was laughing harder than Daisy.

At some point, her face wet with tears from laughing, she returned his look. He held her eyes in his gaze for an extra moment, and another, then she turned back to hear more. When she turned back again, Dewey was gazing into the distance, a faraway look on his face, and she watched him until, finally, he returned to her, and their eyes met again.

It was a little after midnight and everyone had long since gone to bed. Margaret had brought Daisy upstairs and showed her to the guest bedroom. Dewey stayed outside, under the stars, having one last beer. Then another. Finally, he went inside.

He went upstairs and brushed his teeth. He walked quietly down the hall toward his bedroom, passing the guest bedroom. The door was slightly ajar. He paused and looked inside. It was dark and he could see moonlight coming through the window. In the moonlight, he saw Daisy's silhouette. She was standing at the window, looking out.

He knocked gently. "Daisy?"

"Hey, come in."

"You need anything? Glass of water? Extra blanket? Want me to read you a bedtime story?"

She laughed.

"Actually, everything's perfect," said Daisy. "I'm not sure I've ever had so much fun. Thanks so much for everything, Dewey."

"Sure. Okay, well, good. If you need anything, I'm just down the hall."

Dewey started to shut the door.

"Dewey, what's that?" she asked, pointing outside.

He had to cross the room to see what she was talking about. He stood behind her beneath the dormer alcove, though there was barely enough room for the two of them.

A bright half-moon more silver than yellow sat low in the sky. The black ocean shimmered beneath it.

"That's the ocean," Dewey answered.

"Not the ocean, dummy. That."

"Oh, that's the moon."

She turned and looked at him. They were just a few inches apart.

"You know what I'm pointing at," she said.

He leaned forward. She was pointing behind the barn.

"That's a backyard hockey rink."

"Really?"

"Yeah. We used to flood it every winter."

Dewey could see, up close, in the moonlight,

the sharpness of Daisy's nose. She smelled like flowers.

"What are you thinking about?" she asked.

He could feel the warmth coming off of her body in the darkness. His hand brushed against hers, then held it. His eyes, which had been looking off into the distance, moved to hers. He clutched her hand in his, rubbing his thumb along her palm.

"I should probably let you go to sleep."

"Don't you owe me something?" said Daisy.

He shut his eyes, fighting back emotion. It took every ounce of strength, but he didn't move. She put his thumb into the middle of her fist and clenched it tight. Her other hand touched his chest. He opened his eyes. Daisy looked at him as if she was searching for something. His mind was a torrent of emotion. He wanted to say something, yet the scars that crossed his past were like chains now. His stomach tightened as a foreign warmth took him and he was no longer in control.

He looked at her puffy, perfect red lips, at her white teeth. In the moonlight, he could see soft peach fuzz above her lip. She let go of his hand and moved her hand up to his cheek. Their eyes were locked now, and he put his arm around her, holding her lower back. He pulled her closer and pressed against her, continuing to stare. He saw, in that moment, vulnerability, even pain. All of it crossed her face, and he looked away.

Daisy stood on her tiptoes, shut her eyes, and leaned up to him and their lips touched. For a brief moment, he forgot about Robbie, and Holly, and Jessica. He forgot about it all.

After more than a minute, she pulled away.

"I'm not sure we should do this," she whispered.

"I agree."

"You do?"

"Yeah."

"Really?"

"Well, no, not really. But if you don't want to . . ."

"It's not you, Dewey, I just promised myself I wouldn't."

She pressed herself even closer now, as a smile came to her lips, which she attempted to hide by biting her lip.

"Wouldn't do what?"

"Fall for someone like you."

"Is it because I work for your dad?"

She shook her head.

"No. I just promised myself I'd never fall for your type."

She stood on her tiptoes again, brushing her lips against his, not quite kissing him.

"My type?" he said.

"Yeah, your type."

She moved a hand beneath his shirt, rubbing his muscled chest.

"And what is my type?"

"Do I have to spell it out for you?" she said,

pushing Dewey's shirt gently up as her lips again found his.

She tried to stifle a laugh as her other hand found Dewey's belt.

"A professional miniature golfer."

ACKNOWLEDGMENTS

It is with deep gratitude that I express my appreciation to so many individuals who helped during the writing of *First Strike*.

I'll start with a huge thanks to everyone at St. Martin's Press, my publisher, and Macmillan Audio, whose brilliant, hardworking, and nattily attired men and women continually express their faith in me with their enthusiasm for each book. Thank you all, and particularly Sally Richardson, Jennifer Enderlin, Hannah Braaten, George Witte, Jeff Capshew, Vannessa Cronin, Paul Hochman, Justin Velella, Martin Quinn, Alison Ziegler, Joseph Brosnan, Rafal Gibek, Jason Reigal, Ervin Serrano, Robert Allen, Laura Wilson, and Mary Beth Roche.

An even bigger thank-you to Keith Kahla, my editor at St. Martin's Press. I don't know what I would do without Keith. He sees the flaws in the story, the plot, and the characters in a way that I can't and then gracefully offers a path to fixing it all. It's never easy. It's always worth it.

Just as insightful, tough, and patient is my agent, Nicole James. Nicole is much more than an agent, however. She is Keith's partner in figuring out what ails a particular draft, chapter, or scene. At the same time, Nicole somehow also represents me as only a true partner can. More than anything,

Nicole is a friend, always there for me, often times for nothing having to do with my books. For her critical role in my career, I'm grateful beyond words. For her friendship, I don't have words.

Thank you also to my buddy Chris George, whose efforts in Hollywood on my behalf make Captain Ahab look like a quitter.

A sincere thank-you to Marc Gillinov at the Cleveland Clinic, one of the world's preeminent heart surgeons. Marc guided me through the intricacies of heart massage, displaying the same adept touch with my words as he did on the operating table when he saved my life five years ago. Thanks also to Adrian King, my best friend, whose thoughts on various aspects of the plot were vital. Rorke Denver, Michelle Goncalves, Sam, Kelly, and Nick Adams, Sue H., Pam P., and Brad Thor: Thank you. A special thank-you to Alex and Kelly for your love and support.

Most important is my family: Shannon, Charlie, Teddy, Oscar, and Esmé. They had to endure yet another tortured year of me wandering around in boxers and Bean boots talking to myself. The way I get through the tough process of writing a book is by having the love, support, and humor of my family. At night, I read to my youngest, Esmé, before she goes to bed. Every night with her I'm reminded of the way books do so much more than merely entertain when they are shared by two people. I also read to Oscar, though his popularity with the ladies at age twelve offers a tempting distraction for him. I thought I had a few more years of Oscar to myself. Luckily, every day I see the values Shannon and I instilled in him, and when he offers to carry Esmé's hockey bag to the bus stop, when he clears the table without being asked, when he stands up for a teammate, it gives me strength. Teddy, at fourteen, is tall, handsome, and thin, but when I started writing so many years ago he was a little chubby. We called him the "Butterball Turkey." For every ounce of baby fat he lost, however, Teddy gained in brain size. He understands politics better than almost anyone I've ever met. When I was writing *First Strike*, it was Teddy's questions, comments, and insights that enabled me to write what I did. I cherish the memory of lugging that big pudgy dude around when he was younger, but it pales in comparison to the brilliant young man I know now. Charlie, our oldest, is the rock who anchors our family, and his golden heart casts a glow that binds us together. When I started writing, he would bring me coffee in the morning. Now he quietly does his job as an older brother and son, providing a role model to his siblings—and a young gentleman who makes his parents proud every day. Of course, if Charlie is the rock, then Shannon is the sea itself. The one we all rely upon. For me, she's the unbreakable steel and ageless beauty that guides me. Thank you sweetheart for everything.

Center Point Large Print
600 Brooks Road / PO Box 1
Thorndike, ME 04986-0001 USA

(207) 568-3717

US & Canada:
1 800 929-9108
www.centerpointlargeprint.com